# WOULD YOU?

Jesse is worried about her job and fresh out of another unsatisfying relationship. Thank goodness she has her friends: Bryn and Cecile. Bryn's the tough one, and Cecile's the one with the perfect life — with her gorgeous fiancé Zach . . . But then the worst happens, and Cecile's not with them any more. Jesse has to come to terms with her best friend's death, but she begins to fall in love with Zach, who's also reeling with grief. Is Jesse doing the right thing? Can she and Zach ever be happy together, or will Cecile always come between them?

DEANNA KIZIS

◆

# WOULD YOU?

*Complete and Unabridged*

# ULVERSCROFT
*Leicester*

First published in Great Britain in 2006 by
Headline Review, an imprint of
Headline Book Publishing
London

First Large Print Edition
published 2007
by arrangement with
Headline Book Publishing
London

The moral right of the author has been asserted

All characters in this publication are fictitious and any resemblance to real persons, living or dead, is purely coincidental.

British Library CIP Data

Kizis, Deanna
  Would you?.—Large print ed.—
  Ulverscroft large print series: general fiction
  1. Death—California—Los Angeles—Psychological
  aspects—Fiction 2. Female friendship—California—
  Los Angeles—Fiction 3. Large type books
  I. Title
  813.6 [F]

  ISBN 978-1-84782-020-4

Published by
F. A. Thorpe (Publishing)
Anstey, Leicestershire

Set by Words & Graphics Ltd.
Anstey, Leicestershire
Printed and bound in Great Britain by
T. J. International Ltd., Padstow, Cornwall

This book is printed on acid-free paper

*For Julian, who came later*

# Contents

## PART THREE

'When people have taste they may have faults, follies, fads, they may err, they may be human and honest as they please, but they will never cause a scandal!'

Elise de Wolfe,
*The House in Good Taste*

'You got a face with a view'

The Talking Heads

# Part One

# 1

## A Sense of Proportion

When Zach called to tell me my best friend, Cecile, had been in a car accident — hit head on by a taxicab on Beverly Boulevard — my shocked imagination pictured the crash happening in front of the new Design Within Reach, where the old aquarium store used to be. I was wrong. Turns out it was closer to the La Brea intersection, not far from the curry place Cecile and I sometimes went to for samosas which were as addictive as Krispy Kremes, which we'd slather in mango chutney and wash down with cold Taj Mahal beer. I imagined that Cecile's car would cost several thousand dollars to fix, and that she'd have concussion, perhaps, in which case I'd take a couple of days off from the interior design shop where I worked and put cold compresses on her forehead until she felt better. Again, not correct. Cec's car was smashed inward like a stomped beer can. She was in intensive care at Cedars Sinai, where she lay like a pummelled box of blueberries.

At the time, my other closest friend, Bryn,

was sitting on my couch picking at a jar of green olives and looking at me like, *What's wrong?* I told her what Zach had said and she sprang into action; grabbing her keys and wallet. I opened the passenger door to Bryn's car and reached for the seatbelt, then closed my eyes and tried to get a grip. I felt that if I didn't maintain some sense of control, the car would open up and swallow my stomach, my lungs, my arms, my legs, my head. My brain would fall to the leather seat, whirring and clicking, and I'd be stuck riding shotgun in Bryn's Subaru for ever. Looking back on it now, I wonder what I would have said if Bryn had put this scene on pause, so she could tell me that I'd soon lose all sense of propriety? If she told me I'd soon cause others terrible pain even as I experienced, at times, true joy? I didn't know then that I, Jesse Holtz, was what one could call the 'cheerleader friend' — the *sis-boom-bah* supporting cast member who rallied behind those who were prettier, smarter and just generally more *alive* than I was. (There's one of us in almost every group, I'm told.) Nor did I know that I'd soon break every rule upon which our female alliance was based. I didn't know any of that.

*This can't be happening to Cecile,* I thought. She'd always been the charmed friend, leading the charmed life. The friend

I'd trade places with instantly, no question. If one could actually do such a thing, I mean.

⋆   ⋆   ⋆

Only hours before Cecile and I were on the Griffith Park public tennis courts, rectangles of green sandwiched between the 5 Freeway and the park's easternmost edge. It isn't swanky there by any means. There's no clubhouse — just a soda machine and a drinking fountain which the joggers who are always running by use to water their panting dogs — but the bathrooms are clean and the sound of cars passing just beyond the tree line is either distracting or as soothing as ocean waves, depending on how you feel about things.

I watched Cecile attempt to lob a ball — her racket, clutched in her long, suntanned arm, sent the fuzzy orb sailing over the chain-link fence that stood between us and a women's-league soccer game — and I remember thinking, *We'd be playing better if we were keeping score.* Unlike the she-jocks in the field, who were ripping ferociously up and down the grass and delivering kicks that could shatter a knee, Cec and I were rallying, which meant the fun of cooperative mischief — as opposed to competitive play — became the whole point. We wasted court time entertaining one another by wildly swinging our rackets like baseball bats, jumping about, mangling serves, doubling up in laughter.

'Did you *see* that? Could I be *any worse* at this game?' Cecile called over the net.

'We'll never see *that* ball again,' I said, laughing. 'But seriously, you're really good!'

Keeping score, on the other hand, was a whole other game. I didn't generally compete with Cecile of course; like most women, I could size up where I stood in the female looks, wealth and charm pecking order in mere seconds. But the tennis court was the one place in the universe where I had a slight edge. Cecile knew it, too. When we'd play for real, her expression would fix. Her ponytail would get tighter. She'd pull her visor down low on her forehead, as if to say she had only one thing on her mind: *to kick my ass.* Which was fine with me because I had ideas of my own. My jaw would constrict and my brain would crackle with visions of slick counter-moves and brutal fusillade. I'd grip the racket so tightly that my fingers would cramp into a disfigured, achy little claw. I'd call her outs with horrible precision. I'd serve with a violent grunt — such sweet defiance! When the end came, whoever lost would throw her fists down to her sides, lift her chin and scream *'Crrraaaaapppp!'* at the sky.

On that particular Saturday morning (a bright, hot day, even though it was 6 December), we were doing a quick warm-up when Gerry, our beloved, permatan, sixty-five year old tennis instructor, showed up, racket in hand.

'Get in position, Jesse!' he yelled, striding on to court and putting on his sunglasses, which he kept dangling around his neck from a pair of neon Croakies. 'Good. Now get it over the net!'

'OK, Cecile, it's right there! You got it . . . Great!'

'Now Jesse, get moving! Yes? Yes? Yes! Now *that's* tennis, ladies! *That's tennis!'*

★ ★ ★

An hour later, Cecile plonked down on the green wooden bench where we'd dropped our stuff.

'That was so not tennis,' she said, dabbing her face with a towel and bending to stretch her pretty legs.

'You're just annoyed I took that last game off you.' I took a swig of her water and stuck my thumb down the front of my tank top — I was sweating and it made me itch.

'Please, I'm the least competitive person in the world.'

'Only because, tennis aside, you always win.'

'Hey,' Cecile said with a laugh, 'that's true!'

She put her racket inside its case and slung it over her shoulder. Her green eyes were squinting in the sun and her cheeks gleamed with a peachy flush. Her Wilson was nicer than mine. It was a present from Zach, who thought the fact that Cecile had decided to learn a sport — she had a genteel job as fundraiser for the Los Angeles Philharmonic, after all — was the most adorable thing he'd ever heard. Mine was a hand-me-down from Bryn's husband, David. Considering what Taryn, my boss, paid at the shop — I managed Gilded Cage on Robertson, a store that I personally wouldn't even buy a picture frame from — new sports equipment which is manufactured for athletically ambitious-but-won't-ever-be-great players like myself was out of the question.

'Same place?' I asked Cecile, following her swaying tennis skirt into the parking lot.

'Always,' she said. 'I don't care if the wedding's two weeks away. I'm getting the patty melt and fries.'

\* \* \*

I called Bryn as I was pulling out of the driveway.

'Hey screener, it's just me,' I said to her voicemail as I wound my way around Mulholland fountain. On weekends it was commandeered with Latina newlyweds and their petal-sheathed bridesmaids, who would form pastel arcs before the gushing water — a suitable backdrop for a romantic wedding party photo. 'House of Pies. Meet us, OK? Oh and I got the supplies for the place cards because I know you wanted to start those too. Bye.'

Bryn, Cecile and I had disproved the theory that women don't play well in threes. I met them in a literature class freshman year. Cecile, who was seated front and centre, was going on and on about her analysis of the dream sequence in *The Idiot*. I don't remember her take on it, just that I was captivated by her profile — straight nose, tumbling locks straight out of a Renoir painting, and a lush, rose-coloured mouth that looked beguilingly out-of-place, like a lace bra under a school uniform. Cecile was fiddling with a pencil, and she'd occasionally pull a tendril of hair behind her ear. Bryn was splayed in a nearby chair wearing combat boots and an incongruous baby-doll dress. She had a look of intense amusement on her face, and when Cecile finally came up for air, Bryn said, 'Oh would you *please* get over yourself.'

I barked out a laugh that rose into the air and joined theirs — surprising everyone in the room, not to mention myself. After class, Cecile and Bryn invited me to Jabberwocky for a coffee and a study session. I'd spoken to one of them — if not both — every day since.

★  ★  ★

'You're not going to believe how screwed up this case I'm working on is,' Bryn said, joining us at our table at the House of Pies. We were sitting in a booth in a sunny corner which was bright enough for Cecile, who hated dark corners, large enough for Bryn, who liked to sit Indian-style, and nowhere near a mirror because I hated watching myself eat. The booths at the H.O.P. were blue Naugahyde, the tables chipped Formica, the carpet a hideous diamond pattern. We'd been coming here since we migrated to LA after graduation. (Bryn went to law school at USC, and Cecile followed Zach, a food critic who hoped to capitalise on the LA restaurant boom. I, meanwhile, was just born here.) It had got to the point where I knew which waitress would let me substitute Caesar dressing for vinaigrette without charging extra, and who would invariably forget to bring our water.

'There's the sexy bridesmaid,' Cecile said, patting the seat next to her.

'Please, I'm enormous,' Bryn said, sliding into the booth and crossing her feet under her shins.

'What about me?' Cecile said with a moan. 'I'm going to end up getting married in a giant sheet.'

I was easily fifteen pounds heavier — probably more — than both of them, but I'd long since accepted that, where beauty is concerned, perception and reality haven't been introduced.

'So get this,' Bryn said, settling herself in. 'Intuit decided to buy out this smaller company that makes packaging for big corporations — cereal manufacturers and the like. They make an offer, get the company. But here's the thing: *After* the money gets transferred the stockholders decide to hold the funds in an offshore account — '

'Cec,' I said. 'Do you have any idea what she's talking about?'

'I'm too bored to say exactly,' she said.

'You guys suck,' Bryn said, picking up a menu. 'Tell me, then, what crucial issue were you two talking about?'

11

'Fish,' Cecile and I said in unison.

I filled Bryn in on the situation: we all knew Cecile had decided months ago that she wanted to serve salmon at her wedding, which was to take place in the jasmine-scented garden of a Santa Monica hotel in fourteen days. Her logic was that chicken always got too dry, and she didn't really eat red meat. Zach, however, was suddenly anti-fish. He was a steak man, he had announced to Cecile the previous night while she was innocently brushing her teeth. Plus, steak seemed classier to him; more appropriate for a December wedding. She had tried to explain that the menu was already at the printers, the event itself fast approaching, but he had been adamant.

'I think he's intentionally being difficult,' Cecile said. 'Seriously — on some level, he's enjoying seeing me unnerved.'

Bryn's and my eyes met — *rarely* did we get to hear about a Cecile/Zach squabble.

'Look, this was bound to happen,' Bryn said, reaching for a napkin and blowing her nose. 'It's in his job description: Food *critic*.'

I nodded. 'Remember the time we tried to make him a birthday dinner?'

'I prepared for weeks. Still, two months ago I asked Zach point blank, 'Are you going to get all foodie on me about what we eat?' and he says, 'Nah it's your day, whatever you want, blah blah blah . . . ''

'Well, it *is* your day,' Bryn said. 'When I planned our wedding, David wasn't even allowed to speak.'

'Precisely. My day, my menu.'

'Why is that, though?' I said. 'That a wedding's supposedly only about the woman?'

They turned to look at me as though I'd suddenly started barking.

'I'm not talking about you, Cec, I'm just asking. You know how my brother Henry goes out with that guy Hameer? He told me that in some Indian weddings, the *groom* picks out everything, shows up in a fancy car or on a horse wearing this elaborate costume, and then the bride gets to come just to sign the contract.'

'Well, thank you, Jesse, for that cultural lesson in misogyny,' Bryn said.

'Shi'ite Ismailis are actually quite liberal — '

'Ugh.' Cecile put her head in her hands. 'No, I know what you mean. I'm starting to sound like one of those nightmare brides. OK. I refuse to argue about food with my future husband.'

'Who's perfection,' I added.

'Who's perfection.' Cecile smiled. 'You

know what? Show up in a tutu and cat collar and eat steak with your hands. See if I care.'

'Jesse was already planning on that,' Bryn said.

I shrugged. 'It was supposed to be a surprise.'

'Let's talk about something else,' Cec turned in my direction. 'Tell me again why I wouldn't rather be single.'

# 2

## Loft in Translation

Whenever Cecile asked me why she shouldn't date around — not that she'd ever be caught in such a circumstance — I felt obliged to provide her with tales well told in a self-deprecating, breezy tone, as though I were the real-life version of those romantic comedies we were always going to see. In truth, I wasn't a beloved klutz with a misguided plan to scare away 'The One' so I could win a bet at work, nor was I an ugly duckling about to turn into a swan. I was striking out. In the last couple of years alone there was Arty, a production designer who wore John Lennon glasses and was obsessed with an ex-wife from Barcelona who married him for a visa (I was his revenge therapy), Mark, an architect who grew up in Shanghai, got me drunk on Chinese beer, declared his love and moved in with a *male* Japanese T-shirt designer, and Duff, a clothing store owner who said he was divorced, which turned out to be true, but he left out the fact that he was seeing another woman. (I found out when he sent a group email announcing that they'd eloped to Vegas.) That's not mentioning the three or four who didn't last long enough for me to find out whether or not they'd ever be worth mentioning.

Bryn was always exhorting me not to sleep with these guys, giving me lectures on how if I waited, they'd be more inclined to stick around. How could I explain to my militantly girlpower friend that, as pathetic as it was, I'd tried her approach with several men over the years, and they didn't call either? I mean, why deny myself the one thing I knew I *could* get? Namely, laid.

'Well,' I said, taking a sip of coffee before I relayed the latest. 'Ira called the other night at 3 a.m. to see if he could stop by and I must've slept through it. The next day — you're not going to believe this — he accused me of cheating.'

'I'm sorry,' Bryn said, unwrapping a stick of gum. 'Are you even going out with that guy?'

'No. He's told me a million times he doesn't want to be in a relationship.'

'Maybe he wants more, but just doesn't know how to say it,' said Cecile.

'Oh my dear Cecile,' I reached over to pat her slender shoulder. 'Every guy who's ever laid eyes on you has always wanted more, so I know rejection is hard to fathom. My theory is that Ira's just so self-absorbed he honestly feels that I should pine whether he wants me or not.'

'Chuck him,' Bryn said.

I glanced at Cecile to see if she was in agreement but she was staring out the window, distracted by a man walking down the street with a toddler on his shoulders. As he passed, the little girl looked at her reflection in the diner window, her blonde curls gently lifting in the air to the beat of her father's gait.

'Earth to Cec,' I said.

'Sorry. I was just thinking about the wedding. It's distracting, actually. So many details.' She smiled.

'Jesse,' Bryn interrupted, *'Tell me* you're going to get rid of him.'

I looked at Cecile, silently commanding her to help.

'Back off, counsellor,' she said, gently placing a hand over Bryn's. 'You know our Jesse likes to do things *in her own time.'*

\* \* \*

We paid the bill and I ran to Cecile's car to get a scarf I'd left behind a couple of nights before, then kissed her goodbye on the cheek.

17

Cec headed on her ill-fated trip West (if only we'd chatted a moment longer . . . ), as Bryn and I went East to my house to continue with our bridesmaids' duties.

'Do you want me to make coffee?' I called to Bryn as I hurried to the bathroom.

'Are you kidding? I just drank three cups,' she said. 'There must be something I want, though.'

I finished, flushed, and cocked my head to listen. Yes, Bryn was rummaging somewhere in the kitchen. I went to my study — really a dining room which I'd converted into a workspace, with my desk pushed against the windows so I could see the front garden — and grabbed the file I'd made for Cecile's wedding. I rented a one-bedroom in Echo Park, which magazines had been pegging as an up-and-coming neighbourhood for a decade. In actuality not much had changed save a trendy coffee shop and an American apparel store that had opened around the corner. There were still cars on cinder blocks in most of the front yards, and at night the police cruised overhead in their helicopters — 'ghetto birds', the locals called them — shining spotlights into our gardens and generally scaring the living shit out of me.

So far we'd done the engagement party in New York and the bachelorette in Las Vegas, which featured Cecile, of all people, spanking a gay stripper with a rose clenched between her teeth to 'It's Raining Men'. (As she planted another smack on his left butt cheek, Bryn leaned over to me and whispered, 'Halleluiah.') Next we were to start the place cards and put together a packet of things to do for Cecile's out-of-town guests. So far I'd come up with the Museum of Jurassic Technology and the eight-year-old female Elvis impersonator who played at a restaurant in Thai town, but I was starting to worry these weren't what Cec had in mind.

I found Bryn curled up on the Knoll sofa I'd bought for twenty dollars at Goodwill and then had reupholstered. She began rattling off suggestions.

'Getty Museum?' she said, gnawing on an apple. I didn't have the guts to point out that her technique for separating flesh from core reminded me of a mauling one would see on the Discovery Channel.

'Not terribly original, but classic,' I said. 'She'll like it. What else?'

'Dude.' Bryn spit a pip into her palm and placed it on the coffee table. 'Did you make those curtains?'

'Yes. Please get a napkin.'

She ignored me. I was proud of my house, which I paid nothing to rent but only because it looked like a deserted Meths lab when I moved in. The previous tenants had left a pile of trash in the middle of the living room and mould was growing in the bath. The carpet, which I pulled up, disintegrated in my hands where it had rotted. There was a guy who lived two doors down who was constantly cleaning out his garage and dumping a disturbing array of stuff into the street — three refrigerators without their doors, sixteen chair seats missing legs, an anvil, a half-dozen yellow plastic hamster cages, a rack of cheap nylon women's dresses, two mannequins without their heads, a pile of rusty saws, and four hefty green garbage bags stuffed with nothing but old yearbooks. I suspected him of some crime, but I could never figure out what, exactly, he was up to given the sheer randomness of his refuse.

But what my house was missing in local ambience it made up for with kitchen tiling from the twenties, hardwood floors under all that muck (which I'd re-stained myself in a dark chocolate wash), a loft-like floor plan that opened into both the dining room and kitchen, and a small garden in which I planted night-blooming Jasmine, lavender, New Zealand flax, bougainvillea and rosemary. I replaced the bathroom fixtures with vintage hardware I'd found online, and scoured every flea market and secondhand store — sometimes going as far south as Palm Desert and East to Fresno — for a mixture of sixties, seventies, antique, and, occasionally, just interesting furniture. The result was a mix of bold, Crayola colours with rich, matte textures, with the occasional shiny chrome accent piece for glamour. My living room, in particular, was my favourite. I had a rundown Mies van der Rohe sofa that someone in my neighbourhood left on the corner with a cardboard sign that said 'Take Me', two ceramic turquoise lamps with white Oriental-print silk shades, an old Victorian sideboard that I'd lacquered in a lemon-yellow with an enormous, chunky chrome mirror over it and, the best, a mint Verner Panton globe lamp that my mother had given me as a housewarming gift. She'd apparently been keeping it in her closet in the original box since 1969 because she thought it looked 'too Jetsons'. Next up: wallpaper.

Sometimes I wondered what my boss, Taryn, would think of what I'd done with the place, but then I'd remind myself that she made a point of telling me my taste was too 'down market' whenever she got the chance. I'd been waiting for the last six years for the right moment to tell Taryn that, in my opinion, *her* taste was in question. In this fantasy, I'd explain to her that she had no sense of irony, personal style, or emotion. Whenever she decorated a room, it looked contrived. The pieces she chose — always pedigreed, always expensive — weren't exactly the problem; it was that when Taryn put them together they were all matchy-matchy, like it had all come in a set. She didn't understand that decoration was about being more than evocative — you also needed to be *emotive*, to express a feeling or a memory. After I told Taryn all this I'd quit and go on to start my real career. In industrial design maybe? As the head of product development for a chic brand? The details were fuzzy but that wasn't the point. Or at least I didn't feel like it was the point whenever Taryn patronised me with another of her sweeping proclamations. 'Buy the best and you only cry once,' she'd sniff as I tried to get her to look at some samples from a new, experimental line. Or, 'No, no, this fabric is all wrong. I predict we're on the *verge* of a leopard print moment.'

★   ★   ★

I was confirming hotel reservations for Cecile's relatives when the other line started to ring.

'So,' I said, 'the reservation is for six rooms,' *beep*, 'now all of them sleep four,' *beep*, 'but are those with one sofa bed or two actual double —' *beep*.

'I apologise, miss,' the man on the other end of the phone said, his voiced laced with the same brand of professional courtesy that I often used at the store. 'I didn't quite catch that.'

'My other line is ringing just ignore it.' I looked up and saw Bryn mouth the words, *Dump him*. 'I asked if the suites have sofa beds or double —' *beep*.

'Pardon?'

'SOFA BEDS OR —' *beep*. '*Damn it!*' I yelled out in frustration. 'I'm sorry, you know what? I'll just call back.'

I disconnected the line and Bryn was shaking her head. 'Seriously,' she said.

The phone rang again. I picked it up.

'Hello?' I said.

'Jesse?'

That was the call from Zach. From the thickness of his voice, I could tell that he'd been crying.

# 3

## Gimme Shelter

Bryn was out the front door before I'd even put on my shoes. She drove us to the hospital, her jaw set in concentration as she ran red lights, while I fought off negative thoughts that I must have believed, on some level, could affect the outcome. *You're never going to see her again,* I thought. *That's ridiculous. She's going to be OK. If it's a couple of broken legs we'll just deal with it. She'll have to postpone her wedding, but in the grand scheme of things that's nothing.* I caught a glimpse of my face in the side-view mirror; I had that silly expression people wear when they don't know how to behave yet. Should I be shocked? Blubbering? Composed? I wouldn't know what expression to pick without knowing what was happening, and to choose the wrong one would later make me feel like I was either cold-hearted or a hysteric.

We gave the admitting nurse — who sat in a capsule of bullet-proof glass — our names and sat down to wait. While Bryn went outside to try Zach on his mobile, I occupied myself by staring at the swinging doors to the ER. I pictured Cecile walking out, holding an ice pack to her head, her arm in a sling, with a sheepish grin on her face.

'Did I scare you?' she would say, her eyes tired but bright with excitement. 'I'm sorry.'

'Are you crazy?' I'd reply. 'What are you apologising for?'

When Bryn returned I told her about my reverie. Then I worried that what I'd said upset her and said I was sorry.

'Are you crazy?' she said. 'What are you apologising for?'

There was nothing to do but wait.

★ ★ ★

Cecile was a tall girl with posture straighter than a ruler. In college, she preferred the kind of clothes that former prep school girls from Manhattan wore — broken-in chinos, soft rugby shirts, and old boyfriends' sweaters that made her look casting-call perfect against the ostentatiously pretty mountains that overwhelmed the University of Colorado campus. Her teeth were perfect pearls, her body was lithe but not overly attended to, her boobs were enviable — high Cs, and round, not floppy. Cecile was generally oblivious to

25

the fact that she had had what the guys at school referred to as 'a banging body', but she loved eighties music — Prince, in particular — and if any was playing she'd be up and dancing atop a chair with a confidence that only someone with a figure like hers could muster.

Bryn, on the other hand, was Cecile's physical opposite. She was so petite that nobody had ever had the guts to ask for a precise height. Her breasts were like toy teacups, her feet dainty. Where Cec stood ramrod straight, Bryn arched her back into an 'S' shape that stuck out her belly and her rounded bottom — the reason she was named 'Most Likely to Get Pinched' in high school. She wore her black hair in a severe bob with even more severely plucked eyebrows to match. Her skin was so pale that in certain lights it looked blue, and her lips were always stained a deep red. Bryn reminded me of a pop star from Russia. She was, in fact, pre-law from Illinois.

As I stared at my reflection in the hospital's tinted windows, I remembered how, shortly after meeting Bryn and Cec, I used to wonder what people made of us when we walked down the street. A pop star, a movie star, and plain old me, trotting along beside them, sometimes with my arm linked to one of theirs. I wasn't as striking — five-five, one-hundred-and-twenty-something, brown eyes, brown hair. I wore it loose but only because I didn't have any better ideas. I had combination skin and combination style; I was always borrowing Cecile's clothes and letting Bryn do my make-up, two great tastes that didn't really go great together. But eventually I stopped wondering what others thought and gave myself over to my place as their closest friend, confident that Cecile's beauty, Bryn's strength — their bright brand of specialness — would shine on to my upturned face. I basked in their reflected glory like a daisy that loved to be kissed by the sun, especially when planted next to the most exotic of flowers.

Whenever she's tired my mother always says she's 'fading'. Looking at my wan reflection in the hospital window, I could see that I was fading, too. How much of the woman I saw was because of Cecile? I wondered. How fast would I fade away if I lost her?

★　★　★

I bought the least hideous bouquet of carnations and fern they had at the gift shop, figuring if Zach came down he could bring the flowers to Cecile's room. (*If they put her in one. Stop it, stop it, stop it!*) Then Bryn and I just sat there, losing our minds. Every few minutes, she would get up and try to convince the nurse that there *must* be someone who could give us some information. I tried not to dwell on the children playing in the toy area — a sad little enclave of mismatched building blocks and puzzles with pieces missing. I hated to think who they knew on the other side of those doors.

I sensed Bryn's head jerking up and looked at the entrance. David, striding across the waiting room with a small, encouraging smile. It's funny. The first couple of years I knew David, before he and Bryn got hitched, I thought he was either a snob or a bore; turned out he was just shy. His self-consciousness made him meticulous. His brown hair was always neatly combed, and his T-shirt and chinos were spotless, as though he was about to take his class picture. David squatted down in front of us and took each of our hands. His cuticles were immaculate.

'Ladies,' he said.

'And germs,' I replied, motioning to the expectorating gentleman to my left who kept complaining to his wife that he'd already *had* a flu shot.

A doctor stepped out of the ER door and called, 'Bryn Beco?'

'Here!'

David, Bryn and I jumped up in succession. Like those women diving off the side of a pool in old movies, but backwards.

She introduced herself as Dr Marchisan and led us outside. Surprisingly, it was night. With the tinted windows, I hadn't realised. I gripped the collar of my sweatshirt around my neck. I hadn't had time to change out of my tennis clothes. Bryn folded her arms tight across her chest. The doctor had her hair in pigtails that didn't match the deep crow's feet around her eyes. *Young hair*, I thought, amazed that she could be surrounded with trauma day in, day out, and survive it. *Old face*.

'Your friend Cecile has been in a car accident,' Dr Marchisan said. I watched David take a breath, poised to tell her that we already knew that, then decide to hold his tongue.

Perhaps she sensed our impatience, because she dispensed with the niceties, turning to her clipboard and ticking her way through it. 'Cecile has a right clavicle fracture, a right ankle fracture, a compound wrist fracture — that's the right wrist — and a lacerated tendon,' she said. 'There's a right knee laceration with cartilage lost and bone exposed — we can blame the car stereo for that — and two rib fractures. She punctured a lung — other one's still intact, that's positive — but she lacerated her spleen. We'll be taking that out.'

The back of my nose was starting to sting. *Taking that out.* I wasn't sure what that meant long-term, but it couldn't be good. I flicked my eyes over at Bryn and she at me. David was nodding and taking notes. Leave it to David. Always a pad and pen in his pocket.

'The more serious problem,' Dr Marchisan said, speaking more slowly now, so we couldn't possibly mistake her, 'is that Cecile has been unconscious for several hours. Could be a coma, could be a brain injury. This happens with deceleration.' She looked up to see if we knew what she was talking about. We stared back.

'The car stops moving, the skull stops moving — the seatbelt keeps the passenger from hitting the dashboard or the windshield — but the brain keeps going *inside* the skull, and there can be trauma on impact.'

'What?' I blurted.

David shot me a look like, *Not now, Jess. Keep it together.*

Dr Marchisan ignored me and continued.

'We've requested a neurosurgeon from UCLA, who should be here any second now. We've done a CAT, there's some swelling. The bottom line is it's too soon to say how extensive the damage is. We'll know more after the neurosurgeon gets inside to take a peek.'

*Take a peek.* At this, I'm afraid I thought of the most inappropriate joke — the one about the football player who says, 'My doctor told me I had dain brammage, but I don't know what that shit is.'

David asked a question I didn't catch.

'You can only tell so much from a CT,' she replied. 'We'll know more after the surgeon gets here.'

'I'm sorry,' Bryn interrupted. 'But how dire . . . Just tell us . . . I mean, is she . . . What are you saying?'

'I think you need to understand that this is going to be what we here like to call 'a process,'' Marchisan said, folding her clip-board to her chest. 'Right now? There are simply too many variables.' She looked at each of us in turn. 'I suggest going home — the next round of procedures will take days, not hours — but if you want to stay, stay. I or a nurse will come out as soon as there's anything more. Now, I'm sorry, but I have to get back inside.'

Bryn looked at me and pursed her lips together, tight.

'Where the fuck is Zach?' she said, to nobody in particular, and we all filed back inside.

# 4

## House Parties

I guess you could say I saw him first.

It was the second term, during one of our Friday-night party crawls, although I don't remember which house we were in. ('Don't call it a frat,' the pledges used to say. 'Would you call your country a cun — ?' 'OK,' I'd say, holding up my hand, 'you can stop talking now.') I do recall that it was a decrepit Tudor mansion on The Hill, which was the student sector of town. The house had a certain grandeur until you got inside, where the floor was sticky with beer, the wallpaper was peeling, and college students danced atop couches to rap music, only getting off to wriggle on the floor when the DJ played Rock Lobster. (*Down, down, doooooown. Rock!*) Bryn pushed Cecile and me through the crowd, which was bottlenecked at the front door. The air was thick with cigarette smoke. Cec ran into a girl from their dorm who had some gossip about their resident student adviser, so Bryn sent me off in search of beer. When I finally got to the front of the throng of students who were huddled around the keg, there were no more cups.

'Take mine,' a guy said, holding out a clear plastic cup that still had a little amber liquid in the bottom. 'I'm going home soon anyway.'

He was good-looking. Tall with an athletic build, and fit in a skateboarder kind of way, his blondish hair growing out until it curled just above the collar of his broken-in CU T-shirt. His eyes, blue like the swimming pools back home, were framed by long brown lashes. He looked like an actor — one who would play the corruptible young attorney in one film, the down-to-earth firefighter hero in another. He smiled at me. It was an open, engaging smile that, behind its charm, was just a little awkward. I liked everything about Zach on sight; from the way his nose had a light sunburn, to the narrow waist that seemed like it would fit perfectly in the college photo album of our romance that I was already picturing in my head.

'Come on,' he said, wiggling the cup back and forth. 'Succumb to the peer pressure.'

One of his front teeth was slightly crooked. It seemed to me a very flirtatious tooth.

'Why are you leaving?' I asked, taking the cup with a suit-yourself shrug. 'Party's just getting good.' It was only recently that I'd got the confidence to flirt with guys — I had

Bryn's and Cecile's coaching to thank for that — and I was loving every second of the attention it got me. Hell, I would have licked the bottom of his cup if he'd asked.

'It's so just damn loud in here. Wait, let me get that for you.'

He pumped the keg and held the little spout up until the cup was full of slightly warm beer.

'I'm Zach, by the way.'

'*What?*' I held my hand up to my ear.

'*I SAID I'M ZA* — oh, ha ha,' he laughed. 'You almost got me.'

We started talking — what's your major, what's yours — quickly moving to the sand volleyball court behind the house, where it was quieter. There were bales of hay out there to double as benches, a bonfire throwing sparks of ash, and a reasonably undiscovered keg. Every half-hour or so, Zach would refill what was now our cup, and we'd pass it back and forth, the frothy beer going down more easily with every sip. Zach was pre-med, he said, although, frankly, he was just trying to make his father, a cardiologist, happy.

It turned out he was from San Francisco, liked to cook ('I can make a mean risotto,' he said), and was very into mountaineering. We joked about how there were so many West Coasters at school they may as well have called it University of California at Boulder.

'Hellllooooo? Remember us?'

My friends, coming our way. Bryn was wagging a finger at me. *Don't fall for Cecile,* I thought as they approached. I'd learned from past experience. *Don't,* I prayed. *Don't, don't, don't . . .*

'Thanks for the beer, bitch,' Bryn said, hands on her hips.

'Where have you been?' said Cecile. '*Oooh.* Can I have a sip?'

I handed her the cup.

'Zach, may I introduce Cecile Carter and Bryn Beco,' I said.

'Zach Durand.' He stood to shake both of their hands. (*So polite,* I thought.)

'Listen up,' said Bryn, 'we just ran into that girl Sophie from Russian Lit. She knows of another party, so . . . '

I looked at Zach.

'I'm kinda happy here,' he said with a shrug.

'Me too.' I smiled to myself; I'd found the one guy in Colorado who didn't want to follow my friends around like a stray.

'O-*kay*,' said Bryn. 'I guess that just means more boys for us, right, Cec?'

'What else is new,' she said, leaning over to kiss me goodbye on the cheek. (For a split second, I must admit, I wondered what she meant by that. Then I reminded myself Cec would never be intentionally mean.) 'He's a cute one,' she whispered in my ear. Then, standing up, 'Breakfast tomorrow?'

'Sure,' I said. 'Could it be not too early? I'm not a morning person.'

'Yeah,' said Bryn, taking Cecile's hand and walking away, waving over her shoulder. '*Right.*'

★  ★  ★

With the bonfire warming my face and setting his profile aglow, Zach and I had one of those conversations that, at the time, seemed like one of the best I'd ever had in my life, although now I suppose it was fairly standard for college underclassmen. We talked about getting homesick; I thought of my big brother Henry so often that *missing him* became its own distinct category of emotion. But we both loved the fact that Boulder had real seasons, the Aspen trees turning gold in the fall and dropping their leaves all within an hour of one another — as if on cue — with the first winter storm. We talked about not knowing what we wanted to do with our lives, but finding it exhilarating; like this was an adventure, and nothing bad could happen to us before we got the end. I told him about how I'd always wanted to be a painter, but lately I was having a hard time with the critical discourse portion of the class — the part where my work, usually praised by my high school art teacher, Mrs Calderwell, was ripped to shreds by the professor and a coterie of her favourite students who, frankly, I didn't think were that good themselves. We spoke about how much we loved Boulder; how the place had an almost magical allure.

'Did you know it's cursed?' Zach asked, shifting on the hay bale and facing me.

I shook my head.

'When this land was taken from the Native Americans, they put a hex on it.' His whiskers glinted a soft brass in the firelight; I resisted the urge to reach out and touch them. 'Boulder became so dazzling, that from then on anyone who lived here would be trapped for ever in a small paradise that's really a prison.'

'You can check out anytime you like,' I semi-sang, mocking him, 'but you can *never lee-heave.*'

He laughed and told me to shut it.

'Speaking of which,' Zach said, 'are you going to stay for the summer?'

'Staying, I hope. Bryn and Cecile found a cheap sublet on Pennsylvania so I'm trying to convince my parents. Of course they're going to make me get a job.'

'I'm trying to find a place with my buddy David,' he said.

'You will. The Boulder hex demands it.'

'Too true,' Zach said. He broke into a squeaking falsetto: '*Welcome to the Hotel California. Such a lovely place. Such a lovely place . . .* ' As people started to turn around, Zach stood and committed himself, belting The Eagles until the drunken frat boys started clapping. '*Plenty of room at the Hotel California —* '

I was blushing, tugging on his arm. I begged him — *Please, Zach. Please, you must!* — to cut it out. My stomach ached from laughing so hard. He just wouldn't stop.

*  ★  ★  ★

Zach walked me back to my dorm. I was a little drunk. He was a little drunk. I may have been a little drunker than he was, which made me bold. I wasn't confident about my body, my wit, or my looks, but in college I'd discovered that when alcohol was involved and sex was in the air, I loosened up in a way I never had in other areas of my life. Cecile liked to hypothesise that I secretly craved love; that drinking too much gave me permission to throw affection down on my

39

bed, metaphorically speaking, and grab it with both hands. But after all those years of wishing I could get boys to like me in high school, I thought it was possible that I'd just become kind of an easy lay.

When we got to my door, I asked him in.

'No room-mate?' Zach said.

'It's a single.'

He raised an eyebrow and smiled.

I turned the key and before I could turn on a light, his hands were reaching for me. We started to kiss in the dark; our fingers tangled in one another's hair.

Soon my T-shirt was on the floor. Zach's hands were on my back. Then we were on the bed, and I remember thinking how much I liked kissing him, his lips like two ripe strawberries. Every now and then my elbow or knee would bump the brick wall abutting my bed. It scraped. I didn't care. As the kissing got more intense, my hand started to move where I thought Zach wanted it to go.

'Jesse, wait.'

He put his hand over my wrist.

I paused. 'What's wrong?'

In the moonlight coming through my window, his skin looked blue. 'I think we should talk,' he said.

'OK,' I sat up and pulled the sheet around me.

'I really like you,' he began.

'Oh God,' I said, pulling the sheet tighter. 'Whenever a guy starts a sentence with *I really like you*, it's always something. So lemme guess. You're already hooking up with some girl in your dorm.'

Zach shook his head. No.

'You're not looking for a relationship.'

A shrug. Not exactly.

'Just say it.'

'Girlfriend back home,' he said.

'Serious?'

'Well, we've been together since we kissed behind Mr Minor's class at the junior high school dance,' he said.

I bit my lip and looked down at myself, bundled up in a sheet next to some guy who belonged to someone else. I was suddenly ashamed, thinking, *Why do guys always tell you things like this when you're not wearing any clothes?*

'Look, Jesse, I really am sorry,' Zach reached out and touched my arm. (Insult, meet injury.) 'The truth is I want to break up with her — I'm not lying to you — but we've been together for ever and she keeps talking about how she knows we can make it. It's like every time I try to talk to her she just won't hear me and I don't know . . . ' He ran his fingers through his hair. 'I just don't know.'

'So you took me home because you figured I was up for it,' I said, taking the sheet with me as I went to put my T-shirt back on. It left him laying there in his boxers, looking stupid. I couldn't decide if I cared. 'I get it. It's not like you were that far off.'

'Don't say that. I really do like you,' he said. He propped himself on one elbow. 'I'm sorry. I screwed up. I'm an asshole, OK? I'm an asshole.'

I felt around the floor for my T-shirt.

'You're not an asshole,' I said, tugging it over my head and dropping the sheet. 'You're a guy.'

'Gee, thanks.' Zach swung his bare legs over the side of the bed and reached for his shoes. He paused. 'Wait. OK. Here's an idea: what if we just called a time-out? Not to be like this but, I don't think it's going to last, you know? I mean, is it bad that I'd like to think I could call you? That maybe I can sort this out and we can pick up where we left off?'

I stood there, with my bra balled up in my hand, not sure what to do.

'You like me, huh?' I said.

'Seriously. I do. It's dumb, but I feel like I can talk to you.'

I stood there, looking at him. Sizing him up.

42

'Now I feel stupid,' he said.

'No,' I said. 'Don't. Listen,' I said, trying to sound casual, even though inside I was mortified at how easily — once again — I'd almost gone to bed with the *wrong* dude, 'you can call me. Then maybe someday I'll like you back.'

Zach stood, buttoning his trousers, and picked up his jacket from the back of my desk chair.

'You'll like me again. I know you will.' He smiled. 'Jesse, will you please write down your number?'

# 5

## Carpet Diem

I stole a cigarette from David's jacket while Bryn was moving her car out of the emergency-room parking lot. It was crooked like a broken finger. She never got off my back about my smoking, and I almost considered quitting just to get her to shut up about it. But with David, she looked the other way as long as he didn't do it in the house. Something about how he'd promised to quit the moment he got out of writing video game code, which was lonely and tedious work. He wanted to write scripts, which was lonely and tedious but 'creative' work. David was a huge fan of science fiction movies, always going to different conventions, and he would heatedly argue until the end of time that William Shatner was an unsung genius. David, computer geek, halo champion, D & D wizard, was the only man I'd ever seen Bryn bend for.

I snuck outside and found a secluded little concrete nook just to the left of the emergency-room doors. I carefully smoothed out the cigarette's papery skin, gently pushing the tobacco around until it was evenly distributed, before I lit the end with a pilfered match.

As I inhaled, I inspected the indentations the hospital carnations were making in my palm. *Should I call my mother?* I wondered, looking for the moon, which was obscured by the reflection of the city lights in a lightly clouded night sky. *My dad? My brother? What would I tell them? What could they do?*

I felt a tear slide down my face and I wiped it away furtively. If anyone caught me crying, tears would be a harbinger when all anyone wanted was hope. Or sleep. Or for today to be like the day before, when nothing had happened. I heard a voice behind me.

'What do you get when you paint all the cars in the nation pink?'

'You're out,' I said, turning around to see Zach.

'I just saw everyone else inside,' he said. 'I only have a minute.'

He was still wearing his softball clothes. Between his baseball jersey and my tennis skirt, it occurred to me that we must have looked like two lifestyle models from a bad catalogue. Zach's hands were deep in his pockets, and his sandy hair was tweaking out behind his ears like a Gerber baby's. I was struck by how handsome he was, even now. It was the wrong thought and it caught me by surprise, like when you spill a glass of milk even though you're an adult now and those things aren't supposed to happen. Zach was Cecile's fiancé.

'Fiend,' he said, nodding towards the cigarette. He looked tired.

'Sorry,' I muttered. 'Zach, I'm really sorry.'

'What do you get?' He asked again.

'Huh?'

'When you paint all the cars in the nation pink.'

I shook my head. I didn't know.

'A pink carnation.'

I smiled weakly and handed the flowers to him. He peeked at the card and gave a small laugh when he saw what I'd written. *Sorry these are so ugly. Please get better now.*

Zach took the cigarette out of my hand, took a puff, stuck his tongue out like, *blech,* and handed it back.

'The knuckle-heads inside will tell you everything you don't already know, but these doctors play it pretty close to the chest.'

'Is she going to be all right?' I asked.

Zach shrugged. 'Dunno,' he said. 'Hope so. Look, just hang tight, OK? I'll give these to Cecile as soon as I can.'

With that, he gently socked my shoulder

and walked back into the hospital, the electric doors sighing as he passed.

*   *   *

Cecile opened her eyes twelve hours after the accident, but she was still considered a Number Two — just one tick above comatose — on the ludicrously named Rancho Los Amigos scale. (When Zach told me this was what the alertness measurement system was called, I thought he was making another bad joke and replied, '*Olé*.') On her third day she responded to her mother's voice and started breathing on her own, so she was upped to a Three. Of course, Bryn and I weren't allowed to see her making these incremental improvements. Only family in the ICU.

*   *   *

Dispensing second-hand information became something of a ritual over the next two weeks. Namely, passing information on to concerned parties like a game of telephone. Close friends like Laura — our friend from Boulder — and her boyfriend Chaz got called first. Then Cecile's work colleagues, then people who'd drifted out of our lives as they moved from one state to another or, sometimes, from

Hollywood to Brentwood, which was a different kind of world away. We called friends who were writing for reality television shows, friends who had babies and quit their jobs, friends who had broken up altogether. I stood outside the hospital waiting room, mobile phone pressed to my ear, and relayed Zach's request: No visitors. Send flowers. People always wanted to know a surprisingly detailed diagnosis — there invariably was an aunt or a cousin who'd had a similar case — so I memorised her condition like a waiter learning the daily specials. The terms were unjustly beautiful, and difficult to say. Contusion . . . edema . . . hematoma . . .

Nevertheless, every day Bryn and I, desperate to do something — anything — brought a present to the hospital and gave it to Zach. One day it was another bouquet. The next a toy lion holding a heart that said, 'Soon you'll be *roaring* to go!' Eventually we had to get creative so I brought porn.

★ ★ ★

My first summer in Boulder, Bryn, Cecile and I moved into the sub-let that turned into our permanent residence after the owner decided to stay in Portland. It was a Victorian a few blocks north of the university, in the middle of the historic part of town. The ground floor was ours — there was an upstairs studio rented by a grad student we hardly ever saw. We had two bedrooms, one bathroom, a living room, a small yard, and a kitchen with a breakfast fast nook. Cecile, whose parents were willing to pay extra rent, took the smaller bedroom at the front. Bryn and I shared the bigger room at the back, tucked behind the little kitchen. The house was old — sticky door jambs, windows painted shut, and about seven different shades of blue on the walls — but I did my best to make it home. I sanded down the doors, pried windows open and painted walls, fuelled by a month-long diet-pill and soft-drink binge. (I was under the misapprehension that if I lost weight I'd look like Cec. No dice. Paint job looked good, though.) I covered our thrift shop couches with Paisley tapestries, and used old milk bottles as vases. 'Those look pretty, angel,' Cecile would say, stopping to consider some new throw pillows I'd sewn out of vintage scarves. Sometimes she'd bring me iced tea as I worked on a painting in the storage shed, which I'd converted into a small art studio for myself. 'I wish I could make things,' she'd say, nosing around my brushes, broken ferules, stretcher strips, and a stack of new canvases, still enticingly wrapped in cellophane. She'd sit in an old lawn chair, reading a worn romance novel while I painted, occasionally looking up to ask me about a technique, or a colour I was mixing. Once I surprised Cec with a blank canvas set up on my table-top easel. 'Go for it,' I said, sitting her down.

'What should I do?' she asked. I told her we could start with a kind of exercise, in which she had to paint me without looking at the canvas. It would teach her to let go, I explained, to see beauty without being too literal about it. She painted for an hour, finally looking down to see what she'd done.

'My God, no!' she said. 'I made you so ugly!'

She turned the canvas around to show me. My nose took up half of it, and my hair hung in strings around my face like garter snakes. 'I think you've captured a real likeness,' I said.

Cecile shook her head, vowing to leave the 'art stuff' to the professionals. Before she left, she paused at the door. 'You're so pretty, Jesse,' she said. I blushed and told her to get lost. Cec sighed. 'Sometimes I wish I could stick my eyes in your head, so you could look in the mirror and see yourself the way I do. You have no idea how attractive — and how talented — you are.'

★　★　★

We spent the summer drinking beer, swimming in the Boulder reservoir, and napping during the gentle rainstorms that blew in from the mountains in the afternoons. One evening, it was my turn to close Wash, the clothing store where I worked part time. Bryn and Cecile wanted me to meet them at a barbecue that a friend of ours, Laura, had invited us to. I liked Laura. She, like me, was from Los Angeles, and she was into art. However, she knew what she wanted to do with it: graphic design. Laura was always in the Mac lounge on campus, designing flyers for parties, along with posters for the Student Council. I admired how organised she was, and the fact that she wore avant-garde, black-rimmed glasses that declared to the world, *That's right. I'm creative. What the hell are you?*

But that day I was exhausted. My friends didn't work; they didn't have to. Cecile's father was an investment banker, her mother a socialite who was on the board of several Manhattan charities. Bryn's parents were both divorce lawyers in Chicago. (Happily married, go figure.) My parents — who split when I was six — weren't so well off. My mother was a published author who still gave lectures now and then; my father was in commercial real estate, but not the Donald Trump kind.

At the end of a nine-hour shift, I locked up the shop, dragged myself home, and fell asleep watching an old movie on TV. There were cook-outs every night that summer. As I drifted off, I thought, *I'm not missing a thing*.

★ ★ ★

The next morning I was drinking coffee and doing the crossword puzzle on the steps of our back porch when Cecile appeared in the kitchen doorway.

'What happened to you last night?' she said, sitting down on the concrete above me.

'I couldn't rally,' I said, leaning back to rest my head on her knee. 'Was it fun?'

'It was OK.' She scratched her leg. She had a mosquito bite. She frowned in concentration as she scratched, a curl of hair falling into her grassy eyes. 'Jesse?'

'Hm?'

'Remember that guy, Zach?'

'Who?' I said, thinking, *Oh, I remember*.

'The guy you kissed at that frat party last spring but didn't like because he was kind of a mama's boy?'

'Hm.' I closed my eyes as though basking

in the sun. During breakfast with Cec and
Bryn the morning after Zach told me he had
a girlfriend, I told my friends he wasn't my
type. I used all kinds of vague justifications
for this so-called change of heart. Mama's
boy must have been one of them. I was too
mortified to tell Bryn — especially Bryn
— that I'd taken off my underwear before I
even knew his dating status, and I figured that
if he called, I could just tell them I'd changed
my mind. 'Oh yeah,' I said. 'Zach from San
Francisco.'

'Did you think he was nice?' Cec's voice
had a funny twinge in it.

'He seemed OK. Why do you ask?'

'He asked me out.'

I opened my eyes.

'Oh God, Jesse, is that all right?' Cecile
scooted one step down so she was next to me
and grabbed my hand. 'Do you like him? I
thought you said you didn't like him. Did
I make a mistake? I can call him and tell him
never mind.'

'No it's just . . . what happened?'

Cecile took a breath and blew it out. She
looked soap-commercial fresh even though
she must have gone to bed later than I did.
'We started talking at the barbecue,' she said.
'Turns out it was at his place with some guy
named David who Laura knows. So I hung

out for a while. We talked, and then he asked if I wanted to get dinner sometime. I swear I didn't think you'd care. Do you care?'

Cecile was looking at me — her eyes wide in potential horror — and I knew she would back out of the date if I asked her to. I could also tell she liked him.

'No, honey, it's fine,' I said. 'Really. But . . . doesn't he have a girlfriend?'

'Oh my God, I'm so relieved,' she said, leaning forward and hugging me. 'He did have one, yeah. He told me about it: they broke up last spring. Are you *sure* it's OK? Because I told him I was your room-mate — OK, not right away, I'm sorry — but honestly, if you're not cool with it — '

'Don't be silly,' I said. 'We're like, ancient history.'

'So you're *sure* sure? Like one hundred per cent?'

'Stop it, you're bugging me,' I said, picking up my newspaper. 'Just seize the day and let me finish my crossword puzzle.'

'Jesse, you're the *best friend* ever.' Cecile kissed me on the forehead. 'I love you, bunny. I do, I do.'

She yelped with excitement and ran into the house.

'I hope he calls me!' she yelled over her shoulder.

'I do too!' I said.

He did.

★ ★ ★

Zach and Cecile started spending every night together, and soon his deodorant was a regular fixture on our bathroom counter. Around the same time, Bryn and Zach's room-mate, David, began an on-again, off-again thing that I could never keep track of. One minute Bryn adored David, the next she was bored, then adoring him, then bored . . . I told myself I would forget about Zach, and eventually, my wish came true. This was Boulder, after all, a hippie, summer-of-love kind of place where anything went. As the months slid by, I found new guys to have crushes on, new people to grope with in the dark.

When Bryn and David finally got their act together in the senior year and he proposed, I became the only one in our little group who was always showing up at our various snowboarding trips, birthdays and game nights with a different guy on my arm. I told myself it didn't matter. When the guy was gone, I would always have *them*. All of them. 'Men are fleeting,' I told Cecile one night when we stayed up late to talk in the kitchen over leftover pizza and warm diet root beer, 'but my friends are for ever.'

★ ★ ★

Cecile was driving west on Beverly Boulevard when the cab driver lost control and swerved into oncoming traffic. The police report said he was arguing with a passenger in the back seat about which route to take downtown. The driver was killed on impact, but the passenger, miraculously, walked away from the accident and called 911 from her mobile phone. The speed of the cab would be determined by something called friction analysis. Zach had been spending most of his time — when he wasn't talking to Cecile's neurophysiologist — meeting with accident lawyers and a claims investigator.

Day five. As I drove to the hospital, I felt like I couldn't breathe. Like I was being pressed on from all sides. Any minute I feared my mobile would ring and Zach would tell me Cecile was dead or would never walk or speak again. Like white-coated Cassandras, the doctors kept reminding us that it could take weeks, even months, before we'd know the full effects of her injury. There could be chronic fatigue, memory loss, cognitive difficulties, personality changes (how quickly

56

we learn to let the terrible possibilities roll off the tongue). She still wasn't talking. Still no visitors. That afternoon I met a woman, Stella, at the vending machine. Her husband's car had rolled off the 5 Freeway. He, like Cec, had TBI (traumatic brain injury) and for weeks after he regained consciousness he hadn't been himself, screaming at his wife, overturning cafeteria trays, manically pacing the halls, dropping to the floor with seizures. It was a phase that with any luck would pass, the nurses told her, but Stella was worn out. She thought when he woke up, he'd be the same.

'Just pace yourself, that's all I'm saying,' Stella said, laying a shaky hand on my shoulder before she walked away. 'Bones heal faster than brains.'

I watched her go. And then, when the last swish of her denim-clad thighs faded away, I found myself running in the opposite direction. I ran down the hospital corridor, crossed the lobby, climbed the car park stairs, and made a beeline for my car, all with my hand over my mouth. I slammed my car door behind me, and I started bawling, crying like a child cries. *'What the fuck?'* I yelled, to nobody. To the cars. My voice sounded foreign in my ears. I gasped and I started to sputter, tears running down my face and mucus dripping out of my nose. *'WHAT THE FUCK?'* I yelled again.

The car park echoed back to me.

It said, *'Fuck!'*

I started banging my hand against the steering wheel. It hurt. It felt good.

*'What the fuck? What the fuck? What the fuck?'*

When I was finally quiet, I started the car, and I drove home. Tears were still running down my face when I let myself in, got into bed. I cried for Cecile. I cried for Zach, and Bryn, and of course myself. I cried for not even being allowed the small favour of knowing what exactly would become of her.

★　★　★

The following morning I was sitting with an unread magazine in my lap and popping open a soft drink, asking Bryn if it was bad to drink a second can of Red Bull before 10 a.m., when I saw my brother Henry walking briskly towards us down the hospital corridor. He was wheeling his suitcase behind him. He must have come straight from the airport — he'd been producing a segment at the Astrodome in Sacramento — and he was loosening his tie as though he were going to rip his shirt open and reveal a giant 'S.'

Henry grabbed me and pulled me to him. 'God damn it,' he said, reaching another arm out for Bryn, who was getting ready to leave so she could get to the office for a few hours. 'God damn *shit*. Come here, both of you.'

Three bear hugs later, Bryn kissed me goodbye, making me promise I'd call her if there were any changes. Henry dragged me to the cafeteria to get me something proper to eat, tossing the Red Bull in the trash in disgust. He ordered me a veggie omelette with wheat toast and fruit, even though I said I didn't think I could eat.

'Just, seriously,' he held up his hand as I protested. 'Shut up.'

We sat at a faux-oak table in the corner of the cafeteria, diagonally opposite to a group of nurses. 'That one scene was just so unbe*lie*vable,' one of them was saying. 'Anyone knows a head wound like that would bleed so much she'd be *blinded* by her own blood.'

'That chick's hot, though,' said a male nurse. Everyone at the table laughed.

'So,' Henry said, digging into his breakfast and nudging my plate towards me. 'How's everybody holding up?'

'Bryn thinks Zach seems overly anxious about the lawsuit,' I said, taking a bite of my omelette, the first swallow hitting my stomach in a way that was far more satisfying than I was prepared to give it credit for. 'He keeps saying, you know, 'We're not the kind of people who sue everyone in sight . . . But the medical insurance won't let us *not* sue.' '

'That poor guy.'

He shook his head and took a sip of his milk. Henry was the only gay man in the world who drank half a gallon a day as though he was, at any moment, going to be picked by his football coach for first string in the big game.

'So now what?' he asked.

'We wait.'

'And in the meantime?'

As a matter of fact, Zach had given me a couple of jobs to do, and considering my breakdown the day before, I was thankful for any task, no matter how small, just to feel like I was *doing* something. I was to retrieve some insurance files from his home office and pick things up from the drug store — he wanted some socks, a three-pack of T-shirts, stuff like that — while Bryn, ever the lawyer, had requested the wedding vendor contracts; she was hoping she could find a way to prove that Zach and Cecile were entitled to a full refund on all their commitments.

Henry balled his napkin up and tossed it on to the table.

'I'll drive you,' he said.

'Aren't you on a deadline?'

He was always on a deadline.

'Not im-*me*-diately. Look, I can always drink a ton of coffee, make Hameer bring me a takeaway, and take it to the editing bay tonight. Hey.' He reached across the table and stroked the back of my hand with his fingertips. It itched. I ached. 'Everything's going to be OK,' he said.

⋆　⋆　⋆

A couple of months before the accident, Zach and Cecile bought a three-bedroom Craftsman house in Hollywood Dell. It was built in the early 1900s, when developers lured middle-class families West with romantic but affordable architecture that, they said, would rescue them from the woes of industrialisation. Such humble beginnings sold for well over a million now, but the afterglow of big dreams from little places could still be felt on a sunny winter day.

I let us in and Henry whistled softly. I felt the same: There were original post-and-beam ceilings and hand-hewn windows, set off by a generously sized kitchen and a subzero fridge. From the living-room window, you could see a swing in front that overlooked their leafy garden — ferns and bricks covered in moss — and, through French doors at the back of the house, there was an outdoor living room with a hammock stretched between two leafy oak trees. I didn't have to ask Cecile how she could afford it.

I picked up the newspapers off the front path and gave them to Henry to throw away in the dustbin at the side of the house. Walking into the hall, I inhaled a scent that was pure Cecile. Almond-scented lotion. *I should take her some*, I thought. Then I blushed — how silly, how trite. They'd only been in the house a couple of months, so it wasn't really furnished yet. I couldn't help but notice that the furniture from their old apartment looked too sentimentally collegiate for their new home. I heard beeping coming from the bedroom and it took me a moment to realise what it was: Zach's alarm clock must've been set but he hadn't been home to hear it. I walked to their bedroom and turned it off.

'Jesse?' Henry called from the front door. It took him only a dozen strides to get from the entrance, past the dining and living rooms, to the back bedrooms. Unlike the modern condo he shared with Hameer in Studio City, with its thirteen-foot-high ceilings and slate tile that echoed, in Cecile's home — which wasn't small, by any means — Henry looked like a grisly bear in a camping tent. He cocked his head.

'Dog?'

'Happy's at the neighbours'.'

'Ah. Hey, speaking of neighbours,' he said, 'Mom wants to know if you're coming to dinner next Friday.'

I'd completely forgotten. Mom, normally the least sentimental woman in the world, loved Christmas, and liked to have us over pre-holiday for a family dinner so she could show off her tree before we cluttered its perfection with poorly wrapped presents. I hadn't even started buying gifts yet, and it was already the twelfth. I thought of our mom and dad — squabbling, divorced, but still sharing meals every now and then 'for the children' — and shook my head. *Maybe Cecile will be out in time*, I thought. *Then I'll be able to go.* I rested my head on the bedroom door jamb as Henry paused to study a framed picture hanging in the hallway. It was of Cecile, Zach, Bryn, David and I drinking margaritas and wearing stupid sombreros with those little dangly ball things hanging off. Cec's twenty-sixth, two years ago.

'You guys look so young in this one,' he said.

★　★　★

I left Henry investigating the pictures and went into the guest room, where Zach said he'd put his filing cabinet. Rounding the corner, my heart stopped. Hanging off the back of the closet door were four bridesmaid dresses. One for me, one for Bryn, one for Zach's sister Derry, and one for Laura, who had become a graphic designer after all — she worked in a creative agency in Santa Monica, where she lived with her equally groovy stylist boyfriend, Chaz. ('It's a miracle he's not gay,' Henry had muttered after meeting him for the first time.) The dresses were wrapped in plastic; it billowed as I walked into the room. They must have come after Cecile had left for our tennis lesson, or she would have brought mine. I saw the green silk with the ivory ties that we'd picked out at a dressmaker's showroom downtown, a happy day when Bryn and I congratulated Cecile for picking out dresses in a shade of pea green that we'd never want to wear again. A funny noise came out of my throat — a cross between a gurgle and a gasp. Henry came rushing in from the hallway.

'They've already been altered,' I said, shaking my head and pointing, on the verge of tears again. 'We can't take them back.'

'You won't have to.' Henry pulled me in and smoothed my hair. 'Look at me.' He put his hands on both sides of my face. '*You won't have to.*'

# 6

## A Total Genius with Colour

When Cecile got moved to a recovery floor the following Monday, I ran to Savon and bought a box of chocolates and a giant teddy bear that was so big I had to put it in the front seat for the drive. (Got me in the car pool lane, very exciting.) Bryn and I were told that we could visit her alone for ten minutes each. I'd go that morning, Bryn after work. Zach met me at the elevators.

'I have to go downstairs and make some calls,' he said, looking beaten down by the last nine days of worry and stress. His cheeks were hollow and his lips chapped. 'But I'm going to walk you in. She gets a little disoriented — sometimes she doesn't know where she is, but she'll know you. If she starts to throw up, make sure to get a nurse because she could rupture something. The medication's been tricky. She won't talk much and half of what she does say doesn't make much sense anyway, but she can hear fine so don't be afraid to be your charming self. OK?'

'OK.' I watched an extremely elderly

patient in a hospital gown get wheeled by with an IV, her mouth open in such a way that it made her look like a dying fish. 'Jesse,' Zach tried to make eye contact. 'Do you need me to stay with you?'

'No, I got it,' I said. 'Seriously. I just want to see her.'

'Good.'

Zach opened the door of Cecile's room.

'Honey?' he said quietly. 'Jesse's here.'

I stepped inside and saw a person in a hospital bed whom, if Zach hadn't brought me in himself, I would not have recognised.

Cecile's beautiful face was so swollen that she looked like someone had taken an air pump and filled her up like a birthday balloon. Jaw, nose, cheeks, everything was distorted. Her head was wrapped in white gauze. Her hair, which she'd been growing out over the last year for her wedding, was shaved on one side. Wherever there weren't bandages there were painful-looking bruises. Her skin was the colour of weak tea. Her chest was strapped; her wrist in a cast. Her hands were bound to the hospital bed — Zach had said she sometimes lost her bearings, and the nurses did this to keep her from trying to get out of bed. Under the blanket, her body caved inward, like the old lady in the hall.

I went to Cecile, and her eyes started to tear.

'Hi, baby,' I said. 'How's my beautiful girl, huh? Oh, honey. Are you OK my sweet angel?'

She shook her head. No.

Her eyes were wide with fear. I turned to look for Zach, but he was already gone. There was, I saw, a piece of paper taped to the wall across from Cecile's bed with the days X'd off so she would know how long she'd been here, I presumed. Tears started to slide down her cheeks, and it was everything I could do not to start bawling on the spot. I didn't want to frighten her. I swallowed, hard.

Cecile started to shake her head, harder. No, she was telling me. No, no, no. She pulled at the restraints. The IV was slipping at a precarious-looking angle.

'Honey, stop that. Shhh. Calm down. You have to stay still,' I cooed. 'You could hurt yourself. Don't do that.' I lay my hand lightly over the cast on her wrist, remembering that Zach had also said she didn't like to be touched too much — everything hurt. 'Just breathe. You're OK. That's better. See? You're doing much, much better.'

She reached out with her little fingers, nails broken, engagement ring gone. I gave my hand to her and she tapped it.

'What is it, baby?'

When she spoke, her voice was the tiniest of whispers, the pain evident in every breath.

'I want to go skiing,' she said.

I bit my lip.

'*Skiing*,' she insisted.

'I know, honey,' I said gently. 'We'll all go skiing. Soon. Very soon. We're OK. Come on now. We're OK . . . '

It seemed like I'd only been there a few seconds when a nurse came to tell me my visit was up. I gave Cecile a soft kiss on her cast, and pulled the nurse into the hall. I told her about the skiing — what did this mean? Was it bad?

'That's a new one,' she said, chuckling. As I pestered her with questions, the nurse guided me back to the elevator and pressed the button. I didn't even realise this was happening until the doors started to shut and I could see her in kitty-cat print scrubs, walking briskly back down the hall.

★ ★ ★

You'd think over those terrible days that my boss might have called to see how Cecile was doing — she'd met her about four-hundred-and-seventy-five-thousand times, after all. But no. When I woke the next morning, there

69

was another clipped message on my voice-mail: 'Hi, Jesse. How are you? Look, I know it's so hard for you to focus whenever there's drama, but when you get a moment, call me.'

At the sound of Taryn's voice, I wanted to hurl the phone against the wall. Instead, I calmly deleted her, thinking of my dad's advice on how to handle moments like these: *File it away and forget it.* He'd been doing that with my mother — his ex-wife — for decades.

I was into my seventh year at Gilded Cage, and every now and then I tried to conjure up some sort of escape plan that never seemed to materialise. It's hard to say what I was thinking all those years while I was stocking Taryn's store with things that appealed to her terrible taste, but before I knew it, I was looking at the words 'Happy 29th!' written on my birthday cake, and I realised I was suddenly at the age where people expected more of me than I'd actually accomplished. I'd been running on fumes, respect-wise, for years. After all, at twenty-five, people expect you to still act like you're twenty-one. At twenty-seven, people make jokes about how thirty is the new twenty. But at twenty-nine, you find out that's all a lie, and, if you're still working retail, people look at you like, *What happened?* So you file it away and try to

70

forget it. Then you realise that doesn't always work.

*But so what?* I told myself. I didn't have a trust fund. It wasn't like I could just run out and open my own store the way Taryn had. Sure, I was pretty damn decent at interiors, but that didn't mean I could make a living at it; I could barely keep up with the student loans I already had. Besides, if other people didn't like the fact that my temporary job had become semi-permanent, that was their problem. I still had loads of time, right?

Over the next several days, I filed away Taryn's increasingly curdled messages. If she had any inkling how serious Cecile's condition was, she either didn't care or she really did have a plum pit for a heart.

Beep.

'It's Taryn. I know you're under stress, but I just can't say what will happen if I don't get those boards from you before Christmas.'

Beep.

'The meeting with our new client — or have you forgotten Lizzie Biggens? — is in two weeks. I will be here, by the phone, waiting for your call, for the next hour.'

Beep.

'What the hell . . . Jesse?'

Beep.

Taryn Tupping was one of those girls who

went to private school with kids who had last names like Von der Patton and Robidoux. There were rumours that her family had some connection to the *Mayflower*, but I was willing to bet that was sheer bull. She was thin as a whip of liquorice and had straight blond hair which she kept snipped just below her hatchet-shoulder blades. She wore the uniform that LA socialites wore; dark blue tailored designer jeans, pointy shoes, and a usually silky, always expensive, semi-revealing top. There was a gap in her front two teeth that made me think of a cute little squirrel the day I went in for my first interview. Later, that gap would become more and more feral to me. The store, for Taryn, was a vanity gig and my job was to take up all of the slack for none of the glory.

The Biggens in question was a studio executive who was auditioning Gilded Cage to design the interiors for her new Pacific Palisades home. At the initial interview, Biggens announced she wanted a house that was 'thinking outside the box', so she could strike fear and awe in the heart of every agent and studio executive in the land. She would, therefore, be re-interviewing three decorators. The one who got the commission would surely ride the word-of-mouth train well into the next decade, not to mention the fact that with Biggens's connections, her home was a showcase for a glossy spread in a decor magazine. Money and status, the two things closest to Taryn's heart. She loved the thought of bagging Biggens more than she loved herself, and this was really saying something.

Except she was choking. Big time.

'Jesse, I have a surprise,' Taryn tittered, pulling me aside one afternoon after the initial consultation. As though she was doing me a favour, Taryn said that I could 'take a first pass' at the mood board — essentially a giant collage of textile swatches, paint chips, inspirational photographs and tear sheets that evoked both the action decoration and the emotion of the house as we saw it — for the Biggens presentation, which would take place the week after Christmas.

I started to say the deadline was too close to Cec's wedding, which was on the twentieth, not to mention the holiday break, but Taryn waved that away.

'Do one of those textural pieces you're so good at,' she said. 'Because honestly? If you start applying yourself? I think one day you'll be a total genius with colour.'

It was ironic that I worked for a woman like Taryn. When I got to Colorado, I was convinced I would make my living as a painter. Not necessarily one of importance — I had none of the impetuous flair for shocking the masses that it took to become truly esteemed — but as a working artist who showed at galleries and sold a piece now and then. I was passionate, dorkily enough, about still lifes. I think it had something to do with wanting to tease out a sense of order in my surroundings — child of a broken home, mother a promiscuous writer, blah, blah, blah. Whether it was the books in my locker or the vinyl sheen on my mom's sleeping pills, conceptually, I believed, I could capture the significance of these items and imbue them with meaning. Childish, maybe, but in high school I was interested in the bonnet ornaments on all the fancy cars parked outside the local valley mall, the Jacuzzi we had out back that I once saw my mother having sex in with a man I never laid eyes on again. (Nor did she, I expect.) Mrs Calderwell, who let me eat my lunch in her classroom so I could have the studio to myself, stoked my dreams over stale hamburgers from the cafeteria. We'd discuss what each of my paintings meant, and she'd offer touchy-feely but genuine encouragement.

'Oh this one is *very* Jungian,' she'd say, standing back, her bead necklaces clicking as she admired my latest oil of a neighbour's dead pet parakeet. 'The commoditisation of life is a *tremendous* topic. Think of it, Jesse, we're finally awakening to the Earth Mother's critique of our way of living. That's what you were going for, isn't it?'

'Kinda,' I'd mutter.

'You might want to try to add some form of healing energy, though,' she'd say. 'Think colour. Think light. Think balance. Do you see?'

Funnily enough, I sometimes did.

I had to wait until the second term of college to get into Marina Flook's painting class. I'd heard she was brilliant — one of her paintings had been included in the 1992 Whitney Biennial, and she had galleries showing her work in Phoenix, Portland, *and* Denver. I'd never been so impressed.

The first day of class we all brought a portfolio of our work, and I remember Flook was particularly taken with a student named Roger Koplovitz who was into painting Nazi concentration camp schematics on to designer shopping bags. As Professor Flook walked around the room, her Tevos making slaps on the splattered concrete floor while she pulled at the neck of a black turtleneck that was so close in shade to her hair it was hard to see where one finished and the other began, I thought that I would do well, considering the pop culture references in Roger's work. But when she got to my portfolio, Flook flipped a couple of pages and laid a consoling hand on my shoulder, saying, 'There are those of us who are on the verge and those of us who have a bit further to go. But don't worry,' *pat, pat,* 'I can fix you.'

I consulted Flook in her office on everything I painted, hoping it would give me the confidence — the '*bold audacity*' — to become a real artist. But the more questions I asked, the more questions I had. I soon found myself painting exactly what she asked me to paint, yet with every piece I did she seemed only more disgusted with me. '*No!*' she snapped one afternoon, while I was painting the genitals on a nude male model. 'If you feel so dispassionate about your subject — class, pay attention to this — if you feel *no passion* for the *penis*, then don't paint it. Just' — she picked up my brush and smudged over a testicle that I'd spent half an hour trying to shade — 'shadow it out!'

'She's a Flooking phony and a Flooking bitch,' said Bryn that night at the Sink. 'You, Jesse, are *extremely passionate* about the penis.'

Cecile nodded, her green eyes flashing as she picked up a slice of pizza and offered it to me. 'Don't listen to her, Jess, she has no idea what she's talking about.'

Bryn asked if maybe I should just go to the administrator and ask if I could drop the class, and take it from someone else the following term.

'You want her to give up?' Cecile interrupted, slapping her pizza down on her plate. '*Absolutely not*. Jesse, I'd rather see you get an F painting what you want than give that hack the satisfaction.'

I was torn. 'I just want to get it right,' I said. 'I don't know. I'm starting to hate painting as much as I used to hate every other subject. What should I do? I mean, how do I learn to 're-see' a penis?'

Bryn and Cecile met eyes for a moment, and then they said, 'Field research', in unison, dissolving into giggles and ducking when I picked up a pepperoni and threw it at them.

★ ★ ★

Our final project counted for 80 per cent of our grade, because, as Flook liked to say, 'In art there is no room for mediocrity.' Every night, every day, I struggled to come up with an idea that would have a message, a point . . . I pictured myself getting an A. I pictured myself getting an F. If I got an F, I would quit being a painter, because the whole point was to be able to have a vision that could withstand — no, *improve* — with criticism. That was what all the other artists in class said over our lunches in the quad.

Four weeks before the project was due I came up with an idea. This time, I didn't consult Flook. I would create a doll's house — an actual doll's house — of a home in Boulder that had burned down with the family inside. I'd been disturbed by the articles in the paper, perhaps because there was a mother, a father, a son who looked like Henry, and another daughter who had, I thought, a minor resemblance to myself. I planned to recreate their entire environment. Their books, their furniture, their toys — all as it might have been. There was a doll's house shop on the south side of town, and I started going there every other day, begging my parents to bankroll hundreds of dollars worth of miniatures. I wanted detail, *painstaking detail*. I created the rooms in the plywood house, paying attention to layout and point of view, and then I shifted things just a little bit, so the perspective would become unsettling, almost nauseating. While I worked, Cecile visited me. She talked to me about my idea, brought me a sandwich or a Coke. After my model was done, I began painting canvases of it, one room at a time. I tried to be literal. I wanted to see if my concept would work, and, thrillingly, the strange 'off-ness' of the scale was reproducible. The paintings were disturbing. Creepy, even. I considered it a great victory that, upon careful examination, if you were being smart about it, you'd realise the paintings were not of real rooms but of miniature ones. The finishing touch was that I burned the doll's house down, so the model no longer existed except in the portraits I'd created. I titled my series — thrillingly, I thought — 'Case Study Number 4, After the Number Four as it Relates to the Four Members of the Calypso Family.'

Several of the paintings weren't even dry when I brought them to class.

Flook stood in front of the first oil and paused. She walked to the next painting. And the next. And the next. Then she started examining the documentation of my process; the house while it was under construction, the newspaper clippings, the ceremonial burning. She pulled on her turtleneck, and chewed the end of a paintbrush. I tried to stand still, not wanting to distract her from congratulating me on finally learning to 're-see' the circumstances of my childhood life.

'Jessica,' she asked, calling me to her side, 'honestly, I'm at a loss for words. Can you please explain to me what on earth would make you want to paint something that has absolutely no depth?'

I went home and took my paintings to the trash, leaning them up against the side of our house next to the bins. I changed my major to art history the following day, and, as I left the administration office, I saw Koplovitz — that hack, that phony — crossing campus with one of his ridiculous shopping bag pieces. He spotted me and asked if I wanted to come see the off-campus studio he was renting. I had no place else to go and I was curious, so I agreed. We got there, drank too much wine, smoked too much pot, and I had sex with him on a mattress he'd set up in the corner, probably dreaming that someday he'd be a good enough artist to get a girl to do exactly that. I suppose on some level my self-debasement was psych 101. A shrink might say that I felt I couldn't work creatively and with passion, so I decided to *screw* creatively and with passion. Just the same, it would turn out that I was good at that. Better than I could have ever hoped to be.

I never talked to Cecile about switching my major — I couldn't face her disappointment and I didn't want her to try to talk me out of it. She must have read my feelings correctly, because she kept a respectful distance. However, she did launch a kind of silent protest. About ten days after my shameful Koplovitz rendezvous, I let myself into Cec's room, hoping to borrow some of the eyeliner she was always telling me brought out my eyes. The poster she'd kept over her bed — a sentimental black-and-white photograph of a little girl holding a pink rose (the only thing in this dreaded image that had hue to it, like the ten exclamation points an adolescent girl would put in her first love letter) — was gone. Instead, my final project paintings — all of them — had been professionally framed and were hanging there, above Cecile's bed. They were a painful but loving reminder of her unwavering belief in me, and they remained there until college graduation.

# 7

## Breathing Room

On my first day back at work the weather was glorious, and it was as though the world was not only going back to normal, but was also going to be better, even, than it was before. Cecile had improved over the last several days at an astonishing rate. The hospital staff, as if in celebration, were decorating the halls with red and green crêpe paper, cut-outs of Santa Claus, and foil Jewish stars. In my imagination, the doctors would one day publish whole papers on Cecile, and give standing-room-only speeches about her recovery at medical conventions. She was able to speak in her normal voice. She could sit up. She could eat solid food. Little bits and pieces of her memory started coming back. She remembered nothing of the accident, but she did remember having breakfast with Bryn and I shortly before. Because of swelling in the tissue around her brain — a consequence of her surgery, the nurse said — she occasionally forgot things. She'd ask simple stuff, such as, 'What do you call the thing you use to call someone?' ('Telephone, dear,' her mother, the always immaculately groomed Mrs Carter, would say without skipping a beat, while thumbing through a copy of *Vogue*.) Or she'd turn to me and say, 'Could you pass the uh, the um, that, you know, the uh . . . ' ('Vase?' I'd ask. 'Glass? Remote? *Remote!*'). One day, I was visiting when the nurse brought Cecile's lunch — chicken, gravy, and some wilted-looking green beans.

'What's this?' Cecile asked me, frowning at the poultry with a pout that was surprisingly pretty for a girl in a green hospital gown with a shaved head.

'It's chicken,' I said.

'What does it taste like?'

'Oh baby,' I said, not sure if I wanted to laugh or cry. '*Everything* tastes like chicken.'

The doctors assured us this would pass. Cecile had phoned from the hospital that morning and she had sounded terrific. 'I peed!' she yelled. 'All by myself!' I was excited to just *breathe* again.

With everything that had happened, I hadn't set foot in Gilded Cage in nearly two weeks, and I was surprisingly refreshed. I threw open the back door and flicked on the lights, wondering what kind of nastiness Taryntula had been up to lately. Fortunately, she probably wouldn't be in until the afternoon, if at all. I switched on KCRW and got to work, flying through invoices, sorting orders, and arranging for the delivery of some new pieces. I was happy to discover that the brown wool felt I'd picked for a pair of New Regency chairs that had just come back was perfect — a chewy caramel that stood out in stark contrast to their white lacquer arms and legs. I put them out on the floor and tossed some crimson cushions on them: red-hots. On a nearby table I put out a set of Minori China. The caramel, red and blue worked. Fabulous, even. That night, I vowed, I'd go home and start again on the mood board for the Biggens residence. *Everything would be perfect*, I was thinking, *if only Taryn would fall on to something incredibly sharp*. The phone rang. As I picked it up, I saw Zach's number on the caller ID. My heart froze. Then I remembered we were in the clear.

Technically, the following day he and Cecile were supposed to get married, and that was exactly what Zach said he intended to do. He'd picked up his tux. He needed Bryn and me to go to the florist a.s.a.p. to pick out some flowers and he read me his credit card number so fast I had to scramble to get a pen from behind the register. David was going to the liquor store to buy champagne and some sparkling apple juice for Cec. Derry, Laura and Chaz were on board. I asked Zach if he was sure Cecile was up to it and yes, he assured me, he'd talked it over with Cecile's doctors and the nurses were beyond thrilled. She had become, after all, their favourite patient. An apparently hot priest from the hospital whom Cecile had nicknamed Father What-a-Waste would arrive at four to do the honours, and Zach had arranged for a violinist from the Phil to play the march in her room. Zach was on his way now to buy a wedding cake from a cheap-o place downtown, then he'd visit Cecile, who had no idea what was going on.

'I'm going to get the biggest, ugliest, nastiest cake they have,' Zach said. 'I'm getting *married*!'

I told Zach he was a man against whom all others should be measured. And I meant it. I really did.

★　★　★

When Bryn and I walked into Cecile's hospital room in our pea-green bridesmaid dresses, she started to laugh.

'Look at you!' she clapped, delighted, like we were pulling a prank. 'But you can't wear those! You should be saving them for the real wedding.'

'You mean you don't remember what day today is?' Bryn asked, handing Cecile a bouquet.

'Wait,' Cecile said, taking the flowers. 'Are you serious?' she asked, her hands flying to her face. 'Now?'

Bryn and I nodded. 'Jesse?' Bryn said, holding out her hand.

I handed her cosmetics case over and she zipped it open on Cec's bed.

'I'm thinking blushing bride — some peach, some gold on the lids, maybe. How about you, Jess?'

'Definitely. And something glossy for the lips.'

'Oh my God,' Cecile shouted. '*OH MY GOD!*'

At that moment, Derry, Laura and David, Zach's best man, came into the room.

Laura's boyfriend Chaz was the flower girl. He had a floral tiara in his shaggy brown hair, a suit with a *Def Leopard* T-shirt underneath, and a basket from which he threw petals at us. 'Don't say I haven't learned anything from styling all those photo shoots,' he said with a wink. 'I *know* how to throw flowers, you bitches.'

'Stand over there, guys, I'm almost done,' Bryn said, sweeping a little more blusher over Cecile's cheeks. She looked beautiful. Not much hair, but gorgeous just the same. 'Perfect.'

'Wait,' Cecile said, laughing as I pinned a veil on her head. 'Wait! Wait!'

'What, wait?' I said. 'The nurses are going to be in here throwing rice in a minute.'

Bryn signalled for the priest. Father What-a-Waste came in and stood at the edge of Cecile's bed. He asked Cec if she was up for the ceremony.

'Jesus Christ, yes! Sorry. I mean, of course, Father. Holy shit!'

He smiled; it was OK.

From outside the door came the strains of a violinist playing the *Wedding March*.

'Patrick?' Cecile said, when her friend from work walked through the door.

'Hi, princess,' he said.

Zach came next, somberly striding to the music, Cecile's bachelorette veil on his head. Cecile just lost it.

'*Oh my God!*' she gasped, crying and laughing at once, waving her hands like her nails were wet with polish. 'Excuse me, Father. Oh my God. Oh my God. Oh. Phew. Oh, oh, oh . . . '

Zach climbed into bed next to Cecile, and the minister jokingly picked up her chart as though he was going to check it — giving us all a chance to laugh and wipe our eyes before he read them their vows.

'Dearly Beloved, we are gathered here today . . . '

From my place, off to one side, I watched as Cecile and Zach pledged their love for one another, until death did them part. I watched Zach kiss her, gently, one hand on her cheek. And I watched her return that kiss, it passed like a private letter between them — we were not allowed to read all its meanings. It was a kiss between two people who were surviving, and overjoyed about it. I had never experienced a kiss like that. Considering what they'd been through in the last two weeks, I wasn't sure I would want to.

'Now who wants some champagne?' Zach said, holding up a bottle of Veuve Clicquot which we had chilling in a bedpan. I drank until my tongue turned fuzzy. Cecile had apple juice and threw the bouquet from inside the shower, which was the furthest away she could stand, and one of the hospital staff — a pretty night nurse named Carmen Lopez — caught it. Even David, who wasn't one for public displays, had to get a tissue from the bathroom. Cecile beamed at me from across the room and I blew her a kiss.

Two days later, Cecile died in her sleep.

# Part Two

# 8

## Anger, Denial, Depression and Decorating

As I pulled on to the 101 South, I tried to put the nine months that had passed since I saw Cecile's parents at the funeral into perspective. *It takes nine months to have a baby*, I thought. *The school year is nine months.*

After Cecile died, time stopped for a while, like in that movie where Bill Murray had to relive the same day over and over. I went to the store at nine, ate lunch at two, closed at six, was home at seven, read until midnight, lights out at one. On my days off, I hunched in my house, alone, like an intruder. I kept the curtains pulled and the phone turned off. I rearranged furniture, repainted the kitchen and cleaned out closets. I liked organising things. It made me feel calm.

Cecile died of what was called a spontaneous acute subdural hematoma, which was a fancy way of saying that an artery near the surface of her brain burst and killed her before the doctors could stop the bleeding. Nobody was to blame; nothing could have been done. Zach called to tell me as I was opening the shop, and I just stood there. He asked if I would drive to Bryn's house just so he'd know where we both were and I said, 'OK.' He asked if I could help with the arrangements and I said, 'OK.' I was so confused, so utterly surprised, that when he asked if I was sure I was all right I swore to him that I was 'A-OK.'

We did all the usual rituals. The funeral. The wake. I kept to myself for most of it. A few months later, I started trying to act normal again — going out, doing normal things. But on some days, as I went to dinner or listened to music and went on with the business of the living, I felt like something important was slipping away. It was as though I was standing at the edge of a dock and watching my favourite summer shawl undulating away from me on a fast-moving tide. *Why did I have to let her go?* I wondered. *Why couldn't I just jump in and bring her back to me?*

Taryn got the commission off the mood board I had finished last New Year's Eve. I lost myself in the work during the week after Cec's death, when I was anaesthetised with grief and my un-mailed Christmas cards glared at me from a messy stack on my dining-room table. As the months slid by

Taryn conveniently forgot about my contribution, so I was re-relegated to menial tasks, delivering things to Lizzie's house — the one I'd determined how to decorate, thank you very much — and saying nothing whenever Taryn passed one of my ideas off as her own. With my friend in the ground, I just didn't care. I'd been generally aimless, career-wise, for years of course, but without Cec I was worse, even, than I'd been. My days ended with a sense that something inside me was missing, like a sentence without a full stop at the end.

Out of the blue, Bryn got a call from Mr and Mrs Carter, Cec's parents. They were in town and wanted us to meet them at Cicada. As I exited off the freeway, the mid-week lunch traffic moving slowly through the downtown streets, I turned the air-conditioning to full blast; I was praying I wouldn't sweat through my blouse before I even got to the restaurant. It was 105 degrees. Fire weather. Or, as Bryn liked to call it, 'Shit storm weather.' The Santa Ana winds were burning through the dried-out canyons, making fast work of any tossed cigarette that came their way and blowing the flames clear to the Santa Monica beaches, where they'd leave a haze of orange-grey smoke over the ocean — another postcard-perfect California sunset born. I hated the heat only when the seat of my car scalded the backs of my legs, as it had that particular September day. Other than that, I found that high temperatures could be as reassuring as a heat pad thrown over an aching shoulder.

★　★　★

In the twenties, Cicada was a haberdashery for silent-movie stars. As I pulled up to the valet, its façade gleamed with Art Deco chrome. Lalique glass that the owner had imported from France shimmered and onyx marble reflected the late summer sun. My eyes had to adjust when I walked through the large mahogany doors. Inside, thirty-foot-high gold-leaf ceilings soared and brass railings hummed with polish. We'd once celebrated some promotion of Cecile's here, when her parents were visiting years ago. At the time, I couldn't imagine anything more splendid.

Bryn was already at the table. We'd been on the phone all morning exchanging ideas on what we should say, what we should wear. I'd remarked that I'd wished Emily Post had written an entry on how to lunch with grieving parents, and Bryn agreed that the prospect of dining with Mr and Mrs Carter was terrifying. If only Bryn and I could have seen ourselves through Cecile's parents' eyes that day. We would have known that the twinge in the air was not because they resented us — for breathing, for living — but because we were so young it hurt them. We made Mrs Carter think of what she now referred to as 'the accident', and how unfair life (which until then had always seemed to be perfectly fair) had become.

They were waiting.

'Am I late?' I asked, scrambling for my mobile phone to see just how rude I'd been.

'Not at all,' said Mrs Carter. 'I've ordered you an iced tea.'

'Oh, thank you,' I said, reaching up to smooth down my hair, which was already freeing itself from the hurried ponytail I'd tied up not an hour ago. I sat next to Bryn, who said, 'You look cute, cupcake.'

She seemed relaxed, but her eyebrows were up at full mast. *What exactly*, they asked, *are we doing here?*

I checked the table to see if people had already put their napkins in their lap. Yes. I did the same.

Cecile had always handled her parents with a graciousness that I envied; there were never sudden outbursts of in-fighting like there were in my family. Her parents were old world, old money, old fashioned, but she never seemed to feel the need to taunt or revolutionise them. Mrs Carter led us through the business of eating with the relaxed ease of a practiced hostess, asking us what was new in our lives, how David was, how our relatives were — she called them all by name, of course — and reciprocating with the latest in her New York life; which chef was cooking in what restaurant, and what play we couldn't miss should we come to town. She was what I believe the French call an *éminence grise*; a woman who seemed merely ornamental, but was actually in control of everything.

When the waiter arrived to take our plates, Mr Carter cleared his throat, calling the meeting to order.

'Ladies,' he said, taking his glasses off and cleaning them with a napkin. There was, I saw, a speck of shaving cream just under his right ear. Its presence there surprised me. 'I'll be frank. When Cecile ran off to that party school I had no idea what sort of flower children she'd take up with. But — '

'What Mr Carter is trying to say,' Mrs Carter interrupted gently, 'is that we think you were both wonderful friends to our daughter, and we know how much she cared about you.'

Mr Carter nodded, conceding the point. 'Cecile let her intentions be known should something happen,' he said. 'We indulged her. Those imbecilic doctors said her prognosis — '

'We thought she'd be fine,' Mrs Carter said.

Cecile had obviously left Bryn and me something each, I surmised, and the Carters were here to give the items to us. I was afraid the moment I saw her pearls, or Tiffany watch, or whatever it was, crossing the table, I'd start blubbering. So I swore to myself I wouldn't, under any circumstances, let that happen. The Carters — especially Mrs Carter — were very couth. I wanted to be couth, too. That, and I didn't want to upset them.

'Bottom line', said Mr Carter, 'is that Cecile told us what she wanted done with her trust fund. I take it you knew that Cecile had a trust fund?'

We didn't move.

'Most of it went to Zach, of course,' said Mrs Carter. 'But Cecile wanted something to go to each of you, and *I* think that she was wise to do so. Maybe she knew,' she paused, tinking her spoon against her cup of coffee. 'I'd hate to think that she knew.'

She looked at Mr Carter and he slid two envelopes across the table. 'Jessica Holtz' was written on one; 'Bryn Beco' on the other.

'Open them,' she said. 'Please.'

We each reached for our envelopes and pulled out wide, thick cheques; the kind important people kept in leather binders and wrote on with a fountain pen.

My eyes almost popped out of my head. In our hands, Bryn and I each held a cheque for fifty thousand dollars.

'My *lord*,' Bryn gasped.

'This is just . . . I don't even know what to say,' I said.

Bryn and I looked at one another. She nodded.

'We can't accept this,' I said, pushing my cheque back across the table. 'This money belongs in your family.'

'We loved Cecile,' said Bryn, doing the same. 'We can't take her money.'

'It's a gift,' Mrs Carter said. '*Stan*.'

So Mr Carter explained that Cecile's decision was final; we really didn't have a choice. Mrs Carter explained that Cecile had left no specific instructions. 'You are to do with it whatever you wish,' she said. 'We look forward to seeing great things from you.'

I stared at the cheques on the table. Whatever I wanted. As if I'd known, since I quit art school, what I wanted. At the moment, all I wanted was to duck under the table and hide from Mr and Mrs Carter. To get as far away as I could from their shiny wallets and expectations. It wouldn't help anyway; Cecile would be watching. I had vague opinions on whether or not there was an afterlife, but I felt as though she would know if I never put it to good use. What on earth would I do with fifty thousand dollars? I could think of nothing, *nothing*, that would have any meaning at all.

At the behest of some undetectable signal, our waiter appeared to tell us the Carter's limousine had arrived to take them to the airport. Mr Carter laid both his hands flat on the table and pushed himself up out of his chair, flatly refusing our offer to pay the bill.

Bryn and I carefully put our cheques back in their envelopes and self-consciously slid them into our purses. As we walked the Carters out, we tried to make a suitable fuss amid the landmines of guilt and surprise and sadness that surrounded us, exchanging powdery-cheek kisses with each of them, along with hopes that they would have a good flight. We must have expressed our gratitude twenty times from the door of the restaurant to the car, but all Mrs Carter said was, 'You're welcome' and 'We can't wait to hear what you do with it.' As the limo pulled away I could see our 'thank-yous' dancing in its wake, like a swarm of little butterflies with no firm place to land.

# 9

## This is Your Brain on Rugs

Bryn wouldn't stop bugging me about dating again.

'You can't sit around and expect happiness to leap out of the bushes and scream '*Aha!*'' she said a few nights after the Carters' brief visit. I'd buried my cheque in the bottom drawer of my filing cabinet, where it lay with such a presence that late at night it was as though I could hear it breathing, and ever since I had been doing my best to ignore it. Bryn and I were sitting in my living room, nursing a bottle of cold vodka that I put in the freezer for our semi-regular Sunday night bitch and stitch. We'd taken up knitting a few months after the funeral, as though a poncho that in the end would strongly resemble a slice of hairy Swiss cheese could fill the void. The wool yarn I'd picked was itchy in my lap. It was 80 degrees, even though it was almost 9 p.m., and I had no air-conditioning, so we devised a system involving a fan, an open window, and the occasional spritz from a water bottle.

I squirted some water into the fan and let the mist blow back into my face. 'Not interested,' I said, thinking of how the last man I had dated, Ira, had never called me again once I had told him my friend had died. (I guess a girl in mourning isn't much of a booty call.) I was on an extended hiatus, I told B. 'Besides,' I added, 'some guy won't make me feel better about Cecile ... you know ... '

'Dying. *Learn to say it.*' Bryn finished another row of her perfect, tight little stitches. I was behind; still purling and looking at the pattern thinking, *Huh?* 'OK, but he might help you forget about it. At least, in spurts.'

'Spurts.' I squirted the bottle again. Bryn laughed.

'Seriously, all I'm saying is, this isn't *like* you. Where's the little skank we all adore?'

I shrugged. 'She took an early retirement.'

'Can I ask you a question?' Bryn asked.

'That is a question.'

'What do you *do* every night? Bid on furniture on eBay?'

'Sometimes,' I said, turning my face to the fan. 'What do you think of this rug, by the way?'

'It's a rug. What difference does it make?'

'I can't decide. I'd like it to have about thirty-five, forty inches between the edge of the rug and the wall — that's standard — but now I'm having a sofa placement problem, because to get the rug the right distance to the wall and under the front sofa legs you have to put the couch too close to the fireplace, and you know *that*'s going to drive me crazy.'

'Mmmm,' said Bryn.

'I re-caulked the bath last Saturday. That was satisfying.'

'Not exactly the type of caulk I'm referring to.'

I shot her a look that said, *please stop*.

'OK, this is the last thing I'm going to say. I'm not a touchy-feely person. You know that. I don't look at wedding magazines for fun, I think plastic Christmas trees are a great idea and I hate B & Bs. But I don't know how I would get through this if it weren't for David, and I don't know how David would get through this without me.'

'I have y — '

'You need someone *besides* me,' she interrupted. 'Honey, worrying about you is starting to feel like a full-time job.'

'What's *that* supposed to mean?' I dropped my knitting, needles and all, into my lap.

'Nothing,' Bryn said.

I fiddled with my yarn.

'*Nothing*. I'm just . . . concerned. That's

the word I should have used: concerned.'

I had noticed lately that Bryn and David were more affectionate than usual. The previous week they pity-invited me to the movies and I saw Bryn, of all people, sniff the back of David's head while he was buying the tickets. I'd always been the fifth wheel with Cecile and Zach, David and Bryn, and nobody ever seemed to mind. Had the chemistry changed? The atoms of our collective friendship realigning themselves into some new, unfamiliar cell? This thought was so disturbing I forced it from my mind. *I'm being paranoid*, I thought, counting stitches.

As Bryn rambled on about the single men at her law firm, I didn't have the heart to remind her that the kind of comfort she had in mind isn't what dating was designed for. People who don't know you well want to be entertained. What they don't want is to deal with your baggage or your bullshit, and I had both.

★   ★   ★

That week would have been Cecile's thirtieth birthday. Bryn stopped by the shop on the actual day to say hello, just as I was helping our favourite, and only, employee unpack a set of outrageously pink cherry-blossom perfume bottles which Taryn had ordered for a client's equally ostentatious black-lacquer vanity. (That piece, I had to admit, would have been fantastic if only Taryn could stop adding accessories.) May started working at Gilded Cage after Taryn read some article about trends that convinced her she'd do more business if she hired a token hipster Japanese. It was unbelievable that this was how Taryn's mind actually worked, but for once I was grateful; May was generally around to cover for me since she only practiced with her band at night, and she drove Taryn nuts with her Ferris Wheel of hair colours — an unexpected bonus.

When Bryn walked in, May stopped gagging at the perfume bottles to ask B. how she was holding up, considering what day it was. Her serious expression was incongruous with her purple hair, which was in pigtails held with Hello Kitty rubber bands.

'I'm doing well,' Bryn said, placing her hand lightly on May's arm. 'Thank you so much for asking.' As May walked back to the stockroom, her bottom barely covered by a white mini-skirt and her feet in acid-green slouchy eighties boots, I noticed a small smile on her lips. Bryn pinned her grief on like a memorial ribbon; mine clanked around my neck like a cowbell. After lunch with the Carters, B. dutifully deposited her cheque in a market rate account and wrote a card expressing her thanks to Cecile's parents which was post-marked the same day. She and David were thinking about buying a house, which was Bryn's favourite new topic. *Did you know that properties in Silver Lake have appreciated 60 per cent in the last two years?* She'd ask, a copy of the *LA Times* Real Estate section folded under her arm. *Or that some people bought flats in Beverly Hills just so their kids could attend the public high school?*

All I knew was that I still hadn't deposited my cheque. My thank-you note, a draft of which was still on my computer at home, was a jumble of clichés with no mention of what I planned to do with the money. I went over and over in my mind the words that Mrs Carter had said. *I could do with it whatever I wished, and they expected great things from me.* What qualified as a 'great thing?' What would Cecile want me to do?

Snapping her fingers to get my attention, Bryn asked me what my plans were for the night. I told her I had three episodes of *Trading Spaces* on my Tivo and a coupon for a free two-litre bottle of soda if I ordered a medium pepperoni pizza from Domino's. She made a face and said I'd better find someone to date before she found them for me, then ran off to a meeting.

Despite Bryn's prodding, I had little hope that romance would turn my insides from knitting-yarn grey to warm cashmere-pink. Lately, memories of sexual encounters I once found thrilling — confidence-building, even, if only for a short amount of time — had an icky quality. I once read a true story about a man who had a stroke and became convinced his own leg belonged to another person. He'd wake up and try to throw the offensive limb out of his hospital bed — the sight of it repulsed him — only to be shocked when he fell out with it. Like that foreign appendage, the intimate moments I'd shared with men were no longer a part of me. They were ghostly pale and alien; uncomfortable to recollect.

★   ★   ★

'Sorry I'm late,' I said that night, rushing into the restaurant. I'd been running behind as usual, but this time I'd actually made an effort to be on time and was still thwarted. 'The only way you'd know there was a restaurant here is because there's a valet standing outside.'

'I told you it was next to the 99 cent store,' Zach said. 'They make it hard to find so they can keep the riff-raff out.'

'So now I'm a hick?' I pulled out my chair and plopped myself down.

'Just the opposite. You're the only person I've ever met who's actually *from* LA.'

I wasn't dating, but that doesn't mean I wasn't dining. Dining much better than I usually did, in fact, when I *was* dating. Sharing meals with Zach had become a semi-regular thing. I'd hardly seen him the first few months after Cecile died, but then I got an email asking if I wanted to meet him for lunch at a new Japanese restaurant he wanted to write a column about. I accepted, and although the meal was a bit strained — should we talk about Cecile? Not talk about Cecile? — I found that I enjoyed it. In a platonic way, of course. The next week he called again and we met for dinner, sharing small plates of delicacies at a chic French brasserie on Third. Now Zach would call whenever he was going someplace new, which was pretty much all the time. To my surprise, after the first couple of meals, his kind attention made me feel closer to Cecile. As though she wasn't really gone for ever. She was just . . . late.

'Try this.'

Zach handed me a large, ornament-shaped glass filled with a rich burgundy.

'D-lish,' I said, positioning myself and sipping the red liquid, which tasted of warm pomegranate juice and dark chocolate.

'Not bad, right?'

'Well, you're the expert.'

'I am.' Zach sat back, looking pleased with himself. 'I am just that good.'

While he ordered for us — we had to try most of the menu or else he wouldn't be able to properly judge the kitchen — I took a look around. The restaurant was tucked on a hillside and most of it comprised an enormous patio. Moroccan pillows were scattered on teak benches and there were colourful glass lanterns on the tables which tripped the light prismatic. We were sitting on the farthest side of the patio, which was built around an ancient oak tree which had to be at least a hundred years old. While I studied the tree's canopy I felt safe, protected. There was a little bowl of spiced olives on the table. I popped one in my mouth and decided that I liked this restaurant. Very much. I told Zach this and he said I'd make a terrible food critic: you had to eat more than one olive before you made up your mind.

'So?' I said, after the chef stopped by to tell us he was sending over a few dishes he wanted to prepare, just for us. 'This is a sad day, huh? How are you doing?'

Zach took in some air and puffed his cheeks when he blew it out. 'Oh, you know, the usual. I got up, I forced out a couple of hundred words, crawled back into bed and contemplated suicide by excellent wine and hundreds of heirloom tomatoes.'

'Was it really that bad?' I leaned forward in concern.

'No,' he said. 'In fact, today was OK. I visited the cemetery this morning, and then I just tried to act as normal as I could. Don't get me wrong, some days are hell. On others life is just life and everything's OK. But that can be hard too, in a way.'

I knew what he meant.

'You look different,' I said.

'Really?' he motioned to the waiter, mouthing the word, *Bread?*

'Are those new jeans?'

'Oh. Uh, yeah. Do you like them? The saleswoman said they gave me a higher rise.' He laughed. 'Frankly, I have *no* idea what that means.'

'It means they make your butt look amazing.'

Zach reached across his face and scratched under his chin, embarrassed. There was a couple of day's growth there, but it made him look handsome, in a relaxed, Ralph Lauren model kind of way. 'I've started sleeping in the middle of the bed.' He shrugged. 'Supposedly that's positive, according to the shrink everyone makes me go to.'

'Only because you've been through so much.' I took another sip of wine.

'I know. But it's hard. Like, 'Hello, Doctor Beaver' — That's her name, by the way. How Freudian is *that*? — 'No, I haven't taken Cecile's clothes out of the closet yet. Why? I don't know why. Do *you* know why? Why would *you*, doctor, ask *me*, patient, why? Why not?''

I told Zach something about the stuff in the closet reminded me of a poem I liked. He asked if I could recite it.

'*Now?*' I shook my head in horror.

Zach just sat there, waiting.

'OK, fine.' I took a deep breath and lowered my voice so other diners wouldn't have to listen. 'It's something like, 'Home is so sad/It stays as it was left, shaped to the comfort of the last to go/As if to win them back . . . Something, something, something.'' I blushed. 'I can't remember the middle, just that it ends with, 'Look at the pictures and the cutlery/The music in the piano stand/ That vase.''

'It's beautiful.'

'Well, *I* didn't write it. Anyway,' I waved the sudden heaviness in the air away, 'I thought *I* was pathetic for sitting around, looking at pictures of Bryn, Cec and I, and weeping alone, but I guess not. We're quite a pair, aren't we?'

'A match made in heaven,' Zach said. He raised his glass, and we both drank to that.

★   ★   ★

I had the following day off, but instead of lying in bed, nursing my hangover and browsing the latest on-line Pantone colour report — which was what I wanted to do — I was in the car. I'd been summoned to my mother's, whose email said she wanted me to collect paperwork regarding how her estate should be handled in case of her death. I'd replied fine, yes, I'd be there. I didn't bother to point out that she didn't exactly have 'an estate', she had a condo, and she was in perfect health. There wouldn't have been a point; I'd told her about the cheque from Cecile and my mother, ever the novelist, had a knack for writing the things that happened in other people's lives into her own. I reached into my glove compartment for two aspirins, swallowing them dry, and wondered how I'd get through the next few hours.

In the seventies, Elena Holtz wrote a book that was kind of a *Fear of Flying* meets *The Mary Tyler-Moore Show*. It was about a young married woman who confronts her Catholic upbringing, stuffy parents and sexually conventional husband, and escapes from New York to California, where she goes to Berkeley, does a lot of drugs, has a lot of sex, gets a divorce, and writes a best-selling novel. It features a questionable mescaline interlude in Mexico, along with fellatio and other unmentionable acts performed on a Cuban lover named Angel Cervera, a revolutionary ex-pat/misogynist/sexual dynamo. Needless to say, it was meanly autobiographical. There were over half a million copies in print, in more languages than I could remember. Now, Mom occasionally wrote articles for women's magazines and sometimes spoke at colleges for a decent-sized fee. College students still read her book 'for the feminist principles', they would say. But the truth was, my mother's politics had become quaint in a world where being a high-school lesbian was considered precocious. No, I suspected her readership was largely due to the steamy romps with Angel, which shamefully aroused me the time I hid under the bed to read them, at thirteen. As I took the elevator to the fourteenth floor, I imagined what Zach's Dr Beaver would say and laughed.

I walked into Elena's living room and there was a man around my age — thirty, thirty-one — with light brown, closely cropped hair, wearing a powder-blue button-down, chinos and wire-rim glasses that gave him a leftist smarty-pants look. He was sitting on Mom's brown sofa. There was a cup of coffee in his hand and a tape recorder propped up on my backgammon set, which I kept at Elena's to play with Henry's boyfriend Hameer during family dinners.

'Jesse!' my mother said, looking startled when I appeared in the hall. 'Didn't we say Wednesday?'

'You said Tuesday, Mom.'

'I said *Wednesday*. It's right here, in my date book.' She held up the leather Filofax where she'd scribbled, 'WED: JESSE TO DISCUSS ESTATE' in red pen, the letters large enough for her guest to read.

'Sorry,' I mumbled, raising my eyebrows. 'Really, I can't imagine any other reason for your asking me to come here.'

'For *you to ask* me,' she grammatically corrected, shooting me a look that said, *Don't cut off your nose to spite your mother*. She asked me to sit while Matthew fired off the last few questions for his interview, which would become an article he was apparently writing for some on-line website named after a rock. He took great pains to explain his angle to me while he packed up; he saw my mother as a visionary who'd helped to form the self-referential meta movement.

'Cool,' I said, giving my mother a look like, *Please tell me he's not serious.*

*   *   *

A few days later my mother called to tell me she had given Matthew my number.

'He went to *call*,' she said, as if that was an explanation. 'And I happen to believe he's got a very serious, ahem, endowment, if you know what I mean. You should have *seen* the way he — '

'Seriously, mother, if you say one more word, I'm going to throw up in an envelope and mail it to you.'

Elena tended to meddle in my life when I was bored with it, and to be bored with it when I found it meddlesome. But what *did* surprise me was that, when Matthew called the following day and asked me if I wanted to go to a movie, I said yes. It would be my first date in almost a year.

Matthew and I met at the Los Feliz three, where we saw a foreign film with a title I couldn't pronounce in an empty theatre the size of a closet. The conversation before and after the film was as dry as my popcorn, so I assumed we'd mutually blow one another off. But Matthew was persistent. Three messages later we went to see a Cindy Sherman exhibit at LACMA. A couple of days after that, Matthew emailed to ask me to dinner the following Wednesday. I was thinking that I should come up with some excuse, but Henry intervened.

'Mom said he was hot,' was the first thing Henry said when I picked up the phone.

I turned down the TV. 'Oh hey, Hen. He is, by her standards.'

'Meaning?'

'Remember Mom's Latvian poet who lived with us that summer?'

'Catching him sitting naked, on the dryer, while he washed his one pair of trousers literally almost turned me off from being gay.' I could hear ESPN in the background, and realised Henry must've thought this was important: He never called during *Sports Center*. 'Look, sister, all I'm saying is that you've had no fun lately.'

I asked who said a date with this Matthew guy would be fun.

'Nobody, but you're so — '

I heard Hameer yell, '*So bloody boring!*'

Hameer grabbed the phone.

'Have sex, darling, please. You're depressing me.'

With that, the little bastards hung up on me.

★   ★   ★

Hameer was, by far, my favourite of all my brother's boyfriends. He was from London, where his parents — originally from Lahore in Pakistan (his father was a Sunni Muslim, his mother a Shi'ite Ismaili) — moved before he was born. For a Muslim, Hameer was that rare combination of sophisticated, spiritual and openly gay. He was, Bryn, Cecile and I had all agreed, *gorgeous*, with skin the colour of leather-bound books, eyes blacker than a lacquered chinoiserie console, and a rakish grin that hinted at his propensity for mischief. Unlike Henry, who wore brown belts with black shoes, Hameer preferred designer shades, dark jeans, and Hugo Boss dress shirts. He constantly teased me about my clothes (I wasn't much better than Henry, after all), sometimes gave me hair and make-up tips, and occasionally took me dancing. I loved his irreverence, his insistence that nobody in the US could make a curry like his 'mum', and the way he moved on a dance floor as though he were starring in his own personal Bollywood movie. I was a drooling fool for his accent — as was my mother — and I had a mental collection of all the British slang he used: naff, slapper, tosser. My favourite was 'the dog's bollocks', AKA 'the dog's nuts', which is, apparently, an appropriate expression to use when something is especially good.

Henry knew I was smitten. 'But despite what you see on HBO,' he'd cautioned one night last year when we were all out to dinner at my dad's favourite Chinese restaurant, 'every gay guy you see doesn't want to have a commitment ceremony and adopt a kid.'

My dad cleared his throat and said, 'You know, what I've been watching a lot is *The L-word*.' He turned to Henry, '*Great* show.'

My brother gave me a look that said, *Jess, just shoot me now*, when my mother delivered the *coup de grâce*: 'Like most patriarchs, your father believes that Lesbian sex somehow includes him,' she intoned, pouring herself another glass of plum wine. 'Henry, don't you have lipstick lesbian friends who could divest him of this notion?'

★　★　★

Over saag paneer at the Indian restaurant near my house — which, if he'd been there, Hammer would have declared *manky* with a sniff of contempt — Matthew expressed interest in seeing my place. He seemed particularly curious about some Blenko glass I'd collected, although I kept telling him it really wasn't hard to find; there was a store on La Brea that had loads of the stuff. I offered to split the bill, but he insisted on paying. *I guess Bryn was right after all,* I thought, when Matthew pulled out his credit card. *If I don't sleep with a guy on the first date I'm suddenly dipped in gold.*

'So how 'bout it?' Matthew asked when we pulled up outside my house.

'How about what?' I said.

'Asking me in so I can check out the Blenkos.'

I looked up at the dark windows. It *had* been a while. And Bryn would be satisfied that I'd been taken to dinner . . .

'OK,' I said, picking up my doggie bag. 'Why not?'

I gave him the grand tour, answered some questions about how you knew if one of Blenko's candy-coloured vases was made in the seventies or manufactured more recently, then we sat on the couch. Our conversation turned from glass collectables, to eBay, to whether there was a future for, say, actual newsprint when the Internet offered information on demand. I said there was; I believed that the tactile nature of paper — the fact that you could hold it in your hand, or save it — ensured printing would endure. Who wanted to show their grandkids a printed out jpg of something as monumental and important as, say, 9/11? But Matthew said I was dead wrong because of cost and convenience. As he rambled on about skyrocketing paper costs and immediate gratification, I realised it was a conversation he'd obviously had many times before. I was getting bored, but Matthew was just getting started. Finally, he took a sip of his beer and turned to look at me.

'I called your mother to check on some facts for the article the other day,' he began.

'Yeah?' I said.

'She told me about your friend, Camille.'

I looked at him blankly. He didn't catch it.

'Cecile,' I corrected.

'God, sorry. How tacky of me. Cecile. So, you feel awful, right? Like you'll never be able to get close to someone again?' He put his arm up on the back of the couch, just behind my neck. 'Man, I know *exactly* how you feel.'

'Really. Did one of your best friends get hit by a taxi cab?'

'No, I was just . . . speaking metaphorically.'

'Oh. Thanks, Matthew.'

He changed the subject back to the column he was writing about Elena and stumbled on for another ten minutes. As I watched him I started to feel guilty. The guy was just trying to be nice. So when he leaned in to kiss me, I let him.

At first, it was weird. His lips tasted like beer, and they were harder than I'd thought they'd be, like Binder clips. But after a few minutes, I found myself warming up. *Maybe Matthew isn't so bad*, I thought, as his breath got a little faster. *He likes Blenko glass . . .* Matthew's hand trailed from my neck toward my breast. I arched my back a little, granting permission.

He looked deep into my eyes. *Deep into my eyes*, I thought, *what a corny phrase.*

'I have something for you, Jesse,' he said.

Then he leaned back, unzipped his pants and, his exceptionally large penis standing proudly at attention, said, 'You can pull on *that*, Mama.'

★　★　★

'You've *got to be kidding me*,' Zach was laughing so hard I could hear him gasping

121

into the phone. 'Hold on, I need a tissue.'

I heard rustling. Then Zach blowing his nose. He had a cold, and I'd been calling every now and then to check up on him.

'Can you believe it?' I grabbed another rice cake. I was getting close to eating the whole bag, but Zach had been hinting that he wished I didn't smoke so much and I had to do *something*. 'I couldn't get him out of my house fast enough. I was like, coat, shoes, keys, *b'bye*.'

'But you investigated how big it was first, right?'

'Zach, please. I'm eating.'

'That's not a denial.'

'Well, maybe I copped a quick feel.'

'You're joking, right?' His voice turned more serious.

I told him that yes, for once, I actually was joking.

Zach laughed. It was a deep, rich chuckle.

'How'd you meet this jackass?' he asked.

'My mother!' I said, chuckling as he burst out laughing again.

'Oh God.' Zach took a deep breath. 'You know, a story like that only confirms that I can't go back out there.'

I tried to reassure him that there was no rush — nobody expected him to start dating again so soon.

'Ah, let's just say even though I'm in no hurry, everyone else is thinking about it for me.'

'Everyone who?' I polished off the last of my rice cakes and got up to take an exploratory peek in the fridge to see if there was anything else worth nibbling. 'It's only been ten months.'

'Well, there are the girls in the *Times* office. They all have crushes on me.'

'You're modest!' I said.

'No, seriously. My shrink says it's widower fever, and they are *really* forward about it. Like the other day, I went in for a meeting, and this girl from marketing handed me a piece of paper that said, 'When you're ready', with her phone number on it.'

'What's her name?' I asked.

'Raquel Swallow.'

'That's fantastic,' I got up to go to the kitchen, where I poured myself a glass of white wine from the fridge. 'So you see, Dr Beaver, I knew I was in love with Miss Swallow right from the start . . . ' '

There was a long pause.

'What?' I said. 'Bad joke?'

'Oh. God, no.'

'Then what?'

'Nothing.' He coughed. 'It's just Raquel isn't the one I like.'

'Oh, well, I was just kidding.'

Then I thought, *Did be just say 'the one'?*

'Hold on, Zach, is there someone else?'

He didn't say anything.

'Do you have a new *girrrlllfriend?*' I teased.

'Honestly, Jesse, you're worse than my little sister,' he said, clearing his throat. 'No. Of course not.'

'Because if there's someone you're interested in — '

'Change of subject or I'm hanging up on you,' he said, laughing.

'Oh, *come on.* You're not getting off the hook that easily.'

'Phone's on the way to the cradle. Oh no, Jesse about to be disconnected. Bye, bye, Jesse! Byyyeeeeeee!'

'OK, OK,' I said. 'Don't hang up on me. I won't ask again.'

'Phew. I thought I was actually going to have to go through with that.'

★ ★ ★

Bryn and I met for lunch on a cloudy Friday afternoon. September was almost over and the city had finally given itself up to cooler breezes. I'd been so happy that morning when I pulled out a sweater for the first time in months. I was craving something cozy to eat — macaroni cheese, or a nice steaming bowl of chilli — but Bryn insisted we go to a health food place around the corner from her office. Lately, she seemed to be paying more attention to what I ate — because she wanted me to go on more dates, I was sure. Of course she was still on my case about the smoking. *Since when*, I wondered as I frantically chewed gum on the way to the restaurant, *did everyone in the world stop smoking?*

I was pondering the menu of carb-free 'sandwiches' wrapped in lettuce and tofu 'McNuggets'. Bryn already knew what she wanted. She waited with her hands folded over her menu, looking at me with a slightly amused expression.

'So I called to check in on Zach last night,' I said, settling on a salad, which seemed the safest option. 'That cold's nasty.'

'So I've heard,' she said. 'How was he?'

I shrugged. 'Definitely less depressed than he was the week of Cec's birthday. But you know Zach, it can be hard to tell.'

'Still waters, right? David and I had dinner with him right before he got sick. It's sweet. The way he . . . ' Bryn searched for the phrase, looking up at the ceiling.

'Makes sure he spends time with us,' I finished.

'Exactly. David said Zach told him he

wants to make sure we know he isn't out of our life for ever just because Cecile's gone.'

I took a sip of my mint tea, wondering if I should tell Bryn about Zach's possible crush. Then I asked myself why on earth I wouldn't.

'I think he has his eye on someone,' I said. Bryn paused, wiping her mouth with her napkin, which came away with an alarmingly red smudge from her favourite lipstick.

'Really?'

'I asked him last night and he threatened to hang up on me.'

'Hm.' She squeezed lime in her mineral water. 'I guess I can't say I'm surprised. I once read this thing in college that said Queen Victoria set the official standards for mourning after King Albert died. You had to grieve two or three years for a husband, but only three months for a wife.'

'I wonder who it is,' I said.

Bryn narrowed her eyes. 'Someone he works with?' she said. 'An editor, maybe?'

'He wouldn't say.'

'*I* should ask him.'

'Be my guest,' I said. 'But you have to tell me who it is. I'd really like to know.'

'You and me both.'

We spent the rest of lunch talking about other things.

# 10

## May the Forks be With you

It had already been a hectic day. Our upholsterer in Monterey Park covered two Louis XVI chairs in lemon linen when we'd asked for kumquat and he was asking us to pay the shipping charge to send them back, which I felt was out of the question since I'd checked the work order and the mistake was at his end. Meanwhile, a difficult client was refusing to let our photographer in to shoot pictures of her finished living room in Manhattan Beach, which we needed for our portfolio as per the original contract agreement. Taryn was at a day spa, and the only communiqué I had received from her was this:

*To all employees:*
*It's time to once again re-evaluate our appearances. We are, of course, not a fashion boutique. However, lint-free, Los Angeles chic or classic prep clothing is appropriate work attire. Might I suggest that this evening we all take a*

*look in our closets and set aside two separate sections — one for work; one for personal use? I plan to do this myself. (!)*

Taryn xoxo.

'Could this hold a television and DVD player?' a customer asked just as the phone started ringing again. I looked at the caller ID. It was Bryn. The customer was peering inside a Chippendale cabinet made by a master carpenter sometime in the late 1800s.

'Gilded Cage, could you please hold,' I said into the phone before resting it on my shoulder.

'Well, not quite,' I said. 'See, there are no holes.'

'My husband could *drill* holes,' she said. 'My question is whether it's deep enough.'

'I need to talk to you,' Bryn said.

To Bryn, in an official tone, I said: 'Of course, just one moment.'

To the woman: 'I think the point is that it's more decorative than functional? I'm afraid this is a collectable piece.'

The woman was, I couldn't help but notice, carrying her yoga mat in a Louis Vuitton carrying case.

'I think it could be quite the thing,' she said, knocking on the back. 'I need a tape measure'

128

'May?' I called.

She appeared from behind a couch, where she was on her hands and knees trying to plug in a glass lamp that had just arrived. It was so delicate that it looked as though it was made of spun sugar.

'Could you help Ms uh — '

'Mrs Katz.'

'Right. Mrs Katz measure the Chippendale?'

'I'll do my best,' May said, dusting off her knees. She was wearing another one of those outfits that would be better suited to one of her shows, not that I'd ever been to see her play. This time it was a yellow sweatshirt that had been slashed apart and rebuilt with the seams showing, a denim mini-skirt, red tights, and dangerously pointy-toed pumps. Her hair was dyed red as of last night. If I'd put yellow and red together I would have looked like Ronald McDonald, but on May, the outfit worked. She became more interesting — and more beautiful — with every colour clash.

As I retreated into the stockroom I heard May say, 'So whaddya got, flat screen or plasma?'

'What are we talking about?' I said, kicking a box over so I could sit. The place was a mess and it smelled like smoke again. I kept telling May to go outside, but she didn't much consider me an authority figure and I completely understood why.

'David and I had dinner with Zach last night,' Bryn said. 'He cooked.'

'What'd he make?'

'Some kind of scallop thing but that's not the point. Jesse, I think you're the one he has the crush on.'

I burst out laughing.

'Bryn, you've *lost your mind*.'

'That's not what David said.'

'Really?'

Yes, really.

I stopped laughing. If David said there was something to it — David, winner of the least likely to gossip gratuitously award . . .

'OK,' I said, poking behind boxes of dishware for May's bag to see if her cigarettes were inside. 'Go.'

'Chaz and I were in the backyard playing fetch with Happy. David and Zach were in the kitchen doing dishes — '

'Laura's boyfriend was there too?'

'Don't take it personally. Zach's just trying to spread the love. It's horrible, but frankly I think he's more popular as a widower than he's ever been.'

'You're awful.'

'Try honest. So David was telling Zach about the night we went to the movies, and

130

he said something about how I kept pushing you to go on more dates.'

'You practically threw me at that guy at the snack counter,' I said. I found May's bag, pulled out a cigarette and opened the back door, stepping into the alley behind the store. The reception got a little fuzzy but I could still hear. I flicked the lighter and inhaled.

'It was for your own good. So then Zach says something about how he thinks you should go out on more dates too.'

'That's nothing,' I said, plucking a piece of tobacco off the tip of my tongue. 'Zach would say the same thing to my face. In fact,' I gilded the lily a little bit, 'he frequently has.'

'No, that's not — are you *smoking?*'

'Of course not.'

'I thought I heard you exhale.'

I took another puff. 'It's called breathing.'

'*Sorry.* The point is, Zach said something about you being 'pretty', and David said, 'You think', and then, David says, there was this awkward pause and I walked in and Zach changed the subject.'

I snorted and told Bryn this didn't mean a thing.

'Is there something you haven't told me?' she asked. 'The evidence is pure hearsay, but . . . '

'What? *No.* No, no, no, no, no. I would

never. And if I did you'd be the *first* person I'd tell.'

'You could . . . '

'But I wouldn't. Never.' I shifted the phone to the other ear, just as I heard May let out a catastrophic 'Shit!' followed by the sound of glass smashing to the floor. 'Oh, damn it, I think May just knocked something over. I have to go.'

'So you're sure?'

'Of course I'm sure,' I said, putting the cigarette out, wrapping it in tissue, and throwing it in the rubbish. 'Nothing's happened. I go to dinner with Zach because we're friends. Same as you.'

'Because I wouldn't be mad.'

'*Right.*'

'Seriously. I need you to know I wouldn't be mad.'

'OK, OK, you wouldn't be mad.'

From the other room, 'Jesse? Can you come here for a minute?'

'Bryn, I gotta go. I'll talk to you later.'

'OK, sorry, I'm obviously being crazy. Bye.'

'Don't worry about it, love you, bye.'

I rushed back into the store and there was the new lamp, its cotton candy base shattered.

'We *could* tell Taryn it arrived like this,' May whispered so the customer, who was on the phone consulting about the Chippendale with, I could only assume, her drill happy husband, didn't overhear. May was sweeping up the pieces and depositing them back into the shipping box.

'I think we're getting our paycheques docked, May,' I said with a sorry smile. 'But I'll tell you what. Cheeseburgers for lunch, and they're on me.'

*   *   *

On my way home, I bought a six-pack, grabbed the comforter off my bed and sat down on the sun-bleached wicker chair I kept on my front porch, tucking the blanket under my knees. I didn't turn on the light. I wanted to sit in the dark.

I lit a cigarette from the pack I had bought at the liquor store on the way home. The first inhale was like what I imagined a shot of heroin to be; I could feel the ropes in my neck uncoil. But it went downhill from there. I craved the smoke, but I didn't exactly enjoy it the way I used to. Lately, every time I lit a cigarette I couldn't stop obsessing on the sheer insanity of it. After what happened to Cec, how could I knowingly do something that could kill me? Of course, this would make me so upset I'd want another.

I was half listening to the sound of couples chatting while they went in and out of the coffee house around the corner. *Would Cecile mind that Zach and I were having dinner every other week or so?* I wondered. True, we had never spent much time alone before. Over the last nine years, in fact, I don't think we'd ever met for so much as a slice of pizza without Cec for reasons that, to me at least, were obvious. Which was why, after she died, it was originally Bryn who designated herself as Zach's mother hen. On the other hand, Zach and I had always been fond of one another, in our way. Once, at a barbecue in college, he stepped in when my date — who wanted to leave to do a little partying of his own — slurred something about hearing that I was always willing to 'help a guy out'. Before he could get another word out, Zach was firmly leading him by the arm out the door. I heard him say, 'Just give me one reason to punch you and you got it, ass bag', before depositing him out on Pennsylvania Avenue. I stood in the doorway, watching. I was mortified, and slightly amused that Zach would use a gross phrase like 'ass bag' in my defence.

'Hey Jesse, know who sucks?' Zach said, wiping his hands on his jeans as he came up the front steps.

I shook my head.

He handed me his beer and put his arm around my shoulder. '*That guy.*'

We were closer now, but not for any circumspect reasons. I took another puff, and found myself getting a little irritated. *What was this anyway, I thought. Just because Zach and I are friends everyone thinks we're starting something?* Sure, Zach and I were the only single ones in the group, but that didn't mean anything. Wait — *Zach was single.* This bizarre reality suddenly hit me like a slap with a brick. I knew Cecile was gone, but somehow I'd skipped over a tangential fact: he was available now. Just like me.

★ ★ ★

Lizzie Biggens, the star client I'd helped Taryn win, was a large woman, blonde, early forties, with an ample bosom that she referred to as her 'twins'. She liked Dolce & Gabbana suits, cigarettes, Pilates, and that was it, as far as I could tell. Her house was perched on the edge of a Palisades bluff, and as I walked up the flagstone path to the entryway, I marvelled at the structure. It looked as though it had been hewn out of the mountainside; an organic yet geometric shape comprised of glass and stone planes. As I got to the first staircase, I shifted the weight of the carved stone Buddha I was carrying to my other hip. Taryn was too cheap to have the sculpture biked over — the weight, she said, would have driven the cost up to eighty dollars. Thus, he was my enlightened being to bear. When I reached the second flight of stairs, I paused to rest by an enormous flowering cactus, shorter succulents marching up the hill like impassive little green aliens. My spiritual load weighed a ton.

I knocked on the door and Lizzie's first assistant — she had two — answered, wearing a gold T-shirt with graffiti on it which made her look like she was an extra from a rap video and a black headset which made her look like a TimeLife operator. She held up an index finger — don't speak — and shooed me towards the back patio.

'*My Buddha buddy!*' Lizzie cried when I appeared on the patio, which overlooked a gaping canyon filled with pepper trees. 'You can *feel* how old this is,' she said, standing there with a cigarette in one hand, the other on the statue's stomach as though it was pregnant with good karma. Lizzie ignored my struggle to balance the piece without dropping it. 'Looks heavy as hell,' she said, turning away.

I tried to smile and started to set the

Buddha on a teak outdoor dining table.

'Not there,' Lizzie barked. She was still in one of her suits, but her heels were kicked off on to the bamboo matting. She wasn't wearing make-up, which made her face look more haggard than it might have if she weren't in formal business attire. 'I'll show you where I want it,' she said.

'OK,' I said. 'Sorry.'

I was always apologising when I was around Lizzie Biggens.

I followed her cigarette smoke, resisting the urge to bum one, into the house. We passed through several rooms, most of which were furnished with pieces I'd chosen. In the dining room stood a mirrored *étagère* I'd picked out, which held two ceramics of bright orange coral that I'd found in a Goodwill and brought back to Taryn with the secret hope she'd approve. It was my idea to contrast the rugged pieces with the more formal cabinet, which was the kind of thing I'd do all the time if I had the guts to open my own store. I smiled to myself when I saw that Lizzie had taken my suggestion, even though she couldn't have known it was my impulse.

'My studio,' Lizzie said, opening a pair of frosted-glass doors to reveal a room that I'd never seen before. Inside was a bare wood floor. A ballet barre spanned one wall, and there was a balance ball, a Pilates machine, and yoga mats scattered here and there. The main feature was the view — three walls were entirely glass and framed nothing but trees and sky.

'Amazing space,' I said, about to enter.

'Shoes', Lizzie said, looking me up and down, 'off.'

'Oh, sorry.' Without thinking I handed Lizzie the Buddha and bent down to untie my shoelaces. When I went to take it back from her, she had a bemused expression on her face.

'Where do you want him?' I asked.

'In front of the eastern window.' Lizzie walked ahead of me and stood beside the spot. 'We're doing a photo shoot in here next month,' she said as I bent at the knees to set the Buddha on the floor. 'Some fashion magazine wants to do an article on Hollywood VIPs and our fitness regimens.' She thought a moment. 'Personally, I miss the days when that meant four lines of coke, four times a day, and casual sex for lunch.'

I laughed.

'It's going to shoot really well,' I said.

'Right,' she said. 'Now tell me what you really think.'

I looked at Lizzie in surprise; she'd never asked me to do more than throw away cardboard boxes and packing foam. I looked around the plain room, which, with the exception of the view, could have been any yoga studio, anywhere, and told her that, frankly, the room lacked character. 'I'd start with the lighting,' I said. 'It's a fast way to elevate the space beyond what most people expect.' I added that, in fact, we had some oversize chinoiserie lanterns in the store that could look great.

'There are no window treatments,' I said. 'But that's OK. Why spoil the view? But, in terms of the shoot . . . it might be nice if there was a way to bring the outdoors inside, you know?'

'Not exactly,' Lizzie said, turning her back to me as she gazed out over the canyon and smoked, dropping the ashes in her tea.

So I told her about a landscape designer I knew who made some gorgeous indoor/ outdoor planters. Modern pottery in geometric shapes, but with a soft, earthy colour palate. 'Anyway, she designed this one huge steel planter for my friend's law firm and it's stunning,' I said. 'These really unusual cacti arranged geometrically with a Buddha in the centre. It could make this little guy feel a bit more at one with nature, and it's the kind of thing magazines love — could even get you the centre spread.'

'A desert altar,' Lizzie said, turning to look at me as though we were meeting for the first time.

'Why not?' I said, realising, suddenly, that if Taryn knew I'd started talking to Lizzie this way she'd have my head.

'I love it.' She dropped the cigarette in her cup and it made a hiss. 'The highest I'll go for the planter is a thousand. Get it designed so it fits, negotiate a good price and take your commission out of the rest. I need it by 18 November.'

Before I could even say yes, Lizzie spun on her heel, waving over her shoulder at me to follow. I rushed to catch up. When we got to the front door, she looked me up and down.

'You forgot your shoes,' she said, leaving me there to collect my things and show myself out.

★   ★   ★

'So I have a *brilliant* idea,' Bryn said.

'Oh yeah?' I reached over to roll up the window on my ancient Bronco, the only car left in LA that didn't have power windows so I could hear her. I only kept the truck because it was great for moving furniture to and from the flea market. I was on the way back from Biggens, thinking about the commission. I'd have to send Taryn an email about it; I was hoping she'd let me see it through.

'Zach mentioned that you guys are having dinner Saturday night, and he invited David and I to come if that's OK. He wants to cook again.'

'Sounds fun,' I said. I was getting annoyed, the window wouldn't go up, and now I was tugging at the top of it with one hand, driving with another, and I had the cell wedged between my shoulder and my ear.

'But here's the thing. I have a friend in town from San Francisco.'

I stopped tugging.

'What friend?'

'Julie.'

Turning on to Sunset, I searched my mind for a Julie. I didn't recall a Julie. Wait . . . There *was* a Julie O'Malia that Bryn went to law school with. Blonde hair. Tiny waist. Freckles. She was from . . . yes, now I had it . . . Pasadena.

'So anyway,' Bryn continued, 'Zach said I could bring her, but then it seemed weird because, you know, three girls and two guys, so David said he could bring *his* friend, Ethan. I've told you about him. He produces video games? He's really great.'

'Sure,' I said. It was a set up with a

potentially huge dork, but it would make B. happy. 'As long as Zach's into it, I think it's a fine idea.'

'Fantastic. We'll take care of the whole thing. All you'll have to do is show up.'

'Great,' I said.

'Oh, and Jess?'

'Hm?'

'Sorry about yesterday. I shouldn't have pounced on the whole Zach-liking-you thing like that.'

I told her not to worry about it; we'd both been through a lot.

'Thanks. Oh, and wear your green dress. You know, the one with no back?'

I pointed out that it was a bit much for a casual dinner with friends.

'What are you talking about?' Bryn said. 'It looks incredible on you.'

Later that night, as I researched traditional Buddhist altars on the Internet, my mind wandered. *I think it's you,* Bryn had said. Despite her apology, I knew her well enough to be sure that she was trying to hedge her bets by setting both Zach and I up. *Doesn't matter,* I thought. Bryn was a meddler — she liked to be at the centre of things, controlling, yes, but only because where her friends were concerned she was convinced she knew best. *Then again, what if Zach tried something on*

*Saturday night?* As I reached to turn on my printer, I almost laughed out loud. The thought of Zach trying to make a move on his dead wife's best friend was absurd. When I turned off my desk lamp ten minutes later, I was still chuckling.

★ ★ ★

On Saturday night I was making my way up Zach's front path in the green dress, my back getting chilly. I could hear a lively conversation going on inside.

'Oh my God, that's so *funny!*' said an unfamiliar voice. I heard the sound of a cork popping out of a bottle. '*Mmm.* I *love* a fruit-forward varietal.' It was a woman.

I knocked on the door. Zach answered wearing an apron that said, 'Cat: The Other White Meat.'

'What've you got against cats?' I asked, handing him a bottle of wine.

'Hate 'em! Don't we, Happy?'

The dog barked and jumped in a circle, his brown and white patches blurring he spun so fast.

Zach leaned forward and kissed my cheek. A curl of his hair fell over his forehead, brushing my eyelashes. I followed him into the kitchen, where I expected to see Bryn,

David, and the infamous Ethan. But — oh, *hi* — there was just Julie. *Just Julie*, I thought. *Sounds like the name of a bad sitcom.*

'Jesse, right?' she said, pushing her hair off her face with the back of her hand. Julie was as I remembered: Blonde, thin and pretty, in a J. Crew model kind of way. She had the white teeth that reminded me of a row of Chiclets, and blue eyes that had a hint of an attitude that seemed to say, *I may be beautiful, but I also happen to be very bright.* She gave me the old up/down, up/down. 'Look at *you!*' she said, wiping her hands on a tea towel. 'I wish I could get all gussied up like that, but I guess I'm just a jeans and tees kind of girl.'

'Except for that,' I pointed at the apron she was wearing, and smiled. It said, *Thrilla on the Grilla.*

'Oh,' she laughed. 'It's Zach's. Isn't it cute?'

'The cutest.'

'I'd shake your hand but I'm up to my elbows in chicken fat over here.'

Julie motioned towards a raw bird on the cutting board in front of her. There was a large bottle of designer water on the counter alongside a glass of wine. She'd wrapped a paper towel around each. I watched her squirt some water in her mouth.

'Do you need help?' I asked. In the background, I could see yet another apron hanging on a peg: *May the Forks be With You*. Zach went to cooking school in Paris one summer, and he'd been getting them as gifts for as long as I could remember. I wanted that apron. Bad.

'You're not getting near this food,' Zach said with a laugh, pulling a knife out of the chopping block. 'Remember that time we were all on a ski trip and you tried to make French toast?'

'Bad?' Julie asked. *Squirt, squirt.*

'Maple-flavoured mush.' Zach gave me a wink. 'Sit down and make yourself comfortable. Here's a glass of wine,' he handed me a glass of crystal that I recognised from Cecile's bridal registry, 'and some nuts for the nut.'

I sat as instructed and picked at a bowl of pistachios as Zach gave Julie a tutorial on how to stuff a bird, explaining that his special trick was to slide the butter and garlic under the skin, so the meat would get infused with flavour.

'I love to cook,' Julie said, 'but you're just amazing.'

'You cook?' Zach said.

'Where are Bryn and David?' I interrupted.

'They just called a few minutes ago. They're running late,' Zach said.

'I'm staying with my parents so we thought it would be better if I brought my own car,' Julie said, smiling. 'This is gorgeous crystal, isn't it?' she added, nodding at her wine glass. 'I *love* Tiffany's.'

*I'll bet you do*, I thought, trying not to fix her with the death stare.

While Zach mixed some sort of batter — cracking eggs with one hand — I took my glass of wine and went into the living room. Ella Fitzgerald was playing on the stereo and he'd lit candles. I peered at one of the framed pictures on the mantel-piece. It was from their engagement party, about six months before her death. Cecile was laughing, her head thrown back and her blonde hair tumbling over her bare shoulders. Zach was whispering something in her ear, looking freshly scrubbed. *He was a little skinnier then*, I thought. I wondered if Julie had noticed the pictures. Or that, in fact, Cecile was everywhere. The throw pillows on the couch were ones Bryn and I had given her a few Christmases ago. On a side table was a pair of silver candlesticks Henry and Hameer got them as a wedding gift. A lot of the presents had arrived from Bloomingdale's after Cecile died, and Zach kept them — foam peanuts drifting around his floors for weeks, I'd heard — not sure what else to do. I took in the room and I thought, *How could this chick just walk in here and act like she owns the place? Wearing his apron* — I heard a peal of giggling from the kitchen and 'Oh my God, I've never done *this* before!' — *and drinking out of Cecile's wedding crystal.* My feelings took me by surprise; when Bryn brought the whole plan up, I thought I'd be OK with this. But now, Just Julie sounded so gleeful I wanted to run in there and yell, *Hello? Are you aware that this hot hunk of man you think you just discovered lost his wife ten months ago? What do you think this is? An episode of* The Bachelor?

I overheard Zach saying, 'Now, tie the string . . . And you've just trussed your first chicken!' That's when I realised that he *was* the Bachelor, tonight at least. And he was, excuse the phrase, a catch.

I just didn't know what to make of it.

I heard Bryn and David coming up the path. I opened the door, eager suddenly to get a look at this Ethan guy. But it was just the two of them.

'Hi!' Bryn said, hugging me round the neck. 'You look fantastic! Honey, doesn't she look *fantastic?*'

'Fantastic,' David said, leaning over to kiss me on the cheek before he walked into the kitchen.

'So listen, dude,' I heard David say to Zach. 'Ethan couldn't make it.'

I looked at Bryn like, *I beg your pardon?*

'Sorry,' she said. 'Something about a work dinner. I hate men.'

'Zach hates cats,' I said.

'Bryn!' Julie appeared in the doorway and rushed forward for a hug, her still wet hands flipped up at the wrists. 'Oh my God, you look so great! Have you lost weight?'

'Not really, but *you* look fantastic! Look at your arms! They're so buff! David, doesn't she look fantastic?'

'Everyone looks fantastic!' he called from the kitchen, where he was opening a beer.

'Well, I am running the marathon. *Again*,' Julie said, hoisting the water to her mouth and taking a long, emphatic squirt. 'Gotta stay hydrated. It's the most important thing.'

★ ★ ★

There was so much food on the table we had to keep the wine on the counter and the bread on the window sill. Everything was perfectly prepared. The salad's champagne vinaigrette slapped your tongue and told it to pay attention, the roasted chicken was oozing buttery juices, and the grilled polenta was more comforting than corn bread. The

148

conversation sparkled, but I found myself obsessing on my attire. My dress was ridiculous — the green silk screamed guest of honour, not third wheel. I only half listened as Bryn and David described a house they'd seen that they liked.

'It has a six-hundred-foot redwood deck,' Bryn said, 'and you can actually see the Hollywood sign and Griffith Observatory from the bathroom.'

'You need a good view when you're on the loo,' David said, and Bryn playfully rolled her eyes. They both looked happy.

Bryn had directed who would sit where. She put Julie next to Zach, David and herself across from them, and me at the end. Something about this seating arrangement was uncomfortably familiar — I always seemed to end up one chair away from a man. Every time Zach looked at Julie, he cocked his head closer so he could hear what she was saying. His hair had some kind of gel in it that was flaking slightly just at the crown of his head. I wondered if Julie noticed it, but if she did, she didn't care. Zach was courteous. He filled her wine glass, laughed at her jokes. He even refilled her water bottle from the Sparklets dispenser next to the sink. Bryn seemed pleased with herself. David was oblivious.

'Should we play a game?' Zach asked when dinner was finished, and as I helped Bryn clear.

'I love games!' said Julie, clapping her hands. 'What should we play?'

'Celebrity?' David offered.

Everyone agreed that would be fun.

'I want to be on *your* team,' Julie said to Zach, resting a hand on his arm for a little longer than necessary. Up until now, Bryn had been watching their progress with a self-satisfied air. Now she grabbed another plate and stacked it with a loud clatter in the sink. Maybe Julie was taking this a little too far, even for her.

Zach suggested it would be them against Bryn and me. 'We'll take David,' he said. 'He's useless anyway.'

'Fuck you, man,' David said. We all laughed.

★   ★   ★

Bryn and I presented a united front. She sucked in her cheek bones and made a karate chop and said, 'Hee-Yaah!' I yelled out, 'Uma Thurman!'

I said, 'I do a public radio show in a really nasal voice.' She yelled out, 'Ira Glass!'

Zach and Julie had a harder time. She

missed Kurt Cobain, Ewan MacGregor, and Condoleezza Rice. David, who only got Hankie the Christmas Poo because he was obsessed with *South Park*, was an utter failure.

⋆   ⋆   ⋆

'OK, I'm out,' David said after we trounced them in the bonus round. 'Bryn?'

'Yeah, I'm beat.' She stood and stretched. 'Jess, want us to walk you to your car?'

Suddenly everyone was looking at me.

'Oh,' I said. 'Sure, I'll just go grab my bag.'

'Have another glass of wine and hang out,' said Zach.

Julie frowned.

'It is getting late,' I said.

'It's only a quarter to twelve, Cinderella,' Zach said. 'Let these wimps go, and finish the bottle with us.'

'Um,' said Bryn. I could see it dawning on her, finally, that she'd created what was turning out to be an uncomfortable situation. I looked at her like, *What do I do?*

In answer, she said, 'Stay. Have fun. We're old married fuddy-duddies. Just call me tomorrow.'

'The lawyer has finished her closing argument and the case is closed,' Zach said, pointing at me. He seemed pretty tipsy. 'You're staying.'

So I stayed.

'What should we do?' Zach asked after Bryn and David had gone. He refilled Julie's wine glass.

I resisted the urge to say, 'Threesome?'

Julie settled into the couch, taking a sip and saying brightly, 'Gosh, I'm not tired at all. And I'm a lawyer — we're always tired.'

We started talking. About Julie, mostly. The apartment she'd bought in Nob Hill. Her job. She had a lot of clients from Silicon Valley, and people always needed a good contract lawyer. In addition to being a big runner, she also mountain-biked, hiked and was taking flying lessons. We were having a beginning-of-the-evening conversation, except that it was the end of the evening.

'What do you do again?' Julie asked me.

I told her I was a trapeze artist for Cirque du Soleil.

'I thought Bryn said you worked at a shop.'

I told her it was called Gilded Cage.

'On Third?' Julie asked.

'Robertson.'

'I wish I worked somewhere I got a good

discount,' she said. Her eyes were sharp. 'I bet they practically pay you in designer tea towels. Which of course means they can pay you a quarter what you're worth. It's so unfair.'

*Wow,* I thought. *Julie really does love playing games.*

'Boyfriend?' she asked.

'Not at the moment,' I said.

'Oh, poop.' She turned to Zach. 'Don't you have any friends we could set Jesse up with? She's *so* adorable — who wouldn't want to date her?'

I was now in the third person. But to my great relief Zach came to my rescue with an in-joke.

'I think Bryn is giving her way more help than she needs,' he said.

He smiled at me. I smiled back. But Julie was gaily soldiering on.

'Now,' she said, standing up and approaching the mantelpiece. 'Let's take a look at these pictures. Is this you? In college?'

'Sure 'nuff,' Zach said.

'I thought the swoop went out with *Flock of Seagulls.*'

'I was keeping it alive.'

'I met Cecile once, I think.' She leaned forward and looked at a picture of her from the year we all went to Spring Break in

Cancun. 'Wow. She was gorgeous.'

'True that.'

'You're a blondes man.'

Julie was a blonde woman.

Zach didn't answer.

'I'm really sorry about . . . ' Julie took a squirt of her bottled water.

'Thanks.'

She excused herself to go to the bathroom, and I stood to get my things.

'I'd better get going,' I said, heading for my bag, but Zach reached out and took my wrist. His palm was warm.

'Stay,' he said. 'Please. Just a little longer.'

'OK,' I said. 'If you really want me to.'

★   ★   ★

The clock ticked towards one. On the way back from the bathroom I heard Julie stop in the kitchen to fill her water bottle. She was getting drunker yet more hydrated — it's the most important thing — and shooting me glances that said, *Could you please take the hint and get the hell out of this house?*

But every few minutes or so Zach would look at me like, *You're not leaving.*

At a quarter to two, Julie finally gave up. I have to give it to her, she played it well.

'I have to train in the morning so I'm afraid

I have to call it a night,' she said, standing up and smoothing down her jeans. 'Zach, would you mind seeing me out?'

★ ★ ★

He came back rubbing the back of his scalp.

'I thought she was never going to leave,' he said.

'Oh my God!' I said, jumping up off the couch. 'I couldn't tell what was going on. I thought you were like, all set to . . . to . . . '

'To what?' He smiled.

'Make out? Oh God, listen to me.'

'I shouldn't have let her drive,' Zach said, plopping himself down on the couch and putting his feet up on the coffee table.

'No,' I said, sitting back down. 'It's my fault.'

We both laughed and at the same time said, 'No, it's Bryn's fault.'

We were both facing forward, as though there was something to watch on the television, which wasn't on.

'Want to watch a movie?' Zach asked.

'Too tired,' I said. 'Did you get her number?'

'Right here.' He tapped his breast pocket. 'Not that I'm planning to use it.'

I asked why not. She seemed . . . nice.

Zach looked at me and shrugged. 'You know why not,' he said.

I stood up to clear the table.

'I think Cecile would understand,' I said.

'Don't clean. Come on, I'll do it tomorrow.'

I sat again, thinking, *I gotta go. Now.*

'But you're right,' he added. 'She would understand.'

I had taken my shoes off hours ago. Now I self-consciously tucked my feet beneath me. Zach was looking at me. Not necessarily a look I didn't like, but a look just the same. I felt self-conscious. Like I was blinking too much or something.

*What am I doing here?* I asked myself.

Then I realised I very much wanted him to kiss me. My stomach constricted.

*I am a bad person,* I thought. *A really bad person. A bad, bad, bad, horrible person.*

Zach leaned forward to wipe crumbs from the wine cork into little piles on the table, letting them fall off the edge into his hand, his brow tilted downwards, his mouth parted slightly. His hands were chef strong — able to crush walnuts, crack lobster shells — but delicate too, with quick fingers and clean nails. Ashamed of myself, I couldn't help imagining that I was a piece of cork, and his palm was something I could fall into. I could draw his fingers around me . . . He turned his head as though he were going to say something.

'Want me to walk you out?' he said.

'Please.' I snapped back into reality. 'Yes.'

'Are you OK?'

'Yeah. I mean, of course. I'm just . . . out of it. Like really out of it.'

*And*, I thought as Zach stood and opened the door for me, *completely losing my mind*.

# 11

## A Word on Stone Benches

It was freezing on the ride home — the temperature had dropped to forty-five or so, and my skimpy dress was getting its last revenge. I let myself into the house and ran a bath, sinking into a tub that was so hot I wondered for a moment if I needed to jump back out again. I imagined steam coming off my freezing cold toes. *Why didn't I just leave?* I wondered as I leaned back into the water. *Was it really that I wanted something to happen, or could I simply not let Julie have him?* I traced a pattern in the steam on the tiles around my bath, and thought back, to the day of the funeral.

I got there before Bryn, but after Zach. I found him talking to the mortuary director. I didn't want to interrupt so I lingered in the waiting-room for a minute. The funeral home was tastefully disguised as a ranch house, as if you could be duped into forgetting where you were. I parted a lace curtain that hung over a bay window and scanned the grounds. There were no gaudy mausoleums, just neat row after row of tasteful marble headstones with the occasional small crypt. There were well-tended pines and maples, the lawn was immaculate, and here and there were patches of rose bushes with carved stone benches where a person could sit and reflect. The cemetery was understated but classy — very Cecile. I could hear the director asking Zach to follow him so he could sign the appropriate paperwork as I let myself outside. It was hot and smelled vaguely of fertiliser. I walked across the gravel driveway, pondering that satisfying, crunchy sound. Birds were chirping overhead and I could hear bees in a tall hedge. On the other side of the field, a woman and, I presumed, her children were having a picnic next to a headstone. The two little girls were running around and picking flowers out of old arrangements. They brought them back to their mother, who laughed and told them to put them *back*. I couldn't imagine ever laughing again, and yet there was so much life here.

I crossed a grassy field towards the plot Zach had chosen. I knew I was going the right way because it was the only one with a white tent over it. I was surprised when I heard that Zach was in charge of the arrangements, but Bryn explained it to me: even though he had only been Cecile's husband for two days, Zach, not her parents, had the legal responsibility to decide what would happen with her remains. Later, Zach told me this had him in a panic for weeks; he didn't know if she should be cremated or buried, and when the funeral director asked him if he'd like to purchase a headstone for himself so he could reserve a plot next to his wife, he excused himself, ran outside, and wept. I wondered if the Carters were upset that their daughter wasn't flown back to New York, or if they liked the fact that she'd stay where she had hoped to build a life of her own.

My heart splintered when I saw her name — Cecile June Carter-Durand — inscribed on a piece of shiny marble along with the date of her birth and death. It hadn't occurred to me that her name would be engraved into rock that way. I expected a tombstone, of course, just not *her* name on it. I stood there and gawked, not knowing what to do. I heard a car door slam, voices talking in a low murmur. People arriving. One of Cecile's cousins — Stewart, I think his name was — spotted me, fifty yards away. I became self-conscious; I was looking at Cecile's *grave*, which had a ridiculous, unreal quality to it. I thought about how I must have looked like somebody who was grieving — hell, I *was* somebody who was grieving — and wondered whether being aware that you looked like somebody who was grieving meant that you weren't *really* grieving. I was at Cecile's funeral, damn it. I wanted to fall apart. But the only thing I could think of was that, if Cecile had been standing there with me, she would have felt the exact same way. We would have joked about it. I would have said, 'This feels like a bad episode of *Six Feet Under.*'

And she would have said, 'Totally.'

Bryn pulled into the parking lot. I walked back to meet her.

We hugged. We asked one another if we were OK. We made lame jokes. 'Oh yeah! Great! Never better!' Bryn looked around at the helpless gaggle of parents milling around, mothers clutching their purses like lunch-boxes and husbands taking hesitant sips of water out of mini-sized Dixie cups and said, 'Isn't it weird when the grown-ups become the kids and the kids become the grown-ups?'

★   ★   ★

When everyone started to take their places, I panicked; there was Bryn and David, Laura and Chaz, my mother was standing with my father, towards the back, my brother and Hameer next to them. I knew instinctively I was supposed to stand near the headstone like Bryn and David were, but alone? I looked for a place that wouldn't be too conspicuous. A bench, perhaps, where I could sit and be dignified until it was over.

My eyes met Zach's. He was standing a few feet away from the minister who married him. Father What-a-waste. He motioned for me to stand near him. So I did, just a little bit back. He turned his head and looked at me again. Lifted the edges of his lips in a small impersonation of a smile. That was where he wanted me to be, I can't say how I knew but I knew, and so that was where I was. Standing just behind Zach. There, but not there.

*My God*, I thought, as I got out of the tub, a shiver running through me when my feet hit the cold tiles. *How long had this been going on?*

# 12

## The Best-Laid Floor Plans

Why is it that after three — OK, five — glasses of wine the back of my head feels like it has been clamped on to my neck with a bear trap, and my limbs get a strange, vibrating tingle, as though running on an electrical circuit? The morning after dinner at Zach's, I looked in the bathroom mirror and saw that my chapped lips were still stained berry-red from all the wine.

Somehow, in my sleep, I'd resolved to put an end to this before it even began.

*The idea that Zach wanted me to stay for any reason other than to help put the kibosh on Julie is absurd,* I thought as I attacked my tongue with a toothbrush.

*That I would do anything to dishonour my friendship with Cecile is* completely *absurd,* I thought as I pulled on a skirt which I hated, but which was at least clean, with my usual black tank top and a sweater.

*The idea that I would put our friends through something like that is entirely, utterly and irrefutably absurd,* I thought as I unlocked the door to my car.

I slammed the door shut. It made a satisfying, heavy metallic crunch.

*Then again*, I thought, as I pulled out of the driveway, *would it really make us the worst people in the world?*

★   ★   ★

I was driving to the shop when it occurred to me that in every friendship, there's a floor plan, of sorts, which keeps everything in its proper place. The blueprint is negotiated early on and rarely revised. When Cecile was alive, the rules were that I did everything Bryn said, worshipped Cec, and in return Cecile would occasionally take my side so I could win some minor victory — such as where we were going to have dinner, or whether I could go on a date with a man Bryn considered below par. Without Cec to act as counterbalance, I was completely at Bryn's mercy.

I remember there was once a guy named Bjorn — I know, preposterous name — but even though he was kind of cheesy there was something about him that I liked. I spotted him while I was out with Bryn one night, drinking beers on the patio of a bar on Pearl Street. I told her I wanted to ask Bjorn to join us and she turned to get a better look. 'He's a rollerblading enthusiast' she said. 'I saw him the other day, skating next to Boulder Creek with Walkman headphones on.'

I countered, then, that I'd just have to put on elbow pads and dork out — Bjornify myself, as it were.

'Be serious,' she said. 'I mean, come on, Jesse. Do you think so little of yourself?'

I shook my head that no, I didn't. I knew she meant well, but I watched him leave with a smile on my face and hatred — for Bryn? For myself? — in my heart.

I parked in my spot behind the store and unlocked the back door. As I wiped my hair out of my eyes, I could actually smell alcohol evaporating out of my wrist. I turned on the shop lights and computer monitor, and then took a bottle of water out of the mini-fridge in the corner of the stockroom while I waited for the heater to kick in. It was surprisingly frigid outside. On the drive in the weatherman intoned colour-coded air quality warnings — green, beautiful green — which meant no smog. But who cared? Nobody was going to the beach.

The fan whirred on. It took me ten minutes to realise it was blowing cool, not warm, air. I checked the fuse box out back, but nothing seemed amiss. Terrific. I left an urgent message for the repairman, even though I knew he'd probably be booked. It was going to be one of those days.

I sat down to check the email and tried to ignore the cold that was creeping at the back of my neck. The first was from Taryn. It was yet another one of what May and I had started calling her 'xoxo' emails — self-centered, condescending, but signed with hugs and kisses so she would seem like she had a soul. This one said Taryn wouldn't be in today, tomorrow, or possibly Tuesday, as she had decided to stay on in Ojai for a 'fast and cleanse' programme. I wrote back that was fine, and wondered if it would be a good time to ask about the raise she had promised me six months ago which still hadn't materialised. I decided against it. She'd just ignore my email, which would make me feel more defeated than I already did. Next there was junk, junk, junk and then an email from Bryn. The subject line said, 'Chez Zach.' I opened it.

*how was the rest of your night?*
*xx,*
*b.*

I pressed Reply and my fingers hovered over the keyboard. Under normal circumstances,

166

I'd probably write something like, *torture! i thought he was going to kiss me, but then, at the moment of truth, he asked if he could walk me to my car. argh.* But instead I typed: *exhausting. Zach kept insisting i stay because*

My mind skipped ahead to what the email would say next — *because Julie made a play for him. Meanwhile, I'm starting to suffer from my own inappropriate fantasies, so I ended up drunkenly planting myself on Zach's couch so that if Julie wanted to kiss him she'd have to claw me out of the way.*

Finally, I deleted what I'd typed and settled on: *good. i think Zach just wanted company. julie's really nice. how are you?*

I hit Send. This was the first time in recent memory that I'd told Bryn anything other than the cold hard truth.

★ ★ ★

May came in at noon, sneaking up and poking me in the ribs.

'Wake up!' she yelled. 'The bitches are coming!'

'Ow, stop,' I said.

May plopped her bag on the floor and sat on the stool behind the register. She was wearing plastic earrings that made clacking noises whenever she turned her head, a vintage wool dress and leggings tucked into cowboy boots. Mod cowgirl, she informed me, was her 'October look'.

'It was between that and hooker fairy,' she said. (I tried to picture what this would look like and thought, *only May*.) 'Whatcha doin'?'

'Reformatting the invoice files.'

'Wowzers.' She watched me for a moment as I fiddled with what should be in bold and what should be in italics. 'I see what you mean, if you put the due date in italics it really jumps out at you, but then again, it's hard to read.'

'It's called being the manager,' I said.

'It's called busy work. Why is it so friggin' cold in here?'

I handed her the phone and said she should feel free to call the repairman, tell him about her fairy hooker idea and see if it enticed him to make us a priority.

May sighed and picked up a set of silver coasters she wanted me to send to Biggens. 'These aren't so bad,' she said, 'considering Taryntula picked them out.'

I nodded. I didn't want to think, I didn't want to talk. I wanted to work. I was going back and forth with the designer on those planters, and I decided to take some initiative and send Lizzie some pictures of those lanterns we had in stock. Work would save me from fantasising about a life I was never going to have, I felt, with a man I was ashamed I'd even remotely considered.

'When I'm a big rock star, I'm going to buy everything in this store — including Taryn — and set it all on fire,' May said.

'Excellent idea.'

She bounced around for a minute. 'What's with you?' she asked.

'Nothing. I'm a little hung over, but I'm fine.'

'You were with a guy?'

'No guy. Just dinner at Zach's.' I saved my document before I messed it up and looked at May, who was petulantly tapping her toe and nibbling at her cuticles. 'Do I need to find you something to do?'

'No,' she said. 'It's just . . . I'm bored.' She drew it out, like *boooooored*.

'May? Darling? I'm sorry. I have to finish this, then I want to look over our orders to make sure our spring inventory will be up to par. Might I suggest you go find something to break and then you can busy yourself cleaning it up?' I smiled, so she'd know this part was a joke.

'You're the boss.' May spun on the heel of her cowboy boot and turned to look at two women — wealthy thirty-somethings pushing ergonomic baby prams that reminded me of the so-called 'extreme' mountain bikes everyone had in college — who had stopped to peer into the display window.

'Fresh victims,' said May, walking towards the front of the store and laughing in a witch-like cackle as the bell on the door gave a jangly ring.

★ ★ ★

At 2 p.m. I was still in organisational mode — moving from the computer files to the orders to our own website, which needed some updating. I was making notes of what pieces I wanted to add — along with some notes on their history, which I thought our customers would appreciate — for the site when, 'Ahem.'

May was standing in front of me, holding the phone. I had no idea how long she'd been there.

'For you, Miss Thang.'

'Thanks.' I stood and wiped my hands off on my skirt before taking the cordless.

'Hello?'

'So you got home intact.'

It was Zach.

'So hung over I can barely detach my tongue from the roof of my mouth, but in one piece. How are you?'

'I'm good.'

Suddenly I couldn't think of a single thing to say.

'Have you talked to Bryn?' I said.

'Nah,' he said. 'You?'

'Just a quick email this morning. You know, to say hi. What are you up to?'

Zach breathed out, like, *pheffff*. 'Not too much,' he said. 'Working on a piece about the resurgence of interest in artisan cheese for *Details*.'

I told him that sounded interesting.

'I hope so. I have this theory that connoisseurship is really just the newest way to beat the Joneses, not to mention get a date.'

'I'm impressed.'

'Don't be. Anyway . . . Well . . . I was just calling to say hi.'

'OK. Me too.'

*Me too?* I thought. *He* called *me*.

Uncomfortable silence. Uncomfortable silence.

'OK, well then, bye,' he said. He sounded mildly annoyed.

★　★　★

I went home and thought about calling Zach back. *What was that about?* But instead I tried to watch TV. *A Room With a View*, which I'd seen before and enjoyed, was on — the part where one Italian stabbed another right before Helena Bonham-Carter's dishevelled hair-do. The phone rang and I picked up, expecting it to be Bryn or my brother. I felt a wave of relief when I heard Zach say, 'So that was a weird conversation today, huh?'

'What the hell was wrong with us?' I said, lowering the sound.

'Search me,' he said. 'Actually, I might have been overcompensating because I was calling for a reason, and then I felt that maybe it was a bad idea, or maybe *you'd* think it was a bad idea. Wait. Let me start over.' He took a breath. 'OK. I have to go to this work thing on Friday night? It's like this cocktail party for the *LA Times*? All my editors are going to be there and a bunch of our advertisers, and the writers are being asked to shake some hands. *Anyway*. I was wondering if you could possibly come with me . . . Jess?'

'Oh, sorry. I was waiting for you to finish.'

'No. Well. I mean, that's it. I know it probably doesn't sound fun — it sucks, to be honest — but I don't exactly want to go to another one of these things alone.' He laughed. 'You should see how sorry all the editors feel for me. They're constantly asking if they can get me a drink, and the last time I went I got so plowed I had to take a cab home and then realised I'd left my wallet at the bar — '

'Zach, don't worry, I'm there,' I said.

'Are you sure? You're going to get a lot of queer looks.'

'Great, then it will be my usual Friday night.'

'Very funny.'

I was doing my best.

Zach then said he had something else he wanted to ask me. No. To tell me.

'OK.' I shifted my seat on the couch, and tried to prepare myself for what I thought he might say. *We've been friends for a long time . . . Don't want you to get the wrong idea . . .*

'I tried to call you, you know.'

'Today?'

'No,' he said. 'In college. That term after we met. I broke up with Carrie about eight weeks later — '

I told him I didn't remember a Carrie.

'The girlfriend I had back home in San Francisco.'

'Oh. *Now* I remember. The one who wouldn't take no for an answer.'

'Yeah, and look what she missed out on. Anyway, so I did try to call you. But by then you weren't in the dorm any more. You know

I actually tried to track you down? I called Information to see if they had your number, but you weren't listed — '

I thought back. I told him I was fairly certain our college phone was under Bryn's name.

'That must have been it. Then I called California, to see if your mom was listed because I remembered you saying she'd written that book but she wasn't. And *then* I thought about trying her publisher, but I must admit I was starting to feel a little stupid and I gave up.'

'Just like that, huh?' I said.

'Not just like that.'

'You never told me.'

'No,' he said. 'Because . . . ' his voice trailed off.

'Yes?'

'Never mind. It's not important — the point is, I tried.'

I thought for a moment. This *was* news. Useless. But news just the same.

'Look, it's OK,' I said. 'It's not as though after you met Cec I didn't just think, *Well, no point in putting up a fight.*'

He said he didn't know what I meant.

'Please. I think we all know Cecile and I weren't exactly in the same league.'

Zach didn't respond.

'I'm glad you told me, Zach,' I said.

'Phew. OK, well, I have no idea why I'm telling you this now but . . . Good. I guess this is goodnight. See you Friday.'

'See you Friday.'

We hung up, and I turned back to the movie, watching Helena — her curls piled atop her head and tumbling down her back — succumb to an Englishman's kiss that was fraught with import, delivered in the middle of an amber-lit wheat field.

# 13

## Location, Location, Location

Friday evening. I'd been having difficulty picking out an outfit that would convey the right thing. Something that said, *I'm only wearing these butt-hugging pants to express the tasteful sexuality and overall attractiveness as your friend-slash-pseudo-date, not to seduce you.* After talking to Bryn, who said she had offered to go with Zach herself but then had other plans, I realised that unless I wanted to humiliate myself I simply had to proceed with Zach on a purely 'as a good friend' basis. After all, this wouldn't have been the first time I'd misconstrued someone's intentions, and I'd be damned if I was going to do it again with him. Plus, there were his feelings to consider — how vulnerable he was, not to mention the fact that he was still grieving. I was still grieving, too.

*Bam, bam, bam, bam, bam.*

Someone was banging at the door. Zach wasn't due for another half an hour. It had to be my neighbour — five-feet-five inches of bullying college administrator who loved baseball caps, rose bushes and George Michael. He was on a hostile campaign against my bathroom light. Every few weeks or so, he'd come over to announce that the light was shining into his curtain-less kitchen window and disturbing his meal/sleep/*Faith* video re-enactment/whatever.

*Bam, bam, bam, bam.*

'I don't hear you,' I sang quietly. Then there was a foot-kicking *BAM! BAM! BAM!* Oh no you don't.

'*Gregor!*' I yelled, running to the door, planning to give him what for even if it was going to be with one foot in, another foot out of, a pair of tweed pants. 'They're called curtains you friggin' obsessive compul — '

I yanked open the door, and my brother, Henry, was leaning on the door jamb, a newspaper bag over one shoulder and a bemused grin on his face.

'Why would you say 'Friggin'' and not the actual word?' he said. 'I've never understood that. It's not like everyone doesn't know what you mean.'

'Ugh, God. It's you.'

'Nice hello. May I come in?'

I said that he may, stepped aside and tugged my trousers up the other leg.

'What do you think of these?' I asked, doing a truncated model's twirl.

'They're OK.'

'OK?' I looked down at my legs. I didn't want to look super fantastic, but OK wasn't quite what I had in mind either.

'You look fine.'

I made a face.

'You know, if you want to ask fashion questions, you should ask Hameer.'

'You're right,' I said. 'The definition of insanity is asking a guy who thinks an ironed T-shirt is formal wear how you look.'

Henry walked into the kitchen.

'Got any beer?' he asked.

'In the door compartment thingy,' I called. I went back into the bedroom, where I stood looking glumly inside my closet. *Time to get J.A.C.T*, I thought, invoking Bryn's acronym for Jeans-and-a-Cute-Top. I reached for a pair of dark Levi's and a silk blouse. It was the safest choice.

'So Henry,' I yelled, 'to what do I owe this honour?'

'I need advice,' he said. 'Your place is on the way home from ESPN so . . . hey, is that Mom's old armoire?'

'I painted it white and put coral knob pulls on the drawers.' I grabbed my own beer and watched him settle in on the couch. 'I'm going for an Oriental-slash-Miami-Beach-slash-luxe thing. And it holds my CDs. Not that I have time to discuss this now.'

'Huh.' Henry got up and swung a door open, inspecting my shelving. 'Pine?'

'Reclaimed teak, as a matter of fact.'

'Rip 'em yourself?'

'Had a neighbour do it. He's got a pretty complete set of power tools.'

'I'll *bet.*'

'So Henry,' I was still standing, which I hoped would give him a clue that he shouldn't get too comfortable, 'what's up?'

'Cut-to-the-chase. I like that. OK. Hameer proposed last night.'

'Your boyfriend . . . '

'Yes.'

'Proposed marriage?'

'Technically a commitment ceremony,' Henry said, 'aka a now-I'll-never-be-able-to-sleep-with-that-cute-guy-in-my-basketball-league ceremony. A my-life-as-I-know-it-is-over ceremony. A — '

'Henry, please. I get it. Did he get down on one knee?'

Henry nodded. 'Oh. *Uh-huh.* After calling Dad, apparently, and asking for my hand.'

I laughed, picturing this scene. Hameer was a genius. I told Henry so.

He just sat there, nodding.

'So?' I said.

'So what?'

'What did you say?'

'I said I'd have to think about it.'

'You could be a June bride!'

Henry took a deep pull of his beer and burped.

'OK.' I sat down next to him. 'If you say no, does that mean you're breaking up?'

'No,' he shrugged. 'Maybe. He'll be hurt, which is understandable. It's just that I never bought into the whole traditional family, two kids and a dog thing. I mean, *I'm gay*.'

'True.' I looked at the clock. I didn't have much time, but this was important. 'You're gay, yes, but you like football. Beer. Barbeques. Judas Priest. You coach little league. You're basically the most hetero-homosexual I know.'

'That's what Hameer said.' Henry shook his head.

'Look, casual sex is a way to express yourself, but monogamy can provide greater intimacy.'

'That sounds like one of Bryn's.'

'It is one of Bryn's. She said it the other day.'

'Then that's my cue,' Henry said. He stood.

'You're leaving? I just sat down.'

'Yeah, I only wanted to stop by for a second, actually. So you think I should do it?'

'Is this like an exit poll?'

He shrugged.

Then yes, I told him. If he really loved Hameer, and could see himself spending his life with one man, he should say yes.

'Fine,' he said.

'Fine,' I said. 'Now if you're really leaving please f-off.'

I was walking Henry to the door, when he asked, 'So who's the big date with?'

I let him out, explaining I was *not* going on a date.

'You're wearing perfume. Even the most hetero-gay guy in the world noticed.'

'It's a benefit for the *Times*. I'm thinking maybe I can get a little PR going for the shop.'

'Got it.' Henry was almost at the bottom of the porch steps when he turned and said, 'Since when do you care about the shop?'

I thought a moment. Since Biggens had taken an interest in me?

'I'm doing it, you know, for me,' I said. 'And for Zach. I flipped open my mailbox to see if there were any bills in it.

'*Zach, Zach*?' Henry said.

'The very same.' I folded my mail to my chest.

'*Interesting.*'

'Not really,' I muttered, following him down the steps.

'No, Jesse, it *is* interesting.' Henry put his front foot against the stoop. His tie was loose and his beer belly was just barely pushing against his white button-down. It struck me how funny this was: my older brother was going to marry the guy he met while covering the World Cup, thus beating me to the altar by a mile, while I was playing the beard for my best friend's widower, whom I briefly dated in college. How was *that* for alternative lifestyles?

'This has a certain symmetry,' Henry said, squinting against the porch light. He tapped my toe with his foot. 'Seriously. I think it could be good.'

'You're way off base.'

Henry winked. 'Five bucks says you make out.'

'Henry!' I yelled. But he was already walking down the driveway, his hands in his pockets as he whistled, 'Here comes the bride, all dressed in white'.

★ ★ ★

Zach insisted on picking me up. It made more sense than meeting there, he said. When I heard his car pull up, my stomach lurched. I had to remind myself this evening was just a night between two old pals. No big deal.

'Hey!' he said when I opened the door.

'Hey!' I said.

'You look nice.'

I made a face — I looked like I always looked — then I remembered my manners.

'So do you.'

He did, too. Zach had on a crisp dress shirt and a pair of dark blue jeans, with a black blazer that fitted his broad shoulders perfectly. Under more normal circumstances I would have asked if he wanted to come in for a drink, but somehow now this seemed like a come-on, even when, truth was, I felt like I could use another beer. Instead, I said, 'Should we go?'

'Sure.' Zach smiled. 'Let's go.'

We made small-talk in the car. What was going on with him, work-wise. What was going on with me, work-wise. I told him the latest on Taryn — she'd had me overnight courier a set of Frette sheets to her in Ojai, along with two vases from the shop, so she could get a good night's sleep 'in spite of the spa's Sting-goes-to-India décor'.

'That's the most ridiculous thing I've ever heard,' he said.

'On the one hand, I get it. Taryn has a really strong aesthetic and so I guess there's a kind of consistency to her madness.' I'd been known to rearrange the lighting in a hotel room on occasion, I told him. 'And once I put a painting I couldn't stand under the bed.'

'On the other hand . . . ' Zach prompted.

'On the other hand she's about three chairs short of a dining set.'

We pulled into the Music Center's underground car park — a vast labyrinth of parking spaces underneath the downtown theatre complex — and followed waving attendants in orange neon vests who were directing cars. It was a busy night. There was a play at the Dorothy Chandler Pavilion, a concert at the Mark Taper, plus the *Times* party. After what seemed like a dozen turns, we parked the car and walked to the nearest escalator, the beginning of an endless chain of switchbacks that would lead us up, up, up, and back into the world. As we transferred from one landing to another, I frowned at my jeans, which now seemed a little casual compared to all the cocktail-attired women who were heading to the theatre. Zach was putting on a tie which he grabbed from the back seat when we pulled in. Why was I always picking out the wrong clothes? Without Cecile, I was a sartorial disaster. The last escalator delivered us above ground, and we stepped out on to the vast, outdoor plaza.

It took a moment for me to compose

myself. The *Times* party was more of a to-do than Zach had made it out to be. There was a midnight-blue entrance carpet surrounded by lily arrangements which floated atop clear Lucite pedestals. Although the plaza was enormous, crisp yellow silk scrims in carved black lacquer designated the boundaries of the party. At one end, a lit fountain flaunted its water display, slapping the paving stones with percussive splashes; at the other, the round Mark Taper concert hall gleamed bronze from within. It was like stepping into a gigantic, open-air jewellery box.

Zach guided me through the check-in, pocketing his name tag with a wink, and cocked his head at the bar. 'What're you having?'

'Scotch, please,' I said.

'Soda?'

'Neat.'

Zach got the drinks; he was drinking beer.

'Didn't realise you were a Scotch man,' he joked, sounding like an actor in one of those old Hollywood movies. He handed me a tumbler.

I put on my best Dorothy Parker, ' 'One more of these and I'll be under the host.' '

He held his glass up. 'Cheers.'

We clinked.

'Zach!' A very tall, very thin, tan-suited

man with a shiny bald head was approaching with a woman, also exceedingly thin and wearing a white trousersuit. As with owners and their dogs, these two looked alike. *But who was the owner, I wondered, and who was the pooch?*

'Editor number one,' Zach whispered to me, stepping forward with his arm outstretched. 'How's it going, Tom?'

'Not bad, not bad. You know my wife, Stevie.'

'Nice to see you, Zach,' she said. Tom and Stevie then both turned and looked at me expectantly.

'This is Jesse Holtz,' Zach said.

'Hi.' I shook each of their bony hands.

'Nice to meet you,' Stevie said, tapping my arm for a moment with the palm of her hand. She was only about three years older than I was, but she looked like she'd been grown in a completely different pod; the sort of woman who owned an exercise bike and never forgot to take her vitamins. Her hair was cropped short — not of inconsequential, girlish length the way mine was — and she was carrying an expensive-looking quilted leather bag. She had the sort of clothing and accessories Cecile was always lending me when she was alive. As Stevie and I sized one another up, I heard Tom say, 'Listen, Zach, about that fine dining package we're planning to run in April . . . '

Stevie and I were stuck with one another.

'So, Jesse,' she said. 'Where did you and Zach meet?'

'In college,' I said.

'College?' She asked, tilting her head and looking perplexed.

'CU,' I said.

'Then you must have known — I'm sorry, it's really none of my business . . . ' Stevie paused and it dawned on me why she was so uncomfortable: Zach and I had never got our story straight — was I not supposed to mention college? Nevertheless, I was interested, sociologically speaking, to see what Stevie would say next. 'Are you . . . old flames?' she stammered.

I had to put her out of her misery. 'Oh no, not at all.' I smiled. 'We're very old friends. I mean, we've known one another for about ten years.'

'*Oh!*' Stevie nodded, relief unknotting her brow. 'I'm so sorry about Cecile. Were you close?'

'Very.' I took a sip of my drink.

'You know, I always saw her at these functions. I thought she was just lovely. Really. A lovely, lovely girl.'

I told Stevie that she was right: Cecile *was*

a lovely girl, although talking about her in the past tense, even now, was a difficult thing to do.

'What have I missed?' Zach was back at my side. I watched as Stevie tried to involve him in the conversation without bringing up Cecile's death directly.

'Jesse tells me you two met in college. Isn't that fabulous?' she said.

'Fabulous.' Zach looked at me. *What's going on here?* his eyes asked.

'Totally fabulous,' I said with a look back like, *Don't ask.*

★   ★   ★

An hour and a half later I had met three editors and their wives, too many advertisers to recall, one restaurant publicist who kept begging Zach to write up a client's brasserie, and one paranoid chef who kept joking that he hoped Zach would stay away. I'd had three Scotches, four appetizer-sized spinach pies, and a half-dozen chicken skewers. I went back to what Bryn had said when I told her I was going to be Zach's escort.

'And you're thinking this is going to be fun because . . . '

'I'm not thinking it's going to be fun,' I

said. 'I'm doing it because he asked me for a favour.'

'If you say so, honey-bunny,' she answered. Then she told me she loved me and said she had to go — a client had just arrived for her three o'clock. I hung up and wondered, *Was Bryn annoyed with me? Lately it had been hard to tell.*

It *was* fun, however, in a way. As I watched Zach shaking hands and talking food, it occurred to me that I'd never seen him in quite this light. Zach the respectable food critic. Zach the tastemaker. Zach the man. Then again, it was uncomfortable watching people try to figure out who I was and how they should treat me. After explaining how we knew one another for the sixth time, I went to the Ladies', hoping to grab a quick moment to myself, when I heard two women talking at the sink. I watched their feet in the space below the cubicle door.

'Car accident,' said one. She was wearing beige rhinestone pumps.

'No,' said pink shoes. 'She was *gorgeous.*'

'I know. Incredible skin . . . '

Pink shoes said hold on; she had to fix her lip-gloss.

'I always thought he was quite attractive.'

'Zach's a dreamboat,' said the rhinestones. 'He's broken up about everything, of course. It's tragic, really.'

There was something about those bony ankles. Then I realised. Rhinestone shoes was the woman I'd met, Stevie.

'Do you think that woman's really his date?'

I heard a laugh. 'Hardly,' said Stevie. 'I mean, you remember his wife.'

I waited to flush the toilet until I heard them leave.

'Had enough?' Zach asked when I returned.

I nodded that yes, indeed, I'd had enough.

★   ★   ★

We were safely on the escalator. I was watching the back of Zach's head descend when he turned around and caught me staring. I looked away.

'Do you by any chance know where we parked?' he asked.

He meant what floor. 'Oh, uh . . . four?' I said.

'Not six?'

'You know, I have no idea,' I said. 'I thought you were looking.'

'I should have been, but I don't think I was.'

I started to laugh.

Zach started laughing too, embarrassed, and rubbing his chin. 'Crap!' he said, scratching his head. 'Um. OK. Do you want to start at the bottom, or at the top?'

★   ★   ★

There are ten underground floors in the Music Center car park. It's as wide as a football field and a city-block long. Every fifty feet or so there's a concrete wall that blocks your vision, so, if you're lost, you have to walk around the partition to see if your car is on the other side. To make matters worse, each floor is split-level, which hinders your view even more. You get from one half-floor to another along metal staircases that clank when you walk down them. Zach and I looked together for about twenty minutes, and then divided the split-levels between us to save time.

'Jesse?' I heard him call from the level below, his voice echoing off the concrete floor.

'Yeah?'

'I'm sorry about this.'

'It's OK, you didn't do it on purpose.'

There was silence for a moment

'I can't believe I lost the damn car!'

'What if it was stolen?'

Pause.

'At this point that would kind of be a relief.'

I chuckled. My high heels were off now and dangling from my index finger. The bottom of my feet had turned black. There was nobody in sight; we were leaving the party early and the play wasn't out yet. I could hear Zach shuffling on the floor just below. Occasionally I'd hear a hop, which I assumed was Zach jumping up to try to see over the roofs of cars. I had his key ring in my hand, and I kept waving the clicker around, pressing the button to see if his car — a silver Audi that I'd seen a thousand times but now looked like the hundred or so sedans I'd already seen — would hear me.

'Do you want to take a break?'

Zach was peering over the top of a nearby staircase.

I said I thought that was a great idea.

'I'll come to you.'

He bounded up the steps and took my hand, motioning for us sit down on the concrete next to a white Land Cruiser that looked like it had just been waxed.

'Maybe you should get one of these,' I said, leaning on the car next to Zach, stretching my legs out in front of me. His dark blond hair was slightly mussed and his blue eyes looked green in the amber lights.

'Is this gas guzzler really me?' he asked.

'No. But you can see it from far away.'

'Oh, ha ha.'

We were quiet for a minute.

'So this is fun,' I said.

'You know what I like about you, Jesse?' Zach said.

I shook my head.

'You're a terrible liar.'

I was?

'Uh, *yeah*. Remember that time, what was it, your twenty-fourth birthday?'

'The surprise party.'

'Right. Cecile knew the whole way through dinner that you were just pretending not to know the next stop was at our house.'

'*What?* Why did she let me pretend?'

'She thought it was cute. You know, that you were trying not to ruin your surprise for her sake.'

Laura called that afternoon to ask me what time the party was. I don't think she knew it was supposed to be a surprise, I explained.

'Laura then called and told Cecile she thought she'd messed it up before we left to go get you.'

Cec never told me. 'Why doesn't anybody ever *tell* me anything?' I said.

Zach shrugged.

I studied my cuticles, which were dry. I put my hands in my lap. I missed Cecile so much, yet hearing a new story about her made me surprisingly happy. I could still learn things about her, even though she was gone.

'Jesse?'

I looked up. There was a serious expression on Zach's face; his eyes were wide — almost fearful. Before I knew what was happening, he leaned forward and kissed me, gently, on the mouth. His lips were warm. And achingly soft. Like the way a candle feels when you run your finger through the flame. I realised, instantly, that Bryn had been right. I was the girl Zach had a crush on, and I hated to admit it, but I was overjoyed. We kissed tentatively at first. Small, little pecks. But then we fell into the kisses, breathing them in, exhaling them back. *If only I could find a string of reality to grab on to*, I thought. *A rope thrown down these stairwells of kissing that would pull me up, up, up and into the world.* But we didn't stop. If we stopped, we'd have to consider the consequences. We'd have to consider Cecile.

Somewhere outside of myself, I heard a *Bip bip*.

Zach kissed me again. There was another *Bip bip*.

He pulled back.

'Is the car *talking* to us?' he asked, slightly out of breath.

*The keys.* I pulled them out of my jeans pocket, pushing the hair out of my face with the back of my hand, and pushed the button. *Bip bip.*

Zach craned his neck around the top of the four-by-four. 'It's two rows over. I can see it from here.'

'We're saved,' I said.

'What a bummer, huh?' Zach stood and offered me his hand. 'Jesse, can I take you home?'

Months later, I'd wonder about that night. I'd play it over and over in my mind. If we'd known how tenuous the ecosystem that holds a group of friends together really is — if we'd focused on *that* — would we have kissed at all? Who knows? Maybe if we could have seen everything that was to come, we still would have done it. In the Mark Taper car park, on level three, section H.

# 14

## A Little Rearranging

Sometimes, when the traffic has shushed for those few, dark minutes before dawn, I wonder what Los Angeles used to be like. If it was all rolling hills, grassy plains and wild oak trees for miles and miles. If, when the canyons weren't filled with housing developments and their improbably green lawns — sprinklers sneezing aaa-tch-tch-tch-tch, aaa-tch-tch-tch-tch — they were wild and brown, scratchy and thick, and just a little bit dangerous. But even with the Spanish haciendas stampeding their way up the driest hillsides and down into the greenest gulches, the city still delivers moments of magic. Driving around a corner, your headlights flash into the eyes of a passing coyote pup and her mother, who fixes you with a protective stare. Lying in bed in the early morning you can listen to the quiet hoo-hoo-hoos of owls hidden in the eucalyptus trees that grow just beyond the confines of your back yard.

At 6 a.m. I stole away to my front porch to

listen to those dulcet hoos. Nightmares woke me. Horrible ones in which Cecile was still alive and knew I'd kissed Zach. In one of them, I ran into her outside a dark, rotting house with boarded-up windows and doors ripped off the hinges. She was going out and I was going in. I was so ecstatic to see her I ran to hug her, but she pulled back and looked at me queerly, as though she didn't understand my joy, my tears. I asked what she was doing there, and she replied that she was moving but, she said, inspecting the box of belongings I had in my hand, clearly I already knew *that*. She was distant, contemptuous even. Shaking my head, I told her not to be angry. I said we could go back to the way things used to be. I said that I *preferred* it before. 'You didn't,' Cecile said, her eyes hard, like glass. 'You're lying. You've always been lying.'

I called May at nine and got her voicemail, a recording of some punk rock band that thrummed and screamed into the phone until the beep came to the rescue. I said I wouldn't be in until the afternoon, but she could call me on my mobile if anything happened. Sundays were slow — mostly weekend lookely-loos, no interior designers or serious buyers — so she should be fine. At a quarter to ten, I called Bryn.

'Breakfast?' I asked when she answered the phone.

'Mmm,' she said, her voice thick with sleep. 'Pancakes.' Then she said. 'Wait, you mean like, this second?'

'Well . . . ' I looked out the window at a hummingbird, which was zipping about a honeysuckle vine which was growing in the yard. It reminded me of when Henry and I were kids. We'd been told by a neighbour that the delicate funnels really had honey in them, so we rode our bikes to a honeysuckle vine at the top of our cul-de-sac, plucked the yellow flowers off and sucked on their tiny bodies, young enough to believe we could actually taste what we smelled.

'All right,' Bryn growled, giving a dramatic sigh. 'But this is gonna hurt.'

*Like you can't imagine*, I thought as I hung up the phone.

★   ★   ★

I pulled into the House of Pies car park and wished I'd had the presence of mind to suggest someplace else. There were so many memories here. Cecile consoling me after another failed relationship, Cecile telling Bryn and me that Zach had proposed on a weekend in San Diego. Unlike those mornings, when information flowed as quickly as the coffee, I wasn't sure what I was going to say to Bryn. All I knew was that if she seemed even the slightest bit upset I'd have to tell her I planned to tell Zach that this simply wasn't something either one of us could pursue. If, in fact, he hadn't already reached the same conclusion himself.

I stood by the cash till for a minute before I realised Bryn had beaten me there. She was at a table in the back, wearing a hooded navy sweatshirt with a white denim mini-skirt that showed off her taut calves and little ankles.

'So what late-night adventure are we here to deconstruct?' Bryn asked as I sat down across from her. When I opened my mouth and nothing came out she smiled and said, '*Oh.* This must be serious.'

'It's kind of serious,' I said.

'Let's order first, I'm starving.'

Bryn signalled the waitress, who knew us, and who had two cups of coffee already poured, which she set down on the table. Bryn got banana pancakes with syrup, a side of bacon, and hash browns.

'For you, hermana?' the waitress, a Latina who wore her black hair pulled back into a tight ponytail, had her pencil poised in mid-air. I wasn't hungry at all.

'Sourdough toast?' I said. 'Coffee?'

'That's it?' Bryn asked.

'I couldn't sleep this morning so I had a snack.'

'Smells like you had a pack of cigarettes.'

'That, too.'

The waitress left with a shrug and Bryn rested her elbows on the table, cradling her chin on the back of her hands.

'The suspense is killing me,' she said.

I looked at my friend, whom I counted as one of the most wonderful people in my life, and wondered where to begin. *She's so pretty*, I thought.

'I kissed Zach last night,' I said.

Bryn took a sip of her coffee and set the mug down on the table. She cleared her throat.

'OK.'

'I'm sorry,' I said. 'I didn't want to.' What was I saying? 'No, no, I *did* want to. But I didn't want to because of you. And Cecile, of course. But I did it anyway. So. I don't know.' I paused and tried to think what to say next. 'Start yelling at me if you need to, or if you have to be alone I'll understand, but just, well, there it is. The truth.'

Bryn took in a deep breath and looked out of the window.

'I wish I could say I was surprised,' she

finally said. 'I saw this coming. David actually had a talk with Zach about it.'

*What?* said the expression on my face. *When?*

'Earlier this week. Zach seemed to be talking about you a lot, quoting things you said on the phone, taking you to dinner. David and I discussed it and in the end he went to his house and told him to back off.'

Ah, the day of the awkward conversation. One mystery solved. But Bryn had sent David to do something like that without talking to me first? I shouldn't have been surprised, but I was.

'Why would you try to talk him out of liking me?' I said, thinking, *Is this what friends do now?*

'Hold on.' Bryn explained that it wasn't Zach *liking* me that was the problem, exactly. 'I just feel like this is moving a little fast,' she said, 'so I'm concerned. About both of you. I mean, let's put Cecile's death aside for a moment, because it's not your fault she died and I know better than anyone that it certainly wasn't your choice.'

*Right.*

'Focusing on the living, have you really thought this through? What you're getting into? Zach is still in mourning, Jesse.'

'He's a lot better,' I said. 'You must think so, or you never would have tried to set him up with Julie.'

Bryn was caught off guard, perhaps, that I'd gone there. *Fair enough*, her expression said.

'You haven't slept with him, have you?' she leaned forward to study my face.

'No,' I said. I tried to hide that I was insulted; as though this was a fair question.

She sat back. I wasn't sure if she believed me, but she'd chosen not to put me on the witness stand.

I'd promised myself I would not plead my case. Yet all of a sudden I found myself trying to convince her. If there was even a chance that I could be happy with a man like Zach, I began, wouldn't I be a fool to pass that up? Look at my track record, I added, it wasn't as though guys like him were banging down my door.

'I mean, you saw how he was with Cecile when she was in the hospital,' I said. 'You saw how loving, and caring, and, and loving . . . ' I took a sip of my coffee. I was starting to get too emotional for Bryn. She liked rational arguments. 'Don't *I* deserve that? For once?'

Bryn played with her napkin, ripping it into tiny pieces. 'Of *course* you do, Jess,' she said.

Then she shook her head and put the napkin down. 'You know what? Go for it. I was just worried about you guys, that's all.' She smiled.

'Somehow I feel like you don't really mean that.' I was suspicious of this rapid about face from Bryn 'The Pitbull' Beco.

'I'm not crazy about the idea. But look, it's your life. I can't stand in the way.'

Relief washed over me. Shame, too. *How could I be so selfish?* I wondered. But then I thought, *No, I have to do this, I want this more, maybe, than I've ever been able to admit.* 'Oh Bryn.' I reached over to take her hand. 'Look at what I've done to you.'

'To *me?*' she said, laughing lightly. 'Honey, *I'm* fine. This has nothing to do with me beyond my concern for my friends.'

But surely, I argued, this would be an adjustment for her. Bryn shooed the thought away. 'Oh my God, not *at all*,' she said. 'Don't worry about me. I'm always good, you know that.'

'Your pancakes,' the waitress said, arriving with a large plate that was oozing fresh fruit, butter and syrup in front of Bryn.

'Actually, those are for us to share,' Bryn said, sliding the warm, fluffy pile to the middle of the table. She rolled her eyes, and handed me a fork. 'Toast, my ass,' she said, shaking her head and handing me a fork.

The hard part was over, I realised, taking a bite of the food. At least, that's what I wanted to think.

# 15

## A Tile to Remember

When I walked in the shop that afternoon I was hit in the face with the smell of furniture stain; chemical, bitter, and sharp.

'Oh. Hi, Jesse,' Taryn said from behind her desk.

May, who was supposed to be covering for me while I had breakfast with Bryn, was Windex-ing a mirrored *étagère*. She had her hair in pigtails again, but they looked wilted. Behind Taryn's back, she winced, like, *Sorry*.

'I decided to pop in and found May here alone,' Taryn said, typing something on her computer as though she was *extremely* busy. Knowing her she was probably either shopping or checking her horoscope, but her display was guilt inducing just the same. 'I could swear I actually *pay* you to work on the weekend.'

'Oh, I'll happily dock myself today's — ' I started to say.

'Not the point.' Taryn shook her head and met my eyes with a cool, *I'm disappointed-in-you* gaze. Her blonde hair was blow-dried straight — she had an appointment with her hairdresser in Beverly Hills every Friday — and her arms were stringy and tanned under her cream silk camisole from regular Pilates sessions and the careful application of bronzing lotions. I felt ugly all of a sudden, in my linty black tank top and jeans.

'Jesse, nobody knows better than I that it's a *huge* commitment to run a shop.' Taryn stood up and walked to the other side of her desk, her hand flying to her breast. 'I mean, perhaps this is *my* fault. Maybe I'm just giving you *too many* responsibilities. But I think I've found a solution. Guess who's back?'

I looked at her, dumbfounded. Since Debbie left two years ago, it had only been myself and May.

'Our good old friend, Mister Time Clock. Yes, I'm ordering new punch cards this very moment.' She leaned back and pushed a button on the computer screen. I heard the *swoosh* sound her PowerBook made when an email was being sent. 'I know, it's a *little* degrading. But I'm going to punch in and punch out too! It'll be fun! And frankly, it's the only way I can really know when you two are both here.'

As if I wasn't already feeling as big as a parasite on a flea's arse, Taryn then did something that drove me crazy. 'Is that OK with you?' she said. 'You *are* the manager. I wouldn't dream of making a decision without your input.'

I stood there, thinking of the various arguments I could make. All those Wednesdays I worked while she was on another one of her 'spa days', all those Friday afternoons when I'd end up making deliveries to Lizzie's or on my hands and knees among the dusty bolts at Diamond Foam and Fabric in a futile effort to find a damask print for pillows that would match one of Taryn's dreadful drapery creations. I wanted to point out that, frankly, I wasn't overwhelmed, I was *bored*. I could do more. I could have more responsibilities beyond sorting bills, running errands, and helping customers. I'd been in charge of every photo shoot the store had ever had — styling the rooms with flowers and accessories so they would look good on film. I'd been sketching in my spare time; new patterns for custom silk-screened wallpaper, a few suggestions on how we could turn Lizzie's office into a more creative space with a wall of these cool industrial cork tiles I'd found online — she could tack entire scripts up that way if she wanted to. Taryn hated cork, but even Jasper Morrison was designing with it now. I had a whole file to show her, a ton of different ideas.

*If only I could open my own shop,* I thought. But then a voice deep inside said, *Of course, to open a shop you need clients, and more than a bunch of half-baked ideas, not to mention the right space, a deposit on the lease . . .* I thought of the cheque Cecile gave me, but no, if I lost that money on a failed business, I just didn't think I could ever forgive myself. I mean, I was already kissing her husband, what next? Just do something impulsive with the money she'd left me, when I knew owning a store was risky without the client contacts Taryn had? Sure, I was a better decorator, but after all these years of letting Taryntula put her name on my work, who would believe it? *I should look for a house like Bryn,* I thought. *Then again, my mortgage would lock me into this job for ever.*

'Jesse?' Taryn snapped her fingers. 'I asked if this was OK with you.'

'It's fine,' I said.

She nodded, sympathetically. 'But look, don't hesitate to take time off when you need it, OK?' She pointedly shook her head at a stack of mail in her in-tray that I was planning to sort and send to her house tomorrow. 'I know you get so easily overwhelmed.'

★ ★ ★

Zach called me at work just as I was speaking with the heater repairman. Taryn had waved her fingers over the vent behind her chintz desk chair and asked if we'd even noticed that there wasn't any hot air. ('Talk about hot air,' May muttered under her breath. I mentally pleaded with her, *I know, but please don't make this worse than it already is.*) Taking the phone, I left the repairman to continue his investigation of our unit's innards. I snuck into the ally behind the store.

'Is the bitch in the house?' Zach asked, recognising the stress in my voice. The sound of his made me happy, lighter.

'Like you *wouldn't* believe.'

'Maybe this will cheer you up. How about dinner Tuesday night? There's a new Tuscan restaurant I want to write about — the chef's one of my favourites in New York, and this is his first place in LA.'

'Sounds fun,' I said.

'More than that party I dragged you to,' he said. 'And I promise to use the valet. So listen, I have to do an interview in a minute so I can't chat, but I wanted to say that last night was terrific, stop chewing your lip — which I've noticed you do when you're stressed — and don't dress down. This isn't friends hanging out, Jess. It's a date, OK?'

'Okay,' I said. I couldn't help smiling.

Zach hung up the phone, and I clutched it to my chest. I had no idea what I was going to wear. Don't dress down, did that mean dress up? But in LA, even when people were dressed up they still looked effortlessly fabulous. Without Cecile to help, I was all thumbs.

As I turned to put the phone back in the charger, I overheard the repairman giving Taryn the prognosis. ' — clogged beyond belief. See all this fine dust? It needs to be brushed out at least twice a year. Otherwise it overheats and everything shuts down.'

'Oh for goodness sake,' Taryn said, her voice laced in frustration. 'Jesse? May? Could you both please come here?'

★ ★ ★

On Tuesday Zach pulled up outside my house at seven-thirty, right on time. I went outside to greet him, and he opened the car door for me.

He'd placed a white daisy on the front seat.

'How'd that get there?' Zach asked when I found it.

'Mystery elf?' I said, matching his tone and blushing.

'Must be. Zachary the flower-giving mystery elf.'

While he drove I held the daisy in my hand. I was unsure what, exactly, I should do with it. Bring it with me into the restaurant? Put it in my bag? Leave it on the dash? No matter what my choice, I worried that it would die before I got it home. Finally, I wrapped the flower in a piece of tissue paper from my purse and placed it on the back seat.

Zach smiled. 'You don't have to save that,' he said. 'There will be plenty more.'

★　★　★

I was wearing a new dress I'd bought at Bloomingdale's after work the day before. Knowing that I couldn't dress for shit, I opted for something new. I would think of the outfit I wanted to create, just like how I'd think of a room: I wanted something classic, but contemporary. I wanted to create the chic vibe of a well-designed sitting room that you want to drink red wine in. A place where you could talk all night. Something that had black leather, chrome, but a chunky, cosy rug that toned down the hard edges and made it homey. I finally settled on a black shift dress, with modern silver earrings — costume jewellery, but they looked nice — and I splurged on a pair of black leather high-heel boots with a brown wooden heel. The boots were the equivalent of that earthy rug I had in mind, and I have to say, I think it worked. As I finished getting ready, I felt rather pleased with the result.

When we arrived at the restaurant, Zach asked if I would mind if he ordered for both of us.

'Not at all,' I said, putting the menu down with relief. I thought I knew enough about Italian food to at least order it, but the only word I recognised was *risotto*.

Putting the menu aside, Zach summoned the waiter. They spoke to one another with resonant r's, t's, o's, and i's. The place was small, but had a layout that gave it a welcoming feel, with brick walls and mahogany tables. There were tea-lights scattered around, and at one end the open kitchen yawned, the mouth of a wood-fired oven exhaling a heady breath of roasting meats and rising dough. As I turned to look, my elbow scraped on the brick wall behind my chair. The sensation reminded me of the little wounds I would get while I thrashed about on my college dorm-room bed all those years ago. I'd once done that with Zach, in fact. My face felt hot.

The waiter left to fetch us our wine with an

approving nod and Zach and I gawked at one another.

'I like your dress,' he said.

'Thank you,' I said, adjusting the neckline. I thought about telling him my new dressing-as-décor system, but then I worried he'd tease me; after all, Cecile didn't need to play mental games just to get dressed for dinner. His staring was making me self-conscious. Here I was, on our first date, and yet I couldn't find the rhythm that got us there. Zach looked fairly uncomfortable too; I was sure this was my fault. Fortunately there was a way around that: pigging out.

From the first basket of bread, delivered with a bowl filled with homemade ricotta cheese, to the half-dozen courses thereafter, we stuffed our faces. Zach explained each dish. There was warm chicken liver crostini, creamy buratta cheese atop slivers of marinated tomatoes and drizzled with olive oil. We had mashed beans and sage that came with a platter of spicy sausages, their skins taut to bursting. There was something called Ribolita — a kind of bread soup — and we sampled some sort of white fish served in an black iron roasting pan, still hot and spitting salty juices.

As we crammed food into our mouths, I tried to introduce routine topics — his house, my house, Bryn's house search, updates on our respective parents. It wasn't until I asked Zach about why he liked to write about food that the tempo picked up, and we slid into a more rhythmic, conversational beat.

'I just find comfort in it,' Zach said, serving me a second sliver of fish and tearing off another piece of bread, which he put on my plate. 'I always have.' He paused. 'I think it has something to do with my grandmother. She was a fantastic cook — French, but her cooking wasn't like what they teach at Ducasse. Her food was more about what they used to eat in Northern France — cassoulets, *lapin aux pruneaux, carottes à la crème aux herbes.*'

'I know what cassoulet is, but *lapin-oh-proo* — '

'Rabbit roasted with prunes. That's French for comfort food.'

I asked if he saw his grandmother often, and he told me how his parents would go through these stormy patches. His '*mémé*', as he called his grandma, would come and stay. She'd fill the house with her presence, with her *food*. Stack the refrigerator with roast chickens and *pot au chocolat* — kind of like the French take on chocolate pudding, Zach explained.

'I'd sit there and watch her for hours,

drawing in my colouring books on the kitchen floor, just happy to stay out of the fray,' he said.

'The fray?'

'Good old Mom and Dad.' Zach took a bite of food, his wrist strong, solid. On his ring finger, I noticed, there was a white line where his wedding band used to be. *When*, I wondered, *did this happen?* 'She was an alcoholic, and what I guess you'd call manic-depressive, although back then I didn't know they had a name for it. My dad, well, he's a terrific guy, but he has a temper when he drinks a bit more than he probably should.'

I conjured up a mental picture of Mrs Durand, her pale, watery blue eyes watching Cecile's funeral, her arms crossed in front of her, one tiny hand gripping her thin wrist. Afterwards, she put a hand on my arm, the touch stick-like. 'I know,' she'd said. 'I know.'

'Does she still drink?' I said.

'Not a drop.' Zach laughed. 'She plays racquetball.'

'I know what you mean about food, though,' I said. 'Listening to you talk, I'm starting to realise that the way you feel about food is kind of like how I feel about furniture.'

He asked what I meant and I explained

that when I was a kid we had this great house up in Mount Olympus. It was the kind of neighbourhood where Henry and I could ride our bikes up the middle of the street and I loved that house. The Duhrrie rug in my bedroom. The antique dining-room table that my parents had with these whacked-out wire Bertoia chairs. All over the house there were pieces from the different places that my mom and dad had lived. They were groovy bohemians in San Francisco before I was born, then they lived near Lake Michigan for a while, working in a candle store — some of the Eames furniture they picked up was manufactured in Zeeland — then they travelled to India.

'Anyway,' I said, 'when they got divorced, it all got divided up. All those things that looked so lovely in a room together were split apart.'

'So you're trying to put it all back?'

'Well, no.' I smiled. 'I'm not *quite* that crazy. But I guess I'd like to conjure up that time. To recreate the magic of those rooms, in a way. If Taryn would let me. Besides, life is hard. You may as well have a cool space to sit in and cry.'

Zach laughed. Dessert arrived; canelloni stuffed with sweet ricotta and raisins and a dusting of powdered sugar so light it was as though an angel had puckered her lips and

216

breathed over our plates.

'I've always wanted to ask you,' Zach said, 'why don't you just quit? Use the money Cecile gave to you, I don't know, go to interior design school, or become a decorator.'

'I've had more than enough of school,' I said. 'Besides, I want to do something special with the money. You know, something that would be meaningful to Cec.'

Zach leaned forward, spooning up some of the dessert. 'What would that be, though? Jesse, you *can't* do something that will be meaningful to her. That's the sad fact of it. You just have to live your life. That's what she would have wanted you to do.'

I nodded, thinking, *I'm trying, I'm trying.*

* * *

There was a light rain when we left. I watched rivulets run down the passenger window, shot through with the white light of passing traffic until they looked like tiny electric rivers. I thought of Colorado, where you don't see electric rivers in the wind-screen. You see stars.

An unexpected change of motion. Zach had made a left, up into the Hollywood hills — the opposite direction of my house.

'Zach,' I said.

'Come over,' he said.

'Don't you think it's getting late?'

'No.'

I checked the clock on the dash. I was busted. It was only ten-thirty. He was taking me back to his place

As Zach wound through the curved streets, I found myself thinking about inevitability, whether or not it existed. I wondered if Cecile could see me now and, if so, what on earth she made of me.

★ ★ ★

Zach let us in. The house was dark. He walked into the kitchen and switched on a light.

'Take this,' he handed me a bottle of wine. 'And this.'

He handed me a bottle opener.

'Oh, and this' — he laughed as he passed me a throw pillow, then another — 'and this.'

'What are *you* taking?' I asked.

'Wood. Glasses.'

Zach opened the kitchen door and called outside. 'Happy!'

The dog came bounding in, his white and tan wiry coat slicked down and soaking wet.

'Oh no. Happy, why didn't you go into the

garage, huh?' The dog was paying no attention. 'Why didn't you go into the garage?'

I kneeled down to pet Happy and he jumped up and licked my lips, placing his bristly, muddy paws on my new dress.

'*Happy!*' Zach scolded.

'It's OK,' I said. 'I love him.'

'Ah, yeah, but he's not supposed to do that. Listen, I'll towel him off and I'll meet you there, OK?'

'There . . . '

'Not the living room, in the den.'

★　★　★

While I listened to the sound of dog biscuits making metal tinks as it hit the bottom of Happy's aluminium bowl, I felt the den wall for a light and flicked it on. This wasn't a room I'd spent much time in — aside from the time I found our bridesmaid dresses here — but I remembered that, technically, when we finally got around to decorating it properly, this room was going to be 'Zach's'.

('You'll help me do the whole house,' Cecile had said when she told me how much new furniture she wanted to buy. 'And don't say you don't know how, because your taste is perfect, and I know you can do it.')

The den was small and had the look of former-dorm-room meets grown-man-trying-to-show-an-interest-in-furniture. In the corner was one of those black torchère lamps that every college guy in America bought at Target between 1990 and 1995. The walls had built-in bookshelves which were filled primarily with cookbooks — glossy oversized manuals, their spines saturated in edible colours — along with a fairly extensive collection of mystery novels, which I had no idea Zach read. His desk was new, but made to look old, Pottery Barn maybe, and there was a reading chair that I definitely recognised from the Restoration Hardware catalogue. I wondered when Zach had ordered this stuff — I'd never seen it before — and it broke my heart to think of him surfing the Internet, furnishing an empty house he was supposed to share. There was a lovely Chinese rug on the floor — probably something from Cecile's parents — and a nondescript wood table in front of a tile fireplace.

The tiles interested me. They were Batchelder — three-by-three blocks of hand-made ceramic which were glazed a burnt-yellow and embossed with pictures of Mexican haciendas. I was able to identify them from a day when Taryn brought me with her to drop off some heavy vases at a client's house. On the way back to the store, I remarked that the living-room fireplace seemed a little bulky to me. Taryn looked at me as though I'd just rolled in fertilizer.

'Those tiles are quite *valuable*, Jesse,' she said, shifting into patronising lecture mode. Mission scenes were a design feature of Batchelder tile, she told me. That particular set was most likely installed in the twenties, when Batchelder had a shop in Pasadena. He was part of the Arts and Crafts movement.

'You'd be wise not to think of such historical details as 'incongruous',' Taryn said, flipping her hair back and placing her hand back on the steering wheel of her luxury SUV. 'They're *classic*.'

Zach's tiles, I saw, did have more charm than I gave them credit for that day. I wondered if he'd be interested if I relayed their history.

'Ugly as hell, isn't it?' Zach said, walking in with a heavy-looking cord of wood and two wine glasses.

'Actually, I heard they're pretty rare.'

'Really?' He leaned over and opened the fireplace grate. 'Huh.'

'The Arts and Crafts movement?' I was trying not to sound like Taryn's pet parrot. 'In Pasadena?'

'Ah, the Arroyo Seco. Makes sense.' He got on his knees to build a fire. 'Have a seat,' he said. There was no couch, so I put the pillows on the rug in front of the table. From the floor, I watched Zach build an impressive tepee of wood, placing kindling in the centre and getting it all going off just one match. Then I remembered: on college snowboarding trips, he used to brag about his skills. 'Just look at that,' he'd say, walking through the room on the way to bring Cecile a beer. 'Bea-utiful.'

'Nice,' I said.

'Thanks.' Zach got up and turned the Target lamp down until it hummed at low light. 'Just atmosphere,' he said, sitting next to me.

'That lamp is horrible,' I said.

'Really?' He swivelled to look at it.

'Utterly. Gruesome, even.'

'Hm,' he laughed. 'Maybe I need a new decorator.'

I smiled, pointing to a U2 poster he had on the wall. 'Not maybe,' I said. 'You need *serious* help.'

'So.' Zach poured me a glass of wine and handed it to me. He paused a moment and took a deep breath. 'Christ, I'm scared out of my mind right now.'

It was the last thing I expected him to say,

and I loved him for it.

'You are?' I said with relief.

'Oh my God, yeah. Scared shitless. It's like, take your pick. I haven't kissed another woman in ten years? That's huge. I've got seriously dated moves.' He motioned to the wine, the fire. 'Cecile's gone and I can barely stand it — it sits on my chest' — he tapped his solar plexus — 'every day. Sometimes I think maybe I'll just never get over it. Maybe I'll just live with it all on top of me.'

'Zach, I am so sor — '

'No, please don't say you're sorry. Everybody's sorry. I know that. What I was going to say is that I feel like it will go on for ever, except for when I'm with you, Jesse. Then that weight *brightens* a little bit. It's not like Cecile goes away — I never want her to go away. Just, the bad stuff lifts a little, and starts to feel more like it's just a part of me. And . . . well, I think you're beautiful.'

I snickered. 'Like a weed's beautiful.'

*It's plain*, I thought, *but you can count on it to always show up.*

'Funny, too, when you're not beating the crap out of yourself.'

'Cecile was funny,' I said, taking a sip of wine.

Zach gave me a long look. 'Cecile could *appreciate* a good joke,' he said. 'She did not,

223

however, make them very often.'

I thought for a moment. It was, for the most part, true. 'I guess you have to be miserable first, funny's your reward.'

'Then I must be hilarious. I mean, last week a phone solicitor called and asked to speak to my dead wife — he wants to know if she's checked the house for termites recently. What the hell am I supposed to say? Tell some stranger she can't come to the phone, not now, not *ever*? It's awful.'

I nodded. It *was* awful. Probably worse than I could even imagine.

'But the *point*, Jesse, is I have feelings for you now, OK? I do. Maybe it's just really wrong, but I can't help it. *I* know what I want to do. So, are you with me?'

There are moments in life where you have to make a choice. Ever since I've become a so-called grown-up, the options have become more delineated and the consequences more real. In college, it's hard to really screw up. You drink too much? You'll drink less tomorrow. You mess around with the wrong guy? You'll meet a new one by the weekend. You showed up for your test on the wrong day? You can switch the class to a pass/fail. But lately there was no pass/fail. There was yes and there was no. Never kind of. Or maybe. People died. People kept living.

Grown-ups asked other grown-ups direct questions and they expected a direct answer. I was completely unprepared.

But just the same, knowing that it would change everything, and that I wouldn't be able to take it back — not to Zach, not to myself, and definitely not to Cecile — I said, 'Yes.'

*Yes*, I thought. *Yes. Please. Yes.*

Zach exhaled. '*Thank God*,' he said.

He leaned forward and kissed me. Stronger than he did the night in the garage. Deeper. His lips were warm from the fire-place, and when I put my palms on his face, his cheeks were hot.

Soon we were beyond kisses. He unzipped the side of my dress and peeled it back, tugging my bra aside. I responded — my back arching as he kissed my neck and breasts. Wet, hungry kisses travelled over my body, and made an ache grow between my legs. We rolled on the floor, over one another, fibres from the rug clinging to our hair. Zach ran his hand up under the hem of my dress. The thought that Cecile and Zach had done what we were doing crept in but I didn't want to stop. I tried to tell myself that thoughts of her could become a part of everything — a part of our connection, of who we were in that moment and who we hoped to be. Or maybe

I just didn't want to deal with it. Not then.

My underwear was around my ankles, and Zach unzipped his jeans. He was about to slide into me.

'*What are you doing?*' I gasped, sitting halfway up.

'What?' Zach said, freezing, his hands on either side of my neck and his breath coming in short little bursts.

'You're not wearing anything.'

'We're both naked.'

'No, I mean, look it's too soon in general, but you're not *wearing* anything — '

Zach rolled over on to his back and tried to catch his breath.

'A *condom*,' he said, his shoulders shaking. At first I thought he was crying, then I realised it was laughter. 'Holy shit.'

'Do you mean to tell me you've forgotten all about those?'

'I've been in a relationship for so friggin' long — I'm sure I don't even *have* one, unless there's one in my travel bag from, like, 1996.'

I started to giggle. Of course. Trojans hadn't been part of his sexual repertoire for quite some time. Nor had the concept of waiting.

'It's OK,' I said. Then I started to laugh so hard I was crying, my breath coming in painful gags.

'Thanks,' he said, cracking up harder. 'Oh, thanks a *lot*. Yuk it up. Laugh at the rookie.'

After a few minutes, our laughter died down, and we lay there, spent. I sniffled and wiped the tears from my eyes, every now and then one last burst of giggles shaking my shoulders like aftershocks. Eventually, Zach slid his hand up my thigh, between my legs. 'But what if,' he whispered in my ear. 'I mean, would it be OK . . . if we did more of this?'

I cleared my throat. 'Yes, actually,' I murmured, as his hand touched me. 'Please. More of this.'

# 16

## Sofa, So Good

'Must've been *some* dinner,' May said, clocking herself in. She plopped a copy of the *LA Times* on my desk.

I peered over my computer screen to read the first sentence:

Tuscan food, like many of our favourite American dishes, provides comfort with simple ingredients. But why not add some spice, some texture? Some — should I say it? — *sexiness* even? At Siena, country dishes whisper a promise of satisfaction that goes deeper than, say, your average *pappe al pomodoro* . . .

'Sounds like it was sssssaucy,' May said.

'Are you done with this?' I asked, reaching for the paper.

'It's all yours,' she said with a wink.

I watched May head to the back of the shop to work on fabric orders, and I wondered, *Was she on to me?*

'So I couldn't be on to you more,' May said that afternoon, scooting her elbows forward, her olive skin gleaming as she leaned across our table outside the French bakery up the street from the shop and her almond-shaped eyes narrowed. 'You're sleeping with Zach. Am I right or am I right?'

'Actually, you're wrong,' I said, taking a bite of my *croquemonsieur*. We'd hung a 'Back in Ten Minutes' sign on the door and come for a quick lunch. Taryn went postal if the shop smelled like food.

'Bullshit.'

'Swear on my life.'

'I know you're dating him, so there's no point in denying *that*. He's called the shop, what, four times in the last week? Ooooohhhh wait, I get it.' May lit a cigarette, using the lit end to point at me. I resisted the urge to snake one; Zach hated it when I smoked. 'You're seeing him, but you're trying to become one of those everything-but girls.' She twirled her blue-streaked hair and raised her voice an octave. 'Ah give blow jobs more often than ah wash mah face,' she said, in a Southern accent that, on a Japanese-American girl from Seattle, was surprisingly convincing, 'but ah would *nevah* sleep with

229

ah gentleman on the first date!'

'Please,' I said. 'I'm everything *but* an everything-but girl.'

'Then what are you trying to be?'

'Careful,' I said. There was no point in being coy any longer. May was far too persistent and I wanted to tell someone, anyway. 'I'm trying to be very careful.'

May stubbed her cigarette out on the concrete patio before tossing it into a nearby rubbish bin. 'Well, whatever it is you're doing, I just hope one day you'll realise', she got up to pay for a refill on her cappuccino, 'careful just ain't yo' style.'

★　★　★

May couldn't have been more wrong. The pacing of my relationship with Zach, physically speaking, was immensely more satisfying than anything I'd ever experienced. Instead of having sex right away — of crashing together in a voracious heap only to find him bored and impartial five minutes later — we spent our first two weeks together talking, snuggling, kissing. Cecile's yellow Shabby Chic couch — which I objected to on principle and I'd told her had to be replaced when she got back from her honeymoon — was our favourite nesting place. Zach and I talked about work, our passions, dating and the future. We talked about death, how hard it was to fathom, and how there weren't really any rituals for grieving the young; all the traditions we had at our disposal seemed old, musty — for grandparents. One evening over a bottle of Burgundy and crème brûlée that Zach browned with a mini-blowtorch, we vowed to reject those tired conventions and try living *and* grieving at the same time. Why not? Zach was turning thirty at the end of the month, the day before Halloween. I was only twenty-nine. Life wouldn't stay on hold for us even if we had the inclination to stand still, which he didn't, and I was hoping to learn by his example.

After two weeks of quiet bliss, Zach asked me if I would help him redecorate the house. I said yes, immediately thinking of all the things I would like to change, to do. I realised I'd been making plans in my head all along. I'd recently met with a wonderful carpenter who was experimenting with natural joinery — a set of his chunky, rough-hewn chairs would be wonderful in Zach's living room, and there was a designer I'd recommended for Lizzie's bathrooms who could do wonders with the kitchen — he studied engineering, psychology and physiology, so he did these client interviews on functionality, and designed on that basis. *Maybe the sofa can stay,* I thought the night Zach asked me to start working on the house. I reclined into Zach's arms, the down poofyness below me. It was like sitting on a thousand boyfriend's sweaters. *Just not in the living room.*

One night we were walking Happy, whom I'd learned was a Jack Russell terrier — I had never had cause to know dog breeds before. We followed his wiry tail up and down the steep canyon roads where Zach lived. The tropical plants in the neighbourhood were shiny green, like reptiles, from the moisture in the air. We were hand in hand, and I loved the way Zach's easy step fell in with mine.

'I was talking to Laura the other day, trying to explain where I saw this going,' Zach said. (I thought of what our old friend must have looked like at the other end of the phone, the Quark program she used for grapic design on her computer reflecting in her black-frame glasses.)

'What did you say?'

'It's hard to explain without sounding cheesy. But losing Cecile was like losing my own arm. Now' — we waited as Happy paused to sniff the base of a palm tree — 'I feel like maybe we can eke out something good from all that bad stuff . . . Like maybe we can be something beautiful out of something terrible. Does that make sense?'

Zach turned to me, and his blue eyes were soft, vulnerable. No man, not even my own father, had ever looked at me that way.

'Something beautiful,' I said, the sentiment filling me with happiness, with hope. 'I like it, Zach. I really do.'

★   ★   ★

We were like teenagers. We made out in the hallway, on the dining-room table, in the shower even, where we soaped one another up and slipped our bodies together, the sensation *ssssudsy,* as May might have said. We did everything we could — stopping just short of the final act — and we did it everywhere. Except for the bedroom that Zach shared with Cecile. I wasn't ready. Neither was he.

A routine emerged over that first few weeks. Zach would make dinner while I played with the dog or looked for furniture and suppliers for his house. We'd eat in the backyard by candle-light, wrapping ourselves in blankets if it was cold. Then, somewhere between going inside to do the dishes and opening that second bottle of wine, we'd reach for one another and stay wherever we dropped until the thin light of the early morning. Then I'd go home, crawl into bed, and sleep until Zach phoned to tell me how much he missed me — my daily wake-up call.

For the first time in my life, I was an everything-but girl. It was everything I could have hoped it would be, and more.

★   ★   ★

'How do you think our friends are going to react when they see us together?' I asked Zach after those weeks of quiet bliss, when we'd seen no one and gone nowhere besides to one another's house. Tonight, we'd decided, would be the first time I slept over. It was Zach's idea — he felt to wait too long would make it loom in our minds — so I brought an overnight bag with a toothbrush, a clean pair of underwear. I had on the clothes I wanted to wear to the store in the morning, and I was trying, in vane, to keep Happy from covering my black sweater with his clinging little hairs.

'I don't care,' Zach said. He was making what seemed to be a very complex Moroccan dish involving chicken thighs, tomatoes, olives, red wine, garlic, oregano, brown sugar and prunes. It was a 'welcome' dinner, he said. I said thank you. He smiled and said, 'You're welcome.'

There was a bouquet of purple Lily of the Valley on the table — their petals regal against their fuzzy yellow fontanelles. Those, too, were for me.

'Oh come *on*,' I said, taking a sip of wine. 'Of course you care what people think.'

'Seriously. I don't. I've been through enough — I don't need anyone's approval.'

'That's interesting, actually,' I said. 'Maybe you feel impervious to gossip or criticism because you'll get off easier, in the grand scheme of things?'

'How do you figure?' Zach was chopping garlic at such breakneck speed that I worried he'd end up mincing a finger before he even started to bleed.

'Everyone's worried about you, and they should be — '

'No, they shouldn't.'

'*Yes, they should.*'

'It's been almost a year, Jesse.' He threw the garlic into a sauté pan.

'A little more than ten months since the love of your life died after a tragic car accident, two days after you married her.'

We'd decided from the start that we'd say whatever we wanted to one another; it was the only way we would keep ourselves from going crazy with guilt and secrets.

'Who says I only get one love of my life?' he asked, pushing the garlic around with a wooden spoon until it started to brown, releasing its piquant perfume.

'OK. Granted, we all want you to have more than one love in your life.'

'We?'

'Me.'

'Not 'me and Bryn?''

I paused, the wine halfway to my mouth, and smiled.

'How much chit-chatting are you two doing nowadays?' he asked. He was teasing me.

'Daily updates,' I said. It wasn't exactly true. Bryn and I had barely spoken all month save for a few brief check-ins, but she'd been very busy at work with a new case and I didn't want to be a pest.

'Damn, I should get you a present just so you have something new to report.'

'These flowers are more than enough, thank you. But back to the business at hand: you don't care what other people think. Fine. What about me?'

'What *about* you?'

I gave him a look.

'Oh, I get it,' he slid some pitted olives into a pot on the stove and began separating fresh oregano leaves from the stems, 'you're worried that people are going to think you're an opportunistic slut.'

'*Zach.*' I sputtered my wine in horror.

'But I'm right, right?'

'I wouldn't put it that way, but yes. I'm worried about precisely that.'

'Look.' Zach wiped his hands on a tea towel and came around the kitchen island. He rubbed my shoulders. 'You *were* kind of a slut,' he said, tickling me for a moment. 'But in a completely endearing, misunderstood way. Now, you've got me panting after you, and you barely give a taste.' He kissed my neck. 'I think most people will just assume you've finally found the right guy.'

I smiled and looked out the window at the little brass solar lights which cast amber circles on to the front lawn.

'Now you're the real you, Jesse,' Zach said, turning me around so he could look at me. 'You're a great girlfriend and, as always, a supportive friend. Anybody who has a problem is going to have to reckon with me because I won't allow it. We're just looking for a happy ending here. Nobody in their right mind would judge us. OK?'

I nodded. 'OK,' I said, reeling inside that he'd just used the word *girlfriend*. Another first.

'Good.' Zach returned to his garlic, pouring in Madeira wine, which he shook in the frothing pan.

I stood to get the leash and called Happy for a quick walk. I could swear I'd lost a few pounds tromping up and down the Hollywood hills. *The real me*, I thought, as I opened the door. Happy was tugging at the leash, his little legs scrambling in a futile attempt to tug me faster and further along. Part of me wished the real me and the false me had met before now; that way, I could recognise myself when I saw my own reflection in a neighbour's window.

I'd never considered myself a dog person. There were plenty of dogs in Boulder — they ran wild and were dreaded, like their hippie owners — and lately it seemed like they'd all migrated from Colorado to LA. Dog people, as far as I'd seen, were a little dirty. Their cars, their fingers, their clothes — everything had that canine smell. Their houses had hair everywhere, and dogs stained upholstery, chewed on chair legs. Cecile was not, of course, a dog person in this particular way — she loved Happy; fussed over him until he gleamed and toted him around town like a fabulous handbag. I was not so disciplined, and yet Happy was becoming my own favourite accessory, in a way. I cuddled him, walked him, and took him on errands with me when Taryn had me running all over town. (Surprisingly, our suppliers — from the dustiest furniture maker to the snootiest embroidery artisan — seemed to love it when Happy came in for a visit.) My tank tops were already starting to betray me — I was getting fuzzy. Still. I bought him chicken cupcakes, his favourite, from the dog bakery in Beverly Hills. How ridiculous! But I couldn't help myself. Or the way my heart squeezed tighter when I'd hear his little feet clicking his way across Zach's tiled floors.

I liked the real me, I decided, as Happy barked at a woman who lived up the street. She was backing her car out of her driveway — she was in her late thirties or so, with that pulled-together look I was still trying to perfect. (Imagining myself as a stainless-steel kitchen, a modern swimming cabana, the living room of a villa in Tuscany.) There was a toddler screaming his head off in a baby seat in the back. The woman waved. I waved back. The real me was a girl who smiled at neighbours. Who went to fancy dinners and got meals cooked especially for her. Who had a dog. Who'd bought three new dresses in the last month. Who always had a message on her voicemail. Who still hadn't slept with the man who left them. I never knew this part of a relationship could be so good. I savoured every moment with Zach and the real me the way I'd savour the last bite of lobster at a restaurant on the cliffs of a beach in Mexico. To me, the real me was exciting, exotic. She was unlike anyone I'd ever been before.

# 17

## See it, Love it, Buy it

'Hiii-iii! Over here!'

Bryn was waving ecstatically next to an 'In Escrow' sign. She'd put an offer on a house in Mount Washington, using the Cecile money as the down payment. Bryn had done this without hesitation, not even calling me until her signature was already on the paperwork.

'Park in the driveway,' she yelled, giving an enthusiastic *point, point.*

'Look at her,' I said to Zach. 'It's like she already owns the place.'

He laughed. '*Regardez-vous,* a woman who knows what she wants.'

The house was Mediterranean. Walls done in white stucco, a picture window in front, terracotta tiles on the roof. It was perched on a hillside of a neighbourhood not unlike mine — poised on the edge of gentrification — except I suspected that Bryn's was about to tip in the supposedly 'right' direction. The surrounding homes were crazed with schizophrenic tastes and priorities. A Craftsman that canyon bohemians had painted purple and orange hallucinated next to a Miss Havisham-esque country where there were still shredded fourth-of-July decorations hanging around the doorway, which crumpled beside a neatly coiffed Tudor which was being lovingly restored. I was nervous, as I'd seen Bryn last week for lunch, and Zach had met David for drinks a couple of nights ago, but this would be the first time they saw Zach and I 'together'. She'd acted as though it were nothing when she called us, saying we should just come on over, but now I wondered if things would be strained. I squeezed Zach's hand before I got out of the car.

'Wow!' I said, walking up the driveway.

'Can you believe it?' said Bryn. 'In thirty days this is going to be our house. Provided, of course, that I'm satisfied with the contract.'

'Of course,' I said. 'But this is so great.'

'Hi Zach,' Bryn said, leaning forward and kissing his cheek.

'Hi,' he said. 'Congrats.'

'Thanks. Long time no see, but you look good. Come on, I want to give you the grand tour.'

I took Zach's hand and we walked inside.

'This is the living room,' Bryn paused and did a demonstrative curtsey, her little bottom thrusting out and threatening to burst the seams of her *almost* lawyer-appropriate black skirt. She trotted into the next room. 'Here's the kitchen, where I expect Zach to teach me how to make many delicious meals. Notice the double-bin stainless-steel sink, dahlings.'

Zach let go of my hand to peer inside the oven so he could assess some culinary requirement. 'Gas. That's better,' he said.

We continued on.

'The dining room — formal, as you can see.'

'Nice mouldings,' I said.

Bryn snapped her fingers flirtatiously, 'Thank you.'

'And this way' — Bryn led us down a hall — 'is the master bedroom, the master bathroom — the tiles are horrid, Jesse, you're in charge of fixing that. Please note the built-in book-shelves — adorable, no? And if you'll just follow me through here . . . ' she opened another door and stepped inside a smaller bedroom with its own bath. 'The nursery.'

This was a surprise. Knowing Bryn, I was expecting her to say 'home office'.

'Are — are you expecting?' I asked.

'Holy crapballs,' said Zach.

'Good God, no. But David and I have been talking about it and at some point . . . ' She shrugged and smiled.

'Well, it's a great hacienda,' Zach said. 'You guys are going to be really happy here.'

Bryn shook her head and clapped her hands. 'I *know*,' she exclaimed.

We heard a car door slam. 'That must be David,' Bryn said. 'Zach, go say hi and I'll show Jesse the back.'

I followed Bryn to the gently sloping backyard, where there were two lemon trees which scented the air with the crisp bite of citrus. 'This is fantastic,' I said. 'You could even put a pool out here.'

'That's what I was thinking,' Bryn said.

We could hear the guys talking in the kitchen, something about cabinetry.

'David will not stop with the home repair plans,' she said. 'As if my little computer geek could hang a picture without hammering his own thumb.'

I looked through a window and glimpsed David — in his usual uniform of chinos, loafers, and a crisp white T-shirt — measuring a cabinet with a tape he could clip to his belt.

'Seems like he's having fun.'

'We both are. So,' Bryn said, perching on an old Windsor chair which the previous owners had left behind. 'Does the idea of me getting preggers freak you out?'

'Are you kidding?' I said, taking a seat on a stepladder. 'I'd be an auntie. Buying the little one presents, taking pictures at birthday parties, going on trips to the zoo. Have you guys thought about a date to start trying?'

Not exactly, she said, but it would be soon.

'So,' Bryn said, 'what's up with you?'

'Oh,' I exhaled. 'Not too much. Been spending a lot of time with Zach, as you know.'

She asked how it was going.

'Good,' I said. 'Actually, really good. I've never exactly had a boyfriend before, so I don't know how this compares, but . . . Put it this way: the other night we went and played tennis and Zach was helping me with my backhand, kind of hitting me easy balls, and he kept kissing them before he'd hit one over.'

'Awwww,' Bryn said. 'That's cute.'

'Yeah,' I said. 'And I don't know if you're interested, but the night before last we finally, ahem, *did the deed.*'

I waited for Bryn to ask me for details, as was our custom. I'd been bursting with the news. We made love for hours and I found Zach's careful attention bittersweet; it made me realise how little I'd actually expected from men in the past. The only thing was that I couldn't finish. I'd had orgasms before with Zach, when we were just messing around, but like a frustrating game of hide and seek, one minute I was on the brink of satisfaction, the next I was aware of everything from how the pillow felt under my neck to his elbow pinching my side. I wanted to know what Bryn would say — was this normal? Was it because I felt guilty? Because I still hadn't accepted what Zach and I were doing, or was still worried that we were in the wrong? Then again, despite all this, Zach and I were both so moved the first time that when it was done we both started to cry and fell asleep sniffling and holding one another in the dark.

But instead of asking questions, Bryn just said, 'Awwwww. Good for you guys.'

I paused. This was not the expected response.

'Um,' I said. 'Yeah, well, it was . . . fun.'

Bryn sighed. 'Look, Jesse, it's wonderful. You had sex. I'm so happy for both of you. But I just bought a house, you know? This isn't the only thing going on in my life.'

Her tone was defensive.

'Oh wait, no,' I said. 'I'm sorry. I really wasn't trying to steal your thunder I just — '

'Don't worry about it,' she interrupted, standing up and smiling as though this wasn't the most awkward conversation we'd ever had. 'Hey, let's go in, OK? I want to talk to David about setting up a time for the inspection.'

She turned to walk inside, giving my shoulder a quick pat. Then the screen clapped shut behind her and I sat there, stunned and alone.

# 18

## Gilt Complex

Years later, after all of this was past, and I'd realised that neither Bryn, nor Zach — nor Cecile, and particularly not myself — were exactly the people I had thought we were, it occurred to me that all relationships continue to evolve, even the ones we have with the dead.

The first time I let myself into Zach's house it was two days before his birthday. I'd come straight from Lizzie Biggens's and I was exhausted. It seemed she had me doing more and more, and I have to admit, besides one email I sent to Taryn about the planter (which she never replied to) I'd told her about absolutely none of it. This time, Lizzie had called to say she was having a dinner party and the living room needed to be completely 're-edited'. She wanted more space and some autumn accessories, so I ran over with a pile of throws, three vases and pillows from the store which weren't too bad and started pushing the couches around until we were both satisfied.

Zach was at an appointment with Dr Beaver — 'the Beave', he called her. He'd left me a message saying I shouldn't wait, so I let myself in with the spare key I'd had since Cec gave it to me a year before. Without Zach in the house — kissing me, making me laugh, filling the rooms with cooking smells — I didn't know what to do, so I wandered around, not being nosy, exactly, just looking.

That's when Cecile's thing started to become more distinct. That was *her* jewellery, still spilling out of its box on the dresser. Those were her books on the shelves. These were her favourite tea-lights. How was it that I saw these things everyday, and yet I seemed to forget they were there and what they meant? I felt a twinge of shame, and I realised then that I often felt *shame* when I thought of Cecile. Sure, there was still sadness, happiness, loneliness — all of those things made sense. But having shame added to the list was the price exacted on our friendship in exchange for my own happiness.

I fed Happy and took him to play fetch in the backyard. It was a chilly day — grey clouds hiding the sun. Without thinking, I went inside to get a sweatshirt, opening the walk-in closet like I would have done before the accident. There they were: Cecile's clothes, exactly as she'd left them. The last time I'd been in this closet had been to borrow a cocktail dress so that I could attend a Lakers' party with Henry. That day she had done my nails and tweezed my eyebrows. 'My God, Jesse,' she'd teased, 'you could paint a portrait or set a stunning table, but you don't even notice that you're walking around with two hairy caterpillars on your face.'

I stood in the closet, and marvelled at how neat everything was. Her shoes were stuffed with tissue paper. Each item of clothing hung on a wooden hanger, no wire in sight. And then, without even realising it was going to happen, my nostrils started to burn, and my throat swelled shut. I started to cry. A real cry. A *big* cry. My shoulders started shaking, and big plops of saltwater ran down my cheeks. Thinking that maybe you just have to throw yourself a pity party now and then I gave into it. I sat on the closet floor, next to Cec's rows of shoes, and let it roll over me, this weeping. Suddenly I was feeling sorry for myself, and it was self-centred and stupid, but I didn't care.

After a few minutes Happy crept in and laid his favourite toy — the 'lamb man', I called it, because it was made of virgin wool and shaped like a gingerbread cookie — at my feet. He did his best sit for me — *Look at how good I am!* — and thumped his tail. This made me cry harder.

I rubbed the dog's little ears and thought about the Beave. Supposedly it was 'a bad sign' that Zach hadn't cleaned this closet out yet. This made me angry. *How inane,* I thought, wiping my face and looking around at Cecile's lovely trouser suits, her chic dresses. *As if grief was something you do on a schedule, the way you go to a job or take an exam.*

*Enough,* I thought. I got up and I grabbed the lamb man off the floor. I picked a couple of dead leaves off him and I closed the closet door, chasing Happy outside to play.

\*   \*   \*

We spent the day of Zach's birthday in bed eating a quiche lorraine I baked as a surprise (disgusting) and sipping champagne and orange juice (delicious) until we were pleasantly buzzed.

'Think of this bed as a desert island', Zach said, wrapping his softball-tan red arms around me, 'that's surrounded by sharks. To get off, you must jump from my underwear' — he pointed — 'to your socks, to that shoe over there, to the pillow, and that's only for bathroom and kitchen trips. All other exploits off the island lead to' — he grabbed my stomach and munched it — 'certain death.'

We made love twice that day. The second time, I almost had an orgasm. Almost. At the crucial moment, I thought something completely insane — *Did Zach like it better when Cecile was on top or on bottom?* The inappropriateness of trolling my memory for sex tips made me lose the moment, and Zach was too far gone to be stopped. *It's my fault,* I thought afterwards, when Zach lay on top of me, panting. *I never should have faked it the first time.* He had no idea there was something wrong.

When I woke up from our second nap of the day, it was already five, the sun low behind the blooming bougainvillea — my favourite — that grew outside his bedroom window.

'Zach.' I shook him. 'We have to get ready.'

'Ughrf,' he muttered. 'Let an old man sleep.'

'No,' I said, tugging at his arm. 'Up, up. This whole movie thing was your idea now' — I smacked his tush — '*get!*'

'Uh, ow?' he said, and playfully shoved me off the bed.

★ ★ ★

Zach wanted to celebrate his thirtieth among the celebrities buried in Hollywood Forever Cemetery. Every Saturday night, a cinema foundation projected a different black-and-white movie on an enormous white marble mausoleum at the far end of the Fairbanks Lawn, which had a reflecting pond on one side and Paramount Studios on the other. Our friends were all chipping in for a potluck picnic, although I was bringing the booze and the cake. We showered quickly — having a glass of champagne while we got ready — then packed everything up so we could sit on blankets near the graves of Rudolph Valentino and John Huston while toasting his mortality. When Zach told me this is what he wanted to do, I asked if he really wanted to celebrate in a cemetery. He scoffed that there was a connection. 'Jesse, it says it right here on the website: an exclusive screening under and above the stars. It's perfect for us.'

I laughed. In a way, it *was* suitably perverse.

When we got there, Bryn and David were just getting out of their car. Bryn was struggling with a cooler that was practically bigger than she was. It was the night before Halloween, so some people were dressed up. I watched a witch walk by, holding hands with a guy dressed as a garden gnome.

'What's the film tonight?' Bryn asked as we paid our ten-dollar donation fee.

'*The Fall of the House of Usher*,' said Zach.

She leaned over and whispered to David, 'Is that supposed to be ironic?'

I gave her a look, hoping she caught its meaning: *Bryn, my darling, you really need to lighten up.*

Laura and Chaz were already there with a red-checked blanket spread out between two headstones and a lit jack-o'-lantern. So was Eddy, a journalist friend of Zach's, who wrote about — as he called them — 'spirits' (as in the drinks, not ghouls), along with his date, a social services counsellor named Alison, who was plain, but pretty in a girl-who-just-wants-to-keep-from-getting-too-noticed kind of way. She was wearing an orange sweater and black jeans — I was wearing an orange hoodie and a black skirt. I felt like we could share a certain wallflower kinship. I smiled when we shook hands.

'Happy birthday, Zach-a-licious,' Laura said, jumping up from her place against the headstone and giving him a hug. 'Oh, I'm so happy to see you. You too, Jess,' she hugged me next. Laura was the kind of girl who leaned into a hug, like she meant it. Her boyfriend Chaz was reclining on the lawn, a glass of bubbly in hand.

'I'm already drinking,' he said, waving hello and adjusting his pirate's hat.

'Go right ahead,' I said. 'We've been drunk all day.'

I sat down next to Bryn. She held up her glass.

'Should be a nice party, honey,' she said.

'I hope so,' I said.

We sat there, unable to think of anything to say to one another.

'So Bryn,' Laura interrupted, sitting Indian-style between us. 'Tell me everything about your new house.'

'Well,' Bryn began, 'it's a Mediterranean with a gigantic back yard . . . '

I'd already heard all this. As the sun went down, the granite gravestones turned cold and gleaming, while the scattered palm trees against the dimming sky looked like skinny girls with crazy hair-dos. At one end of the field, a DJ was spinning electronic jazz tunes, mixed in with the occasional haunted-house howl or eeking bat sound. You'd think it would be creepy to have a picnic just off the cemetery's 'Path of Remembrance', but something about the glamorous grounds — the freshly clipped grass, the ceremonial landscaping and marble mausoleums — made it almost romantic. Everywhere there were cool-looking couples, along with the occasional pair of eccentrics, drinking red wine out of plastic cups and eating sandwiches and candy from picnic baskets. I overheard David telling Chaz about the great June bug infestation of 2004; the audience — Bryn, Cecile and I included — got swarmed by thousands of the little insects which came up out of the night, everyone running screaming to their cars as though it was the fourth plague of Egypt. Apparently that was an isolated incident, but the sense of harmless danger still gave me a creeping tickle at the small of my back.

'We should do the cake before the movie starts,' I said to nobody in particular.

'Got it,' Bryn said, standing. She walked over to her cooler, reached in, and produced a truly glorious-looking pastry creation.

'Oh no,' I whispered, going over to her. I looked over my shoulder at Zach; he was deeply involved in a conversation with Laura and David — something about David's writing a video game about Zombie aliens. 'I brought a cake too.'

'Oh,' Bryn said, her smile freezing for just a moment. 'No biggie, we'll serve both.'

'Yeah, but . . . ' I started to say. I was going to remind her that I'd said in my email she should bring cheese and French bread or crackers. Wasn't the girlfriend supposed to bring the cake?

'Jesse,' she interrupted. 'Relax. It's just a cake. He's my friend too, and I wanted to do this.'

'You're right,' I smiled. 'I have matches. Candles.' I reached for my bag.

'Done and done,' she said brightly, holding up her own.

When Bryn appeared with her cake, candles lit, with me trailing behind holding a white cake with cream-cheese frosting which I'd bought at Ralph's, Zach's face lit up. 'Oh my God,' he said. 'What a surprise. Bryn, you shouldn't have.'

'Your favourite from Bluebird,' she said. 'Raspberry torte with a white chocolate crème. I picked it up this morning.'

Zach look past Bryn at me, standing there with my lame cake on a cardboard tray.

'What's this, *two* cakes?' Zach said. Mine was a little smushed and, thinking it would be funny, I'd bought the one with Yoda on it.

I shrugged and mumbled, 'Well, this one's more like a joke cake,' I said. *Ha, ha,* I thought. *Hilarious.* Zach winked and said, 'Cute.'

I had paper plates. Bryn brought brightly coloured melamine ones. I brought plastic knives and forks; she had silverware. I didn't bother to open my bottle of champagne — technically sparkling wine. She had Veuve Clicquot. As I pulled out some napkins, I heard Zach whisper to Bryn: 'Thank you so much for planning all this.'

'I wanted everything to be special,' she said. 'The way Cecile would have made it.'

For the first time in my life, I wanted to slap her.

Zach nodded and gave her a hug. I looked up and Eddy's girlfriend, Alison, was staring at me. I looked away.

Laura was the only person who ate a piece of my cake. I took this for what it was — a gesture meant to keep the peace between Bryn and I. I wondered why we'd never become closer. Then I wondered if maybe Laura had felt left out all those years since college, when Bryn, Cecile and I were so wrapped up in our threesome that we only included her in birthdays, holidays, things like that.

In a way, I could see why Bryn hadn't thought to ask me what I wanted to do for Zach's birthday. We'd been to a dozen parties which Cecile had planned for him, and of course Cec never would have bought a cake from the freezer-box section at her local grocery store. Then again, when Laura scooted over to tell me she loved nothing more than a good old-fashioned birthday cake like we used to get when we were kids, I just couldn't bring myself to let it go. I kept going over and over the mental picture of Bryn smiling and telling me to 'relax'. We'd never treated one another like this before.

★ ★ ★

The darker it got, the drunker I became. The drunker I became, the more supernatural the ambience. I could hear people rustling in the dark among the headstones, looking for their companions. 'Arnie? Arnie, is that you?'

I snuck my bottle of sparkling wine — which I'd half finished — into my bag and took it to the Ladies' with me. I was going to dispose of the evidence, but on a whim I gave it to a Goth couple who were sitting towards the back under a tree. ('Cool,' one of them said vaguely when I handed it to them.) When I came out of the Ladies', Alison was washing her hands at the sink.

'Hey, there,' she said, smiling at me.

'Oh, hi,' I said, happy to see a friendly face.

She pulled out some paper towels and handed me one.

'Zach seems like he's having a good time.'

'Yeah,' I said, taking it and thanking her.

We left the Ladies' together. 'I'm going to

have a quick smoke,' Alison said, motioning to a nearby bench.

'Actually,' I bit my lip at the pack in her hand as she started to turn away. I'd promised Zach as one of his birthday presents that I would never smoke another cigarette as long as I lived. 'If you don't mind, I'd love one of those.'

'So,' Alison lit my cigarette. We were sitting beside a grave for FAMOUS PERSON TK, waving away the occasional mosquito. 'How did you and Zach meet?'

'Oh,' I said. 'Um, well, he was married to Cecile — '

'Eddy mentioned that.' Alison frowned. 'Poor guy. It must have been so hard for him.'

'Yeah.' For no reason, I added, 'I was friends with her.'

'Oh,' Alison said. I waited for her to say something else. Offer condolences, maybe. She didn't.

'I mean, really good friends.' I said. 'And well, after she died, Zach and I started getting a lot closer.'

Still no response.

'I know, it's crazy,' I took another drag. I wanted to stop talking, but I couldn't. In my drunken state, it was almost as though I was standing outside of myself, watching myself speak. Like I was trying to see how this would

260

sound to a stranger. 'Because I really loved Cecile, you know? And now sometimes I think it's weird, but other times I think maybe it's OK. We all have to keep going, don't we? I mean, you can't just stop the way you feel so ... it probably makes other people uncomfortable though. You should just not say anything and process it if it does that. To you, I mean.'

I was quiet for a minute, hoping this verbal diarrhoea was over. Then I heard myself say, 'Actually, that's the thing I hate the most. When people are uncomfortable but feel like they have to cover it up? But — and this is such a *huge* relief — our friends, for the most part, have been really, really open and understanding. Supportive, even.'

Alison nodded. She'd say something now. Something kind.

'OK,' she said. 'Should we go back?'

I followed Alison back to the picnic site. I could tell from the way she thrust her head forward, craning her neck this way and that while she eagerly looked for our spot, that I'd committed a major act of over-sharing. It was my fault; I was so eager to connect with someone, I'd told a stranger my sordid history with Zach — *was* it a sordid history? — when she hadn't even asked.

We got back to Zach's house well after midnight. He'd barely spoken to me all evening. I had a gift stashed upstairs — a sixties chrome bulb lamp for his desk which had cost me half a month's salary — but I was too annoyed to give it to him.

Zach threw his keys on the kitchen work surface.

'I'm beat,' he said. 'Want a cup of tea?'

I didn't respond.

'What's with you?' he asked.

I shrugged.

'We barely spoke tonight,' I said evenly. I was trying not to sound too confrontational.

'Really?' He went to fill the kettle. It seemed like he was stalling.

I nodded. 'I think, once, you asked me if I wanted a beer, but that's pretty much it.'

Zach thought about it for a moment. 'OK.' He held his hands up like, *you got me.* 'Maybe I was a bit distant. I just felt like everyone was watching us and it made me self-conscious. I don't know if I felt judged or . . . Actually? It was probably mostly *me* judging me, and just a little bit of everyone else. Do you know what I mean?'

I took a deep breath. I did know. But wasn't he the one who said he didn't give a shit what anyone else thought?

'Look, I understand,' I said. 'Put it this way: I couldn't *believe* Bryn.'

Zach looked surprised. He asked what I was talking about.

'The way she basically lorded herself over me, over the party. I mean, who brings a birthday cake to another girl's party for her boyfriend?'

'What are you talking about?' Zach said. He switched on the kettle. 'She didn't mean it like that. Bryn just likes to take charge. You know how she is.'

'Sure, but — '

'But *what*?'

As Zach put out two mugs, I heard my voice catch in anger. 'But this wasn't just another one of Bryn's unconsciously rude moments, Zach. She brought that cake on purpose. It was a power play at my expense, and I don't know what I did to deserve it in the first place.'

'God.' Zach shook his head. 'You're being such a girl right now and you have no idea.'

'What's that supposed to mean?'

'Frankly? It means that you're being bitchy, paranoid and petty.'

My eyes widened in horror. As I saw it, Zach was hanging me out to dry for the second time that night.

Seeing how upset I was getting, Zach took a deep breath, then came over and laid his hands on my shoulders. I thought he was coming to console me. 'You need to relax, Jesse,' He said. 'Sometimes a cake is just a cake.'

My body went stiff.

'Stop it,' I said. 'Don't.'

I left the room and started getting ready for bed, yanking off my skirt and balling up my hoodie and tossing it on the floor. I was tempted to go home, but I was scared what would happen if I did. We'd never fought before. My hands were shaking. I was so mad at Zach for not taking my side.

Then again, I started to worry as I brushed my teeth, what if I was imagining it? I knew the ways women could rip one another apart, I went to junior high. What if Zach was right? Maybe it *was* me? *If that's the case,* I thought as I got into bed, *then I hope Bryn hadn't noticed how angry I was.* I didn't want us to be in a fight too.

Zach came in and changed into his boxers and a T-shirt. Somewhere in the house, the heater clicked on. He got into bed next to me and shivered. Then I felt his fingers start to stroke my hair.

'Forget the party,' he whispered. 'You're just tired, honey. You're imagining things.'

He kept stroking me, and even though I was furious, eventually I began to relax, to allow myself to be touched. He whispered he was sorry into my hair — he shouldn't have used the word bitchy. He kissed my shoulder, my palm, the crook of my elbow.

'I love you,' he said. 'And I promise, next time, I'll tell the whole world the same if you want me to.'

It was the first time he had ever said he loved me, and I felt my anger dissolve. As I let myself go deeper and deeper into the words, his stroking, my anger turned into passion. I allowed myself to be gathered up in his arms, and then we solved a certain problem of mine. Multiple times.

# 19

## Do You Know the Way to Good Feng Shui?

'What're you doing for Thanksgiving?' Zach asked on one of the rare nights we'd decided to spend apart. Since that fight, the air had cleared, and we'd had two weeks of renewed bliss. The renovation I was doing on Zach's kitchen was almost complete, and we went out to drinks with Laura and Chaz a couple of times. It seemed like we were both starting to feel more comfortable around other people. Bryn, on the other hand, remained nearly impossible to reach, which in her emails she kept blaming on some big case.

'Dunno,' I said. I picked up my gym bag, which was stuffed with dirty clothes which had accumulated at his house. 'My mom and dad are planning on going to Henry's, who's taking a stab at domesticity, but I could probably be persuaded to skip Hameer's turkey curry. Why?'

'My parents have invited us up for dinner.' Zach said that he was thinking we could drive up to the city for the night and come back the following day so I wouldn't have to miss too much work.

I shook the bag's contents out on to the kitchen floor, musty garments tumbling out. My house was starting to show signs of neglect — weeds growing between the bricks in the back garden, dust bunnies scuttling across the wood floors when I walked through the living room.

I shifted the phone from one ear to the other.

'When did you tell your parents we're dating?' I said.

'I didn't,' he said. 'My sister did.'

I thought of Zach's sister — nineteen years old, in the middle of her freshman year at Berkley, if I was remembering that right. Derry had dirty blonde, curly hair like Zach's and similar freckles.

'I had no idea you were going to tell your family this soon.'

'I wouldn't consider almost two months soon.'

I asked him how they took it.

'They're more worried about you than they are about me, trust me.'

'And Derry?'

'Oh fine.' I could hear him washing dishes, and I could picture the scene — Zach in his old sweatpants from college, flip-flops on his feet. 'She's a tough kid. I mean, she loved

Cecile — she was only nine when we started dating if you can believe that — so it's a little weird. But she's eager to be included in 'adult matters'. Put it this way, if I hadn't told her, she'd have accused me of trying to cheat her out of the *experience*.'

I told Zach that if that was the case then I guess there was no way I could say no. Besides, with Henry's wedding at the end of December, it wasn't like I didn't have some serious family time coming up anyway. Zach sounded happy. Said he wanted his parents to see how great everything was going so they'd stop sending him care packages in the mail as though he were in some sort of summer camp for the bereaved.

'Are you sure you can get the time off?' he asked.

'I really can't see why Taryn would care,' I said. 'It's not like I'm allowed to do anything of importance there anyway.'

After we rang off, I sent Taryn an email asking if I could have Thursday and Friday free. She was planning to have the store open the day after Thanksgiving, I knew, so I gently pointed out that I'd worked on one of my days off five times in the last couple of months.

Her reply was surprisingly prompt.

'Of course,' it said.

*Wow,* I thought. *That was easy.*

That night, I opened the calendar on my home computer to fill in dates. I typed *Thanksgiving, Zach's parents'* on the appropriate Thursday, *day off* on Friday, then turned to December. *Henry's Wedding Day* went in on Saturday the eleventh. Of course there was Christmas to consider — I wondered if Taryn would consent to giving me the week of New Year's off so Zach and I could plan something? My eyes fell on 21 December and my heart sank. The one-year anniversary of Cecile's death. I took this in for a moment and my mind turned to Zach. *Would he want to be together? Be alone? Would he want to visit the cemetery?* I surveyed the calendar and realised it was like an emotional graph with peaks and valleys of what I was going to feel and when. *Thanksgiving:* nervous. *Wedding:* happy. *The day Cecile died:* sad. *New Year's Eve:* happy. I wanted to revise it. I wanted the calendar to say *Happy! Happy! Happy!* on every day. Was that so wrong?

★   ★   ★

On Wednesday morning, as I was faxing an order to a textile designer, Taryn informed me that I was 'officially' on probation and if I didn't clean up my act, I'd be fired.

'Taryn, if this has to do with my taking Friday off, then why on earth did you say it was al — '

'That has nothing to do with it, Jesse,' she snapped. My surprised expression reflected in the mirrored designer sunglasses she'd chosen to wear inside.

Apparently the whole thing started a week before: I'd gone to Lizzie's to deliver the planter, which was perfect for the yoga studio — it brought a jewel-like, succulent green colour into the room, harmonising the inside of the house with the exterior.

'Turned out good,' Lizzie had said, walking out of the room. She forgot she was already smoking, and shook another cigarette out of a pack she always had in her hand. She left lit cigarettes in ashtrays all around the house like a trail of breadcrumbs. I wanted to dig some of the butts out and stuff them in my mouth. Disgusting. I had to persevere or this is what I'd become.

'Lizzie?' I said, following her out into the living room. 'If you're not crazy about it just tell me. We can have it fixed.'

'No, no. I love the planter. That room's done. But in general' — she held her hands up and frowned — 'something's missing.'

I thought about it for a moment, finally

asking if the problem was that the piece felt too random — did she want to tie it in with the rest of the house?

'Say more,' Lizzie demanded.

'Well, if you repeat the planter, it could become more of a statement, like a pattern,' I said. I took a sip of chai she'd insisted her assistant make for me — an honour that I'd never had before. I told Lizzie I repeated patterns myself; in my case with vintage prints of hummingbirds. I had them in every room, but in different frames, with different trims . . . in a way, the birds took visitors on a visual path. 'See, when you repeat a theme, it gives the house continuity, and it can also give it sentimental value,' I said.

'I *abhor* sentimentality,' Lizzie said. I could see she was getting frustrated, but I decided to keep going.

'Let me put it another way. A movie is just pictures on a screen if it doesn't mean anything. This house is *your* canvas, and you should have things in it that mean something to you. What in this house', I asked Lizzie, 'gives you pleasure. Or peace?'

She looked at me like I was crazy. She put her hands on her hips, and eventually said, with great reluctance, 'The Buddha.'

'Great. What else?'

Again, a long pause. I was really pushing

271

my luck. 'Is this that feng shui crap?' she asked.

'Kind of, but not really. So?' I prompted.

'Of course not. This is all just stuff I bought in a day, you know that. Everything here is replaceable.'

'Then *that's* your problem,' I said. 'You need more elements in this house that can hold some meaning for you.' After all, I told her, this was her home. *Meaning was what was missing.*

I left Lizzie in a ponderous mood. I wondered if she would take any of my advice. If she really loved the planter, we'd get her more, but frankly, I didn't think that would be enough to make her really love the house.

It wasn't until late that night that my mobile phone rang. Looking at Zach like, *Who could that be? You're right here.* I picked it up and heard the snick of a cigarette lighter.

'I'm in my storage unit. It's like something out of fucking *Silence of the Lambs.*'

'Lizzie?' I said. 'Is that you?'

'Milk-glass,' she said.

'What?'

'My mother gave me her entire collection of Depression-era *milk-glass.* She loved the stuff. I mean, I can remember when she bought the vase I'm holding in my hands right now. And my father's desk-set from his office in 1970. Came across that. Brass, wood, marble. I don't know who made it but I think this might be a nice set. Can you do something with this junk?'

'Definitely,' I said, thinking of how good that milk-glass would look on her ultra-modern black lacquer sideboard. As for her desk, it was covered with cheap plastic stuff she'd stolen from the studio. Whatever her dad's desk accessories looked like, they couldn't hurt. I promised Lizzie I'd come over the next day after work and inspect her haul.

So there I was, withering under Taryn's mirrored gaze as she accused me of trying to steal Biggens from her.

'Imagine how *hurt* I was,' Taryn said, 'when I called Lizzie today to ask her how she liked some fabric swatches I sent over and she asked me what *Jesse* thought.'

*Oh shit.*

'I sent you an email with my plans for the planter,' I stammered.

'*Your* plans? They're never your plans. They're my plans, because she's my client. And while we're on the subject? I don't have *time* to read every little missive you send.'

Taryn demanded all my files on the Biggens residence. She'd talked to Lizzie that

273

morning and was going straight over after our 'chat' to sort out 'the mess I'd dumped in her lap'. As if this weren't insulting enough, the store would be taking 75 per cent of my commission on the planters — plural now, because Lizzie told Taryn she intended to order two more, plus a fountain in it for the patio. I could keep the rest. It would come to about 150 dollars.

During this rant, I stood there. It was pathetic, I admit that. But what did I think would happen? Just because I'd been allowed to order some pottery and push a few chairs around for Lizzie everything would change? Of course Lizzie would call Taryn for her approval. Seeing my dismay, Taryn's eyes softened, and her hand flew to her breast.

'Oh Jesse,' Taryn said. 'It's probably *my* fault. I'm obviously not giving you enough guidance. But I wouldn't be a good boss if I didn't at least *try* to teach you how things should be done, would I?'

I smiled and nodded. And then I said. 'Oh, Taryn. You're right.' I picked up my purse. 'It probably *is* your fault.'

With that, I grabbed my time card and punched out.

★ ★ ★

'I was magnificent!' I told Zach. I'd found him in his living room, reading a stack of cooking magazines. Happy, excited by my tone, jumped up on a chair and tried to lick my face.

'Happy, *down*,' he said.

'Oh let him,' I said.

Zach groaned. 'His hair gets everywhere.'

'He was allowed on the furniture before, wasn't he?' I said.

The argument worked, but I had a sense I wouldn't be able to evoke the dog rules that were in place when Cecile was alive for much longer.

'So you *finally* quit,' Zach said, smiling and standing to give me a hug. 'Congratulations. I can't tell you how proud I am of — '

'Hold on,' I said. 'I never said I quit.'

'What?' He froze.

'I didn't. But I walked out.' I smiled like *stay with me here*.

'And then?'

'Well I . . . called from my mobile just to say that I was sorry if there had been a misunderstanding and I'd verbally inform her of special client requests in the future.'

Zach's expression was incredulous. He had a *Gourmet* in his hand, which was now hanging limply by his side.

'I don't *know*,' I said, for no reason since

he hadn't actually asked me anything.

'I can't believe you, Jesse.' Zach slapped the magazine down on the table and walked to the kitchen to get himself, I could tell already, a beer.

'What's the problem?' I said, following him.

'Your boss is *Satan*,' he said, yanking open the refrigerator. 'I can't even *listen* to the stories any more because they all point in the same direction: quit. You don't need the money — Cecile left you plenty. You're not learning anything there. So why do you stay? I mean, do you have to just roll over? Is it just more important to you that everyone else gets what they want? Because let me be the first to tell you, it's not kind, Jesse, it's sad.'

'I'm *sorry*,' I said.

'Don't say you're sorry!' He was shouting now.

'Jesus, Zach. Don't yell at me,' I said. My eyes stung. I was trying not to cry. 'It's my job. It's my *choice*.' My voice started getting shrill. 'Maybe it will get *better* from here.'

Zach yelled something about that being as likely as monkeys flying out of his butt.

'OK. Fine,' I said. 'You're probably right. But I stood up to Taryn today. That was a big deal for me.' *Why couldn't he commend me for that, at least?* I thought. What, I

276

demanded to know, was I going to live off? I didn't want to quit and start using Cecile's money for groceries and student loans. If I decided to quit, I said, I wanted to have a plan. That's all. 'Look, Zach,' I added. 'I'm not like you. You're always *boom, boom, boom*. I'm writing this article, tear out the kitchen, let's go on a date, I don't care what other people think. And then you drink a few beers until you forget about the consequences. I can't do that.'

'All that would be fine, Jesse, if you weren't the queen of procrastination,' Zach said, taking a rebellious swig of his beer. He pointed a finger at me. 'Watching you try to make a decision is like watching the grass grow.'

That did it.

'You know what? I'm going home so you can do just that,' I said. With that, I opened the door and walked out, for the second time that day.

★ ★ ★

I was about halfway home — my car flying down Beverly — when the thought crept in that I wanted to drive back to Zach's, bang down the door, and beg forgiveness. Would we still be driving to his parents' house for

Thanksgiving in the morning? If not, would he even call to tell me? Then again, I told myself, if I went back, Zach might think I'd just proven his point: Jesse, the pushover. The fearful defender of the status quo. That I would not allow. *Besides*, I thought, *I'm not exactly sorry, so why am I in such a rush to apologise?*

I got home and sat in the bath for a while. I stared at the white-tiled walls. I kept turning the water off to see if I'd heard the phone ringing, but no. The part that really burned me up, I thought, as I splashed hot water on my face, was that when Cecile was alive, nobody cared whether I quit my job. Nobody expected me to do anything. She got all the glory, and I existed. It didn't seem fair, to me, that now I was expected to do more.

I got into my bed, which I hadn't slept in in a month, and pulled the covers over my head even though it was only 8 p.m. It was surprisingly hard not to call Zach and attempt to smooth everything over. Like an addict who needed a fix, I curled up in a little ball and squeezed my eyes shut. I tried to pretend that I was Cecile, master of the silent-treatment, hoping that if I pretended maybe it would actually come to be.

# 20

## They Shoot Couches, Don't They?

It's funny how one fight can lead right into another. They don't seem related, and yet, like parking tickets, once you get one, they just keep coming.

I was at Zach's waiting for him to finish packing the car. He'd called me that morning and I tried to think of his apology as a personal victory even though, to be honest, he sounded as though he was keeping the peace more than surrendering.

I went to the kitchen, taking down a few cans of Happy's food and putting them in a shopping bag.

'The dog's staying,' Zach said, appearing in the kitchen doorway.

'Here?' I paused, a can in my hand.

'I'm putting food on the floor. The neighbour's kid is going to let Happy out in the morning and at night.'

'You want to leave the dog alone for *two* days?' I asked, looking down at Happy, who wagged his tail, clearly not appreciating the gravity of his situation.

'What?' Zach said.

'He's a dog, Zach, not a plant. He needs love, affection.'

'I never realised you were such a dog freak.'

'I'm not,' I said. 'I just feel bad.'

Zach sighed, sizing up, I supposed, how much grief it would cause him to tell me no.

'OK, have it your way,' he said with a sigh. 'But you're walking him.'

It wasn't until Happy threw up on the back seat of Zach's car that he got mad.

'Damn it,' he said, twisting round to see how bad the damage was, the car swerving dangerously to the left as he did so.

'Zach,' I said, alarmed. 'Keep your eyes on the road.'

'While the dog ruins the seats? Jesus, Cec — I mean Jesse. You and that damn dog.'

'I'll clean it up,' I said. 'Zach, just pull over. I'll take care of everything.'

Half a dispenser of McDonald's napkins later, he was speaking to me again.

'I'm sorry about the calling you Cecile thing,' he said, as we walked back to the car.

'And for snapping at me,' I said.

'And for snapping at you. And at the dog, OK? Really, I am sorry.'

I looked out towards the highway, eighteen-wheelers and four-by-fours speeding by. As their mechanical wind lifted my hair, I said something optimistic, hoping that we would stop arguing soon. 'I think we're both just under a lot of stress,' I said. 'All we have to do is bust through it and everything will be fine.'

★  ★  ★

*Even Taryn would be impressed by this house*, I thought as we pulled up outside the Durands'. It was a Queen Anne, the Victorian style you'd see on a million San Francisco postcards. Her front atrium — I say her, because like an ornate sailing boat, it was pregnant with feminine flounces — had arched picture windows filled with ferns and fichus. Her façade was painted dove-grey with trim in a carefully chosen white the colour of fresh cream, with the occasional touch of ebony. Compared to the more gaudily painted homes on her block — we passed one in aubergine, lime-green, and flamingo-pink, another in canary-yellow, burgundy and royal blue — Zach's parents' house had a reserved, elegant charm; a Grace Kelly in a sea of Pamela Andersons.

'Go on,' Zach said, when we reached the ornately etched glass door. 'Ring the bell.'

I pushed a brass button and heard chimes somewhere deep inside the house.

'I'll get it!'

Footsteps running down a flight of stairs. A door flinging open. There was Derry, all five-foot-nine of her. She had on blue jeans, a logo'd T-shirt, and Converse tennis shoes. An iPod was clipped to the belt of her jeans. Her features were pretty but slightly distorted — the way young faces sometimes are before they fill out — and her lithe, nineteen-year-old body declared that she could eat pizza and hamburgers all day and she'd still be skin stretched over bones, her elbows and knees like four pointy doorknobs.

'Zachy!' Derry yelled, rushing into her brother's arms. He dropped our luggage.

'Hey D-girl,' Zach said, giving her a hug until she abruptly released him and turned to me.

'Hey, Jesse,' Derry said, backing up. She stole a glance at my shoes that reminded me — instantly — of what it was like to be that age. I expected a hug — in the past, I'd always got one — but not this time. 'You brought the dog. Goodie, goodie.' She leaned forward to nuzzle Happy, who was tucked under my arm and wriggling to get free. I handed him over.

'My God, Derry, you're even taller than you were last time I saw you,' I said.

'Yeah, well. Got milk,' she said, scratching her cheek and grimacing. 'Come in.' She suddenly sprang back into the house, leaving the door wide open behind her, and ran down the hall. 'Come in, come in, come in, *come innnnnnnnnnnnnnnnnnnnnn!'*

Zach and I followed the familiar smell of roasting turkey into the kitchen, where we found Mrs Durand, basting and wearing an apron in a French Country print. What was it with this family and aprons? She straightened up and wiped her hands on a tea towel — which she then refolded again, I noticed, and set neatly back on the counter — before greeting me as though we'd never met before. When I shook her hand, it was like holding a limp little bird.

'How are you, Mom?' Zach said, stepping forward to give her a kiss on the cheek.

'I can't complain,' she said. 'Although I am worried this turkey is going to dry out before your father gets home from the hospital.'

'Mr Durand's working today?' I asked.

'He's always working,' she said.

She was making quite a spread. Turkey, mashed and sweet potatoes, salad, asparagus, homemade cranberry sauce. I offered to help, but Mrs Durand refused, instead shooing us out of the kitchen. There was already a tray in the living room with refreshments; that's what she called them, refreshments.

Thanksgivings at my house were casual

affairs. Dad, Henry and I would hang around in our sweats, drink beer, and watch the game. I'd play some rowdy rounds of backgammon with Hameer, and then we'd eat dinner in our bare feet. As Zach led me to the living room we passed the table — formally set, with some sort of gourd display in the middle. Thanksgiving would not be informal at Zach's house.

★　★　★

When Dr Durand arrived home, he came into the living room, gave his son a hug and wished me a happy Thanksgiving before asking how much trouble he was in for being late. I went to the kitchen and insisted that Mrs Durand let me help her put the turkey and all the accoutrements on the table. Dr Durand said a quick grace and then Zach's mother neatly plated all our food.

We were dining at a large French Country farm table, eating off porcelain with a lemon-yellow glaze. I loved the house's exterior, but I hated the décor. Instead of chairs, Mrs Durand used couches. These, in particular, were hideous creations; overstuffed Pierre Deux floral prints that were buried in pillows. Everywhere I looked there was pattern: on the chairs were petit-point roosters, the wallpaper was striped, the curtains were toile — gentlemen in hats and ladies in parasols waving to passengers in hot air balloons. I seemed to remember that Zach's mother was a native San Franciscan, but it appeared that she'd taken her husband's French heritage along with his family name.

As we ate (*the turkey is dry*, I thought), Derry told us about her new boyfriend, a *'genius'* computer programmer who was trying to transfer into the video game programme at USC.

'There's a degree for that?' Dr Durand asked, shifting his bulk forward. He was a tall man, and thickly built. Zach had his Gallic jaw, although Dr Durand's was heavier. Due to his French accent he occasionally dropped an 'H'.

'*Please*, Dad,' Derry said with a roll of her eyes. 'They have a *whole school.*' She turned to Zach, 'Of course, *everyone* thinks it's terribly risqué that Keshawn is African-American' — she sniggered — 'but I refuse to even *acknowledge* that kind of bigotry.'

'By 'everyone', Derry means us,' Dr Durand said to me with a wink.

'This house is *not* bigoted, Derry,' said Mrs Durand, putting down her knife and fork. 'I just don't want you traipsing around the city together. God only knows what kind of, oh, what do you call them, Armand?'

'White supremacists,' he said, sliding a piece turkey on to his fork.

She nodded. '*Supremacist gangs* you might run into.'

Derry snorted. Her mother ignored it.

Throughout dinner Mrs Durand was as dry to me as that stuffed bird. Her wrists looked like they would snap as she lifted another turkey leg on to Zach's plate; even her yams weren't sweet. She'd changed for dinner into a pair of chinos and a stiff-ironed white button-down shirt that tsk-tsked at me whenever she moved, and I could tell from the way she breathed through her nostrils every time I spoke that my presence was intolerable, as though there were something pointy under her skin.

Still, I kept trying to break through. I asked her where she got her gravy recipe. I complimented the terrible gourd display. She just wasn't having any of it. She had a soft spot for the dog, though. Before dinner she fed Happy his own plate of turkey, and he was now sleeping heavily at her feet, his little pink belly going up and down. Of course the dog was another reminder that I was here and Cecile wasn't. It dawned on me that maybe that's why Zach had been so reluctant to bring Happy along.

'More turkey?' Mrs Durand asked me.

'Definitely,' I said. 'The gravy is really delicious.'

'You forgot the lime for the water, Mom,' Derry said.

'Oh, sorry, Derry,' Mrs Durand got up. To me, she said, 'We're a dry household, I'm afraid.' As in, *I know what you want — and frankly, so do I — but consider this our mutual punishment.*

'I'll take a whiskey and Coke,' Zach said, as his mother disappeared through the door to the kitchen.

'Me too,' said Derry, giving her brother a wink.

'Actually, mineral water is perfect,' I said. Even though Mrs Durand was a bitch, I wasn't sure if I liked their teasing — Zach had told me she was a reformed alcoholic, and she did have the air of a person who'd inflicted her drinking on her children, and now felt resigned to take whatever punishment they meted out in return. As they continued to try to rile her, I could see Mrs Durand through the doorway, pulling a large knife out of a nearby wooden holder. *Oh no!* I thought. *Not the big knife!*

'You know what? Make it a vodka soda,' Zach yelled towards the kitchen.

'And a . . . a . . . Guinness!' shouted Derry, dissolving in giggles.

'Zach.' Dr Durand said it low. It sounded like *Zaq*. He shook his head once, frowning. 'Don't encourage your sister.'

Mrs Durand appeared in the doorway with the limes on a little yellow plate with strawberries painted on it. I hated to admit it, but there was something about this that actually *moved* me. I took two — so it would look like it was worth the trouble — and thanked her.

★　★　★

After dinner, Zach slid his arms around my waist as I was leaving the bathroom.

'You did great,' he said, planting a small kiss on my neck.

'Didn't feel great,' I said.

'My parents have always liked you,' he said. 'Derry thinks you're awesome.'

I shot him a look like, *yeah right*.

'What?' he said.

I didn't tell him that during dinner, Derry had kicked my ankle and bumped my elbow several times, each time giving me a look like, *Say something, I dare ya. I dare you.*

'So listen,' Zach said. 'The little sis just informed me that she has a fake I.D., and I have to say, I don't care. I need a drink. Are you up for a quick outing?'

'Sure,' I said, not pausing to consider whether we should be taking a minor — the daughter of an alcoholic, no less — out to a bar. I only thought of how relaxing a tall, ice-cold beer and a room full of strangers would be. 'Just let me grab my jacket from upstairs.'

I started to climb the spindled stairwell to Zach's room but stopped halfway, distracted by the family photos that were hanging on the wall. There was a shot of Zach in little league — proud in his uniform. Derry in braces on Christmas morning, cradling a Cabbage Patch doll. The family on a trip to Paris, all wearing matching berets. Cecile was in at least half a dozen pictures. There was a snapshot of her at the same cherry dinner table, about to take a bite of dessert. Another was of Cecile and Derry — when Derry couldn't have been older than thirteen — building a sandcastle at the beach. Zach's shadow fell just to the right of them from where he stood to take the picture. In another, Zach and Cecile were curled up on his mother's couch, sipping mugs of what looked like hot cocoa on a Christmas morning, the tree lit up behind them. Looking at pictures of a man you're sleeping with and another woman is always interesting — such a provocative mix of jealousy and curiosity, the mysterious and the familiar. I wasn't envious of Cecile exactly, but I was surprised to find that even though she was one of my best friends, I could never have known how happy she looked when she was with Zach's family.

At the top of the stairs were some framed clips from the *San Francisco Society Gazette*. Apparently Mrs Durand contributed French recipes for their food column. Each article was carefully mounted under the paper's front-page banner, along with the tagline *San Francisco: not just an address, a wonderful way of life.*

As I pondered a recipe for *Fillets of Sole Crécys*, I imagined what the tagline would be if *my* picture hung on that wall: *Jesse Holtz: not just a girlfriend, a wonderful way to torment your mother.*

★   ★   ★

The bar was on Fillmore, only a few blocks from the house, Zach said. The minute we stepped outside, he and Derry went back to their relaxed banter. I took the opportunity to unscrew the fake smile I'd had on my lips since we'd put my bag in his old bedroom.

The cool air had a tiny spray of ocean in it; a welcome change from the hairdryer breeze we got in Los Angeles.

Derry skipped ahead, telling us about a friend of hers whose parents were sending her to live with friends in Europe to 'just be' for a year before she started college. 'Life is so *fucking* unfair,' Derry said, clearly thrilled to be cursing in front of her big brother.

'Well, you know what they say,' Zach said smiling, 'The state fair is in Pomona.'

'Har, har, har.' Derry lit a cigarette, and glanced quickly at Zach to see what he would do.

'Mmm, cancer sticks,' he said. 'Great call, little sister.'

'I smoke because it makes me look *cool*,' she said mockingly.

'Just know that it's harder to quit than it is to start. Jesse knows what I'm talking about. How long has it been, Jess?'

*Two days*, I thought.

'Five weeks,' I said.

Derry scowled, saying. 'Chill out, why don't you? I'm just a social smoker.'

'In here,' Zach opened a heavy-wood frame door for us. The sound of a jukebox spilled out on to the street. After a little pushing and shoving, we found three bar stools in the back by the pool table.

'What're you two fine young ladies having?' Zach asked.

'Whatever's on tap is fine,' I said.

'I'll have a rum and Coke?' Derry said, her voice floating up at the end with a question mark that would have any waitress asking for ID if this place had table service, which it didn't.

Zach left for the bar, so I turned to Derry. Boys, if I remembered this right, were always the safest bet where teenagers were concerned.

'So,' I said, swivelling in my seat, 'Will you keep seeing Keshawn if he transfers to USC?'

'Dunno,' Derry said, not meeting my gaze but glancing around the bar. 'You know, freshman year, lots of cute guys. I might not want to be tied down.'

I smiled, thinking of how many times I'd said this during college. And after.

'Zach said you still work at that furniture store,' Derry said.

'That's right.'

'Do you like it?'

'Um, I like the *idea* of it, I just don't like my boss so much.'

Derry frowned. 'I once had a boss at this swimsuit store where I worked over on Union? He was a *total perv*. He used to ask all the employees if we would model new

292

swimsuits for him. It was so funny — the new girls would always do it, like, twice before they caught on.'

'My God. Did you go to the police?' I leaned forward.

Derry shrugged and slumped back in her chair. 'It wasn't that big of a deal.'

★　★　★

An hour later, Zach and Derry were playing pool. I was on my third beer and feeling no pain. It was good to be out of town, I decided, even if Derry and her mother found me as appealing as a soggy Frito. Los Angeles, and all the problems that went with my life there, felt more than a five-hour drive away. Even the beer tasted better. I was trying to follow Zach and Derry's conversation as Led Zeppelin blared. They were down to the eight ball, Zach's turn.

'Loser buys the next round,' he called out as he lined up his shot.

'Oh my God, Zach, that is *so* fucking unfair!' Derry yelled, hitting him in the butt with her cue. 'You can't make a bet at the *end* of the game.'

She shoved him again and he missed.

'Ha!'

'Now's your chance, you dirty little cheat.'

Zach stepped aside. 'Shut me out.'

'No problem, dick wad.'

Derry sashayed to a position behind the white ball, stopping briefly to drain the last of her rum and Coke out of the bottom of her glass — her fourth? As she moved around the table, men in the room stopped to watch her, their eyes slowly travelling up and down her body. She was too young, as of yet, to totally appreciate what she was doing to them. Whenever Zach would glance around the room, the men looked away.

'You're dead meat,' Derry said. She lined up her cue with the eight ball and the corner pocket, pulling it back. She thrust the cue forward and hit the white ball with a loud smack, sending it careening into a side pocket. Scratch.

★　★　★

'She's a cute kid, isn't she?' Zach said.

'I can't believe how much energy she has,' I said. 'It makes me feel old.'

'Me too.'

We were sitting in a booth, side by side. Derry was in the Ladies'. Zach had his hand on my knee, and its presence there made me wonder whether or not we'd be able to get away with having sex in his parents' house.

*They don't call it make-up sex for nothing*, I thought as I took another sip of my beer.

'Do you think we were like that at her age?' Zach asked. 'Because I seem to remember being a little less worldly.'

'Are you kidding? Remember that time we were all doing the mall crawl on Halloween and you were so high on mushrooms you locked yourself in your car?'

Zach laughed. 'I was seriously messed up. People's costumes were so terrifying I had to roll down the car window to take a piss. Now, you were . . . ' He looked at the ceiling, trying to remember. 'Alanis Morissette.'

'With that horrible wig, and I kept bitching about every guy I saw. It was cathartic.'

'What was I?'

I thought back for a moment . . .

'Gay porn star. With David, right?'

'And the salamis down our pants to prove it.'

'I still can't believe you got him to wear that.'

'*He* still can't believe I got him to wear that.'

'Hey,' I looked around the bar. 'Do you feel like Derry's been in the Ladies' for a long time?'

'Yeah, actually,' Zach leaned forward to take a peek at the front door. No Derry.

'Should I check on her?'

Zach said that would be a good idea. When I stood and brushed by him, he delivered a playful smack on my ass.

'I think we're going to need some time alone later,' he said.

I said, 'Don't forget to bring that salami.'

* * *

'Derry?' I pushed open the bathroom door. There was a girl in dark purple lipstick at the sink, washing her hands. She gave me a look like I was disturbing her and jerked a paper towel out of its aluminium dispenser. One of the stall doors — the floor-to-ceiling kind — was locked. I knocked on it.

'Derry? Are you in there?'

There was silence. Then, 'I'll be out in a minute.'

'Are you OK?'

No response.

'Derry?' I knocked again. 'What's going on?'

No answer. I could hear her breathing heavily. I knocked again, this time a little harder.

'Open the door,' I said.

I couldn't be sure, but I could swear I heard a muffled retch.

'Derry,' *knock knock knock.* 'Answer me or I'm getting your brother.'

A moment passed, then the door swung open and I was hit with the smell of stomach acid. Derry quickly hunched back over the toilet and started to heave.

'Derry!' I said, jumping in. I reached for her hair, which had slid out of its ponytail and was sliding forward.

'Uh-oh,' she said. Then, '*Huh-llll aaaaghr-rrrrrrrrrkkkkk. Huh-llllaaaaghrrrrrrrrrrkkkkk.* Shit,' she moaned. 'Shit . . . '

'It's OK, Derry, just let it out.'

'*Huh-llllaaaaghrrrrrrrrrrkkkkk,*' her bony shoulders heaved, and I stroked them while holding her hair back with one hand.

'That's good,' I said. 'Get it out.'

Derry's back, getting sweaty through her T-shirt, started to shake.

'Oh, sweetie,' I said. 'Don't. It's our fault — we never should have let you drink so much.'

She coughed and took in huge gulps of air. Then she spit.

'I think I'm done for now,' she said.

'OK.'

Derry straightened up and reached for some toilet paper. I was surprised when I saw there were actual tears streaming down her face.

'Derry?' I was alarmed. I reached for her. 'Are you OK?'

She shook her head, the tears flowing freely, and drunkenly swatted my hands away.

'My God, has something happened?'

'Has something *happened?*' she asked incredulously, her mouth pulling into a gasping, gaping mess. 'Cecile is *dead*, and her 'best friend' is fucking my brother, and *you* ask *me* if something's *happened?*'

I jerked my hand off her arm as though it burned.

'Derry,' I said. 'Don't say that.'

'Why *not?*' she asked, blowing her nose with a wad of toilet paper. She was swaying a little, even though she was propped up against the wall. It was clear that she was still very, very drunk. It was also clear that this was more than the rum and Cokes talking. 'I *loved her,*' Derry said, pointing a weaving finger at me. 'Don't you *get* that? *She was like a sister to me.*'

'Derry, I am so sorry. Please. I had no idea all this was upsetting you this way or I would have . . . I would have . . . ' I searched my mind for what I would have done.

'Just, get out, OK?' Derry coughed, and lurched. She was about to start throwing up again. *'Get the fuck out!'* She flapped a hand at me as she turned back to the toilet. *'Go!'*

&#42; &#42; &#42;

Twenty minutes later, Derry emerged from the bathroom. Zach had paid the tab and I was holding her sweatshirt. Without saying a word she walked past us and out the front door, stumbling on the curb. Zach got there in time to catch her.

'Whoa there, little girl,' he said, putting his arm around her waist. 'Looks like you could use a little help.'

I held the sweatshirt out and Derry sneered, looking away.

'I'll take that,' Zach said. 'Thanks.'

I walked behind them so she wouldn't have to look at me on the way home.

&#42; &#42; &#42;

We snuck Derry into the house. Somewhere there was a television on, but Zach's parents didn't come out to greet us, thank God. Derry was barely conscious by then, leaning heavily against her brother and stumbling up the stairs. Zach helped her lie down on her bed while I got a cold face cloth and tried as best I could to clean her face. As I wiped her brow, my hands were shaking. She was passing out.

'Are you all right?' Zach whispered. I

thought of the bathroom encounter, which I hadn't mentioned. I didn't know how he would take it, and considering how he'd reacted when I told him I thought Bryn was upset with me I didn't know if I *wanted* to know.

'Just tired,' I said. 'Does Derry wear pyjamas?'

'How would I know?' he said. 'Damn it. My mother is going to *kill* me.'

'Well, get me her sweats, there on the chair, and I can put her in those.'

Zach got up and picked the navy blue sweatpants off the top of a pile of clothes which were stacked on a butterfly chair. He handed them to me, and then stood there awkwardly.

'I can undress her, just go brush your teeth or something,' I said.

'You sure?' he asked.

'Of course.'

'Derry?' I asked once he'd left. 'I'm just going to get you changed, OK?'

She nodded, eyes closed. '*Mm. Mm-hm.*'

I unbuttoned Derry's jeans, slipped off her tennis shoes, and started tugging her trousers off. I'd done this for Bryn or Cecile at least half a dozen times, and they'd done it for me. Once, I came home from a date so plastered that when the girls tried to get me ready for bed, they found the guy's retainer tangled in my hair. I can still remember their hilarity while they told the story over cornflakes the next morning, while I popped aspirin and begged them to please keep their voices down.

I tugged Derry's sweats up around her waist, and picked the quilt up off the floor. As I tucked her in, she groaned.

'I'm sorry, Derry,' I whispered, before turning off the light. 'You're right: Life is *so* fucking unfair.'

★   ★   ★

Zach was already downstairs when I woke the next morning. He'd slept in the den, and I had tried to stay awake to see if he would sneak into my room, but I probably only lasted five minutes or so. I could hear the clatter of dishes in the kitchen and the air smelled of French Roast. When I opened my eyes, there was a California Gull hovering in the window, probably on his way to find breakfast in the bay. Zach's bedroom was how he must have left it when he'd gone to Boulder. There were some soccer trophies on the wall, a *The Clash* rock poster. His desk — the roll-top kind — was cluttered with a can of ballpoint pens and chewed-up pencils. I smiled when I saw there was a bottle of

Tipp-Ex on one of the desk's little correspondence shelves. *God*, I thought. *Remember Tipp-Ex?*

I went to the bathroom, which Zach and Derry shared, and saw that there were two towels already on the floor, along with Derry's sweatpants. Somewhere in this house, there was an extremely pissed-off teenager who hated me and had a hangover to boot. I washed my face and braced myself for flying cutlery when I showed myself at the kitchen table.

After brushing my teeth, I put on my comfortable jeans — we'd be driving back right after breakfast — and a sweater. I put on a little bit of make-up. I wasn't in a hurry to face anyone.

I closed the door to Zach's room, and started down the hall.

'Is someone out there?'

Dr Durand, calling from his study.

I stopped and wondered if I could sneak by. No.

'It's just Jesse,' I said.

'Could you come in here a moment please?'

I closed my eyes. Apparently my punishment would start on the upper floors, and I would descend like Dante deeper and deeper into hell.

I pushed the heavy wood door open. Inside, Dr Durand was seated at a modern glass-and-steel rod desk. Unlike the rest of the house there was neither bunting nor tassel in sight — his wife had clearly been banned from this room. He was sitting in an ergonomic chair, his glasses perched on his nose, looking at his computer.

'The Internet's ruined my life,' Dr Durand said, motioning for me to take a seat in one of the chrome-and-leather chairs that were placed across from his desk. 'I used to wake up on Sunday mornings, glance at a couple of front-page headlines just to make sure I wouldn't be the last to know that the world was coming to an end, and I'd get on with my day. Go on a jog. Do some gardening. Now, I have to know everything — the box office report, the 'Top Ten Lies Cheaters Always Tell', even what's new with Julia Roberts.'

I smiled.

'So how are things going down in La-la land?' Dr Durand asked.

'Fine,' I said, thinking, *I hate that term.* 'Good.'

'I had an interesting conversation with my daughter this morning. She had a 'friend' who wanted to know if surgeons knew hangover tricks.'

I bit my lip. 'That's not totally my fault,' I

said. It came out with a bit more tone than I'd have liked — in fact, it surprised me — but if this family objected so seriously to my presence, then why on earth had they invited me in the first place? 'Although I admit that my being here has thrown Derry for a bit of a loop.'

'Oh I heard,' he said, waving his hand dismissively. 'Derry's flair for drama is entertaining, when it's not out-and-out exhausting. Actually, her behaviour got me thinking about my patients.'

'How so?' I said this out of politeness, because the good doctor's breezy tone was starting to piss me off. *Just get to whatever lecture you have in store so I can go downstairs, have a cup of coffee, and get my sorry ass home,* I thought.

'Heart surgeons interact a lot with our patients, with our patients' families. More than, say, neurosurgeons. Of course, one of the hardest things to do is to tell a wife or a husband that a patient's died in surgery.' He paused.

'I imagine,' I said, 'that that would be really difficult.'

'It's something you get better at, I'm afraid. But I've found that telling a loved one something so terrible forms a kind of *bond*. A surprising bond, I think. Because eventually it morphs into something uplifting. Life-affirming, even. For years after, I'll bump into the wives and husbands that I've had to speak to. In the hospital lift. In the car park. They tell me how they are, who broke their leg, who's pregnant, who needs a test for this or that. And quite often they tell me about who's new in their lives. That they've got engaged, or just got back from a vacation. Sometimes it's someone from their past. Or they simply joined Match.com. And some-times — more often than you'd think — my former patient's brother has married his widow, or a woman's best friend is now dating her widower. They tell me these so-called peculiar outcomes as though they're amazed, and more than a little embarrassed. So I tell them how *glad* I am that they are doing so well. Do you understand, Jesse, why a surgeon would be glad that they are doing so well?'

'Why?' Now I really did want to know.

'Because they're *alive*. And I like life. You could say that I think of myself as being in the life business.'

I looked out the window. I needed a second or I was going to throw myself on this kind man's feet and start bawling.

'Thank you, Dr Durand.' I said.

'My pleasure.'

He turned back to his computer, and clicked something on the screen.

'Here's one: 'New Study Says Smoking Pot Helps Heart'.'

He chuckled. '*That* sounds like a fun way to put me out of a job.'

# 21

## A Matter of Life and Desk

A week later I had finally almost forgotten about that trip. I was sitting at Zach's kitchen table, reading the paper and drinking a cup of coffee, when I came across an article about a group of psychology professors who tried to figure out how people got together. They did hundreds of interviews on how couples met and found that, a lot of the time, people simply picked the person who was closest to them — scientific proof of the phrase *geographically desirable*, I suppose. A woman, it turns out, is more likely to go out with the guy who rents the apartment next door to her than she is the one who rents the place two doors down. A man is more likely to marry his secretary than he is a woman who works in the office across the street. Proximity is the key. Why this was, the psychologists couldn't determine. Maybe intimacy requires forced locality to work, or maybe we're all just really lazy.

It occurred to me then that Zach believed fervently in coupling. He believed that couples were happier than non-couples, and that the things couples do together are better than the things non-couples do. He thought couple-sex could be more satisfying — and more experimental — than casual sex, because of built-up trust and an intimate knowledge of the other person's body. (I wasn't entirely sure I believed this was a universal truth, but I *really wanted* to.) Financially, couples had the advantage over non-couples, because the proportions of, say, a head of lettuce were better suited to two than they were to one, or because car-pooling is wiser. ('I know,' Zach admitted when he mentioned the lettuce thing to me one evening, 'I'm insane.') There seemed — at first, anyway — to be very little about coupling that Zach *didn't* like.

Zach imposed a certain order on the world. He was a fervent believer in recycling and, thus, insisted on buying the scratchiest toilet paper known to man from Trader Joe's, or he'd look at me in horror if I bought a six-pack of dispensable water bottles instead of filling an old one from the dispenser. He said he appreciated my interest in furniture, but occasionally we argued about whether shelter was as essential as food. ('It's not like you can *eat* a chair,' he'd say when I tried to convince him it was worthwhile to invest in a particular piece for the house. 'One can't exactly live on fois gras either,' I'd counter.) When it came to food, Zach was a borderline control freak. He grew his own basil in the garden and if caterpillars ate it he became so enraged his face would turn red, and if a restaurant served him a dish that was even the slightest bit cold, the review would be beyond chilly.

Some of the things I learned about Zach surprised me. For example, he didn't *like* Happy much. Animals, to Zach, were for cooking, working, skinning, and producing milk or eggs. He would never admit this, of course, because Cecile loved that dog as though she'd given birth to him and now he was under Zach's care until death did them part. But I could tell he was losing interest in his role as the dog's caretaker, and that he felt guilty because when I wasn't around Happy became so starved for affection he became a nuisance — eating socks, digging into the rubbish, humping legs of people and chairs. When it got to be too much Zach would lock him out, in the garden and Happy would yelp until even I wanted to scream. Only then could I convince Zach to let Happy curl up on the couch with me while we watched a movie — provided his allotted space was covered with a terry-cloth towel. Cecile had never used a towel, and so this was evidence, for me, that I couldn't manage Zach as well as she could. (At times like these, I would remember hazy moments when Cecile would complain that Zach was being controlling, but at the time I shrugged her remarks off as the cute complaining that happy couples often do.)

Then again, Zach was the most thoughtful man I'd ever met. I told him one night that I'd acquired a taste for Pimm's from a summer studying abroad, and my heart leapt when I found that he'd started stocking it in the cupboard. If I said there was a television show I wanted to watch, he'd tape it for me. If I said there was a meal I was in the mood for he'd prepare it. If I said I wanted to sleep he'd tuck me in. He gave me well-chosen gifts: a leather handbag, a pair of pearl-drop earrings. All the fancy dinners, the thoughtful presents, everything I'd ever pined for, I had.

I can't say exactly when it started to worry me that I loved Zach, yet I didn't seem to be able to *feel* like I was in love with him — the sensation came as a tremendous surprise.

It started sometime in early December. As the temperature dropped I'd catch myself doing things like staring at Zach while he was asleep. He slept with his hands pressed together under one cheek like a child in prayer. *If I concentrated hard enough on this tender scene, I wondered, would it make me feel more smitten than I did of late?* I was yearning to yearn for him, that's the best way to explain it.

Then there was the lip-balm incident. It was the kind of thing Zach was always doing. My lips had become chapped from the dry heat at his house, and he'd noticed. He gave it to me over dinner at a new, gourmet sushi restaurant so rigid that the chef, not you, chose what you would eat. 'It's just a little thing I picked up, no big deal,' he said, sliding the small glass jar across the table. I looked at the salve — the label said it contained real aloe, verbena, and sage — and read the small card attached to it: 'Love always, Zach.' Suddenly, my throat tightened and my eyes started to sting. I excused myself and ran to the Ladies', the chef scowling at my disrespect as I went. I locked myself in a stall, sat on the toilet and tried to breathe. *What was wrong with me?* I felt like I was being squeezed. I sat there for a few minutes and tried to catch my breath. I knew I had to go back to the table or Zach would be worried. So I smoothed some of the lip balm on — creamy, delicately perfumed. It made my lips 'dewy', which Cecile had always said was the equivalent of a dermatological touch-down. I blew my nose, and returned to the table, claiming I'd had a sudden allergy attack. As we finished dinner, I chatted with Zach about the service, the décor, and the freshness of the briny seared sea scallops.

Later that night, when Zach slipped himself inside me with murmurings of ardour and devotion, I told him I loved him, too. I was alive, and Cecile wasn't, and I had everything she'd lost. *How selfish I am not to be enjoying this*, I thought as we made love. *How sad*.

★ ★ ★

The next day at work, while May helped a customer who was interested in a chandelier for her toilet (I couldn't believe we were still carrying chandeliers — wasn't Target doing a line of those by now?), I decided that *I* was the problem. This relationship was a good thing. I adored Zach, didn't I? I definitely respected him and liked him, no question. I thought he was handsome. I cared for him, deeply. I was just in a rut ... All that pressure ... The problem — this was so obvious — was me. So I wrote some theories on why I was being so cold down on a piece of paper:

- I don't know what it's like to be in a relationship, and my inexperience is holding me back.
- I am afraid of real intimacy.
- Cecile: guilt.
- Outside disapproval. (Bryn)
- If I can learn to let go and be happy, I will.

Because I *was* happy, I thought, finishing my list, folding it, and tucking it in my wallet so I could look at it whenever the need arose. Zach and I said we would create something beautiful, out of something so terrible. All I needed to figure out was why suddenly this didn't feel like such a great plan.

★ ★ ★

'Have you talked to Bryn lately?' I asked Zach that night. We were at The Grove, a fabricated outdoor mall which rivalled the cheesy landscaping of a Vegas hotel with its fake cobblestone streets, embellished façades, and a fountain that sang *That's Amore* while spouting gigantic, arching columns of water in time to the music. The Christmas decorations were up — plastic icicles hanging off the olde worlde street lamps and an enormous tree in the 'town square' — and the irony was thick. Zach hated it there and loved

313

to point out that I, the California vintage modernist junkie, hypocritically liked The Grove. *Guilty as charged*, I thought, as we passed some children marvelling at the twinkling lights that were reflected in the fake creek. I took comfort in the mega chain stores with festive window displays that were exactly the same all over the world, and I got a cheap thrill from that preposterous trolley car with a bell that sounded — *ding ding* — when a wandering toddler was about to get pulverised on its tracks. In terms of design, The Grove for me was like a satisfying, albeit futureless, one-night stand.

Zach furrowed his brow and pushed his hands deeper into his cargo jacket, trying to remember when he'd last heard from my so-called best friend. 'Last Wednesday, maybe?' he said. 'I can't remember.'

We boarded an escalator which would take us to the second floor of Crate and Barrel. We were looking for a new desk for his office. Although I'd tried to get Zach to consider something with a little more character, he was adamant.

'I like the end tables you've picked out for the living room, I agreed to that crazy mirror in the den. I can even live with the colour swatches you have taped up on every wall in my house, but I *refuse* to spend a lot of money on a piece of furniture that, to me, is really just a glorified computer stand,' he said.

This went against everything I believed in. Yes, I liked The Grove. I did not, however, buy my furniture there. But I tried not to make myself crazy over it. I thought of Zach's dad's desk, and the clear demilitarised zone between his study and the rest of the house, which was Zach's mom's chintz domain.

When we got back from our trip to San Francisco, I'd sent Bryn what I hoped was a breezy, non-judgemental email. I was eager to put Zach's birthday behind us, if, indeed, there was anything to it in the first place.

*How was your Thanksgiving?* I wrote. *We had a good time in SF, although Zach's sister got kind of upset — crying, drinking, puking (!) I know it's not true but I felt responsible. Miss you. J.*

Bryn's response: *David made a turkey and it was actually not so bad. Re: Zach's fam., don't worry, they live far enough away not to give you too much grief. Kiss, kiss. B.*

Since then, every time I called her office she was in a meeting or on a conference call. Whenever she called back it was at the exact moment that I was in the shower or out to lunch. It was almost as though she was timing it that way.

'How was she?' I asked.

'Fine,' Zach said, getting off the escalator and stopping for a moment to get his bearings. 'Working. Nothing special.'

'And David?'

'He's eaten the same thing for lunch every day since freshman year — not much changes.'

Zach paused in front of a glass and aluminium contraption. As he slid a drawer in and out, he looked up at me and I wrinkled my nose. He laughed.

'I don't want to say Bryn's avoiding me, but she's seemed a little . . . what's the word . . . *distant*?' I said.

'Come on, you're not on this again.'

I grit my teeth and tried to bite back the challenge that was on my lips. We'd been getting along lately, and I wanted to keep it that way. Zach put his arms around my waist and leaned into me from behind. I tried to stop myself from pulling away. *Why was it that lately I felt so stilted around him?*

'Has it ever occurred to you that maybe you don't need to talk to Bryn as much as you used to?' he asked as we ambled past the sea-grass rugs and sleeper sofa collection.

I asked him what he meant.

316

'You have me,' Zach said, pulling me closer.

I smiled. It was a fake smile. I paused before an oak desk that had nice lines — it would make sense in a Craftsman house, at least. 'I understand the sentiment,' I said. 'But I can't tell you about you.'

Zach released me. 'Then why don't you just ask her if there's something wrong?'

It was such an obvious suggestion. Maybe I hadn't tried hard enough since that day when Bryn showed us the new house. Bryn and I would talk. Instantly I felt a bit better.

'We have knitting night on Sunday,' I said. 'I'll do it then.'

'Good.' Zach kissed me on the neck and rapped the desk with his knuckles. 'I like this one. Can you live with it?'

'Yeah, actually. I like it too,' I said. 'Just . . . promise me that you'll let me find you a different chair.'

★   ★   ★

The following morning, Taryn launched into another one of her torture sessions.

'I'm going to go away for New Year's, so I'll need you and May to work the week that I'm in Paris,' she said. 'Problem?' Her voice snapped like the bubble wrap we used to protect breakables during shipping.

'No problem,' I said, wondering if this was, considering my mood, a good thing; Zach had been talking about going on a romantic trip to Mexico and I wasn't so sure if I was in a romantic kind of mood.

'Because you *did* take some time off after Thanksgiving.'

*Oooh, one whole day*, I thought. As if she could read my mind, Taryn added, 'Not to mention that last Christmas, you were . . . not able to be here.' She looked sad for a moment. 'Because of your friend.'

I raised my eyebrows. Taryntula changed the subject. 'So, I'll be away, and also I have a bunch of client gifts that need to go out *before* Christmas. I'm thinking we should send out these cunning shell caviar spoons . . . '

As Taryn droned on I tried not to grind my teeth. Suddenly, she'd stopped speaking, and was looking at me expectantly.

'Are you going to get that?' she said.

'Oh.' The phone was ringing. I picked it up. 'Gilded Cage.'

'It's Bryn. Can you talk?'

*Finally.* I looked at Taryn, who was getting up to speak with a customer who'd just walked in. The woman was, I saw, exactly the kind of client Taryn liked to handle personally: early thirties, an expensive handbag, hair like Meg Ryan's, and a top-of-the-line PDA clutched in one hand.

'I think so,' I said, walking to the back of the store. 'How *are* you?'

'Ugh, God, you have no idea what the last week and a half has been like,' Bryn said. 'One of the firm's biggest clients is taking over another firm and we have so much paperwork to get through, not to mention that I have a deadline tomorrow to file a — actually, you know what? Nevermind. I wanted to call about Sunday.'

'Our bitch and stitch — I was thinking that we could order in some Indian and — '

'Is it OK if we reschedule?' Bryn interrupted. 'It's just that it's got to the point where David's been making jokes that he always wanted to live alone. I mean, he's been dealing with *everything* around the move while I haven't done so much as put away a dish. I was hoping he and I could actually unpack a cardboard box or two on Sunday before he donates all my crap to charity.'

'Oh,' I said. 'I was looking forward to seeing you but . . . '

'Me *too*,' she said. 'Drag, huh?'

I asked her if there was something wrong.

'Like what?' she said. Suddenly she sounded annoyed. But before I could answer she said, 'Hold on a second.' Bryn cupped her hand over the mouthpiece. I could hear a muffled voice — someone from her office — speaking in a rushed, professional tone. 'You know what?' Bryn said. 'I've got to take this, but talk soon, OK?'

'O-kay.' I hoped she would pick up on the irritation in my voice.

'Ciao!' she said, hanging up.

*Ciao?*

★   ★   ★

Zach had a softball game and then a meeting with a magazine editor who was in town from New York that Sunday. (Zach liked to say that only editors don't think twice about asking a writer to work on the weekend; in their eyes, every day in a writer's life is the weekend.) I decided to take Happy to my place and spend the day doing things I'd neglected, like buying fresh produce at the Hollywood Farmer's Market and finally finishing the varnish on a Haywood Wakefield dresser I'd found at the Rose Bowl flea market. I was toying with the idea of giving the dresser to Bryn as a housewarming gift. *If I ever saw her again*, I thought.

I expected to have to fill my time alone to keep from getting bored, but as I fought my way through the stands selling goat cheese and hothouse-grown cucumbers, I found I was enjoying myself. Competition was fierce at the Hollywood farmer's market. Sundays brought out every metal-head roadie, unemployed director, burlesque dancer, tweaking film editor, haggard screen-writer, and former-drug-dealer-turned-Bikram-Yoga instructor within a ten-mile radius, and each one was an epicure who knew their French Raclette from their Trappist monk's chimay. My only explanation for this was that creative types had time on their hands. As a result, they could cook the crap out of almost anything.

Zach called several times on my mobile that afternoon. For some reason, I didn't feel like answering. I let it ring until my voicemail kicked in.

When I got home, I was still energised, so I put all the food away, then I added another coat of varnish to the dresser, humming while I worked. I took a long, hot shower, ate my dinner, walked Happy, and then I started cleaning. Over the din of the vacuum cleaner, I occasionally heard the ring of the phone. Zach, I was sure. Probably done with his meeting by now and wondering what I was doing for dinner. But again, I ignored it. Being in my own house was like reacquainting myself with a long-lost friend. When the last dust creature munched up in the belly of my vacuum filter it was only nine o'clock. *I could knit,* I thought, which made me think of Bryn and the evening we were supposed to have. Suddenly, I realised how upset I was with her. I walked into the kitchen, thinking maybe it was time for me to just call her up and demand an explanation. As I picked up the receiver, my eyes fell on one of May's flyers, sitting on top of a stack of unpaid bills. It read:

*Don't Be a Hater*
*Support The Radness*
*at*
*The Echo*
*10 p.m. Sunday — Free show!*

I dropped the phone in the cradle and looked at the clock. I had just enough time to get there if I didn't change. When May had handed the flyer to me last week, I made excuses as to why I couldn't come.

'I'm just so busy,' I'd said.

I hurriedly grabbed a black cardigan and went to find my bag.

★  ★  ★

The moment I stepped into The Echo, I was struck by how long it had been since I'd actually been out at night beyond dinner with Zach. The club was packed with people — all in their late twenties and early thirties, dressed in that 'Rainbow dresses and cowboy boots aren't weird, they're cool' kind of way. I pulled at my cardigan, and wished I were a more inspired dresser. Even David would have fitted in better than I did; his dorky look only got more chic with every passing Death Cab for Cutie album.

The club's interior left a lot to be desired; the walls were coated in paint the colour of a bruise, and the ceilings were covered with acoustic padding. A worn black leather bar ran along one wall, where people were standing, three-deep, to place orders. Every now and then, a head would pop up out of the throng to yell at a friend: 'What do you want?' At the front of the room was a small stage with a drum set, an electric guitar, a bass, and an upright piano crammed on to it. The show hadn't started yet, but rock music was playing loudly on speakers overhead.

Excited with anticipation and happy to be out around *people*, I decided to get something strong. A vodka soda. No, a whiskey. After a minute or two, I got the bartender's attention by holding up a ten.

'Cash,' she said. '*Finally.*' She palmed the money, and then passed my drink — dripping, amber, cold — over the groaning patrons' heads.

At that moment, the lights dimmed and a spotlight hit the stage. A few people whistled. '*Woooooooo!*' the crowd hooted, sounding like the owls that flew over my garden. '*Wooooooooooooooooo!*'

May walked onstage, followed by two male band members in identical old black T-shirts, Converse tennis shoes, and skinny jeans. Her hair was dyed an impossible orange. She was wearing a navy-and-white-striped sailor dress with red boots. May sat at the piano bench and pulled the microphone towards her. 'Woo-hoo to you too,' she said, smirking. The crowd clapped and laughed.

Somewhere in the club, a man's voice yelled out, 'Do the curtains match the drapes?'

Without a pause, May said into the mike, 'When I let 'em grow in. This song's called 'The Park'.'

She struck the first notes of a song and started to sing. The notes were low, sweet, yet guttural. As she sang, May set an almost reluctant pace with the piano keys. Eventually, the bassist and the drummer joined in, matching her slow beat. Her music, to my untrained ears, sounded like one-part folk, one-part punk, one-part songbird, all seductively curled around one another like an acoustic threesome. The song was about being in love with a new guy and spending a day in the park with him, blissfully not knowing then that the relationship was heading towards certain doom. May didn't play to the crowd as much as I'd assumed she would. She kept her head turned towards the keys, her mouth serious, her eyes a little vacant. *I'm not here to charm you, or to seduce you, or to even notice you,* her demeanour said. *Just follow me.* It was lovely.

It wasn't until about four or five songs in, when May strapped an electric guitar around her shoulder, that she revealed more of herself. Slowly her songs picked up their tempo and her game face fell away. With the guitar slung low and her wrist whipping back and forth in front of her cocked hips, she almost looked like she was playing with herself, with us. Sweat started to trickle down one side of her face, and May's cries got more insistent as the song sped forward. But even then, she never lost her grip on the song, the audience, the stage. With her feet firmly planted on the floorboards, May kept her hooks in sight, and the melodies of the songs were infectious enough to hum.

I was astounded. So was, I noticed, a man standing not far from me. He was tall, and had a little bit of pudge around the middle. Early thirties. Not classically handsome, the way Zach was, but a nice-enough-looking guy. He had brown hair that was a little mussed, and a V-neck sweater over a T-shirt. The way he stood, with his hands in his well-worn jeans pockets, his shoulders relaxed, and his head cocked while he listened to the music made me almost believe he was leaning on a fence post in the middle of nowhere, even though we were standing on a crowded dance floor. He had brown eyes. I was surprised, considering that he certainly wasn't the flashiest guy in the club, when I saw that his sweater was bunched up behind a fairly large brass belt buckle. It said 'WYATT'. As I stared, the man tipped his beer bottle towards his mouth, turned his head, and looked right at me.

★　★　★

I lingered after May's set was over. I hoped I wouldn't be intruding if I just said hello and told her how much I enjoyed it.

'Fuck *off* you actually came?' May hollered when she rounded the corner from the stage.

She took a running start, dodged a few patrons, and jumped into my arms, wrapping her legs around my waist.

'Hi!' I said, staggering back as May hugged me. She let go and slid her legs to the floor. She'd exchanged her dress for a hoodie and jeans. Her hair was in a sweaty ponytail.

'You were amazing.' I was hoping she could tell I was being genuine.

'Well, *duh*,' she said. 'I kept telling you to come. Hold on, there are some people I want you to meet.' She grabbed me by the wrist and yanked me across the room, occasionally taking my drink and gulping down a sip. 'Oooh, this is yummy. I love the rough stuff. Hey, Adam?'

May tapped one of the T-shirt-and-skinny-jeans guys — the guitarist. He turned around.

'This is my — you're kind of almost my boss, right? — Jesse. This is Adam, our guitarist.'

'Hey,' he cocked his head back at me in greeting. 'May talks a lot about you.'

'Really?' I said, surprised.

'She says you're cool.'

'Well,' I borrowed May's line, '*duh*.'

She smiled then pulled me away, saying, 'That's Devo, our drummer, over there but, oh crap, he's talking to that psycho-girlfriend of his, so forget it. Hm, who else? Oh, Wyatt!

Wyatt, come here, I want you to meet someone.'

The guy who caught me staring during her show turned around.

'There you are, sexy beast,' he said to May, a grin spreading across his face. He planted a kiss on her cheek. 'Great job tonight. Seriously. Best yet.'

'*Thank* you.' May beamed, brushing his hair back. 'So Jesse here works at the Cage with me.'

Wyatt shook my hand. 'Do you hate that girl — what's her name? Taryn? As much as May does?' he said.

'More,' I said. 'I think.'

'Not fucking possible.' May helped herself to another gulp of my drink, then turned to say hi to another friend.

'May tells me you're a painter,' Wyatt said. For a moment, I didn't even realise he was talking to me. I didn't consider myself a painter any more.

'Oh,' I said. 'I really don't do creative stuff any more.'

'But you work in interior décor,' Wyatt said. In his slightly fraying sweater, he reminded me of a big teddy bear. Not particularly my type, but he seemed like a sweet enough guy.

'Yes, but, that's purely decorative.'

'Oh, I get it.' Wyatt shook his head. 'You went to art school.'

He had an accent. I thought, *Yew grew uhp in Tex-as.*

I said that yes, I had gone to art school. For a little while.

He smacked my shoulder lightly, like *See? I knew it.* 'Had you pegged,' he said, laughing.

'I'm sorry, what are we talking about?'

'That whole division between what's design, what's art. What's functional, what's craft,' he said. 'Don't you think it's all just crap the teacher says to look smart? Like dazzle camouflage, it' — he searched the acoustic ceiling for the words — 'prevents you from recognising that the professor is, in fact, not smart. Maybe even a hack. Why would you buy into that?'

'Um,' I tried to think of the appropriate answer, surprised that the teddy bear was starting this sort of debate. 'No, I see what you're saying,' I said. 'But there are rules behind what exactly a piece of work — a sculpture versus, say, a sketch of a building — *is.*'

Wyatt leaned in. 'But wasn't it Brancusi who said, 'Architecture *is* inhabited sculpture?' '

*You fucker,* I thought. I wanted to come back with a high-falutin art quote, but nothing came to mind that would help with my position. Not only that, I hated people like Professor Flook and Taryn, yet here I was talking about rules. When had I started to sound just like them?

'You'll have to excuse Wyatt here,' May interrupted. Sometime in the last minute or so, she must have started listening. 'He's an opinionated son of a bitch. Darling?' She placed a hand on his shoulder. 'Stop being such a prick and get me a drink?' Her ponytail swayed atop her head.

'Sure.' Wyatt smiled at her. He turned to me. 'What about you, Purely Decorative. Want to buy me a refill?'

I mumbled something about needing to get home.

'Zach coming over?' May asked.

'Yeah,' I lied.

'OK,' May looked disappointed for a moment. 'But thanks for coming,' she said. 'Seriously, this is so exciting. We'll talk tomorrow, OK?'

I said OK. As I walked to the door, I paused. I thought I felt eyes on me. I turned to look over my shoulder and Wyatt was standing at the bar, staring at me. This time, it was he who turned away.

# 22

## Widow Shopping

Taryn was on her annual December trip to Hawaii, and I wasn't allowed to do so much as send Biggens an instant message, so with nothing better to do, I spent my mornings flicking foam peanuts at an heirloom vase and yelling 'Score!' whenever I got one. May, meanwhile, pestered me with questions.

'Do you just, like, want to rip his clothes off every five seconds, and is that weird for you since you knew him before?' she asked, digging into a bag of potato crisps she'd dumped out on Taryn's desk and slurping orange juice.

'It was weird,' I said, wincing — *Who ate crisps and drank orange juice at the same time?* 'I guess it's still awkward, sometimes. I don't know,' I shook my head. 'It's not like I think about sex every time I see him, anyway.' I watched in horror as May then popped a piece of gum in her mouth, adding another handful of chips. 'What are you *doing?*' I asked.

'I like it when the gum's crunchy, plus you

get the salty and the sweet.'

I retched. She shrugged. 'That's interesting,' she said, nodding. 'Because now that I think about it, you don't seem to talk about him as much as you did a month ago.'

I shrugged. 'I don't have as much to say as I did a month ago.'

'Or maybe you're not as into him as you used to be.'

I almost spat out my soda. Thank you, May, but I think it's a little more complicated than that.'

'OK, easy,' May said. 'I'm just asking. But just for fun. Say you wanted to get out, how would you do it?'

I said I guessed I'd just tell him I wanted to break up.

'Oh, no. It's not that simple. What I *mean* is, say you wanted to break up with Zach, *how could you do it*, considering the circumstances?'

'I guess I never thought about it.' This was true. Breaking up was simply not an option that I'd ever considered. I'd always assumed that we'd work out. In fact, lately it seemed like we *had* to work out.

'You should've come up with an out clause,' she said, cracking her gum. 'You know, something worked out in advance. That's what I did with my guitarist, that guy

Adam, when we dated a few years ago, so if we broke up we could still work together. See, without one, Zach can't break up with you, because you're his deceased wife's best friend, and you can't break up with him, because you don't dis the widower, you got me?'

May handed me the bag, and I took some crisps. You don't dis the widower. *You know,* I thought, *she could be on to something.*

'May?' I asked. 'Do you want to come to my brother's wedding?'

Bryn had sent her regrets to Henry on the reply card, with the caveat that she might stop by if she could 'fit it in'. I hadn't heard back from her since she had cancelled knitting night. When Henry told me he got her card, I hung up the phone, furious enough to vow that I wouldn't even try to get Bryn on the phone. This was the last straw. She obviously didn't want anything to do with me any more, and I was sick of fighting it, sick of being upset about it, sick of even thinking about it. In a way, deciding not to focus any more than I already had over what, inexplicably, seemed to be the end of a ten-year-friend-ship with Bryn, made it feel final, in a way. I tried to take this on the chin, but the truth was, I was miserable. Even though I was furious, I missed her.

'Took you long enough to ask,' May said. 'To what do I owe this sudden honour?'

I wondered if I should tell her what I was really thinking, or if it would sound too sappy. Then, I thought, *Go for broke.*

'I'd like to be friends,' I said, feeling like I was asking May out on a date. 'I mean, if you're interested. If it's not, you know, uncomfortable with us working together.'

'Jesse, sometimes you really kill me, you know that?' May said, sticking her gum in the empty chip bag and tossing it in the rubbish. 'It's been so long since you've gone outside your little college social circle, you've become blind to the obvious: we already *are* friends.'

★   ★   ★

I had the following day off, so Zach came with me to pick up the Cuisinart ice-cream maker Hameer had on his wedding list, and then to grab the set of football-shaped beach towels Henry had put on his own. I got the gifts wrapped at the mall — the wedding was only a week away and forgetting to buy paper and ribbon would be so typical. Next, we went to Best Buy to look at new dishwashers for Zach's kitchen. His house looked great, I thought. I was thinking about taking some pictures; see if there was any chance I could drum up any interest with a shelter magazine. I wondered which one of my body parts Taryn would chop off then.

As we strolled the aisle — the new dishwashers souped-up like hot rods with stainless steel and chrome — something on Zach's hand caught my eye: it was his wedding ring. I thought for a moment and realised I hadn't seen it in months. The white line that used to be on his finger from where the band was had faded long ago.

'What's this about?' I asked, tapping the ring lightly with my index finger.

'This?' he said, twisting it with his other hand. 'Oh, nothing. Just something I'd like to do for a while. Do you want me to take it off?'

'No,' I said, wondering if I meant it, then deciding that, yes, in fact, I did. 'Do you want to talk about it?' I asked.

Zach shoved his hands in his pockets, his blue eyes clouded as he turned away to read the spec on a deluxe washer that had 'whisper' insulation. 'What's there to talk about, exactly?' he said.

I told him I didn't know, exactly, and smiled, trying to lighten things up a little. 'Your feelings?' I said.

'I feel great.'

'Zach, come on. I don't expect you to feel great all the time.' I reached for his hand.

'But I do,' he said. He peered inside another washer.

I asked him what Dr Beaver had said about the ring.

'Hm? Oh. I stopped going.'

I turned to face him. 'But you're not home until late on Tuesdays. Where do you go?'

I saw a flash of annoyance cross his face. 'Nowhere,' he said. 'Out.' Then he smiled. 'Look, I think I can decide whether or not I need a shrink, right?'

I nodded. 'OK,' I said, thinking, *He stopped seeing the Beaver? When? Why?*

★   ★   ★

On Friday night, we invited Laura and Chaz over for dinner. We hadn't seen them since Zach's birthday, and they were the only couple who seemed to have adjusted to the fact that we were dating. It had been a fun enough night — Laura told me all about a new design project she was doing for a charity, and I assiduously avoided Bryn as a topic — but then, after dinner, Zach got belligerent during a game of *Star Wars* Trivial Pursuit.

'It *wasn't* Tantooine,' he said, leaning forward across the board.

'It was,' said Chaz.

'Oh yeah,' said Laura, taking off her glasses to clean them with the edge of her blouse. 'Remember? They ask Lea where the rebels are, she says Tantooine, then they blow up Alderon.'

Chaz nodded. 'Besides, it says so on the card right here.'

'Card's fuckin' wrong, man.' Zach shook his head.

'Honey?' I said, looking at Laura like, *Is he that drunk?* Zach ignored me.

'Let's put on the movie,' Zach said, trying to stand up and tripping over an ottoman.

'Zach, come on, dude,' Chaz said. 'Let it go.'

'No, I can find it.' Zach weaved his way over to the DVDs.

'Zach,' I said.

'Fuck you, guys, I can *find* it.'

Laura looked at me and widened her eyes. Then she tugged Chaz on the arm. 'I think maybe we should go home,' she said. 'I'm getting kinda tired.'

'Yeah, sure.' Chaz stood, dropped the Trivial Pursuit card on the table and pulled on his black leather coat. He was angry — I could tell — but trying not to let it get the better of him. 'Try to get some shut-eye, buddy,' Chaz said, patting Zach on the back.

'Whatever,' Zach said.

When the door closed, I turned to him.

'What the hell was that about?' I said.

'Chaz can be such a prick,' he said.

That's funny, I told him. I'd never noticed *Chaz* being a prick.

'Well,' he snapped, 'then *you* haven't been paying much attention.'

★　★　★

It wasn't until right before I fell asleep — with Zach passed out next to me and breathing heavily — that I realised he was right; not about Chaz, but I *hadn't* been paying much attention. I'd totally forgotten that the year anniversary of Cecile's death was at the end of the month.

★　★　★

'Do you have a grief section?' I asked the girl behind the bookstore cash till. It was during my lunch break, and I planned to grab a muffin or something in the café while I flicked through a couple of chapters. The salesgirl looked up from her magazine and glared at me — she reminded me of Derry and I resisted the urge to duck behind the calendar display — then she directed me to the second floor where I found a whole bookcase full of well-stacked shelves on mourning, the books taken out and replaced in no particular order. Misery — a popular topic, apparently — was divided into all sorts of categories. Grieving a parent, grieving a pet, grieving a spouse . . .

That morning, I could have sworn I'd heard Zach crying in the shower. He was driving me crazy; it was like I was trapped in some spiral of grief that no longer felt right. After all, the terrible images of Cecile's hospital stay were being slowly replaced by memories of happier times. One I particularly liked to think about was from the time I got her tickets to a U2 concert for her birthday. We drove to the Greek amphitheatre and parked, the traffic pulling in behind us until we were blocked in twenty-deep. I grabbed our tickets and noticed something odd — everywhere I looked there was another long-haired, stoned-out-of-his-mind rocker in a black mesh T-shirt. Turns out the potheads were one step ahead of me: we were a week late. That night was not U2, it was Metallica. When I realised what had happened, Cecile laughed until her stomach started to ache. Then we realised we were blocked in, and I stood there, shaking my head, when my best friend had to go pee in the bushes thanks to me. But then, things looked up. With the throbbing guitar in the background, we sat on the bonnet of my car and got drunk on Jim Beam with a bunch of head bangers who'd come just to tailgate in the car park and listen to the music. We stuffed our faces with a bag of potato crisps I found in the back seat, chasing it down with the borrowed Beam while we traded jokes with some guy nicknamed 'Hesh-ish'. We laughed and danced on the grass, at which point Cecile pressed her forehead drunkenly to mine, saying, 'This was the best birthday I have. *Ever*. Had.'

But with Zach — it was different. I was getting better. He was falling apart. I thought of what May had said, *You don't dis the widower*. She was right: I couldn't leave him, even though our relationship seemed to be getting harder with each passing day. But I had to do something.

Even so, the book titles struck me as rather funny — *Bereavement for Beginners; Anger, Denial, Depression, and Dating*; and, my personal favourite, *Widow Schmidow!* I sat in one of the store's oversized chairs and flipped through a few. In *Too Young to Wear Black*, a chapter caught my eye: 'Widow Shopping: When You're Ready to Begin Anew'. I scanned a page:

When someone close to us passes on, we often wonder why whatever higher power we believe in didn't take *us* instead. We may feel we can never replace our lost spouse, or we may find ourselves eager to date. When Melissa lost Stewart, she was afraid of getting left again, so she used that as an excuse to stay at home. But when Mohamed lost Shania, he was eager to enjoy dates with an attractive new temp in his office. However, he would later feel too guilty to tell his friends he was sexually active. In this next exercise . . .

The author, Dr Eloise Lois Anderson, Ph.D. went on to caution against moving on too soon. 'There is no hard and fast rule,' she counselled, 'but you wouldn't ask a teenager to drive cross-country before he'd gone to driving school, would you?'

Instead, Dr Eloise Lois Anderson, Ph.D. recommended pottery classes ('find new interests') and avoiding alcohol ('a depressive cocktail for any young widow'). For those who were already dating, she got practical ('Stock up on lubricant; you may find it hard to relax the first time you make love with someone new'), and recommended yoga ('meditation can help you accept a new partner, with the added benefit of relieving stress'). I closed the book and tried to imagine my telling Zach maybe all he needed was a little KY, or couldn't have his wine with dinner. Or doing mountain pose with him in yoga class, with my instructor Akasha, whom I hadn't seen in months, come to think of it, regarding us both with that dreamy yet condescending look in her eye, admonishing him to force his breath out of his nose like a snorting yak from the old country. The book was ridiculous, but I finished my muffin and bought *Too Young to Wear Black* anyway, plunking down my twenty-four ninety-five with a feeling of resigned defeat.

# 23

## Best in Tents

If the arrival of Hameer and Henry's wedding week swept me away from the curtain of anger and sadness that had enveloped Zach, I couldn't help but enjoy the break. Hameer's relatives, some Iranian, some Indian, were arriving daily. It was a challenge just to keep their names straight. One day Hameer's parents, Vipal and Yusri, arrived from London, the next Aunt Mohini and Uncle Aamir from England, then four cousins who now lived in New York, three of whom brought *their* wives and children. We had introduction dinners or cocktail parties almost every night. Hameer's relatives were enchanting. Academics, doctors, or lawyers . . . Henry was a completely different guy with them: gallant, respectful. It was a side of my brother I never saw with our parents; he was usually hiding behind the sports pages while my mother and father bickered.

During my lunch breaks, meanwhile, I was busy running to the prop studio where I was getting everything Hameer needed, décor-wise. He wanted the wedding to incorporate aspects of his Iranian heritage and his Indian heritage, 'mixed with a bit of glam', so I'd ordered tea tables, Moroccan lanterns, and leather poofs. I'd rented a Maharaja tent, and Hameer needed appropriate dishware for all kinds of traditional dishes.

This was not easy to pull off in Los Angeles. Nor, because he and my brother were gay, could you throw a party like that in most parts of the world. Many of Hameer's family members had refused to come, in fact, saying that a wedding between two men was not, in fact, a cause for celebration. 'So I'm a bender,' Hameer said one night, a toothy grin breaking over his face as he raised a glass of wine to clink Henry's. 'Cheers, mate, cheers.'

The first night, Henry introduced all the parents (my father and his father shook hands with a knowing look that said, *Look, buddy, this isn't exactly how I pictured this moment either*). Zach was jovial; constantly leaning over to give me kisses on the cheek, charming my mother with stories about travelling in France after culinary school. But the following evening, Aunt Hadil — Hameer's mother's oldest sister, if I was remembering that right — cornered Zach. 'I heard about your wife, poor girl,' she said, taking his arm and pulling him down to her height. She was in her seventies, and when she moved, the gold bangles on her wrists clinked. 'In my culture we try to remember what the Prophet Muhammad said when his own son died: 'The eyes shed tears and the heart is grieved, but we will not say anything except which pleases our Lord'.' She patted Zach's hand.

'That's beautiful, Aunt Hadil,' I said, expecting Zach to indulge her too. But instead he said a curt 'Right' and excused himself to get a drink.

'She had no friggin' idea what she was talking about,' Zach said on the way home. He was gripping the steering wheel so tightly, I thought, *He'd pull that away from the dash if he could.*

'Zach,' I said. 'She's a sweet, elderly woman, for goodness' sake. Cut the lady a little slack.'

'She's old and so it's OK for her to talk about my dead wife?'

'You may lash out, hold grudges, yell — even if these are things you never did before,' Dr Anderson cooed in the back of my mind. When we got to the house I heard myself asking Zach if he'd ever thought about doing yoga. He paused in the foyer, Happy running between us, looking for a friendly rub hello.

'You know,' I said. 'New interests could be

*good* for you. Hobbies can help with the acceptance of a new mate, not to mention alleviate stress.'

Zach kissed me on the forehead as though he was listening, but before he retreated down the hallway he looked at me like *I* was the one who was losing my mind.

★ ★ ★

The day of the wedding, I wouldn't let Zach see me until I was completely dressed, as though I, not Henry, was the bride.

A few days before, Hameer, his mother, Yusri, and Henry had dragged me to a dress shop in Artesia so that I could pick out my sari. It was Hameer's idea, and when I walked in and saw the salesgirls standing on a platform and offering silks shimmering with metallic threads, I thought I would die of embarrassment. 'You guys,' I said, turning to Henry. 'These are beautiful but come *on*, I'm going to look like I'm wearing a Halloween costume.'

'My wedding,' Hameer said, snapping his fingers at me. 'My day.'

Henry laughed. 'You're on your own, *I Dream of Genie*.'

I shook my head, saying, 'Fine, but you're going to be *really sari*.'

Hameer pretended to gag.

Picturing myself as an exotic tea room, I finally chose an amber silk edged in gold, the undergarment a brilliant emerald-green sleeveless blouse which ended just below the bust. Yusri came into the dressing room with me to show me how to tie it, wrapping the petticoat snugly around my waist, tucking the pleats, and laying the pallav over my left shoulder. When she was done, she led me outside, and I saw myself in the mirror. I was astonished. I'd been transformed. I wasn't plain or smudgy — I was exotic, an *Arabian Nights* princess ready to charm a king. Liberated from the ho-hum, safe cocktail dresses that I'd been collecting in a heap at Zach's house after all those dinners, my curves were, well, curvy. The silk clung in all the right places. My single exposed shoulder was transformed into a ripe apricot of flesh and the gold threads flushed my face with life. I wanted to clap and dance around I was so pleased. Instead I stood there, stunned. I hadn't felt that pretty in so long. Maybe ever.

'Well?' Hameer said. 'What do you think?'

'It's the dog's bollocks,' I said, throwing my arms around him, and laughing when Yusri turned to her son in dismay. 'Son,' she said in her tony British accent, 'What *have* you been teaching this girl?'

I surveyed my work in Zach's bathroom mirror. My make-up (also chosen by Hameer — who insisted he had to 'Queer Eye' me from head to toe) and hair seemed correct. I hoped I had the pallav right.

'Are you ready?' I called out through a crack in the bathroom door.

'Whenever you are,' Zach said.

I stepped into the living room, my sari silk whispering and the open-toe gold sandals I'd splurged on clicking on the floor tiles. 'Well?' I said. 'What do you think?'

Zach smiled, his face peachy gold in the early evening light. He was so handsome at that moment, in a black suit with a yellow tie, the flecks matching the highlights in his sun-streaked hair. 'Jesse,' he said. 'You're beautiful.'

'Thank you,' I said, taking his arm. I was so proud that I didn't even notice this was the first time — since childhood, probably — that I'd accepted a compliment without grimace, joke, eye roll, or goof. It was the closest I had ever come to grace.

⋆  ⋆  ⋆

Nobody had said anything about a horse.

My mother, father, Zach and I were seated with one hundred or so other guests inside the Maharaja tent in the grounds of a Silver Lake estate. The mansion, built in the thirties for two silent-screen stars, hulked above us, staring — supposedly haunted — while floating candles glinted in the tiled swimming pool. Every now and then the little hairs on the back of my neck would prick. I wondered if someone could, indeed, be watching me. Someone, hopefully, who wasn't a ghost.

Zach was sitting to my right. My parents on my left. Raihan, a friend of Henry and Hameer's, was front and centre, facing us. He was a professor of Qu'ran studies in San Francisco. He also happened to be homosexual and would be performing the ceremony.

*Clip-clop, clip-clop* . . . People turned to see where the sound was coming from, and there were Henry and Hameer, each riding a black stallion. Both of them were wearing *shalwaarni* — white silk frock coats with a shirt underneath, with baggy white trousers and *cusr* (or, as Zach had been calling them all week, 'Ali Baba shoes'). They had Turbans on, and when they appeared the congregation gasped at their glamour, their astonishing masculine beauty.

Hameer and my brother, who was wearing a sheepish grin, dismounted. Everyone sat.

'Marriage is highly regarded in both the

Indian and the Persian cultures,' Raihan began. 'A loving relationship is encouraged by the Qu'ran, which describes a husband and wife — or, in this case, husband and husband' — people laughed softly — 'as being like garments to one another, thereby offering each other warmth, protection, and intimacy. I've always liked that.'

He went on to explain that the Islamic marriage ceremony was, literally, the signing of a contract. Of course, they could not legally wed, so the contract was in this case letters that Hameer and Henry had written to one another. As he led them through their documents, Raihan spoke quietly to Henry and Hameer. I watched their eyes, tender, humorous, delighted. I felt sorry for Hameer's relatives who weren't there to bear witness, to see that their love for one another was right and pure. After the letters were signed, Hameer and Henry kissed and embraced, then turned to face us, laughing, embarrassed, overjoyed. I remembered, with a smile, when Henry had told us that the service would be mercifully short.

'Please follow the newly married couple to our *waleema* — the celebratory feast,' Raihan said. 'And don't worry — there will be booze. Alcohol is, after all, an Arabic word.'

350

'That was *so friggin' rad!*'

May grabbed me from behind, and pulled me in for a hug. She took a look around the dining tent and gave my handiwork her compliments. I had to admit, it *was* perfect. The party was fit for a sultan — no, *two* sultans.

May laughed when she saw the little coloured beads she'd helped me string on the seating cards, saying, 'I love the fact that we did this under the watchful eye of Taryn's mister time clock.'

'Don't you know it,' I said.

'I hope this is strong enough for ya.'

I turned around to see who'd spoken. Wyatt, bearing drinks.

'Jesse,' he said, handing a vodka and tonic to May. 'Congratulations.'

'Thanks,' I said. It hadn't occurred to me that Wyatt would be May's date. Then again, they were friends and she wasn't seeing anyone.

'I'm Zach.'

'Oh, I'm sorry, Zach, this is Wyatt. Wyatt, Zach. And Zach, you know May.'

She hugged him hello.

While everyone discussed the ceremony — the traditions, the difference between a

Catholic, Jewish, or Buddhist wedding — I wondered, *Why was I so thrown by this guy?* Wyatt made me nervous. I was still embarrassed by my avocation of rules where art was concerned — not to mention a little irritated at him for debating me into a corner. Unlike the night we first met, when he had seemed so relaxed that he looked like he was reclining even when standing up, he looked fussed over, a little boy in his first suit. Still, I didn't want to get stuck in another conversation with him and looking like an idiot again, so I turned to Zach and asked if he wanted to come spend a few minutes with my parents.

'Sure, I want to congratulate them,' he said.

As I walked away, I saw Wyatt lean in and whisper something in May's ear. She threw back her head and laughed.

$\star$　$\star$　$\star$

We were watching Henry and Hameer dance. Henry was trying to lead — doing some appalling stuff — and Hameer was starting to rebel.

'Hameer has some *moves*,' I said, watching him trying to show Henry how to shake it to the Bhangra beats.

'Move in with me,' Zach said.

'What?'

I turned away from Hameer dipping my brother — I wasn't sure I'd caught what Zach was saying.

'You could use a break from paying your rent anyway — ' he shook his head. 'Wait. No. It's not that.'

He had a list of reasons: I'd been doing the decorating, I should get to enjoy it . . . I spent every night there . . . He loved me . . . I loved him . . . Zach squeezed my hand. 'Say yes, Jesse. Please? You know you should.'

I was caught completely off guard. I wanted to say that I wasn't sure. I wanted to say I needed time to think. But then I spotted Bryn, walking in with a gift in her hand, towing David behind her. It was more complicated than that — because I was desperate to find a way to make it work, and I was still convinced that I'd essentially be the devil if I backed out now — but maybe it was true. Maybe just one *little* part of me did it just to spite her.

★　★　★

'There you are,' Bryn said, walking up to us.

'You made it,' I said.

'Yeah, I had to work until late but we

decided to swing by in case there was cake.' She leaned forward and gave me a small kiss. 'Congratulations,' she said.

'Thank you,' I said.

David was standing there, holding Bryn's hand. He looked uncomfortable. Like he'd been told he had to take a side, and there was only one available to him: his wife's.

'Did you say hello to Henry and Hameer?' I asked.

'I will as soon as they get off the dance floor,' Bryn said, looking at them. 'They're adorable.'

I smiled. They really were.

'Guess what?' said Zach.

David said, 'Chicken butt.'

'Wrong. We're moving in together.' Zach was beaming. He was also — when did this not happen lately? — a little tipsy.

'Dude, that's great,' David said, forgetting himself and clapping Zach on the back.

Bryn licked her lips. Despite how much I wanted to grab her and shake her and yell, *What are we doing? We're friends! Don't you get it?* I have to admit that I enjoyed watching her try to mask her expression. It was a power that Bryn had always had and I had never had; the ability to say and do what she wanted then sit back and enjoy the show. I thought of all those times she'd butted in, told me what to do while I tried to deflect her. I thought of how many times in the last few months I'd checked my voicemail, hoping for a message from her that wasn't there.

'This is big news,' she said. Her voice was flat. 'I guess double congratulations are in order.'

'Thank you,' I said. David and Zach looked at each other and a look of understanding passed between them. *Uh-oh*, it said. *Girl shit*.

Before we could discuss it further, Hameer grabbed me from behind.

'Come dance, my princess,' he said, tugging me. 'This is Mohammed Raffi — the Elvis of India.'

'Who knew there *was* such a thing?' I said, flashing what I hoped was a dazzling smile at Bryn as I spun into his arms.

I spent the rest of the night laughing, drinking, and dancing. May, Wyatt, my parents, Hameer's cousins — even Zach — came out on to the floor at the belly dancer's behest (there were both male and female, to represent all the demographics). Zach and I talked about the move-in, and the more champagne I drank, the more contagious his enthusiasm became. Maybe this would work out after all, I thought. I didn't know what time Bryn left. Or David. I drank so much I didn't know about anything.

# 24

## House Proud

When the one-year anniversary of Cec's death finally arrived, Zach insisted he just needed the day to himself. So I went to the cemetery on my own in the morning and left flowers — Bryn had been there already, I saw; there was a bouquet of tulips, her favourite — and then I went to work. I tried to spend the day thinking about the things I loved best about Cec, but concern for Zach kept creeping in. I resisted the urge to call at least twenty times that day. It wasn't until I saw him that night that I could ask him how he was.

To my surprise, he said, 'Relieved', and pulled me into his arms. 'I think it was scarier leading up to it, than it actually was to go *through* it. Does that make sense?'

I nodded. It did make sense.

'I know I've been kind of a pain lately,' he said.

'That's not true,' I lied. 'You've been fine.'

'Just don't leave me, Jess,' he whispered into my hair. 'I really do love you, you know?'

'I know.'

'Do you love me?'

My first thought was No. Then Yes. Then I don't know.

I said, 'Of course I do.'

★   ★   ★

The holidays came and went without much fanfare on either Zach's or my part (he went to his parents, while I decided for once it would be safer to stick with my own). One afternoon in early January I was on my way to pick up some dining chairs that I'd ordered from a design collective in San Francisco for Zach's house. We'd just had the floor re-done in reclaimed teak after months of waiting for the carpenter to be available, and I had a meeting with the guy who was going to make the curtains later. Every day seemed like one long to-do list: I was moving into Zach's in a week, and the sensation was like being slowly encased in concrete.

I was driving down Los Feliz when I realised I was thinking about May's friend Wyatt, whom I hadn't seen since the wedding. We'd made a connection of sorts at one point during the waleema. Henry and Hameer were still dancing, May was talking to Hameer's cousin Wadji, and Zach was in the bar talking sports, so Wyatt and I found ourselves sitting on poofs, discussing his work as a contractor. I'd had no idea that's what he did for a living — I'd figured him for a screenwriter; he had that kind of presumptuous, sloppy way of dressing that seemed to say, *I can wear this because I make more money than you.* But no, he did residential properties, he said. And commercial. A lot of store design, in fact.

'Why is that?' I asked.

'Well, the city's just getting denser,' he said. He was sure I'd noticed that LA wasn't a walking city like New York, but we finally did have some real neighbourhoods emerging beyond the local strip mall. 'People need shelving, display, flooring, lighting. Who am I to turn them away?'

'You must be making a killing.'

'I'm doing OK, for a day job.'

I bit. 'Day job?'

'I'm a sculptor,' Wyatt said.

Flashback to the *I don't do creative work any more* debacle at The Echo. Suddenly it all started to fit together. 'Do you show?'

He shrugged. 'I have a gallery representing me in New York, another one deals for me in London. I had a piece in the Whitney biennial last year, but . . . anyway. I just fired my LA rep — we weren't really *feeling* one another, as the kids would say.'

I looked at him like, *wow*. Unlike with Flook, I had a reason to be impressed this time.

Wyatt shrugged, embarrassed. His drawl, after a few drinks, was stronger than I remembered it. His soft belly was pushing against the buttons of his dress shirt. He smiled, and his crow's feet — from the noonday Austin sun, I supposed — crinkled. The effect was appealing. I guessed he was about thirty-two — 'age appropriate,' Bryn would have said, if we were speaking any more, which we weren't. It was surprising then to think that Wyatt was such a jerk the night we met.

As if he could read my mind, Wyatt said, 'Sorry for starting that whole debate at the show, by the way.'

I laughed. 'What *was* that?'

'I don't know.' He shook his head. 'I guess May just said you were really good at decor, and I hate it when people put themselves down.'

I looked him like, *Please, what a crock.*

'OK, you got me. I was showing off a little.'

'Why?' I asked.

He looked at me for a moment — a long look. And then he shook his head, grinning. He wasn't going to say. 'Did you really believe what you said that night?'

'No,' I admitted. 'I didn't.'

'Then . . . '

'I guess I don't think of what I do as art,' I said. 'But I do believe that we need a place to nest.'

He grimaced at my word choice.

'Do you want me to keep going or not?' I leaned back like, *Well?*

'By all means.'

'OK. We have, you know, car accidents, divorce, terrorists bombing the subways. It's silly to think you can make a difference, right? But I do believe there's a reason why people — why *I* — just want a nice place to live. Someplace that reflects the world the way I wish it really was. Or maybe even someplace that reflects the way I really wish *I* were.'

'Now you're talking,' he said, slapping his knee. 'I'm glad I picked on you.' He sat forward and pointed at me. 'You've got that vibe. Like if you're not challenged you'll just sit there and pick away at yourself.'

'Well,' I countered, 'I wouldn't go *that* far.'

His eyes travelled downwards, over the now slightly damp silk of my Indian dress, clinging because I'd been dancing to Mohammed Raffi for too long. ('Do it like *this*,' Hameer's cousin said, showing me how to twist my wrists the Indian way. 'Think, *Screw in the light bulb. Screw in the light bulb.*')

'But look at you now,' Wyatt said.

I blushed and thought of the first time I met Wyatt, when I sized him up as a harmless teddy bear. *Maybe not so harmless,* I thought. Then I thought, *Too bad he's not my type.*

So I was driving along, thinking about that night, and that's when I saw it: a For Lease sign in the window of a storefront on Hillhurst. It was so unlike me, but I suddenly stamped on the brakes and pulled the car over.

Just.

Like.

*That.*

★   ★   ★

Zach walked in the door and I ran to greet him. 'I . . . am . . . going . . . to . . . open . . . my . . . *own store!*' I yelled, karate chopping the air. 'Accckrrrrradahahaha!'

'What?' he said, stopping in place his expression totally confused.

'*I'm going to open my own store!*' I whooped again and jumped.

'What kind of store?'

Zach set some files and magazines down on the dining-room table. He looked exhausted.

He'd taken on some extra reviews that month, plus his column. But if he wasn't thrilled by my news, it didn't register. Not right away.

'Furniture,' I said, like, *What else?*

I grabbed his arm and pulled him into his office.

'I've been using your desk, I hope that's OK,' I said, grabbing a pad. I told him about the bungalow I'd seen that afternoon. The bougainvillea growing over the front door had me at hello. Kellygreen vines clung to the white wood slat exterior and long trails drooped over the front bay window, heavy with window-box flowers that looked like hot pink origami. I could hear a radio on inside, so I tentatively opened the door and called out to see who was there. It was the landlord, making a couple of minor repairs, so he let me come in to take a look. The store was, essentially, a little house. A bungalow that I suspected was probably once a part of the first Disney studio before they moved to Anaheim. Inside, the walls were painted plain white, and there were windows on all four exposures. A main room ran the entire front of the house, and in the back there was a little bedroom (now a stockroom), a bathroom and a tiny efficiency kitchen.

'And look,' I said to Zach. 'Here's a list

— just some ideas, really — of what it would take to start it all up. I've already filled out an application on the lease!'

I began to explain my vision. A store — a small store, so the overheads would be minimal — in which I'd curate the pieces myself, many of which, if they were vintage, I could strip and reinterpret so they had a modern twist. I had all the resources I needed already — I knew upholsterers, woodworkers, auto shops that did powder coat, lacquer specialists, dead-stock vintage fabric sellers, plus there was all the stuff I knew how to do on my own.

'Thank God I had the presence of mind to take my binder home because when Taryn hears, she's going to repossess my Rolodex,' I said, waving it in the air so Zach could see. 'It has every one of my contacts in it, all the ideas she's rejected.' Plus, I explained, I had literally a whole shed behind my house full of furniture from the Rose Bowl, from garage sales, all over, really, that I could start working on. Things I never got around to putting in my house, things that wouldn't really work at his place. I could rework, then sell my whole collection. 'Oh, and I was thinking,' I said. 'For new pieces? Why not run the shop like a gallery? That's the curate part: I could talk to artists, furniture builders

— I know how to talk to these people. I went to art school. What do you think of that?' I asked. 'The idea that I'm actually *curating* the store? Or is it too snooty as a concept? Because after Taryn, I don't want to be snooty.'

'Jesse, hold on.' Zach sank into his desk chair and ran his hands through his hair. 'Slow down, OK? How are you going to pay for all this?'

'With the Cecile money, of course.' She said I could use it for whatever I wanted, I reminded him. 'I know she would like this idea,' I said. 'She always said she thought I was good. She even wanted me to decorate this house. And you like what I've done, don't you?'

'Sure,' he said. 'But whatever happened to you wanting to have a solid plan? I mean, people go under all the time. Fifty thousand is a decent amount of dough, but you'd have your lease to consider, whether you're hiring employees, you'll need insurance . . . '

I told him I knew how to run a store — even Taryn would say it. I did *everything* at Cage — dealt with payroll, insurance, orders, taxes . . . If I really needed more money in, say, eight or twelve months, then I was thinking I could start doing workshops to teach people the principles of home décor, when to break them, when to follow them. DIY tricks. All the stuff I wanted Taryn to do but she was too much of a snob for. 'You have *no idea* how patronising and intimidating Gilded Cage is,' I said. 'I mean, most people walk out of there feeling like they have no taste, not like they'd found this fantastic resource.' I could even do residence consultations, I said. Taryn charges two hundred an *hour* for that kind of thing, and she doesn't even *do* anything. *I* do it. 'Look at Biggens!' I said.

'Huh,' Zach said. 'You've put a lot of thought into this for one day. Hey, have you fed Happy?'

I looked at the dog. 'No,' I said. 'I haven't fed either one of us, but I will. Aren't you excited for me?' I added. 'I thought you wanted me to quit my job.'

'I am,' he said. 'Excited. I'm just . . . When do you plan on handing in your resignation?'

'Tomorrow.'

'Moving fast,' he said.

Only if we were going to consider six years of sitting on my ass fast, I pointed out.

Zach blinked, then asked if I was still moving in.

'Of course,' I said. 'Nothing's going to change. Except that I'll be a happier person. This will be good for us. There's been something missing — from *me*. I can't explain it, but I've felt *trapped* somehow. Passionless. This will change all that. So just, you know, be happy for me.'

Zach said he was. Happy for me. As I went to feed the poor dog, who was standing in the kitchen like, *Remember me?* I tried to believe him.

# 25

## Flower Power

Wyatt's phone call was May's handiwork. I called her first thing the next day to tell her my plan ('*It's about friggin' time!*' she shouted into the phone) and he called that afternoon. Apparently, he was willing to take a look at the space I'd applied for, and tell me what it might need in terms of a redesign.

'That would be great,' I said. 'When can you go?'

'Let me check my calendar,' I heard Wyatt ruffle some pages on his desk. 'How about . . . Now?'

We decided to meet at a taco stand not far from the store. May was supposed to open anyway; I didn't have to get to Gilded Cage until after lunch.

I drove to Los Feliz and fought a small battle with my own feelings of self-doubt, which of course were never far away. First of all, I'd committed myself to something that — despite my assurances to Zach — I wasn't totally sure I was qualified to do. And now I was going to latch on to May's friend for help. But I was going to need all the support I could get. Besides, he *was* a contractor.

When I got to Yuca's, Wyatt was seated at one of the plastic tables outside. The building that housed the kitchen and countertop was tiny — the size of a closet, but freestanding. I had Happy with me, and the owner quickly came outside to yell at me, saying that I had to tie him to a parking meter — she didn't want my dog pissing where people ate.

'That wasn't very nice,' I said, sitting across from Wyatt after finding the dog a spot in the shade. 'Happy's trained.'

'Yeah, Rosita's kinda intense, but taste this.'

He held out a pile of mess — roasted pork, eggs and salsa spilling out of a flour tortilla on to the table. *Heavy stuff for brunch,* I thought, noticing that Wyatt had a spot from some black beans on his T-shirt. I turned my face away like *Thanks but no thanks,* but he kept coming after me with that burrito, saying 'C'mon, give it a try for yer good ol' pal Wyatt . . . ' I finally took a small nibble just to appease him, and was shocked when the fresh shreds of cilantro, chopped onions, and savoury roast hit my tongue.

'Holy crap, that's incredible,' I said.

'Spicy,' he said, taking another bite and smacking his lips. 'And delicious.'

He offered me another bite but I shook my head, I was too nervous to eat. So he crammed the rest in his mouth and said, 'Well, then, let's get your little dog and get over there.'

It sounded like, *Wey-ell then, let's git yer little dog and git over ther.*

Wyatt tossed his napkin on the table, stood, and then bent down and let Happy lick his face. I gagged at this disgusting scene — Wyatt with his eyes closed, letting the dog clean up what the napkin missed. He opened his eyes and winked at me.

I don't know why, but I blushed.

★　★　★

I opened the door with a key the landlord had left for me under a flower pot outside and gave Wyatt a quick tour. 'But here's the best part,' I said, striding back into the living room, where I opened a pair of French windows on the western wall. 'A garden,' I said.

'Phew,' Wyatt whistled. 'This is bigger'n Dallas.'

The first time I stepped out there I was, quite literally, blown away. Hydrangeas were growing against one wall. The trellis was loaded with jasmine. There was even a lemon tree. The other six hundred feet or so, however, was just dirt. Despite the garden's charm, the one thing that made me nervous was that I just didn't see how the space could be useful. I didn't think I'd be able to afford to splurge on new soil and drip lines just so customers could get a peek at some grass while they shopped. That's what I'd told May, at least, before she took matters into her own hands and called Wyatt.

'Well,' Wyatt said, shoving is hands in his pockets. (*Wey-ell.*) 'You *do* know a contractor who could build, not to brag, a pretty friggin' great patio out here, with shelving for some, say, California pottery? Maybe a small garden space where you could sell architectural planters. I heard you have an interest in those. And you'd still have room out here to display furniture.'

'An outdoor living room,' I whispered, nodding. 'It's the *ne plus ultra* of California living.' (The *ne plus ultra* — did I just say that? I mentally promised myself I'd never use a Taryn phrase like this again.) Still, where better than my own shop to show people how great outdoor rooms could be? Not to mention that I could hold my workshops out here, maybe serve a little wine and cheese. I could plant flowers — flowers everywhere! — and see if Wyatt could also build an outdoor fireplace . . .

Wyatt and I started bouncing ideas back and forth. The built-ins could be ripped out and replaced with modern shelving, which would give the store a more contemporary, less country, look. We talked about putting faux beams in the ceiling, then wiring it so I could display lamps. The main counter would be easy — even pressboard could look good — maybe poured concrete on the floor, if I didn't want to spend money on boards.

'How much would you do all this for?' I asked, thinking of Zach's warning: fifty thousand might not be enough to quit my job and get this project off the ground.

Wyatt leaned against a window sill and chewed on one of his nails for a second. While he thought, I noticed that his body — so different from Zach's — looked soft under his worn jeans. 'Let's say you hosted an opening for my new sculptures,' he said. '*If* you kicked back your commission until we reached ten thousand and after that only charged ten per cent?' he said. 'It'd be free, not including the materials.'

'That's generous,' I said.

'You're right.'

I thought for a moment. Then said, 'How about the deal is I don't take commission until we reach ten thousand and then my commission will be fifteen.'

'Fifteen per cent?' Wyatt cocked his head.

*That's right, cowboy.* I thought. *I ain't gonna be underestimated no more.*

He smiled and held out his hand and I took it. His fingers were big, and his palm was warm.

'You got yourself a deal.'

★ ★ ★

I dashed to work, hoping Taryn would be there. No. I waited all day — we needed to talk — while chatting May's ear off about the shop. I told her everything — what it looked like, all of Wyatt's plans, all my ideas. 'You have to give your friend a big wet kiss for me later,' I said.

'Ew!' May gagged and almost dropped a Ginori bowl from Italy. '*Blech.* He's, like, my brother or something.'

I took the bowl from her, and placed it on a sideboard.

'You don't find him attractive, then,' I said, feeling slightly disappointed for some reason.

'Ugh,' she grimaced. She looked like an animated character that had just swallowed a bomb, her cheeks puffed out in horror. 'Wyatt and I have known one another since I moved out here. He was my first neighbour. I mean, he's a great guy but' — she shivered — 'Gak, don't *ever* say something like that again.'

★   ★   ★

Zach wanted me to pick up some Hoisin sauce from a Vietnamese deli he liked on the way home, so I dashed there and picked it up along with some shrimp chips I knew he liked. That's when I got the call. My application had been approved. All I had to do, if I was really going to do this, that is, was give the landlord the go-ahead to cash my cheque. It was too late for me to get to the bank now, I told him, but I could do it first thing in the morning.

★   ★   ★

When I got home that night, Zach was nowhere to be found. He finally walked in at eight, just as I was starting to worry.

'Where were you?' I asked. He seemed to disappear like this several times a week, but I was trying not to pry. We'd been getting along. For the most part.

'Just driving around,' he said.

'I tried you on your mobile.'

'It ran out of battery.'

Zach asked me what I'd been up to all day,

373

and I told him about the redesign plans. He just sat there, picking at lint on the sofa, saying *Uh-huh, uh-huh, uh-huh.*

*   *   *

The next morning, I stopped by my place, which was partly packed up for my move. I got the cheque from the Carters — the Cecile money — from the bottom drawer of my desk. When I opened it and saw Cecile's dad's handwriting, I felt a quick pang of guilt. Then, I shook my head. *No more,* I thought. I closed my eyes. 'Thank you, baby,' I whispered to Cecile. 'I love you.' Then I slipped the cheque into my wallet, and drove to the bank.

'I'm here to open a new account,' I said, slapping the cheque on to a clerk's desk.

'How wonderful,' she said, even though she couldn't have cared less. I smiled anyway.

Because it *was* wonderful. One of the most wonderful moments of my life.

*   *   *

For the next three days I got to the store early. Taryn was due to come in each day but she never showed. With the extra time, I cleaned the computer with rubbing alcohol and Q-tips. I filed all the old paperwork, dusted the tables and wiped every glass knick-knack. I vacuumed, and checked to make sure the stock-room was in perfect order. May kept asking me why I bothered — why not just stop showing up altogether and let Taryn figure it out? But there was no way I was going to shrink out like a guilty child who'd stolen the last cookie. I wanted to face Taryn in person, and I'd wait as long as it took.

On the fourth day, when I flipped the sign from closed to open, the place was immaculate. I racked my brain trying to think of something I hadn't done; I wasn't going to give Taryn the satisfaction of thinking she'd be better off without me.

She arrived after two.

'Hi girls,' she said, looking at me with eyes as flat as a fish on *Shark Week*. In one hand she was clutching an Iced Vanilla, the drink of choice for LA social queens. When she went to take a sip, it slurped. Empty. 'Jesse, pop down the street and get me another one of these, would you?' She asked. 'Oh, and a chai, too, I have a meeting here in twenty minutes.'

I nodded. Sure thing.

I went to the Coffee Bean, got the chai and Taryn's drink — I made it a large, what the hell — and paid the ten-dollar bill with my own money, which was customary. When I returned, I placed both beverages on Taryn's desk, remembering to wrap hers in a napkin the way she liked it. ('Water rings', she liked to say, 'show the world you don't expect any better.')

I waited for some acknowledgement that I'd just fetched her afternoon pick-me-up and paid for it. Nothing.

'Taryn?' I said.

'Hm,' She was browsing through a catalogue for a wine-tasting cruise in the Adriatic.

'There's something important I need to tell you.'

'Shoot,' she turned a page.

'I left you several messages over the past week, saying it was urgent?'

'Oh?' her expression was blank. 'I didn't listen to them.'

I smiled. She wasn't even going to be courteous enough to lie any more.

'OK, well. I'm opening my own store,' I placed a postcard I'd had printed up at Kinko's the night before with a picture of a blooming bougainvillea vine on the front, and a 20 per cent-off discount coupon on the back, effective after 1 February, which would be, I prayed, my opening date. 'As you can see, it's not far off, so I have to give my notice, effective immediately.'

Taryn didn't pick up the card. Her jaw flexed.

'What's this?' she said, laughing. 'But you have no clue, Jesse, *none*, on how to run a shop.'

'I disagree,' I said, staying calm. 'After all, I've been running your business for the last six years.'

Taryn smiled. 'Please. That is *so* not true.'

Actually, I said, it was.

Taryn's tongue pressed into the gap in her two front teeth. It made her tongue looked forked. *Here it comes*, I thought.

Her eyes turned soft, lipid. Two little globules of phony regret.

'Oh Jesse,' she said, placing a hand on her breast. 'I had no *idea* you were so unhappy. My God, I mean, I *knew* you were upset when I said you couldn't have the whole Lizzie commission, but, sweetie, she wasn't . . . oh, how do I put this? . . . showing much *faith* in you as a designer. I stepped in because, without me, you were about to get your ass chewed off and I couldn't let that happen. I *know* how hard you would have taken it and I wanted to spare you that at least.'

'Whose ass was I about to chew?' Lizzie

said, stepping into the shop. 'I was outside wrapping up a call when I heard you say my name.' She saw her chai on Taryn's desk and stepped forward to pick it up. She took a sip. 'So. Tell me, who's the unlucky victim this time?'

It was my one chance.

'Lizzie,' I said, handing her my postcard, 'I know you have loyalties here, but I just wanted to let you know that I'm opening my own shop. So if you ever need anything, don't hesitate to call.'

'Jesse,' Taryn said, rising, 'I know I must have done *something* to make you act this insane, but *surely* you're not serious. Lizzie, I am *so* sorry. It's recently become clear to me that I *really* need to learn how to vet employees.'

'Don't apologise,' Lizzie said, taking a sip of her drink. And then she did the unthinkable. She handed me back my card. I was mortified, but I tried to take it in my stride. It was a long shot, after all. 'Listen, Taryn, this appears to be a bad time,' she said, as I took the card back, my face burning red.

'Of course Lizzie,' Taryn gave me a look like *ha ha*, and flipped open her calendar. 'Just tell me what works for you and we can reschedule.'

Lizzie ignored this and turned towards the door.

'Taryn, darling,' Lizzie said, 'if there's one thing my friends have learned, it's that you don't ever use my name in vain. I was happy with Jesse's work, and if she's leaving, I'm simply going to have to hire her myself.' She turned to me. 'People as wealthy as I am don't keep track of phone numbers — that's what I have two assistants for. I've decided to buy a house that just opened next door to Carrie Fisher's and, well, she's a friend, so, call my office. We need to talk.'

# 26

## Banish the Beige

May was editing my possessions with the zeal of a *New Yorker* fact-checker. 'My God, Jesse,' she said, opening a dresser drawer. 'How many black tank tops do you *have?*'

I looked at her holding up six limp garments in her little hands, and then down at myself. I was wearing the seventh.

'They go with everything,' I said.

May shook her head. 'I'm throwing out the ratty ones,' she said. 'Which leaves you with three.'

I looked at her like, *Three?*

'I'll take you shopping sometime,' she said. 'Because, frankly, you could use the help.'

I laughed and said she was welcome to try, but I thought of all Cecile's past efforts and the truth was, I'd probably just buy more black tank tops.

We'd finished packing up my living room, kitchen and office. There were boxes stacked in the hall, and stuffed rubbish bags everywhere. It turns out I was quite the pack rat. Even though my house — on the surface

— looked clean, it seemed as though every drawer May opened, and every cabinet she peeked into, was crammed with junk.

'So you and Wyatt seem to have hit it off,' May said, tossing out old bottle after bottle of beige nail polish — Cecile had liked to say that it was the only kind that didn't look cheap, but I could never seem to get the pale shade right so I'd accumulated quite a collection — into the garbage.

It was true. I'd been having confabs with Wyatt almost every night. Sometimes we worked so late that we ate at the shop, our Mexican takeaway balanced on scrap lumber, sawdust in my hair from helping him with the easier tasks. I liked watching Wyatt work, and I was learning a lot too. He was making tongue-and-groove shelves for the store, and his attention to detail flattered me somehow. The night before, I met him at his loft at the Brewery downtown. Once used to manufacture beer, the Brewery was now public-funded artist's housing. Which isn't to say it's some sort of hippie commune. Just the opposite; artists had been making improvements at the Brewery for over a decade. Wyatt's loft was a two-storey modern box of glass, exposed brick, and steel. On the upper floor — really more like a large balcony overlooking the living room/studio space

— were the sleeping quarters, where he had a king-sized bed, the white pillows and a down quilt billowing like Cool Whip. It was all cleaner somehow than I expected it to be.

I was there to help him figure out what we'd use for his opening. Looking back, I think I was picturing that his work would be like Wyatt, the person. Something a little rugged, hand-hewn. Instead, his sculptures were as intricate as they were intimate. Most were cast resins. One of them was of a bird's nest that was attached, bottom to wall, and blooming outwards, like a flower. The fine detail surprised me. The way the nest was so delicately woven, the sticks thin as angel-hair pasta, containing two almost sentimentally shaded blue eggs. One of them had a tiny brown crack, and something was just about to emerge — dead or alive was hard to say. 'What is this called?' I asked, stepping forward to take a closer look.

'*Let's Get Back Together*,' Wyatt said.

'A girl?' I asked.

'A girl.' He shrugged. There were other pieces which were equally beautiful and delicate. Nature was a running theme, but with a modern edge — a snaggle of twigs with a trapped moth inside, a hollow cactus, thorns pointing inwards.

I got a little drunk after that. We shared a

pizza, and planned under the influence, me laying on his giant sofa, a pad in front of me while we talked about the store. Wyatt played music from home on the stereo; Whiskeytown and The Old 97s booming out of speakers which were hidden in the loft's pristine, soaring white walls. Part of me wanted to ask Wyatt if he would curl up on the sofa with me. Another part of me knew I never would because I was with Zach. And yet another part of me just wished he was a little bit better looking. *I'm so awful sometimes*, I thought.

When Wyatt walked me to my car, I told him again how much I liked his work.

'I like your work too, Jesse.' He reached out to brush something from my face.

I shivered.

'Eyelash,' he said.

I started digging in my bag, looking for my keys. 'Wyatt, thank you so much. For everything.'

★   ★   ★

'Helloooo? *Jesse?*' May was looking at me. I was standing in the middle of my bedroom, I realised, holding a set of Moroccan tea-lights from Hameer that I was supposed to be wrapping in tissue and placing in the box.

May rolled her eyes and turned back to the dresser. 'Be a little more out of it, why don't you?' She stood aside so I could see the contents of another drawer; this one stuffed with almost identical black cardigans and shook her head. 'So I was saying that Wyatt thinks the bougainvillea's — how do you say that, exactly?'

Boo-gan-veee-ah.

'Right. Is going to turn out great.'

I said I hoped so.

'I know you hate it when I press you on stuff like this, but I can't resist: is there something going on between you guys?'

No, I assured May, there wasn't anything going on. *He said my name before I left and he sent chills zinging down the backs of my legs*, I thought. *But I got in my car. And I drove home. And I'm sure I'm going to fall back in love with Zach any day now. And that's all that matters.*

★ ★ ★

That week Zach started making at least two dozen . . . I wasn't even sure what to call them. Hints? Explorations? Whatever they were, they concerned 'after' or, as that rap guy, André 3000, would say, 'Forever ever?' Each time, I considered running out the door to buy a pack of cigarettes, and I have to say, a couple of times I did just that.

'After you move in, maybe we can start making things a *little* more official,' Zach said one evening, while we were cleaning out one of his kitchen cabinets to make room for my dishes.

Then, as I was getting ready to go to the store the next morning, my 'To-do' list growing to two pages, Zach said, 'Say a hypothetical couple wanted to have a hypothetical wedding, how long would this hypothetical couple wait to have children?' I told him they would probably wait a long time, considering everything.

'The store really seems to be taking up a lot of your time,' he said, pouring himself a cup of coffee. 'Want one?' he asked.

I shook my head. I had to get going. 'Look, you said it would be a lot of work and you were right,' I said, getting up and kissing him on the cheek. 'But I think it will be worth it, don't you?'

Zach nodded. 'Sure.'

I paused. 'What's bothering you about all this? Just tell me.'

'Nothing.' He took a sip of his coffee. 'I'm just trying to make sure we're staying on the right track.'

He left the room to go to his study and

start working on an article, leaving me standing there, wondering what the right track was. How do you know when you're on the right track? How to explain that my work life, at least, was *finally* going somewhere and I just had to focus on it because I was afraid that if I didn't, all this energy could just evaporate, like it did back in art school, all those years ago? I looked down at my pad and realised I'd been doodling while Zach and I were talking. The doodle was in a circle, like Wyatt's bird nest. Like this:

As I drove to Home Depot to pick up some sandpaper and extra outlets that Wyatt was going to install, I thought of Dr Anderson, whose book was unfolding like my own personal cautionary tale, whenever I locked myself in the bathroom to consult it.

Many bereaved men are not accustomed to having an emotional crisis, or refuse to seek support from their male friends. As a result, men often look for a female companion to share the load. However, such women are often desperate themselves for security and affection, so to my widower patients, I caution: buyer beware!

Thinking about this made me so angry that when I got to the hardware store, I went to the dumpster out the back, threw it in the rubbish, and poured the rest of my coffee over it.

'Take that,' I muttered. 'You mean, mean lady.'

I slammed down the bin lid. Dr Anderson simply had no idea what she was talking about.

# 27

## Hold Everything

It was hard for me to turn the key and lock the door to my house for the last time. When I drove away, I saw that the jasmine vine in the front was finally starting to bloom, and I realised that I'd finally finished it; the house was perfect. Not surprisingly, it was rented to a young couple who were moving from New York the same day the landlord posted a picture at the Brite Spot.

Henry was driving the rental truck. Hameer was following us in their packed Range Rover. Henry turned to me, his gold wedding band shining in the sunlight coming through the passenger window.

'So,' he said, 'I guess you decided to move in, huh?'

'How observant,' I said.

He looked out the window as we passed Western, his glasses were dirty, and he was starting to resemble our dad, I realised. Henry and I were getting older. He rapped on the passenger window.

'It's funny. I always think of you as living in

Echo Park. It's shabby, but it has so much potential.'

I socked him. 'Not any more, baby. I live in Hollywood Dell now with the movie stars and their Juicy Couture-clothed nannies.'

We drove for a minute in silence.

'Are you happy?' he asked.

'Very,' I said. 'The store looks fantastic, I can't wait for it to be finished — '

'No, I mean with Zach.'

'Well, I'm moving in, aren't I?'

Henry tapped the steering wheel and said, 'I just really want you to be happy.'

I put my hand over his and tried to explain: Zach was a good man. We'd just been having a hard time. I wanted to stick with this. I didn't want to drift around any more, and besides, I'd lost Cecile, then I'd lost Bryn. I didn't want to lose Zach too.

Henry looked sad. I wanted to cheer him up.

'Hey, speaking of Hollywood, remember the time we were watching *Mommy Dearest* and Elena came in and I was like, 'That's *you*, Mommy!' '

'You had a twisted sense of humour for a six-year-old. She cried for a week.'

'And then Mom made you turn gay.'

He sighed.

'And then Mom made me turn gay.'

★ ★ ★

Henry and I were wobbling up the front path with my Mies sofa as Hameer looked on, drinking a Jamba juice and barking directions.

'Hold it! Hold it!' Zach said, when we were about to carry the sofa through the front door.

'Zach, this is really heavy,' I said.

'Set it down.'

We did, and Henry looked at me like, *I knew this wasn't going to work out.*

'Darling.' Zach stepped forward and wrapped one arm around my back, the other under my knees. He hoisted me up and carried me through the hall. 'Welcome to your new casa.'

'Henry tried to do that with me when we moved in,' Hameer said. 'And he dropped me in a pile of dog shit from our neighbour's poodle.'

★ ★ ★

We ordered in some pizza and put Henry and Hameer to work. The first order of business was to rearrange the furniture — again — so my stuff could fit. I'd already graphed it out on paper so I had a sense of what should go where. ('What can I say?' I asked Henry when he told me I was clearly OCD. 'That kind of thing is *fun* for me.')

'I was thinking the couch would work under the window,' I said, standing where I wanted it, my sweaty ponytail sticking to my neck. 'And, Zach, we can use your end tables — the ones in the living room — as nightstands, which will actually look pretty good once we change the bedding.'

'*Uh-huh*,' said Zach. He was standing in the middle of the room and trying to visualise it. 'Hm. But why not just *keep* my end tables in the living room, and keep my night tables in the bedroom, since then both things are doing what they're actually for?'

'Well,' I said, putting my hands on my hips. 'See the thing is, your end tables are actually, technically, telephone tables. You probably didn't know that when you bought them. It's just that they're too high to go next to my couch, which is more modern. It's about proportion, see. The top of the table shouldn't be higher than the armrest of the sofa.'

Zach gave me a queer look. 'I thought you said the other day that you weren't going to think about rules any more.'

'*Touché*.' I smiled. I was sure Zach was just teasing me. 'But with principles, it's about context. About being able to forecast the end result. Kind of like a chef — you can't do fusion unless you know a little something about the two dishes you want to put together, right? Point is, these tables are going to look great in your bedroom, and your nightstands are pine anyway, so — '

'What's wrong with pine?'

I tried to think of a way to say it.

'It's Z Gallery rehashing old Pottery Barn crap for crass Yanks stuck in 1990,' Hameer said, taking a bite of pizza and sitting on one of my boxes where he'd have an uninterrupted view of Zach's and my first argument about the house.

'*Thank* you, Hameer.'

He smiled. 'Respect.'

'Well, all right, then, Jess,' Zach said, turning to walk away. 'I'll be in my study, working on a column, while you, Hameer and Henry decide what to do with my crass Yank taste.'

'*Zach.*' I followed him down the hall, but he didn't turn around. 'Zach, come back!' He shut the door. I turned and looked at Henry. 'He's just tired,' I said.

We were all just tired.

★ ★ ★

Henry and I moved in the rest of my stuff while Zach pouted in the other room. I let him. We'd talked about this, hadn't we? He'd said I could do what I wanted with the house, and since when did Zach care about end tables anyway? It was almost as though he was being intentionally stubborn.

When the last box was in the house, both Henry and Hameer kissed me goodbye and wished me luck ('I love you, but I'm never moving that sofa again,' Henry said, giving me one of his legendary hugs). I found myself clinging to him like I hadn't since that day when he came to the hospital to rescue me. I didn't want them to go.

★　★　★

I rapped on the study door.

'Zach?'

No answer.

'Can I come in?'

'Hm.'

'Hi,' I said, cracking the door open and trying to smile in an *I come in peace* kind of way. He didn't take his eyes off his computer.

'I was wondering if maybe you could give me a hand?' I said. 'I mean, I don't know exactly where you want me to put what.'

He focused on a spot on the wall above his

desk as though I was the most exasperating person in the world.

'You obviously want to put it wherever *you* want to put it, so what do you need me for?' he asked the spot.

'Zach, I'm sorry. Look, maybe I got carried away. I just really want to make this place feel like my home too, you know? And I guess that means I have to move some stuff around. This is what I *do*.'

He shrugged. 'OK,' he said, finally looking at me. 'All right. Fine.'

'Fine, like, 'fine', or fine, like, 'f-off'?'

'Fine like fine,' he said. 'Everything's fine.'

I perched on the edge of his desk. 'You don't think we're making a mistake, do you?'

'Of course not,' he said, placing a hand on one of my knees. 'But here, you hate this lamp, right?' He stood and picked up the black torchère lamp that I'd loathed since the first time I'd laid eyes on it, the night that we'd kissed for hours on the oriental rug. (Was that really only six months ago? It felt like years.) 'It's gone.'

'Zach, you don't have to . . . '

'Come on, it's like an exorcism. It'll be fun.'

He carried the lamp through the hall and out the front door, Happy running behind him and nipping at the cord. Zach placed it on the curb, and said, 'I cast thee out of this house, oh evil Target lamp for — what did Hameer say again?'

'Crass Yanks.'

'Crass Yanks like me who have no taste.'

He turned to face me, a grin on his face.

'Good?' he asked.

I had to say, the sight of that hideous fixture kicked to the curb certainly wasn't *bad*.

★   ★   ★

For the rest of the afternoon, Zach indulged my inner demons by helping me move rugs, sort through which chairs were staying and which were going, and move a pair of enormous bookcases to three different locations until I decided which I liked better. I loved this house — the Craftsman beams, the woodwork around the windows. Now, I was going to live here. I just had to figure out a way to make it all fit together, to shuffle our belongings until I came up with a winning hand.

For me, this was having a great time. For Zach, it was an exercise in patience. The sky darkened, and I got to work on the lighting while he made dinner — a sauté pan filled with *tortilla Española*. We ate standing up

— I had too many boxes on the dining-room table. Finally, with eggs and Spanish red wine in my belly, I decided I had to stop moving furniture, for now, and put away at least one box of clothing so I'd have something to wear in the morning.

I made myself and Zach a cup of tea while he started moving our castaways out to the back for a humongous garage sale we were planning for the weekend. I dragged the box marked 'winter clothing' into the bedroom, pulling out a stack of wooden hangers I'd bought at Ikea. I opened the box and started sliding things on to the hangers, laying each item of clothing on the bed until I had a decent-sized stack. Zach giving me the walk-in was a treat; I'd never had one before. I hooked the clothes over my index finger and opened the closet door, and then I stopped cold, confused by what I saw.

Cecile's things were still on the rails. Her shoes — all of them — were on the floor in a neat little row. Her dresses — cocktail, work, wedding dress, even, preserved in its vinyl bag — were at one end of the closet. I set my stuff on the floor, and stood there, shocked. *Everything* she owned, from her pyjamas to her tennis gear, was exactly as she'd left it.

I backed out into the bedroom and tried to catch my breath. I had no idea what to think;

I'd assumed Zach had cleaned the closet sometime between the last time I was in it — the day I dashed in to get a sweatshirt out of habit and ended up sobbing on the floor — and the day I was moving in.

'Zach?' I called, standing and reaching out to touch a black cocktail dress that was one of Cecile's favourites.

'Yeah?' I heard him say from the front of the house.

'Could you come in here a minute?'

He appeared in the bedroom doorway.

'What are you doing?' he asked.

I turned to face him. 'I thought you said you cleaned out the closet? I mean, where is all my stuff supposed to go?'

'Oh. Right,' he said. 'I was going to, but then in the end I decided to clean out space for you in *my* closet. Which you and I, the rational couple, can share. See?' He crossed the room and slid back the door on his closet, a rack behind sliding doors on the opposite wall. I looked, and there were about two feet for me, sandwiched between a rack for his shoes, a bunch of suit bags and a shelf holding his luggage.

'I'm not the biggest clothing junkie in the world, but that's not going to be enough room,' I said.

'OK. Then I'll move the luggage out to the

garage, and I have a bunch of clothes I have to get rid of anyway, so I'll just sell them at the garage sale.'

'But what about this *entire* closet here with Cecile's stuff in it? I mean . . . ' I dropped my hands to my sides. What was I supposed to say? That now that I'd packed up my old life and thrown away the key I found this a little unnerving? How could I make Zach understand?

'What are you saying, Jesse, you want me to just junk all my dead wife's stuff so we don't waste any precious closet space? Not that we *need* more closet space. Or, OK, how about this? Let's sell it all at the garage sale! That'll be fun, watching strangers pick up Cecile's things and haggle to buy them for seventy-five cents.' His voice was angry, my head snapped back at the force of it.

'Zach, I'm not suggesting you sell Cecile's clothes. I understand your wanting to save her things. Whatever you need to do. But I'm sorry, I can't live next to a — a *shrine* of her shoes and handbags. I mean, why didn't you pack it up, at least, and store it?'

'I told you, I changed my mind,' he muttered.

'What?'

'*I. Changed. My. MIND!*' He slammed his fist down on the dresser.

I looked at Zach, startled by the shouting. His jaw was set, his eyes glaring. He was *pissed*. He looked crazed, his clothes stained with sweat, his jeans dusty. I got the scary sense that if I pushed him one more inch, he'd be capable of almost anything. And I didn't want that. I, especially, didn't want to be the reason for that.

'All right,' I said, trying to think how to handle this. 'Let's both just calm down. Maybe we can strike, I don't know, some kind of compromise.'

'No,' he said.

*No?*

'No,' he repeated. 'N-O, no. Her stuff is staying, exactly where it is, now, and *maybe* for ever.'

He stormed out of the room. Zach, I noticed, was getting really good at leaving rooms.

★   ★   ★

I found him sitting on the couch, staring, irate, at his nightstands now end tables.

I asked him if he was OK.

I said that maybe we should have some tea, and talk this through.

Zach shook his head at me.

'Jesse,' he said, turning to face me. 'I have

done all this' — he twirled his fingers around the room — 'before. I have moved in together. I've argued about closet space. I've proposed. I had the engagement party, and I got married while my wife was in a goddamn hospital bed. I worked my ass off to get there.' He was pacing now. 'I even went to a relationship counsellor with Cec — '

I looked surprised. She had never mentioned this.

'Yeah, chew on that, we went to a relationship counsellor, because I wanted to have kids and she wanted to wait, and your 'best friend' never breathed a word to you about it. Big deal. And now' — he stopped — 'I want to *move on with my life*. Why can't this just be fucking *easy*?'

'Because nothing's just easy,' I stammered, thinking of all I'd been doing to try to make everything work. I started to say something about how we could do this part together. We'd agreed, from the very beginning.

'If you want to talk about what we agreed,' he interrupted, 'then what about all the times you were telling me I could have all the space I needed, and all the time I needed, and now, when I'm telling you how *I* want this to be done, you're giving me nothing but *bullshit*!'

He was so angry, his words felt like slaps. I was standing in the middle of the living room, holding my breath. I felt like I was standing on a plate of razor-thin glass.

'Wanting to give you time, and space, Zach, isn't the same thing as letting you make all the decisions,' I said carefully.

'Well that's convenient, because until very recently, you were more than content to let everyone else make all your decisions for you.'

These words stung. Was that how he saw me? Malleable, like a throw pillow, or a rug that could get moved from place to place, tying a room together but with no say in the matter? I also knew that what he said was true.

Wait, *was* true. His assessment of me was not true, I realised, any more.

'You're right,' I sat down next to him on the couch, shoving aside some pieces of newspaper May and I had used to wrap my vases. I told him that yes, I'd been acting that way for a very long time. 'But Zach, I've changed — don't you see?' I tried to reach for his hand. 'And *you're* the one who's helped me. Talking to me about my job, telling me I was beautiful, and talented, and that I had something to offer . . . so why can't we grow together? I thought this was what this was all about.'

Zach stood up, leaving my outstretched

hand hanging, literally, in the air. 'I have to be honest, Jesse,' he said, shaking his head. 'I just want everything to go smoothly. I want to get married. I want to have a family — '

'But you're a guy,' I stammered. 'It's not like you're running out of eggs. You have nothing but time.'

'More excuses,' he said. 'Shall I spell it out for you, Jess? I want what was *robbed from me a year ago on Beverly Boulevard*. And if you don't understand that then, well, I guess we're shit out of luck.'

I put my head in my hands. I was starting to cry, in frustration. This move was a terrible mistake, I'd known it all along, and I ignored it, and here we were. Why was it, I wondered, that the harder I tried to make him happy, the worse the situation became?

'Shit out of luck,' I said out loud, although I was talking about myself, not us. I'd given up my house, moved in all my things. I asked Zach if he meant that. And he started to laugh. It was a laugh full of contempt, and at that moment I hated him for it. Everything was quiet except for his laughter. This was not the real Zach, I knew it. This was not the man I'd come to know. But I also knew that whatever deep wounds I'd been helping him tape shut were opening up. And they were making him cruel.

'Where do you go every week?' I asked, even though I thought I knew the answer. 'Instead of to Dr Beaver?'

He looked at me in defiance. 'To the cemetery,' he said. 'To visit Cecile. *Is that OK with you?*'

I didn't speak. I couldn't.

Zach turned to leave the room, and I thought, *Yes, please go. I need a moment to think, to breathe.* But then, suddenly, he came back and pointed at me, his blue eyes filled with rage.

'You know what, you can blame me all you want, but you're the one who wanted this, remember? You've always wanted this, and now that you have it, you've got all kinds of bullshit complaints. That's *you*, Jesse. Not me. Do you remember how much you wanted to be here?'

I nodded. Tears streaming down my face. I did remember. I remembered how much I wanted the dinners, the presents, the house, the dog, the relationship. I wanted everything that Cecile had and I didn't, and I'd been willing to sacrifice everything about my old life — Bryn, in particular — to get it. Now this was where we were. What we were. My nose was starting to run, but I let it. I wanted us both to see reality. To see the truth.

'But this isn't working, Zach,' I said,

standing up. 'Let's just call it for what is' — I waved my arms around the boxes and balls of newspaper that were all over the room — 'a great big mess.'

'Oh, don't you threaten to pull the trigger now,' he said. 'We both know you won't.'

I looked at Zach, and I could see his hurt. It was all over his face. It was in the way his mouth twisted, it was in the taut cords of his neck, it was in the whites of his eyes, which were turning red. There was so much anger, so much sadness, so much longing. But not for me.

I could never pull the trigger in the past, Zach said. He was right. So I pulled it.

*   *   *

I knocked on May's door at 1 a.m. She had a studio in a converted warehouse behind some downtown bar, and it had taken me a half-hour just to find it. She opened the door, took one look at me, tear-stained, in my dirty moving clothes, and said, 'I was going to give it a month at least.'

'May,' I said, 'What just happened?'

'Get your butt in here,' she said, 'and tell me.'

I told her everything. How it started not today, but sometime after Thanksgiving. I just didn't *feel* it after a while. I felt like I was taking care of him, and that was OK at first, but then it wasn't. I felt like I loved him as a friend — God, I felt like such an asshole for using that phrase — but not as a lover. And then, to make matters worse, I moved in, and now I'd broken his heart. When I told Zach that I wanted to break up, he just looked at me like I was grotesque.

'Get out,' he said.

So I tried to explain myself, the words coming out in a jumble. About how alone I felt, about the night Derry screamed at me, about how Bryn hated me now, about how I thought I loved him but if this was what it was going to take then it was true: I didn't love him enough. The fact that I thought this was what I wanted had become infested, somehow, with everything else, and now it was gone. Even he had to feel it — we weren't ready, we couldn't do this. Zach held up his palm, like, *Stop*. He was crying now. For a moment I thought maybe he'd at least tell me I was right. Maybe he'd admit that we were making a huge mistake.

But instead, he said, 'I want you to leave. And the only thing I want from you, *ever*, is that I just want you to promise that you will *never* try to come back.'

While I told her all this between gigantic,

gulping sobs, May sat Indian-style in the centre of her living room, nodding. She had on Snoopy pyjamas, her hair was in rollers, and she had on rainbow-striped socks. She was like the neo-punk little sister I'd never had.

'So you left?' she asked, pouring me a cup of green tea.

'Yeah,' I nodded. 'I didn't even take my toothbrush. Jesus, May,' I buried my face in a throw pillow I'd been clutching. 'You should have seen his face. It was horrible.'

'He'll be OK.'

'Yeah, right.' I nodded. 'Because he's on such solid footing as it is.'

'Oh please,' she said, pointing out that I was homeless, heart-broken, and unemployed. 'I'm *proud* of you. I mean, I thought you needed to shake things up, but this is fantastic.'

May got up and went to the kitchen. She came back with a tall glass of wine and handed it to me. Tea, she said, wasn't really going to cut it.

'Look, I didn't really know Cecile,' she said. 'But for what it's worth, she wouldn't have wanted you trying to take her place, turning a blind eye to the fact that he isn't done mourning her. Nobody's the bad guy here. It was just too hard.'

'It *was* hard,' I said, the pressure, the weight of what I was up against lifting a little. I'd been bent over under the pressure to be someone I was never going to be.

'Come on, you can sleep in my bed with me tonight.' May said, standing up.

'The floor is fine.'

'The floor is filthy,' she said. She was right — there were haphazard stacks of *The New York Times* here and there, and when I'd walked to the bathroom earlier to get a tissue, I'd impaled my bare foot on a single discarded, plastic unicorn earring. 'We'll just snuggle up in here — but no hot lezbo action.'

I laughed for the first time that night.

'By the way,' May said, turning down her sheets and fluffing a pillow for me. 'I handed in my resignation this afternoon.' She tossed me a pair of Smurf pyjamas and climbed under the covers. 'Which means I need a pay cheque, and you're it.'

'May,' I said, 'The store isn't even open yet.'

'Well, bi-atch, you'd better get yourself together. Because you have your first employee.'

# Part Three

# 28

## Do It Yourself

I was in the back, making coffee — which I was practically living on I had so much work to do every day — when I heard a crash, and then a wail: 'Jesseee! Can you come here a minute?'

I walked on to the floor and there was May, holding what was left of a set of vintage Georg Jensen dishware that I'd found buried under old bathrobes at a garage sale. They were a truly amazing find — bold, graphic, black-and-white plates that were having another moment.

'I *suck!*' May yelled, spinning around and waving dishes in frustration, her pigtails whipping her face. 'I suck! I suck, I suck, I suck!'

'May,' I said, 'please just lower the plates, and back away slowly before you break another.'

She was beside herself. 'You should fire me,' she said. 'I'm a mess.'

'Calm down, it can be replaced,' I said, grabbing the dustpan and getting on my knees to sweep up the mess.

'It can't,' she said, shaking her bleached white hair and stomping her little feet, which were encased in green vinyl heels. 'They're old!'

There was a website, I told her, that specialised in replacements. They had a warehouse full of literally thousands of pieces of hard-to-find china. 'They'll have this,' I said.

May stopped her whirly frustration dance. 'What?' she said. 'Why didn't you tell Taryn about that back when she broke that Limoges tureen?'

I winked.

'Oh,' May said, shaking her head and laughing. 'The force is strong with you, Master Jedi.'

★   ★   ★

Since the opening three months before, the store had been beyond all-consuming — the roofs leaked during a slew of rainstorms that hit the city one after another, then a pipe burst, then the heater broke (bad memory for me) and yet, despite it all, the store was doing better than I'd hoped. I'd sold most of the furniture that had been gathering dust in my old storage shed and May and I were scrambling to restock. We had the opening for Wyatt — and sold most of the sculptures that first night. Wyatt looked so unpredictably dashing that evening, in jeans and a white button-down, a tie loosely hanging from his neck, the spring air fluffing his brown hair and his big fingers floating in demonstration as he talked about his work. There was a moment, as Wyatt was talking to an art critic from the *LA Weekly*, when he looked at me — a long look, not unlike the one he gave me at May's rock show — and it took my breath away. I smiled, and turned to pour another customer a complimentary glass of champagne, floating one perfect bougainvillea blossom on the top.

Lizzie had me crazed with work. Her new home was a Wallace Neff with frescos on the ceiling and a traditional garden. She wanted the house to be more personal — a place that would conjure up the childhood summers that she'd spent with her father at their beach house in Montecito — which meant she was now micromanaging the décor the same way she ran her production company. She'd changed her mind five times over a set of coral pendant lamps which I'd found for her at an estate sale, and had sent back a settee we'd already had covered for her. Despite all the hassles, I liked Lizzie, and the referrals had been incredible.

The best part of all was that I was, finally, not smoking — not because anyone else wanted me to quit, but because *I* wanted to.

I'd sent Bryn a postcard about the store opening, but she and David didn't show. Instead, she sent a bouquet of flowers with a card that read, *She would be proud of you. Bryn.* I missed her terribly, particularly during the first week that the store was open. I was constantly rushing to the phone to call her and tell her some new bit of news. Even then I couldn't believe that our friendship had turned out to be so tenuous, so fragile. I thought we could weather anything, and it seemed so sad to think that Cecile's death — and my actions following it — had disrupted the ecosystem that we'd created. I still felt like the opposite should have been true, but for some reason — a concrete explanation that still eluded me — this wasn't so. I tried to think of her card as at least positive in that we didn't hate one another. I kept it in the cash till, underneath the change drawer.

Taryn, meanwhile, still had not been to the store, but I could swear one night, as I was working late, that I saw her BMW drive by slowly outside. I couldn't be sure it was her, but just for fun, I waved.

★ ★ ★

About a week after we broke up I went to Zach's house with a moving truck, Henry grumbling that we were officially in a fight. I'd emailed that I was coming and Zach wasn't home when we got there; he left a note saying to put the key on the table when I was done. After reading the note, Henry laid a hand on my shoulder. 'You're doing the right thing,' he said.

But two months later, I was at the shop, watching a photographer I'd hired for the bougainvillea website that I wanted to launch, and I got an email from Zach. It said, simply, 'Would you like to meet me and Happy for a hike on Sunday?' Immediately I accepted the invitation. Even though I didn't know what it would be like for us to see one another again, I really missed that damn dog.

★ ★ ★

We met at Runyon Canyon, where dogs are allowed on the dirt hillside trail without a leash. It was a beautiful May day — seventy-five degrees, only the occasional wisp of white cloud in the sky. A winter of heavy rain had caused no end of damage; one house near the one I was renting in Silver Lake actually slid

415

down a ravine, the owner having just enough time to grab his dog and leap out the front door. But the curtains of water had scrubbed the sky clean to a brilliant blue, and the wildflowers were riotous with saturated colour, a pageant of life on display. I walked to the heavy iron gates that stood open at the base of the canyon, and everywhere I looked owners were releasing their dogs, laughing as they took off with slobbery glee. I found Zach by the old pool house where Errol Flynn had stayed during a bitter divorce, years before the estate was donated to the city. Zach let Happy go, and the dog zoomed my way, barking and jumping in frantic circles that seemed to say, *Hurrah! Hurrah!* and *Where have you been, nice lady?* I leaned down and Happy covered my face with his butterfly kisses. I hugged his wriggly little body, so glad to see him I had to blink a few times to keep from actually starting to cry. When Happy had finally had enough of me he started to dash around, sniffing this and that, lifting his leg, I went to say hello to his owner.

Zach looked good. There was colour in his cheeks again, no bags under his blue eyes and he'd got a new, hipper haircut. When we hugged I could smell all the things that were familiar — his soap, his brand of detergent, his shampoo. He was wearing his wedding band. This made sense to me.

'Hi,' I said. 'You look great.'

'You do too,' he said, stepping back to look at me. 'I'm really glad to see you.'

We started walking, catching up on the easier things at first. I told him about the store, the customers, my new place. The house was in the worst location, I said, because it was actually only accessible by these long public concrete steps; you had to park on the street above. Of course, that's why I could afford the rent.

'I've seen those steps,' he said. 'I've always wondered what those are for.'

'Oh!' I said, glad someone had finally brought this up. 'It's interesting, actually. They were built back in the days of the red car, so people could walk straight up to the trolley stop and not have to switch back and forth down winding roads.'

Zach laughed. 'Of course you knew that.'

I asked what was going on in his life, and he said he was finishing some articles and was planning a trip to France, where he was thinking about enrolling in some cooking courses. He had plenty of money, so he didn't need to work right now, and he felt like he needed some time on his own, in a new place, with new challenges.

'Do you think you'll ever be a chef?'

'I don't know,' he said, shrugging. 'But if I do open my own restaurant, I know who will decorate it.'

I made a joke: considering the end table debacle, thanks, but no thanks. I was relieved when he smiled and said he thought I would do a good job.

Zach and I were panting our way past the deserted weedy tennis courts that had been there since the forties, when we turned to the larger subjects at hand.

'So, I've been seeing Dr Beaver again,' Zach said.

'Twice a month?' I asked.

'Try twice a week.'

He told me that he didn't think, as absurd as this sounded, that he'd even come close to accepting Cecile's death, even now. It was ironic, he said, that you could move on, on the outside, but stay so frozen on the inside. I nodded. I knew what he meant. Why did we fight it?

'I guess where I was, it seemed like being in some sort of prison,' he said. 'I wanted out, you know? But Dr Beaver is always telling me you can't go up, around, or under grief. You have to just bust through.' He rolled his eyes, like he couldn't believe he was talking this way. 'And it *is* getting better. Sometimes I miss Cecile so much, I wake up in the middle of the night terrified — literally scared and paranoid as though someone is in the house. It's not very manly,' he shrugged. 'But other times I realise I need to be miserable. I need this time to think about her. To dream about her. To *miss* her. It's important.'

Zach was quiet for a moment. I could hear the breeze rustling the oak trees. 'You know, I did use you — at least a little bit — to avoid . . . *everything*,' he said. 'I think I thought what happened to me gave me the right to do and say whatever I wanted. Like taking care of myself was the only important thing. I'm sorry.'

It was OK, I told him. In a way, I'd used him a little bit too.

Zach looked at me, surprised. Not at what I'd said, but the fact I'd copped to it. 'I won't disagree,' he said. 'But just out of curiosity, for what, exactly?'

'Well, for a lot of the same reasons you did — anything to ignore Cecile's death, and how little I was doing with my life — but also because I'd always wanted what she had. I didn't do it consciously, but . . . I guess I'm not that great a person.'

Zach laughed. *None of us*, he told me, *is that great a person.*

'I was in love with you, though,' he said. He told me he wanted me to know that his

419

feelings were real, they just . . .

I nodded, and I told him I understood. It wasn't like I didn't love him either. I did. And then . . . But I told him I didn't have any regrets. Not really.

When he told me he'd started going to yoga, I burst out laughing.

'Down dog,' he said. 'It really *does* help alleviate stress.'

And, he added, he'd gone out to dinner twice with my yoga teacher.

'Akasha?' I asked. He nodded. 'Jesus Christ, Zach! Are you *ever* going to go out with a woman I didn't somehow introduce you to?'

'Apparently not,' he said. Actually, he didn't know if it was going anywhere. He didn't know if he was ready, but she seemed nice, and, he added, she sure looked flexible. He'd been fantasising about inviting her to France for a week, but this time, he was going to carefully weigh the pros and cons before he said anything.

Zach asked if I'd spoken to Bryn. I sighed and told him no. Had he?

He said that he had, and she knew we'd broken up. He'd had dinner with her and David a couple of times, but lately he'd been focusing more on next steps. Of course, he thought they would always be good friends.

When Zach said this, I tried not to feel hurt and left out, but I did. I told him about her card, and that I'd accepted that the friendship was over. Besides, I was still angry with her for the way she'd behaved when we started dating. I just didn't see anyway around that, so . . .

'You have to be careful about anger, though,' Zach said. 'It will eat you alive, trust me. The only way around it is forgiveness.'

What, I wanted to know, did he have to forgive?

His list was longer than I thought it would be — that Cecile died. That he survived. That *I* survived. 'Watching you live your own life — especially when you decided to open the store — when hers was over, it really pissed me off. I know that doesn't make any sense, but it's true. I was livid.'

I told him that I thought the situation between Bryn and I was, unfortunately, a little different.

'Jesse, there's something I need to tell you.'

'Go for it,' I said, taking the water bottle from him and pausing to catch my breath while Happy stopped to inspect a clump of wild vines. I started to walk again, but Zach took my arm, stopping me.

'Has it ever occurred to you that you idolised your friendship with Cecile and Bryn maybe just a little bit too much?'

I said of course I'd considered it. Over the last few months it had slowly dawned on me that, in a way, every time I revelled in how beautiful Cecile and Bryn were, how smart, how confident, another part of me put myself down.

'Right, but that's what it did to *you*. I mean what it did to them.'

'I'm sorry?' I tried to keep my expression composed. I was still enjoying this tramp up a wooded trail, but I was starting to feel defensive. Like, *Oh, so this is really about what a jerk I am?*

'Don't get mad, Jess, OK? It's just, I know that Bryn abandoned you. I know that she was cold, judgemental, even. But have you *really* tried to understand that maybe you and I were just too *hard* for her? It's like, because you were all friends so long you *demanded* complete understanding, and when it got more complicated than that, you refused to see it. With both of them.'

'Zach,' I said, taking a deep breath, trying to believe that he was trying to help. I called Happy over — he was getting dangerously close to some poison oak. 'I'm sure you have a point, OK?' I said, bending down to stroke the dog, who panted and wagged his tail. 'And I promise to think about it. But my friendship with Bryn *was* pretty darn close to perfect before she started punishing me for things I just don't feel responsible for. And Cecile, in particular, changed my life. She took me under her wing, in a way. She was generous, and kind.'

'Not all the time.'

I gave him a look like, *Right.*

'She knew, you know.'

'Knew what?' Overhead, a falcon cruised across the tree-lined sky, searching the brush for some prey. A squirrel, maybe. A tasty lizard. A juicy mouse.

'What happened between us the night we met.'

I turned to look at him.

'What are you talking about?'

'I told her the whole story at the barbecue,' Zach said, stuffing his hands in his pockets. 'That we hooked up, that I promised I'd call you, that then, when I finally broke up with my high school girlfriend, I *did* try to call, but then I couldn't find you. Don't get me wrong, I had an instant crush on Cecile. Who didn't? But I wanted to be straight, and I figured since you guys were room-mates, she'd never go out with me anyway. In fact, I thought the most likely thing that would happen was that you'd get in touch after hearing I'd tried to track you down.'

I asked him what happened then, reminding myself I had to breathe. There was a knot forming in my stomach.

'A few days later, Cecile called me — '

'*She* called *you?*'

'Yes. She said you guys had talked it over, and you weren't interested any more, so she was wondering if we could go out on a date.'

'This is a true story.'

I didn't doubt him. I just said it as a matter of fact, even though I could still hear Cecile's voice from that day she told me she saw Zach at a barbecue. *We talked*, she'd said, *and then he asked if I wanted to get dinner sometime. I swear I didn't think you'd care. Do you care?*

Zach nodded and sighed.

'Then there was a night, months later — I don't know if you remember it, but Cec got really drunk and she told me what she'd done. To be honest, I think she thought I'd find it a little bit funny — that she was so into me she lied — but, actually, we got in a fight about it and she slept on the couch.'

I remembered. The night she'd passed out. The night Zach came outside to talk to me, and I'd asked him to stop peeling the paint off the kitchen door.

Why, I wanted to know, was he telling me this now?

424

'I just want you to understand that we're all human, Jesse. Even Cecile. Sometimes she could be manipulative — she knew everyone loved her, so she capitalised on that when she needed to. We do what we have to do. Sometimes she was an amazing friend, and sometimes she had other priorities. Bryn's the same way: she means well, and then she does harm. I just thought you should think about it.'

We didn't talk much on the way down. We stuck to pointing out different sights — the Capitol Records building in the city basin below, a bird's nest in a pine tree. Happy was tired now, trotting along and huffing, every now and then stopping by my side for a drink of water, which I gave him by filling a plastic bag from the water bottle and holding it so he could stick his snout deep inside, emerging with his nose dripping wet.

When we got to the car, Zach asked if I wanted to play tennis sometime soon.

'You know Cecile was always saying you were pretty friggin' good,' he said. 'And I agree.'

'Yeah,' I laughed. 'I was better than her. At tennis.'

He squeezed my hand. 'At lots of things,' he said, handing me the dog leash. 'Just not everything.'

I stood there holding Happy and Zach said hold on, he had to get something out of the car. He opened the boot and pulled out a duffel bag, handing it to me.

'What's this?' I asked.

'Food, toys, leash.'

My jaw dropped. 'Zach — ' I started to say.

'Don't argue, Jesse,' he said, shaking his head. 'You know you want him.'

I nodded, it was true.

With that, Zach gave Happy a pat on the head and told him to be good. Then he got in the car, waved, and drove away. I couldn't be sure, but I don't think it was that easy for him to say goodbye to the dog. But I was glad he did. As Zach's Audi rounded a corner I looked down at my new pooch and he looked up at me, wagging his tail. 'You know,' I said softly, reaching down to pick him up and bury my face behind his ears. 'I always did have a crush on you.'

# 29

## Bless This Mess

A couple of weeks later I was walking up the front steps. There was fresh landscaping — flowers marching in neat little rows — and a new fence. Everything looked pretty good, I thought. I could see a new couch in the living room, and what looked like some new floor lamps. *Bryn's been busy,* I thought.

I knocked on the door, and when she opened it, I presented her with my bouquet.

'Basil, sage, pineapple cilantro. Uh, this one is oregano, that's thyme, and this is tarragon. They're cuttings from my garden. For your garden.'

She stared at me, in that steely, lawyerly way. I instantly thought, *Uh-oh, maybe this isn't going to work.*

Somehow Bryn looked different. She looked . . . fat. Like, really fat.

'Holy shit!' I yelled. 'Are you pregnant?'

Her face broke into a smile, and then she started to laugh, nodding.

'Jesse,' she yelled. She threw her arms around my neck, and I could feel her swelling belly pressing against mine, solid as a basketball. 'You're here, you're here,' she said. It took me a moment to realise she was actually crying. Crying in a way that I've never seen her do in the eleven years that she'd been my friend, my partner in crime, my big mama boss lady. I could feel her tears sinking through my T-shirt; the herbs were getting crushed. 'Oh my God, Jesse,' she said, her shoulders shaking. 'I've missed you so much.'

Bryn pulled me inside and, wiping her nose, insisted on giving me a tour of the house even as I begged her to sit and let me get her something. She pulled me from room to room, much as she'd done all those months ago. 'I've redone the tiles in the kitchen,' she said, 'all the fixtures have been replaced.' Then the living room, then the bedrooms. She was proud of her work, but uncertain. ('Do you really like those drapes, though?' she kept asking. 'Are you *sure*?)' Finally she took a seat in the back garden. I got her a pillow for her back, and laughed as she gingerly set herself down.

'Look,' she said, squeezing her chest. 'I have *boobs*.'

I smiled, watching her jiggle herself around — she was both fascinated and horrified. 'That you do,' I agreed.

She was five months gone, with a girl. Did Zach know? I asked. He did, Bryn said, but they'd only told him last week; the pregnancy had been touch-and-go from the start, so she and David kept it quiet as long as they could.

Immediately I wanted to know what was going on, and she told me everything. Bryn had been working sixty hours a week, and one afternoon she fainted in her office during a meeting. Her doctor said she had something called pregnancy-induced hypertension, and was now insisting that she stay home, no working, until she delivered. 'I've been sitting on my fat ass for a month now,' she said, 'and I'm bored to tears. But supposedly the pregnancy is going better now so that's good, at least.'

David, meanwhile, had a new job as a writer's assistant at a television production company and things were going really well. Ultimately, Bryn was thinking about easing her caseload, but she wasn't sure about it, since she'd always been so ambitious. Maybe, she said, she'd go into practice for herself, although that brought up a whole other set of problems. I told her not to worry, if anyone could figure all this out, she could.

Bryn told me that she'd been a month pregnant, in fact, when she came to Henry's wedding. 'I wanted to tell you,' she said. 'And then you told me you and Zach were moving in together and I was so furious. So I left.'

For the first time, there was some tension in the air. OK, I thought, mentally preparing myself, *you have to do this part.*

'I want you to tell me,' I said. 'Why I made you so angry, and how I let you down. And then I'd like to do the same with you.'

Bryn looked at me like, *Uh, are you sure about that?*

I nodded. We had always been so close, I explained, but we never tested our friendship — never *allowed* it to be examined, to be questioned. For me, it was about fear. I wouldn't stand up to her. That was my fault. But I believed that if we just went for it, who knew? Maybe we'd be better than we ever were. Or, maybe we'd just be OK again. Which was what I wanted, more than anything.

So Bryn told me her side of the story. She wasn't as OK with my dating Zach as she'd said she was. 'It was so typical me,' she said. 'Refusing not to admit that I was upset, glossing everything over,' she laughed. 'And then trying to steer it all in a direction that suited me, to boot.' She talked about how, to be fair to herself, she was still reeling from Cecile's death, but was uncomfortable talking to me about it because then it seemed like she

wasn't supporting Zach's and my relationship. She said the first time she saw us
together, it hurt so much she wanted to
scream. Eventually, she started blaming me
for that, too.

'You can't control the whole world, honey,'
I said.

'I know,' she said. 'But why the fuck *not?*'

'I hated you that day at Zach's birthday,' I
admitted.

She nodded. 'I know. I'm sorry.'

I told her I was sorry — really sorry — too.
Maybe I knew, on some level, that she wasn't
ready for Zach and I to be dating, yet when
she gave me the green light, I just accepted it
because it was what I wanted to hear.

Bryn said the worst part was later, when
she realised *she'd* been such a bitch —
avoiding me, keeping me at a distance
— when she didn't know if I would forgive
her.

I forgave her, I said. I did. Of course I did.
But did she?

Bryn nodded. Then she smiled.

'You can be a real pain-in-the-ass, you
know that?' I said.

Bryn sniffled, and wiped her yes. 'You too,'
she said. 'A frigging *huge* pain in the ass.'

We looked at one another, and I knew that
we were both thinking of Cecile. I wondered

431

if Bryn and I would ever have got into such a huge mess if she'd been alive. Then I realised we might have, actually. There had been something imbalanced about us. Cecile kept us in check, but who knows how long she would have wanted to. For all we knew, she'd tired of it long ago.

'Hey, did you know that crafty little minx stole my almost-college-boyfriend?' I said.

Bryn burst out giggling. 'Uh-huh,' she said. 'Oh my God, that Cecile *was* a manipulative one, wasn't she? Turning those big eyes on and hypnotising everyone in sight.'

I nodded. *Oh yeah, full of surprises.*

'I miss her, though,' I said.

Bryn nodded. 'Me too. But that's OK.'

★ ★ ★

I left an hour later, when Bryn was starting to look sleepy. I promised I'd be back in a few days to check in on her and see how she was doing with those plants.

'Maybe we can also watch a movie?' Bryn asked. She looked so vulnerable, almost like a little girl in her maternity sweat pants, her little feet in flip flops, the red polish chipping off.

'Definitely,' I said. 'Although I'm so busy at work you wouldn't believe it.'

She got the joke. 'Oh, screw you. And bring food. Lots and lots of food. David has me on some macrobiotic diet he read about in *Oprah*. It's the *worst thing in the world.*'

I promised that I would come bearing edible gifts.

I walked down the steps to my car. Wyatt and I had big plans that night to put up some new drywall in the cottage I was renting, maybe sand down a few chairs. We'd spent every evening together for the last couple of weeks, ever since he kissed me suddenly in the lumber section at Home Depot. (It gave a whole new meaning to the phrase, 'Assistance in two-by-fours, aisle four.') Sometimes, while he built shelves, or hung pictures, I'd catch myself staring at him, a dripping paintbrush in my hand as I admired the skill he had with a power drill. The next time I came to see Bryn, I'd be able to tell her all about how I found myself falling in love with some tubby guy from Texas. About how much I loved to cuddle with his big belly, which would slowly lift me up and down while we watched TV. About how the soft lines around his eyes were so delicate and beautiful they made me want to cry.

I pawed around the bottom of my bag for my car keys and I heard a buzzing coming from a flowering cactus outside Bryn's house.

I turned to find its origin, and there was a humming bird, zipping from spiky flower to spiky flower. A whirling zip of iridescence, it dodged thorns, swept past leathery stalks, and plunged it's thin, needle-of-a-beak deep into each plumy bloom, buzzing off to another, then another, then another. *It's so nice out today*, I thought. It reminded me of that morning — now a year and a half ago — when Cecile and I played tennis. It was hot that day, even though it was almost Christmas. Beautiful, talented, wiley Cecile. For ten years I preferred to live in her shadow, and yet I wilted there. The only regret I had was that I hadn't tried harder to grow, to shine, to *live* while she was alive. We could have stood side by side, Cecile and I. For I had to believe — I *did* believe — that's what she really wanted for me. That's why she hung my paintings over her bed so many years ago. That's why she left me the money. I had to admit it; I was at least partly responsible for making it so easy for her to take a man from me back when we were in college. Back then, if I had known, I would have let her. But I wouldn't now. Never again.

I got in the car and grinned. Summer was coming — I could tell from how hot the car seat was on the back of my legs. As I reached for my sunglasses, I made a mental note to ask Wyatt if we could install an air-conditioner at the shop. There were many long, hot June days ahead, when the air would scorch like the inside of a barbecue, when the movie stars would slather themselves in tanning oil by Lizzie's pool, when I would put the finishing touch on a client's house and shut the door thinking, *Yes, this is done.* Bryn was going to name her baby *Willa Cecile Beco*, and there would be days when I would play with Willa and breathe her baby smell, when David, Bryn, Wyatt and I would go out to dinner, when Bryn and I would laugh and get in a big old fight and make up and laugh again. There were seemingly endless, sunny, hot days. Then again, there were no guarantees.

Of course, there were more important things to think about at the moment, I reminded myself as I pulled up to the stop sign at the end of Bryn's street. 'What shade of pink,' I wondered aloud, 'should we paint the baby's room?'

# Acknowledgements

How fortunate I am to be surrounded by such a talented group of cohorts. Thank you to Jennifer Rudolph-Walsh and Michael Shereksy at the William Morris Agency. Karen Kostolnyik at Warner Books. My kind but not *too* kind readers Julian Cautherley, Eve Epstein, Gayle Forman, Kate Mayfield, and Kirsten Smith (excellent writers all). Thank you to Raihan Shaikh-Khaleel, for being a brilliant wanker. My family — Bernice, George, Lindsey, and Bea — for having fab taste in furniture. Adrienne and Leo Fay, for their awe-inspiring support and kindness. (How do they do it?) Matt, for understanding. And, of course, to Jeanne: we miss you every day.

We do hope that you have enjoyed reading this large print book.

Did you know that all of our titles are available for purchase?

We publish a wide range of high quality large print books including:
**Romances, Mysteries, Classics**
**General Fiction**
**Non Fiction and Westerns**

Special interest titles available in large print are:
**The Little Oxford Dictionary**
**Music Book**
**Song Book**
**Hymn Book**
**Service Book**

Also available from us courtesy of Oxford University Press:
**Young Readers' Dictionary**
**(large print edition)**
**Young Readers' Thesaurus**
**(large print edition)**

For further information or a free brochure, please contact us at:
**Ulverscroft Large Print Books Ltd.,**
**The Green, Bradgate Road, Anstey,**
**Leicester, LE7 7FU, England.**
**Tel:** (00 44) 0116 236 4325
**Fax:** (00 44) 0116 234 0205

## BULLETPROOF SUZY

### Ian Brotherhood

Francine Brallahan, aka Bulletproof Suzy, is a highly intelligent, if somewhat violent, member of the urban underclass. She is also leader of a band of Liaison Officers — citizens recruited by the government to enforce payment of unpopular taxes. Suzy's middle-class friend Louise disapproves, and they fall out — but when Louise is found murdered, Suzy and her crew take it upon themselves to find the killer and exact retribution. Unfortunately though, there are a couple of complications to contend with . . .

# QUARTER TONES

## Susan Mann

When Ana returns to the cottage of her youth in the seaside village of Noordhoek, near Cape Town, it's to sort out her late father's affairs. But it soon becomes clear that more is at stake ... After living in London, her return to South Africa distances her already strained marriage to Michael. She is welcomed by her neighbour, Franz van der Veer, an architect searching for redemption. This is further complicated by the arrival of his eccentric brother, Daniel. Against a tangle of childhood memories, scarred histories and renewed hope, Ana confronts the death of her father, and her questions of guilt and belonging.

# THIRTEEN

## Sebastian Beaumont

Stephen Bardot, a taxi driver working the exhausting night shift in Brighton, begins to experience alterations to his perception of reality . . . He regularly takes Valerie from 13 Wish Road to the Cornerstone Community Centre. She is terminally ill, so when he is no longer asked to collect her, he fears that she is dead. Making enquiries about her he discovers that her address does not exist — there is no number thirteen at Wish Road. Life gets weirder and he must walk away from the twilight world of Thirteen. But Thirteen has no intention of letting him go . . .

# BED REST

## Sarah Bilston

Quinn 'Q' Boothroyd is a busy, successful young English lawyer, married to the gorgeous Tom and living in New York. But when her doctor tells her she has to spend the last three months of her pregnancy on bed rest, Quinn is thrown into a tailspin by the idea of losing her social and professional life. Initially bored and frustrated, Quinn gradually finds herself re-examining her world — her marriage, relationships with family and friends, and her job. Indeed, bed rest produces some very surprising, funny and touching results . . .

# THE AMNESIA CLINIC

## James Scudamore

In Quito, Ecuador, English boy Anti and his classmate Fabián are friends. Fabián lives with his eccentric Uncle Suarez. Suarez tells wonderful stories, and soon the boys, sharing his passion, are united entirely through the medium of story-telling. One subject is taboo: Fabián's parents. But when details surrounding their disappearance emerge, Anti consoles his friend with a story suggesting that Fabián's mother may be living at a bizarre hospital for patients with memory loss. With reality losing its grip, the boys embark on a quixotic voyage across Ecuador in search of an 'Amnesia Clinic' that may or may not exist . . .

# THE SOLITUDE OF THOMAS CAVE

## Georgina Harding

It is August 1616, and in the Arctic, the crew of the whaling ship *Heartsease* must return home before the winter ice closes in. All, that is, save Thomas Cave. He makes a wager that he will remain there alone until the next season. So, left with provisions, shelter, and a journal, Cave's lonely contest with the realities and the phantasms of the Arctic winter begins. He is vulnerable to blizzards, avalanches, bears — and his own demons: his fear and his memories. In this wilderness his past returns to him: the woman he'd loved, and the grief that drove him north.